Covert Ops Force: War Criminal

Gary A Wilson

Covert Ops Force Series # 2

I0549436

Covert Ops Force: War Criminal
Published by Nightstalker Press
Albuquerque, NM, USA
www.nightstalkerpress.vpweb.com

Edited by Rachel Blackbirdsong
Book cover design by Gary A Wilson
Author photo by Maria R. Wilson
ISBN 13: 978-0-9863719-6-7
Copyright © 2015 Gary A Wilson

Foreword:

This novel is completely fictional in nature. The military units, weapons and aircraft do not exist at this time. Any resemblances to events or persons, living or dead are purely coincidental.

The scientific theories presented in this book are partially based on research, the remainder based on literary license.

Mr. Spock and Sulu are fictional characters from Star Trek TV series, created by Gene Roddenberry.

Le Roy Jethro Gibbs is a character on NCIS

Aprilozene is a fictional sleep agent

"Tell a lie, make it big, tell it often enough and people will take it for the truth." Paraphrased from a quote by Joseph Goebbels (1897 – 1945)

Dedications:

To my wife, Maria: Thanks for always standing by me in the good times and the bad times. I love you

To my intrepid editor Rachel Blackbirdsong: You deserve a vacation for making sense of my ramblings.

INTRODUCTION

Taqua Four – Covert Ops Time index 12.30.2221

It all began when I led a Covert Ops mission back in time to rescue our captured pilots and prevent the Terran Empire, a cruel and oppressive regime from an alternate reality, from destroying the last few remaining members of the Human, Henoki and Bwentani Alliance.

We rescued the captured pilots, including my son-in-law Pomar (Commander) Zerellus and one of my oldest and closest friends, Major Ricardo Pasqualle.

Imperial First Trooper Mike Dickinson, a ruthless interrogator, had just gotten the key to our defenses when Major Dave Walsh, Major Ray Watson and my daughter, Captain Anamiok 'Ana' Tucker, along with Techian engineer Bat'ai prevented the Empire from gaining access to our defense systems while planting a computer virus into their main frame.

I killed Dickinson by strapping him into and turning on the Neural Shock Device, which he had used to torture and kill hundreds of Alliance pilots and soldiers.

We returned the pilots we'd rescued to Alliance headquarters and were about to go back to the present when a major temporal shockwave caught us while we were in the vortex and propelled us two years into the future, in the year 2221.

When we emerged from the vortex, Earth was destroyed by the Cho'Kai. We found human, Henoki and Bwentani people living on Bwentani Prime, which had been originally destroyed by the Empire, but was now restored because the timeline was altered.

We landed on Bwentani Prime and were immediately arrested by the Celestus Council, who are in an alliance with the Cho'Kai.

We were imprisoned I was sentenced to death along with former Celestus Prasin (Leader) Palonius and General Ryan Dickinson.

However, we escaped from maximum security and sought temporary refuge in the Henoki Colony. They were under threat of attack by not only the Celestus/Cho'Kai Alliance, but a cult of Henoki who worshipped the Dark Underworld deity, *Dev'cha*.

So we came up with a plan to protect the Henoki, Bwentani and the remaining humans from retaliation:

Celestus Headquarters – 08.01. 2221

Lyle, Quennok and Berellus stand in front of a podium, ready to read a prepared statement for the cameras of the Celestus Communications network.

They have come to the headquarters under a flag of truce to inform Jen'Pway they are ready to sign the surrender papers and submit themselves to the authority of the Celestus Council.

Quennok steps forward and says "On behalf of the Henoki Citadel, I Quennok, leader of the Henoki people hereby state that now and forevermore condemn the Terran Colonel Robert Steven Tucker as a war criminal and Anamiok Tucker as an enemy of the Henoki people.

Berellus steps forward and says "On behalf of the Bwentani Imperium, I Berellus, leader of the Bwentani citizenry, also condemn Robert Steven Tucker as a war criminal and an enemy of the Bwentani. Pomar Rillius and my son Zerellus are also wanted for treason."

Lyle follows the others, but hesitates before he speaks. "I, General Lyle Richard Kensington, Commander of the Terran task force, attached to the Bwentani Defense Force, condemn former Colonel Robert Steven Tucker as a war criminal for repeatedly carrying out unauthorized military actions against the Celestus Alliance and the Cho'Kai, murder of officials in the Terran Empire and treason against the human race. His current whereabouts are unknown, but a warrant has been issued for his arrest and once captured, he will be extradited to the Celestus Alliance for trial and after he is convicted, he will be sentenced to the maximum penalty under their laws. I have also detained the forces under his command and they will stand trial for complicity, however they will be granted leniency because they are following the orders of a superior officer and though commended for their loyalty, will face re-education to comply with Celestus law."

Branded a war criminal by three of my closest friends, I, along with a handful of operatives, my family and others, including Palonius have escaped from Bwentani Prime. We have found a safe haven in the Taquan solar system which is inside the Quenvarus Nebula, located twenty thousand light years from the Celestus Alliance. Here we will rebuild our forces, recruit allies and plan an offensive against an enemy that is even more dangerous than the Terran Empire.

Report filed by Robert Steven Tucker.
30 December ,2221

CHAPTER 1

Covert Ops Command Center- Taqua Four - Time Index 01.10.2222.1500

General Ryan Dickinson, the Ops Force Commander and his grandson, Covert Ops team leader Mike Dickinson discuss their lack of progress in finding the Golgrof Clans along with Chief Engineer Bat'ai and Anamiok 'Ana' Tucker, Robert's daughter.

Ana is four months pregnant and has been restricted to duty in the command center.

Ryan looks at a star chart and sees that nearly every inhabited sector within one hundred light years has been searched for the elusive mercenaries.

"Mike, it's been four months, yer tellin' me they're nowhere ta be found?"

"Grampa, they don't have a home planet or organized government. They live in clans an' move 'round 'lookin' fer conflicts."

"I have been attempting to locate them, General. I have been experiencing no luck," Bat'ai tells them.

Ana reports, "Sir, I have attempted to send a general message, with no success."

"Kinda hard ta do when we don't know what kind o' comm system they're usin'," Ryan replies.

Commander Ray Watson enters the command center looking uncharacteristically concerned.

He walks over to Ana. "Darlin', yer father's in the infirmary. He was shot."

"What happened, *Hu'Neok* (godfather)?" Clearly upset, she tries to calm herself down to protect her baby.

"We were reconnin' a detention center, the Celestians somehow got tipped off and nearly had us in an ambush. He had me git the team back ta the WA-13 while he held 'em off. His vest malfunctioned and he caught a round in the chest. The crazy bastard knocked off a few more before I dragged 'im inta the Widow Maker an' we skinned out."

"What 'bout Dave?" asks Ryan.

Ray chuckles while shaking his head. "That other crazy sum'bitch stayed behind ta git more Intel."

"*Hu'Neok*, is my father all right?"

"Doc Burke is patchin' 'im up as we speak."

They leave the command center and go to the infirmary, where they see Robert sitting on the table being bandaged for a bullet wound to the upper right chest. He looks like he is in a foul mood.

Ana walks over to him, holds his hand and says a quiet prayer to the Henoki deity *Ama'diok*.

"I'm all right, sweetheart," he assures her.

"Bob, what happened?" Ryan asks.

"A Celestus sniper grazed me."

"It was more than that, General," Doctor Elizabeth Burke replies. She turns to Ryan, "The Colonel was shot and the round entered his chest and exited through the back. He needs rest."

"No offense doc, but I've been hit worse than this." He tries to put his shirt on, but grunts in pain.

"Bob, I kin order ya ta stay, but I know ya won't, so I'll use the next best threat, I'll have yer wife an' daughter confine ya ta quarters," Ryan tells him.

Robert laughs, and then winces. "OK, no more missions until Doctor Burke clears me." He turns to Elizabeth. "Is that acceptable, doc?"

She sighs. "That's better than what I usually get when you or Colonel Walsh are brought in."

Robert chuckles. "I know. Let's go."

"Bob, yer hurt," Ryan admonishes.

"I've hurt myself worse shaving."

"Ya shave yer chest, Bob? We need ta have a talk, son," Ray quips.

Robert glares, and then 'flips the bird' at him.

Robert's wife, Linaiok enters the infirmary, having heard what happened to her husband.

"*A'nok*" (Spouse) Linaiok says as she goes to him.

"I'm all right, Lin. It's just a scratch."

She glares at him. "Robert Steven Tucker, do not lie to me."

Ray whispers, "Aw shit." He discreetly motions to the others that they should leave.

Robert insists, "I'm fine, Lin."

She pokes the wound, causing him to flinch, then lifts the back of the shirt and sees that it was a 'through and through.'

"You are staying here until Doctor Elizabeth clears you."

"Yes, Ma'am. Ya know, I don't fear much in life, but seeing you pissed is one of 'em."

Linaiok almost manages to laugh, but sighs instead. "*A'nok*, you have managed to get yourself injured on almost every mission. You will not do us any good if you are killed."

Robert exhales deeply. "Lin, the Celestians are starting to crack down on our people, especially our forces that refuse to cooperate. We're trying to gather Intel to get them out."

"And they always manage to find you."

"Lyle knows me almost better than I know myself."

"He knows you are working to free our warriors. They will have ambushes waiting for you."

"That's why it's time to change strategies. Ray, what kind of Intel are we picking up from our surveillance?"

Ray chuckles, "Mainly 'bout you, Bob. They think we're still on Bwentani Prime."

"Good. Elizabeth says I don't need to stay here, let's go."

Once again, Linaiok glares at him.

Robert motions to Elizabeth and says "Doc, please tell her I'm good to go."

"The Colonel will be cleared for duty in the morning. His, shall we say unique physiology, will help him recover quickly from his wounds."

"Your great, great, great grandfather told us that when we disappeared in the temporal vortex, exposure to it slowed down our aging process. You discovered more?"

"Yes, from the files Bat'ai obtained I learned that exposure to the vortex has rewritten your DNA at the quantum cellular level. Meaning, that it not only changed the way you age, but how your body heals itself through spontaneous cellular regeneration. Your daughter and her unborn child will also have this."

"And there's no way to reverse this."

"Not without killing you."

"I thought as much. Thanks, Doc."

Robert and Linaiok leave the infirmary and go to the command center where Ryan, Mike and Bat'ai study a chart of this region of the galaxy, which spans one thousand light years in each direction.

He says to Mike, "Report."

Mike shows him where advanced cultures are located, and also details the locations of the friendly and not so friendly species. "I've made contact with a buncha people, sir. Most o' 'em support what we're doin', but don't have the forces ta fight, an' a few threatened ta whup our asses if we went back. Zerellus fired a few near their ships ta straighten 'em out."

"I assume it's a no-go on locating the Golgrof."

"Yes, Sir."

"Ryan, I think we should stop looking for them and concentrate on getting our people out."

"Yer right, Bob," Ryan replies. "Ana, set an automated greetin' on all frequencies. If they answer, great, if not, then we lost nothing but a few bucks on the phone bill."

Ana laughs, "Yes, sir."

Robert changes the subject. "We have to set up an extraction for Dave and his team. They were on us heavy this last mission. So, either they've improved their Intel—"

"Or they have someone spyin' on us," Ray counters.

"Raymond, I have run security sweeps and they do not have listening devices, nor do they know that our operation center is here," Bat'ai states.

"*Hu'Neh*, you said General Kensington knows how you operate, my *Hu'che'Neh* (grandfather) and Prime Minister Berellus know you as well," Ana points out.

"I know, Ana. Sometimes I wonder if it was a mistake altering their memories and not altering their knowledge of our ops," Robert replies.

"Robert, according to Rillius, it could have damaged their long-term memories if we tried to alter them too much."

"I know, Bat'ai, but how do we go up against someone who knows us almost as well as we know ourselves? He was our CO for almost two hundred years."

"You asked that same question when we were fighting your quantum reality doubles from the Terran Empire."

"And how did we defeat them?"

"By doing what is unexpected."

"Hell, Lyle knows every ops scenario we kin throw at 'em. What in blazes kin we do that he wouldn't 'spect?" Ryan asks.

"Kill him," Robert replies.

Everyone in the command center looks at Robert as if he has lost his mind.

"Whoa, son, I know yer supposed ta be number one on the Celestus Alliance's most wanted list, but killin' Lyle?

That jest ain't right, an' I aughta open a can o' whup ass fer even suggestin' that," Ray says.

"I'm with Ray on this one, Bob," Ryan states.

Robert looks at them squarely. "It's unexpected-"

"An' will git ya the firin' squad."

"If we do it right, it will give us the break we need."

Ryan eyes him. "Ya better let us know what's rattlin' in that skull o' yers."

Robert lays out what he has in mind. He tells them that the first part of the mission involves rendezvousing with the other top sniper in the Covert Ops Force, Colonel Dave Walsh.

CHAPTER 2

Cave –Bwentani Prime – Time Index 01.11.2222

Dave and his covert ops team have taken refuge in a cave in a remote mountain region in the Renallius providence, having evaded Celestian and human forces loyal to General Kensington.

One of the ops team members, Sergeant Dan Morris hears someone approaching the cave, and gives hand signals to the team, who train their weapons on the entrance.

They relax when the extraction team enters.

"Stand down, Sergeant," Robert tells him.

"Sir."

Dave goes over and shakes Robert's hand.

"Good to see you in one piece."

"Sorry you guys had to wait."

"You had to get the team out. Besides we got good Intel after you led them away from the Detention Center."

"Good, your team can brief Ryan when they get back. Zerellus will bring them back to base. We have another op, I'll brief you on the way."

"Understood. Sergeant, you're in charge, bring the team back to HQ."

Robert states, "Pomar (Commander) Zerellus is standing by. Follow the signal to his transport."

"Yes, sir," Morris replies.

He leads the ops and extraction teams out of the cave. Dave notices that it's only himself and Robert remaining.

"What kind of op are we running?"

"Sniper." He pauses and states, " Lyle's the target."

"Bob, with all due respect, are you out of your fucking mind? He is our commanding officer and our friend."

"And the reason our ops are being compromised. Up until now, they have been one step ahead of us on every op we run because Lyle knows our doctrine inside and out. We take Lyle out of the equation and they'll be in the dark."

"And we throw away everything we have been fighting for. I want no part of it."

"You have no choice. It's an order. From Ryan."

"And after this, you'll have my resignation."

"I don't like it any more than you do. Shit, if you had to kill me to save our people, I would be more disappointed if you didn't take the shot."

"Then you better give me one of those soulless bastard pills you've been taking."

Robert mutters, "Let's get it over with."

Dave and Robert go to a waiting WA-13 and get in.

Special Forces Operatives Mike Dickinson and Rillius are in the jump seats, dressed in tactical gear and wearing invisibility vests.

Robert gets in the pilot's station. Bat'ai activates the quantum shields along with a scattering field to make it impossible to track them. Their destination: the Celestus Alliance headquarters in the Glenarius providence.

Imperium Headquarters Bwentani Capitol

Robert and Dave are in their sniper outfits, on opposite rooftops waiting for their target to leave the headquarters.

Robert keys his mike. "Sniper one in position."

"Sniper two in position," Dave replies.

They calibrate their rifles, check the wind and distance for the optimal shot to take down one of the top leaders in the Celestus Alliance.

"Do you want me to take the shot, Bob?"

"Only if I don't have a clean one."

"I see movement by the door."

Robert trains his sniper scope on the front entrance of the headquarters and sees Celestus leader Jen'Pway, Bwentani leader Berellus and Terran military leader Lyle Kensington exit the building. They are surrounded by Celestus security.

"No joy," Dave says.

Robert tells him, "Target acquired. Taking down target in three...two...one."

He sets his sights just behind Lyle's ear, releases his breath and then squeezes the trigger.

A heavily muffled shot rings out and Lyle suddenly goes down in a heap.

"Return to the building! Lock down the base, Tucker is here, find him!" Jen'Pway commands.

The remaining leaders are quickly returned to the building while Celestus forces are deployed to apprehend the Terran assassin.

Lyle's body suddenly disappears.

"Let's get out of here," Robert says.

Robert and Dave get out of their gilley suits and leave them on the roof. They both leave something on the suits: A playing card, with a Joker on it. Written on the card is their 'signature':

THE JOKE'S ON YOU

They return to the WA-13, lift off and open a portal to return to Taqua Four.

CHAPTER 3

Covert Ops headquarters

Robert and Dave are being debriefed by Ryan.

Dave is still angered about the mission and he is about to live up to his threat to resign his commission, when Elizabeth enters the briefing room.

"General Kensington is stable and once he's conscious, his memory will be restored," she tells him.

Dave is stunned. "Lyle's alive?"

"I shot him with a tranq round that looked like a bullet. I loaded yours with the same round in case I didn't have a shot."

"Why the hell didn't you tell me?"

"We couldn't take any chances, Dave. We had to make sure there were no security leaks to tip them off."

"You think I'm a leak?"

"Of course not, but the Celestians could have had some kind of surveillance in the cave and I had to make your outrage look real."

"We swept for bugs when we went in."

"The *Dev'cha* are working with the Celestians. We have Henoki and Bwentani ops team members and they are susceptible to having their minds probed."

"You think they've been tipping off the Celestians?"

"That and Lyle knowing our operations."

"At least he's on our side now."

"What about Berellus and Quennok?"

"They're going to tighten security, so we'll have to figure out another way to get them out. Don't think they'll let us get close enough to use the sniper ploy again."

"Are they safe where they are?" Ryan asks.

"From what we've seen, all three of them were. The only reason we got Lyle out of there was he was tipping off the Celestians on how we run our ops," Robert replies.

"I think we put the fear into them, if we're willing to take out our own leader, then they know they could be next," Dave says.

"Exactly, so we better lay low and see how they respond."

Bat'ai enters the room. "We may not have to wait long, Robert. Jen'Pway is about to address the Alliance on the communications network."

Ryan orders "Put it on the big screen, son."

Celestus Prime

Jen'Pway is standing at a podium, surrounded by security. There are Celestian troops on the roof tops. Quennok and Berellus are by his side, somber and silent.

He pulls out a prepared statement and reads it.

"It is with a heavy heart that I must announce the sudden demise of Terran Commander Lyle Kensington. He died of natural causes and he will be buried with full Celestian honors. We will observe a period of mourning and our condolences to our friends, the Terrans for the loss of a great man."

Covert Ops Headquarters

"Kin ya believe that horse shit?" Ryan exclaims.

"They have to keep the air of invincibility. They're like the Terran Empire, and like them, it can be used to take them down," Robert replies.

"Tell ya what, I'd pay top dollar ta be a fly on the wall in that room," Ryan quips.

Robert chuckles and says, "Me, too."

Ryan asks, "Bat'ai, did ya git the ghost program up an' runnin' yet?"

"Raymond and I have the program developed, but we have not been able to get into their system, General."

"I planted hidden cameras in Jen'Pway office when I grabbed our gear." Robert states. He types in a command and Jen'Pway's office appears on the screen. He is seen yelling at Kal'Pen. Berellus and Quennok are also in the office, visibly shaken.

"Do you wish for me to turn the volume up?"

Robert laughs. "No, B. I think we know why he's pissed off." Elizabeth enters the command center. "Doc, is Lyle up to answering a few questions?"

She glares at him and replies, "He is conscious and not too happy with you, Colonel."

Robert chuckles, "Didn't think he would be."

They leave the briefing room to go to the infirmary.

They arrive at the infirmary and see Lyle sitting up in the hospital bed, with his head bandaged."

"Nice to see that you still care, Bob," Lyle tells him with a sarcastic tone.

"Sorry, Lyle had to make it look real."

"What the hell did you hit me with?"

"A tranquillizer housed inside a soft .308 round."

"Never heard it coming."

"A new muzzle that Dave developed."

Lyle eyes Dave. "So, you were both in on it?"

"For the record, Lyle, I was completely against it." says Dave, defensively.

Robert 'coughs', "Kiss ass."

"Yeah, right," Lyle responds skeptically.

The others laugh.

"What do ya remember, Lyle?" Ryan asks.

"We were discussing setting up the base on Taqua Four." Suddenly he looks around and realizes they are not on

Bwentani Prime. He asks "You mean?"

"We're here."

"You could not have done this overnight."

"You've been under for four months."

"Then why the hell don't I remember anything?"

"Doctor Burke restored your original memories. Rillius will have to reactivate those memories when you've fully recovered."

"The same thing we did when we pulled Captains Foster and Pasqualle out from their cover inside Empire?"

"Yeah, sorry I had to have this done, Lyle, but it's kept our forces safe and their focus fixed firmly on me."

"Well, you could have warned me."

"We were vulnerable and the *Dev'cha* were leaking information to Jen'Pway. The only way to protect our people was to convince the Celestians that you, Quennok and Berellus declared me a war criminal. By the same token the only way to get you out was to convince them I killed you."

"When are you going to pull them out?"

"Eventually, but right now they're locked down, and we need to start diverting attention. Now that you're no longer schooling them on our tactics, maybe we can make progress," Robert says chiding him.

"Bob, you know I would never betray you guys."

"I know, just busting your chops."

"I don't know whether to give you a medal, promotion or a court-martial."

"Hell, why not all three? It wouldn't be the first time."

Lyle laughs, and then groans.

Elizabeth tells them, "The General needs rest. That round you used may not have penetrated the skull and caused brain damage, but it did have a concussive effect, so he has to be monitored for side effects and should be ready for duty in twenty-four hours."

"Well then I guess just continue what you're doing and bring me up to speed at 1500 hours."

"Yes, sir," they reply in unison before leaving the infirmary. Robert stops Elizabeth in the hall, and whispers something to her. She nods, and then goes back into the cubicle.

He returns to the Command Center and tells Bat'ai to sweep for listening devices and make sure that Lyle wasn't implanted with a tracking or listening device.

"There is no sign of tracking or listening devices, Robert," Bat'ai tells him.

"Good. Do you think my wife and Liaok have been sufficiently trained to let me get Ray back into the field?"

"Yes and your daughter has been a real help."

"Great. I'm going to be debriefing Dave Walsh's team. Keep monitoring Jen'Pway's office and let me know of any changes."

"Yes, Robert."

Robert nods and leaves the Command Center.

Jen'Pway's office

Jen'Pway is furious at the latest blatant attack by the Covert Ops Force. While he is grateful he wasn't the target of the assassination, the fact they killed one of their own people reinforces the belief the humans are barbarians and can't be trusted.

Berellus and Quennok are also in the office, equally outraged by this; their feelings of betrayal have been justified.

"How was he able to get onto our base and kill the Terran without us even detecting him?" Jen'Pway asks.

"The same way they escaped from the detention center, Prasin," Kal'Pen replies.

"Incompetence."

"No, Prasin. There is a rumor that they possess advanced technology from another reality; a device that can theoretically render them invisible."

"Tucker escaped through a ventilation shaft and freed the others when he stole his equipment out of my office and attacked our guards," Jen'Pway replies.

"Sir, then how did he make it through our security without being seen?"

Jen'Pway replies, "As I stated, incompetence, they were executed. Did I make a mistake in sparing you?"

"No, Prasin."

"Then this subject will not be brought up again. The Cho'Kai leader is coming and will want an answer for what happened. Go to the Detention Center and bring me a Terran to execute for killing the Terran Ambassador."

"Yes, sir."

Kal'Pen leaves.

"Prasin, what if what Kal'Pen is saying is true?" Berellus asks.

"Bring in the Zenaren. They have the ability to track anyone, even if they are using camouflaging technology. Do so as quietly as possible. Wait until after Ka'Nef has left. He may perceive this as weakness on our part and they will station their warriors here. Their presence could incite the people to stage an insurrection."

They hear a beep as a Celestus Sentry appears on the screen.

"Sir, a Cho'Kai transport has arrived. Their leader and a squadron of Warriors are on the way to your office."

"Escort them in."

"Their leader says that he does not trust our warriors and wants to talk to you about this morning's incident."

Jen'Pway utters a Kallaxian curse and shuts off the wall monitor.

"Shall we leave?" Quennok asks.

"No. We have to present a united front and explain that this was the work of a lone dissident. Do not mention Tucker or his team as the assassins," Jen'Pway commands.

Quennok and Berellus nod in agreement.

Cho'Kai leader Ka'Nef, his son Kn'Ri and a contingent of Cho'Kai warriors enter.

Jen'Pway bows. "Ka'Nef, it is an …"

Ka'Nef interrupts, clearly angered at Jen'Pway.

"The Terran named Tucker, where is he?"

"The assassin was a lone dissident."

"That may work for your weak-willed people, but do not insult my Intelligence, or my father's," Kn'Ri admonishes.

"It was the Terran named Tucker. He killed his own commanding officer, General Kensington," Quennok states.

Jen'Pway glares at him.

"Tucker is a cunning warrior and a Cho'Kai at heart," Ka'Nef says in a genuine tone of respect for an enemy.

"We are searching for him. I have called in the best trackers in the Alliance, the Zenaren," Jen'Pway states.

"Resolve this quickly, or else your alliance will have a new leader," Kn'Ri says adamantly.

The Cho'Kai leave.

Covert Ops Command Center

Robert, Dave and Ray look shocked when they see Ka'Nef while they were spying on his conversation with Jen'Pway.

Robert says in a tone of disbelief, "I killed that son of a bitch. How the hell is he alive?"

Bat'ai informs him, "When you went back and altered the past, Robert. You never went on a mission to the Cho'Kai base, so you did not kill him."

Ray sighs and shakes his head. "So we're back at dad gum square one."

"We are still trying to figure out to what extent the timeline has been altered," Bat'ai replies.

"How 'bout that Texas two-step we did an' ended up two years in the future?" Ray inquires.

Bat'ai states, "It was the culmination of multiple changes in the temporal timeline by the Empire and our going back in time. It has affected not only our reality, but the Empire's home reality and possibly others as well." He types in a command and performs a quantum level scan of the barriers separating the different realities.

Robert sighs. "How bad did we fuck things up, Bat'ai?"

"It appears that the quantum barrier is stable."

"What about where the Imperial bastards came from?"

"The Empire's home reality seems to have evolved into a benevolent dictatorship because the Triumvirate never existed there."

"Well at least some good came out of our fuck up," Dave snarks.

"David, before the Triumvirate altered our history, barely two million humans survived a thermalitic attack instigated by an Imperial battle cruiser."

"What's a thermalitic attack?" Robert asks.

"It was a weapon developed by the Empire designed to destroy the atmosphere and render a planet uninhabitable."

"Why didn't they still have it when the timeline was altered?"

"They eliminated the parents of the person who developed their weapon and ours."

"Keith Sykes?"

"Yes, Robert."

Robert verifies, "And since the Triumvirate is dead, it's now a fixed point in time?"

"Yes."

"I'll tell you one thing; I sure as hell don't want our old timeline back," Dave says.

"Amen to that."

"Ya ain't jokin' son."

"B, call Ryan and Ricardo, have them meet us in the Ops briefing room in five minutes."

"Yes, Robert," Bat'ai replies. He opens a channel to Ryan and Colonel Ricardo Pasqualle, Chief Tactical and Training Officer, while Robert, Dave and Ray leave the command center, passing through a security shield, which confirms their identity.

Cho'Kai Base – edge of Bwentani system

Ka'Nef and his son enter a bay, which has been set up as a crude medical center.

They walk to Doctor 'John Burke', who is the Imperial Chief Medical Officer and one of the few survivors of the massive assault by Alliance Forces shortly after the Covert Ops Force altered their history.

"Doctor, any change in their status?" Ka'Nef asks.

'Burke' replies, "I have managed to stabilize them physically, but they remain in a coma. I do not have the medical expertise to reverse it."

"You have studied Terran medicine," Kn'Ri scoffs.

"My application of medicine mainly involves inflicting pain to extract information, not curing disease."

"Doctor, I suggest you find a way to revive them. The renegade Terran named Tucker just killed their own leader, and they show signs of putting together a counter offensive. The Celestians are incompetent and will be quickly defeated in battle."

"If we could capture one of their medical officers, along with the Techian who upgrades their technology, we may be able to achieve your goal," 'Burke' suggests.

"A cunning suggestion," Ka'Nef replies. He turns to his son. "Kn'Ri, contact the Henoki cult leader."

"Dev'pok?"

"Yes, their spies have been supplying us with vital information on their missions, limiting their success. They may be able to locate the enemy base of operations."

"Yes, *Sabon* (Father)." Kn'Ri leaves.

"I shall leave you to your work, doctor. Notify me of any change, one way or the other."

"Yes, Ka'Nef."

Ka'Nef leaves.

'Burke' returns to what he was doing: monitoring the stasis chambers, which the Cho'Kai plundered during the invasion of Earth shortly before its destruction. He checks the vital signs of surviving Terran Empire Commanders 'Robert Tucker, 'Ray Watson', Vince 'Colretti' along with captured Kabrelian scientist Talak'Vin.

CHAPTER 4

Covert Ops briefing room – 1500 hours

The Senior Staff reviews their ops strategy, along with the newest piece of Intelligence they've received: Ka'Nef is once again the Cho'Kai leader and they are going to increase their presence on Bwentani Prime, and what it means to their people.

Robert addresses Lyle, "During your time with the Celestus Alliance, what kind of influence did Ka'Nef have in Celestus Operations?"

"Truth be known, Bob, he never met with Jen'Pway or the Council. He always sent either his son or one of his commanders," Lyle states.

"Guess shootin' Lyle must've really pissed 'im off," Ray cracks.

The staff laughs for a moment, before returning to the seriousness of the situation.

Robert nods, "That's not far from the truth, Ray. When they were allied with the Empire, they would let the Triumvirate do their dirty work while they did the fighting. The Celestus Council is not known for their brutality and I'm guessing that Ka'Nef's patience is wearing thin with them."

Lyle nods in agreement. "One time he did send his son, Kn'Ri to execute a Celestus Council member for failing to carry out a Cho'Kai directive. I heard that Jen'Pway was sick for a week."

"That mother fucker has no problem having our people executed, but he gets squeamish when it's one of his own," Dave growls, disgustedly.

"What surprised the hell outta me is that he didn't go ahead and execute Jen'Pway," Robert muses.

"Because Jen'Pway keeps the people obedient and productive," answers Lyle.

Ray scoffs. "Since when did the Chicken Chokers start givin' a hoot 'n' hell 'bout people cooperatin'?"

"Bwentani Prime has the raw materials needed to fuel their propulsion system. When I was forced to convert their system, it all but eliminated their need to destroy a planet to replenish their resources," Bat'ai says with a slight tone of guilt.

"So the bastards blew up our planet out of spite?"

"Yes, David. I also modified their DNA to this reality."

"True, but in the process you saved billions of lives, B. There is nothing to be ashamed of," Robert says assuredly.

"Thank you, Robert." Bat'ai sighs, before continuing "I checked the schematics for the reverse polarity weapon you used to defeat the Cho'Kai in the alternate timeline. It will not work."

"Why not?' asks Lyle.

"It is incompatible with the technology they currently possesses. It appears they are not the same Cho'Kai you faced ten years ago."

"How the hell did that happen?" Robert exclaims angrily.

"I could go into a long and technical explanation, but simply put; we can only manipulate time and reality so much before it rebels against us."

"Is that what caused the temporal shock wave?" asks Robert.

Bat'ai states, "Yes, plus the Triumvirate, who instigated the phenomenon in the first place no longer exists."

"So it's a fixed point in time?" asks Ray.

"Yes, Raymond. Though as someone who has experienced at least a half dozen changes in this reality alone, this one seems to be the most bearable."

"So you're suggesting that we don't try and change the past?" Robert asks.

"Yes, Robert, unless it is to simply restore this reality," Bat'ai replies.

Ray furrows his brows. "So if we tried ta go back an' take out the Chicken Chokers?—"

"We would experience a temporal shock wave that would make the previous one seem like a small ripple on a pond," Robert interrupts.

"That's an apt metaphor Robert, since it would tear apart the quantum structure of this reality and possibly others as well."

"Let's be glad those maniacs aren't around anymore."

"You ain't kidding, Dave." Robert chuckles, before asking, "Bat'ai, so if I'm to understand what you're saying is that this reality is out of temporal balance?"

"Yes, Robert."

"How would we restore it?"

"By going back and changing the original event."

"I thought you said this was a fixed point?"

"I am referring to the event that started the whole chain of events which led to our being here today," Bat'ai states. As he looks from face to face he realizes that he has totally confused the rest of the staff. He smiles to himself before continuing his explanation, "When you all disappeared in the Bermuda Triangle."

Lyle looks skeptical. "You mean that if they hadn't been drawn into that temporal vortex, none of this would have happened?"

"It makes sense, Lyle," Robert says. "If we hadn't been called into action against the Coalition at New Providence Island, the Henoki assassin wouldn't have opened the vortex and we wouldn't have had our DNA altered."

"Correct, except for one detail, Robert. The assassin was not Henoki, he was a Kallaxian."

This revelation stuns the rest of the staff.

"Doctor Burke's ancestor performed the autopsy and we preserved the body. When we made contact with Quennok and Berellus, they confirmed it was a Henoki assassin from a rogue faction, probably the *Dev'cha*, used to create distrust between us. It was the basis of the alliance we made," Robert says still in shock by this turn of events.

"It was before the quantum DNA scanner was perfected," Bat'ai tells them.

Robert asks, "Have you run a scan to make sure we don't have any Kallaxians or any other spies onboard?"

"We are running continual scans, Robert."

"That's reassuring."

"So I can assume we're not going to go back and reset the temporal timeline, so to speak?" Lyle asks.

"I would say only as a last result, an Omega Defense," Robert replies.

"I shall research the optimal time to implement it. I must warn you, if we go through with it, you will have no recollection of the past one hundred and ninety seven years and your DNA would revert back to normal. You would live a normal human life span of one hundred and twenty years," Bat'ai cautions.

Robert sighs as the realization suddenly hits him, "Which would mean I wouldn't marry Lin and Ana wouldn't exist.'"

"More than likely, Robert."

"Things would have ta be really FUBAR fer us ta do that," Ray says.

Bat'ai furrows his brows, "FUBAR?"

"Fucked up beyond all repair," Robert replies. "In other words, a black hole would have to open up and suck us all in," he says, half joking.

"We actually did experience something like that, Robert," Bat'ai says in all seriousness. "The Terran Empire fired a thermalitic weapon in our reality. Since the weapon did not originate here, it opened a quantum black hole.

Fortunately we developed probes and satellites that contained it. You called it Quantum Armageddon."

"And I'm going to guess that the people that designed the probes and satellites no longer exist," Lyle states.

Bat'ai replies, "I am the only person remaining, General. We have the schematics on file and we have the technology to reproduce it."

"The Cho'Kai and the Celestians don't possess the time travel technology so we're safe," says Dave.

"Their subatomic disintegrator weapon is almost as dangerous. I think it's time to do a covert op and at least attempt to put it out of commission," asserts Robert.

"The Cho'Kai have pretty much stayed out of our hair, if we provoke them, they could retaliate against our people," Lyle cautions.

"With Ka'Nef getting involved, I have a feeling the Cho'Kai are going to start asserting themselves anyway, Lyle," Robert replies.

Lyle exhales deeply. "I hope you're wrong, Bob, but I know better than to go against your instincts."

"A sabotage mission would be asking for trouble, but if we can do a stealth recon and gather Intel, that would at give us a clue as to what they're planning to do," Robert suggests.

Lyle orders, "Put an op together, have Ryan and Ricardo get Intel from Bat'ai and run it by me when you're ready."

"We'll have a plan by 0700 tomorrow.

"Dismissed."

Dave activates his neural link, "Ops Two to Alpha One come in."

"Go ahead, Ops Two," Mike replies."

"Alpha team report to the training room. Hot ops."

"Be there in two shakes o' a rattlesnake."

Robert and Dave chuckle at Mike's colorful response and then go to the command center to get a layout of the Cho'Kai base.

CHAPTER 5

Cho'Kai Command Center

Ka'Nef and Kn'Ri meet with the leader of the Henoki *Dev'cha* cult, Dev'pok to reward him for his loyal service to the Cho'Kai.

"You and the Celestians have been unsuccessful in the apprehension of the Terran renegade Robert Tucker and his forces," Ka'Nef states.

"Their base is too well hidden, your lordship," Dev'pok replies, his speech sporadic because he is not used to speaking verbally and the Cho'Kai's telepathy is not developed enough to comprehend mental communication.

"You have supplied sufficient information to set up numerous ambushes and traps. The Celestians have been too incompetent to capture them. I am charging you and your warriors with finding and either capturing or eliminating them."

"I will reserve the honor of killing the Terran to you, Ka'Nef. I only request that we dispose of his abomination of an offspring."

"That honor is yours, Dev'pok."

He is about to reply, when he suddenly bears an unusual expression on his face. At the same instant, the gemstone in the middle of his pendant starts glowing blue.

"Ka'Nef, I sense a presence that does not belong here," Dev'pok states. He pauses, and with a look of disgust says, "It is a blasphemous Henoki and a Bwentani."

Ka'Nef addresses a warrior at the control station, "We have intruders, lock down the base; all warriors seek out and apprehend them."

"Yes, Ka'Nef," Ta'Rin replies. He presses a button that activates an alarm, then grabs his weapon and leaves the command center, chanting their battle mantra, *Ka'ni'dei* (Fight and kill.)

"I offer my services to locate the intruder. The Terrans developed technology to make themselves invisible, but I may be able to locate the infidel even if he is unseen," says Dev'pok.

"Go with my son."

He bows to Ka'Nef and follows Kn'Ri to a weapons rack. They each grab a rifle and leave the command center to aid in the search.

Ka'Nef goes to the control panel and presses a button, which activates the 'natural environment' of the Cho'Kai home world: swirling gasses, electrical charges and fluctuations that will short circuit all non-Cho'Kai technology.

Cho'Kai landing bay

The covert ops team leaves the camouflaged WA-13 and are about to begin the recon of the base, when an alarm goes off with a warning in the Cho'Kai language that there was an intruder in the base.

The team quickly returns to the WA-13 and shuts the door.

"How the fuck did they know we were here?" Robert shouts as he and the others turn off their invisibility vests.

"I do not know," Bat'ai replies from the tactical station. He checks his scanner and says "It appears we have another problem."

Robert is about to ask, when the stations in the WA-13 begin to fluctuate.

The invisibility shields fail, making the Outlaw visible and vulnerable.

"What the hell happened?"

As Bat'ai works on restoring the systems, he responds, "They have produced their natural environment and it has caused our shields to fail. We are quite visible."

Robert looks out of the main windows and sees a squad of Cho'Kai warriors approaching.

"Shit! We have a greeting party. Do we have weapons?"

Ray tries to activate the Fusion Generated Pulse Beam Weapon. "Pulse beam weapon ain't workin', Bob."

"Can you fix it?"

Bat'ai replies, "It may take a moment."

"We don't have a moment!"

Dave opens the weapons locker and pulls out some conventional weapons, along with a couple of sniper rifles.

"Bob, we'll get on the roof and pick off as many as we can while Mike and his team secures the dock."

Robert nods in agreement, and then opens a hatch leading to the roof of the WA-13. He immediately becomes disoriented and closes the hatch.

"They somehow reproduced their atmosphere here." Robert tells them. "Now we know why no one has attempted a recon mission before now."

Bat'ai reboots the WA-13 main computer and manages to get partial shields online. He also gets the scanners operational and does a sweep of the Cho'Kai dock.

"Robert, there is an environmental control panel along the south wall, approximately one thousand meters from our location. If we can disable it, we would be able to open a vortex and escape."

Robert sighs. "I'm a pretty good shot, but their damn environment is too disorienting."

"Our zero G suits should work," Dave tells him.

"OK, I'll take out the controls and pick off as many as I can. Secure the dock and set up some special surprises for them."

"Good hunting," Dave says.

Robert gets into a specially designed suit to combat the Cho'Kai environment, slings his rifle over his shoulder, opens the hatch, and climbs onto the roof of the WA-13.

He sets up his rifle and gets into a prone position.

"OK, B. gimme a reading," Robert says into the mike of the zero g suit.

"Two hundred ten degrees South West, fourth panel to the right of the junction."

Robert sets his rifle and adjusts his scope to locate the panel. After locating it, he trains the rifle on it and says, "Taking the shot." Then he takes a breath, releases it, and squeezes the trigger.

A muffled shot rings out and the panel explodes, shorting out the environmental controls.

Robert feels himself becoming lighter and realizes that he disabled the system completely.

"I did too good of a job, B. There's no gravity out here."

"Our propulsion system is back online, along with the shields, we are able to leave. I am activating the shields and equalizing the pressure." Bat'ai states.

"Good work."

A few seconds later he hears a hiss, and then the top hatch opens. Robert sends his rifle down and gets back in just as the Cho'Kai enter. They begin to open fire at the WA-13, but suddenly drop dead because of the lack of a breathable atmosphere.

One of the Cho'Kai manages to activate a heavy steel door, which seals the dock.

"Can we open a portal?" Robert asks.

"The vortex activator is still inoperative, but we do have weapons, Robert," Bat'ai states.

"Blast the fucking doors!"

"Ya got it, son!" Ray replies.

Robert gets in the pilot's seat, presses the quick start to activate the engines and the WA-13 lifts off.

Ray targets a wall and fires the Pulse Beam Weapon.

Outside of the Cho'Kai base

A section of the base explodes outwards, followed by the WA-13 exiting through the gaping hole.

A squadron of Cho'Kai fighters leaves from a different dock, joined by Celestus fighters from Bwentani Prime and Zenaren hunting ships from the nearby Kurai system.

Robert sees what is happening and grunts "We got everyone and their fucking uncle after us. Is the vortex activator operational?"

"The Cho'Kai environment has done considerable damage to most of our systems. I will need at least a day to get everything operational."

"They got us outgunned 'bout a hunnred ta one, Bob. We wouldn't last five minutes in a fire fight," Ray tells him.

"Do we at least have the quantum shields?"

"Yes, they are at twenty-five percent efficiency. I can cloak us, but can only do so for about an hour."

"How far can we get in an hour?"

Bat'ai informs him, "Our maximum velocity is eighty percent of light speed. We may be able to get to the Kabrel system before the shields start to fail."

"Is the Kabrel system under their control?" Robert asks.

"The Kabrel system is uninhabited. The sole planet in the system that could sustain life was destroyed almost two years ago."

Bat'ai detects Zenaren ships matching their course.

"Robert, we have four Zenaren ships following us."

"Those bastards have the ability to track us even in stealth mode," Robert replies.

"Raymond, employ a scattering field and launch a decoy to confuse their scanners," Rillius suggests.

"I'm on it," Ray replies.

"I think some zero G mines would dissuade them from following us," Dave says.

Ray presses a button, which releases a dozen six foot diameter mines, which float in place, nearly undetectable by conventional scanners.

The Zenaren enter the area where the escaped ship was last reported.

The ship's commander, Sullix orders his weapons officer, Volix to activate their enhanced scanners, which are sensitive to the ion wake caused by spaceships.

The scanners pick up the faint trail left by the WA-13.

Volix is about to communicate his findings, when two ships suddenly explode simultaneously, followed closely by the third.

"Sir, they have deployed zero gravity mines, one is fifty meters off our port bow," he urgently states.

"Evasive maneuvers," Sullix commands.

The ship attempts to evade the mines, but they pass within ten meters, which causes the mine to magnetize and attach itself to the ship and a light begins to flash.

Ten seconds later, the last Zenaren ship explodes.

Bat'ai watches the last ship on the screen go dark.

"That was the last Zenaren ship Robert. There isn't another one within a million kilometers," Bat'ai reports.

"Shields, Mr. Worf," Robert cracks."

Bat'ai looks very confused look by what Robert has just said and turns to Rillius, who shrugs his shoulders.

The team laughs as Bat'ai activates the stealth shields and Robert sets a course for the Kabrelian moon.

Cho'Kai Base

Ka'Nef is furious about Tucker and his people being on his station, and not only escaping, but causing extensive damage to a dock. He also finds out that they eluded capture and destroyed four Zenaren ships, and that their current whereabouts are unknown.

As he paces in the command center cursing in his native language, Kn'Ri realizes that it is wise to keep his distance from his father until he calms down.

He motions to Dev'pok and they walk out of the command center.

"I feel my warning was inadequate," Dev'pok confesses.

"The fault is not yours. We have underestimated the cunning of the Terran and his men," Kn'Ri replies.

"Terrans can be extremely treacherous."

"There is one who could help us to apprehend them. But his medical condition is beyond our abilities."

"Henoki medicine is advanced," Dev'pok states.

"I thought your people renounced medical knowledge."

"Our ancestors did. We are more practical."

"Do you have such a physician?"

"Not among my people, but there is a doctor that follows the teachings of their false god. I may be able to arrange for her to be brought here."

"They allow a woman to do such thing? They are only good for preparing sustenance and breeding," Kn'Ri scoffs.

"If her presence would offend you, I shall search for another doctor," Dev'pok says apologetically.

Kn'Ri chuckles. "No, that will not be necessary, bring the doctor. I suggest you depart. My father will be quite aggravated for a time."

Dev'pok bows his head to Kn'Ri and leaves.

Kn'Ri is about to go back into the command center, when he sees a warrior thrown out of there, slams against the wall and collapses to the ground, dead.

He decides to go inspect the dock and make sure the repair crews fix the damaged dock or they will suffer the same fate as the unfortunate warrior, who just happened to be at his duty station.

He picks up his pace, when he hears his father's cursing echo in the hallway.

CHAPTER 6

Moon orbiting Kabrel six

Robert pilots the WA-13 to a large cave located on the dark side of the Kabrelian moon. Bat'ai activates a field to contain the artificial atmosphere provided by the Outlaw.

Ray, Rillius and Bat'ai are checking over the computer and the defensive systems, while Robert, Dave, Mike and the ops team provide security at the entrance of the cave.

The team medic, Cal'vek and Rillius walk to where Dave and Robert have set up a make shift observation post.

"Sir, I think it was our fault we were discovered," Cal'vek confesses.

"What do you mean, Cal?" Robert replies.

"When we entered the Cho'Kai hangar, I felt a very powerful presence probe my mind."

"Mine as well, Robert," Rillius states.

Dave replies, "According to the Intel supplied to us, the Cho'Kai possesses limited telepathic abilities."

"Sir, it may have been a *Dev'cha*," Cal'vek replies.

"On the Cho'Kai station? I thought when Quennok allied with the Celestians, it made the *Dev'cha* irrelevant."

"Apparently the Cho'Kai have a different view of them then they used to. It could also explain how they have been bird dogging our ops," Robert hypothesizes.

"So you shot Lyle for nothing," Dave teases.

Robert chuckles. "Yeah, let's not tell Lyle about that."

Cal'vek tells them with a tone of shame, "Sir, I will resign if I am putting our team in danger."

Robert assures his medic, "Cal, you are a valuable asset to our team and to our mission. Doctor Burke has been requiring more help in the medical section. With a few years of schooling, you can be certified as a doctor."

"I would enjoy that, sir," Cal'vek happily replies.

Rillius says, "*Binzah*, I feel that until we can determine if the *Dev'cha* have been compromising our missions, we should exclude the Henoki and Bwentani operatives from our covert missions and transfer them to our conventional units."

"Good idea. You and Zerellus can run conventional ops with your forces."

Rillius nods, "Agreed.

"How are Ray and Bat'ai doing?" Robert asks.

"They have managed to restore full weapons and shields. Communications and quantum systems are still affected."

"So in other words, we can't open a vortex or even call for back up," Dave replies.

"I am afraid so, David."

"Great, at full speed we'll get back in about twenty thousand years," Dave cracks.

"Not necessarily, David," Bat'ai replies as he walks to the temporary command center.

Robert asks, "You got the quantum vortex working?"

"No, Robert. I found an alternative method of travel employed by the Kurai," Bat'ai states.

Dave scoffs. "The Kurai? Those bastards are allied with the Zenaren."

"In this reality, David. In the alternate timeline, they were our allies and you were friends with their leader, Kaleel."

Robert nods. "What's this alternate means of travel?"

"It is an artificial wormhole."

"How is this different from the quantum vortex that the WA-13 uses?" Rillius asks.

"The technology we use has the ability to transport us from one point to another instantly. The Kurai wormhole is basically the same, but on a much smaller scale."

"What kind of technology do you require?"

"I can create it by modifying the Pulse Beam Weapon."

"How far of a jump can you make with it?"

"It is difficult to be precise, but the Kurai have achieved jumps of up to one thousand light years using technology inferior to the WA-13," Bat'ai replies.

"A single jump would get us out of range of the Cho'Kai and everyone else who wants a piece of us," Robert replies.

"How long will it take?"

"I can create it in a few seconds."

"Bob, come in," Ray calls Robert on his neural link.

Robert taps his neural link. "What's up, Ray?"

"We better git the hell outta dodge. Dunno how they did it, but them sum'bitches found us an' they're sendin' everything they got our way."

"We're Oscar Mike (On the move)." Robert yells to the team, "We have incoming hostiles, haul ass back to the ship!"

Robert and Dave grab the computer and monitoring equipment and move quickly to the WA-13. They reach the Outlaw, toss the equipment in the cabin, then wait by the doors until the ops team gets in. Then they get in and secure the cabin.

"Punch it, Ray!"

"Ya got it, son," Ray replies.

He fires up the engines to the WA-13 and pilots the craft out of the cavern.

Bat'ai sits at the weapons station and begins the equation to open the wormhole.

Robert asks, "B, can you control the destination?"

"Not as accurately as the regular quantum vortex."

"Is there a way to get us within one hundred thousand kilometers of the Cho'Kai base?"

"I believe I can accomplish that."

"Ya wanna go back there? Are ya outta o' yer Longhorn skull?" Ray admonishes.

"Ray, that base is different than the last two that we have reconned. They were affected by the time change the same way we were and we have to find out how."

"Are our shield an' weapons workin'?"

"They are fully functional, Raymond. I can open another wormhole in less than ten seconds," Bat'ai assures him.

Robert is about to reply, when an alarm goes off at the tactical station. He mans the console and checks the scanner. He sees at least fifty blips on the screen.

"We got company, they'll be on us in less than a minute," Robert reports.

Bat'ai finishes the equation and presses the fire control for the Pulse beam weapon. "Wait five seconds, and then enter the vortex, Raymond."

A wormhole forms in front of the WA-13. Ray mentally counts down from five, and then pilots the Outlaw into the wormhole.

Bwentani system - one thousand kilometers from Cho'Kai Base.

The wormhole opens and the WA-13 emerges. The teams sees that they are too close and have been detected by the base. The external weapons on the station begin to rotate towards them.

"Shit!" Robert exclaims. Bat'ai is about to reply, but Robert stops him. "I know, B. I'll make the scan and we'll get the hell outta here!"

Bat'ai quickly enters the calculations for the next jump, and then stands up. "I can perform the scan quicker. When I complete it, press the flashing button on the panel and it will open a wormhole."

"Ya better make it quick, they're fixin' ta open a big can o' whup ass on us," Ray warns from the pilot's station.

Bat'ai sits at the tactical station, runs a quantum level scan of the base. After he finishes, he says "Open the wormhole, Robert."

Robert presses the button and the wormhole opens.

Ray pilots the WA-13 towards the wormhole. They are stopped five hundred meters from the event horizon. The wormhole dissipates ten seconds later.

"The Cho'Kai has us in an Immobilizer Beam."

Robert exclaims, "Shit! How the hell did they get past the shields?"

"I do not know. I shall attempt to disrupt them," says Bat'ai.

"Let me at the fire controls," Robert says.

Bat'ai stands up as Robert goes to the controls, resets the Pulse Beam Weapons and aims at the tower emitting the Immobilizer Beam.

The weapon destroys the tower transmitting the beam.

"Ya better open the dad gum wormhole, they're fixin' ta blast us ta smithereens," Ray yells.

"Get us the hell out of here; we'll make the jump from somewhere else."

"Ya got it, son," Ray replies. He sets the engines to maximum and the WA-13 flies away from the Cho'Kai base.

Robert gets up and moves aside so that Bat'ai can return to the weapons station. Bat'ai enters calculations for the next wormhole.

Ray pilots the Outlaw into the vortex, sending them five thousand light years away from the Bwentani system, safe from the Cho'Kai and Celestians.

"This jump has drained the weapons and propulsion systems. We will have to wait thirty minutes for the system to re charge," says Bat'ai.

"Great, we're sitting ducks for the Cho'Kai and Celestians," Robert sighs.

"We are quite safe, Robert. We are five thousand light years from the Bwentani system."

"Where the hell are we?"

Mike looks out the main viewer and says, "The Hadar system."

"How do you know?" Robert asks.

"It looks exactly the same as the Empire realm."

Dave looks out the main viewer. "Any unfriendlies?"

Mike replies, "It was an Imperial stronghold there. Here, couldn't tell ya."

"Let's not take any chances. Set shields to maximum and let's have a look around," Robert says.

Dave eyes him. "Do you think that's such a good idea?"

"Well we have thirty minutes to kill; besides, when was the last time we just did some good old fashion exploration?"

"Uh, never."

Robert nods. "We may as well start. Besides, this may be a good place to set up another base just in case we're unable to get the quantum vortex back online, or we run into this problem again."

Dave nods. "Good point. OK, is it just me, or did the Cho'Kai just use our own immobilizer beam against us?"

Robert nods in agreement. "Yeah, and when the hell did they develop the technology to recreate their atmosphere inside the station?"

Bat'ai looks uneasy. "Robert, David. I know how they accomplished it."

"How?"

"Talak'Vin."

"That's impossible. Our Intel says he was killed almost two years ago by the Cho'Kai on his home world."

"When we altered history, the Empire may have captured him and planned to use him the way they used me until the Alliance attacked the Empire. We may have to prepare ourselves in the event some of the Imperial leaders survived."

Robert shakes his head in disbelief. "The Triumvirate? They were killed in the attack."

"Did they get visual confirmation?" Bat'ai asks.

"The temporal shockwave could've wreaked havoc. But why haven't we heard anything before now?"

"They could have been incapacitated." Bat'ai checks the status on the weapons system. "We still have twenty-five minutes. There is a planet that can support life and appears to be uninhabited. We can make a quick survey, then come back and fully explore it later."

"Yeah, it'll be nice to explore a planet without being shot at," Robert says.

"As long as ya keep the Star Trek jokes ta yerself," Ray cracks.

Robert chuckles. "No promises"

Ray shakes his head, and then pilots the WA-13 to the fourth planet of the Hadar System, where they discover the remains of an Imperial Base.

A scan of the garrison reveals it has been deserted for almost two hundred years. They land at the headquarters and recon the building.

Once it has been cleared, Bat'ai and the team enter the command center, where they see an antiquated database.

Bat'ai gets the system operational and they discover that when they altered time, somehow the Imperial stronghold was brought into this reality and that they fought their way across this sector of space, ending up invading Earth around the same time the Cho'Kai attacked in 2217.

"What do you think, Bob? We have a readymade base," Dave says,

"Seems off the beaten path and they probably wouldn't think of looking in a deserted Imperial strong hold."

"Should we leave the team to secure the base?"

"No, if they get in trouble, we wouldn't be able to get to them in time."

Dave nods in agreement.

"We are ready to make the next jump. I feel I may be able to get us a lot closer to the Taquan system."

"I'm ready to get out of here," Robert quips.

They return to the WA-13. Robert gets in the pilot's seat activates the engines.

He suddenly becomes light headed and says, "Ray, you better take the helm."

"What's the matter, Bob?" Ray asks.

"I got dizzy. It passed, but I don't want to take any chances."

"Ya better have Liz take a look at ya."

"I'll be OK, just a headache."

Robert stands and lets Ray sit at the pilot's station. He sits in a jump seat with the ops team and rubs his temples, having a difficult time getting over the sudden bout of vertigo.

Bat'ai uses a scattering beam to mask their trail, opens a wormhole and they make the jump, ending up six thousand light years from their base.

After a third jump they successfully return to the Taquan system, and consider themselves fortunate to escape an enemy that is a lot more dangerous than any they have ever faced before.

CHAPTER 7

Cho'Kai base – R&D lab

Doctor Talak'Vin has recovered from the injuries he sustained when the Alliance Forces attacked the Imperial Base in Washington, DC shortly after the Covert Ops team altered history.

He still requires several hours a day to regenerate in the stasis chamber, but he is still able to assist the Cho'Kai in upgrading their technology based on his theories and data he stole from the Special Ops Force in a different timeline.

Ka'Nef, Kn'Ri and 'Burke' enter the lab.

'Burke' uses a device to measure Talak'Vin's vitals and general health. 'Burke' checks the device and nods with approval. "You are getting stronger, Doctor Talak. Soon you won't need the stasis chamber at all."

"I am indebted to you, Doctor." He turns to Ka'Nef. "And I am grateful to you as well, sir."

"You have accomplished in four months what our people have not been able to do in a thousand years," Ka'Nef replies.

"I studied the Special Ops Force database when they encountered your people in the other reality. They took advantage of a design flaw in your propulsion system and were able to send you back to your native dimension. I have corrected the flaw so their device is no longer useful," responds Talak'Vin

"Recreating our atmosphere to nullify their technology also ensures they will not be able to sneak onto the base again."

A warrior enters the lab and salutes Ka'Nef.

"Sir, the Terrans attempted to enter the base again. We had them in the device the Kabrelian invented, but they were able to destroy it and escape."

Ka'Nef looks momentarily furious and is about to 'kill the messenger' when he suddenly takes a deep breath, and asks. "Where are they now?"

"They are not within rage of the tracking device."

"That has a range of one thousand light years. That is not possible. Their quantum device is offline and they could only travel a few light years at maximum speed," Talak'Vin replies.

"What about their technology that can make them invisible?

"Their stealth technology? I have rendered it useless, Kn'Ri," Talak'Vin pauses before stating, "There is only one method they could have employed. An antiquated form of travel used by the Kurai, which created, for a lack of a better term, forms a spatial wave and the ship would travel on it until it dissipated."

"How far can they travel?" Ka'Nef asks

"Properly applied, about a thousand light years."

"They are out of range of our fighters, *Sabon*," Kn'Ri states.

Talak'Vin informs Ka'Nef, "The Celestians have the Terran's technology, but do not possess the means to travel that distance. The Zenaren employ a similar technology. They may be able to track them, if there is a trail."

"Contact them."

"At once *Sabon*," Kn'Ri states. He leaves the lab.

'Burke' clears his throat. "If you no longer require my services; I wish to return to the lab and attempt to bring the others out of their coma." After receiving an affirmation, he leaves the lab.

Talak'Vin waits until 'Burke' is out of ear shot before speaking. "Ka'Nef, I feel that I should warn you about bringing those men out of their coma. They are very unreliable and will betray you the first chance they get."

"We had no intention of doing so," he replies. "The Terrans we are confronting are treacherous and the Imperial Terrans are without honor. We learned they were going to attack us before the other Terrans destroyed them."

"Then why do you keep them alive?"

"I am using them to bait the renegade Terran into a trap." Talak'Vin appears confused. "You have supplied me with the information that Tucker recorded about his genetic double, along with his hatred for him. I will have that fool Jen'Pway announce that the rulers of the Terran Empire survived and they are signing an alliance with the Celestians. Tucker will be motivated to stop this at any cost."

"A brilliant plan, sir. Imperial Commander Tucker is also responsible for altering history and making this timeline a reality."

"If we adhered to our Code of Battle, I would have been obligated to form an alliance with them, but Terrans have a limited sense of honor and will fight to win by any means necessary; so we have to adapt to effectively combat them."

"I will study the scan I made while they were vulnerable in the landing bay and adapt your systems to fully combat them."

"I shall leave you to your work."

Ka'Nef leaves the lab, then telepathically calls his son and senior advisors to formulate a strategy to capture Tucker and break the will of the surviving human military, along with both the rebel forces eluding the Celestians, and those being held in their 're-education centers'.

CHAPTER 8

Command Center – Taqua Four

The senior command studies the Cho'Kai base, along with data they retrieved from the Imperial base, and a quantum DNA scan of the people on board.

They are stunned to find four human life signs with the Imperial DNA signature, a Kabrelian, and fifty Henoki signatures, which are all slightly different from the DNA profile they have on record.

"They have to be *Dev'cha*, sir," Cal'vek states. They evolved differently from the rest of our people. Their telepathy is more advanced because of living under the ocean and forsaking dry land."

"That's why they could sense you even when we were in stealth mode," Robert replies.

"Yes, sir," Cal'vek replies shamefully.

"Cal, please don't blame yourself about this, we went in blind and were lucky to get out in one piece. Now we have better Intel."

"Yeah an' their dad gum technology is actually ahead o' ours. Shit, they were hard ta handle when we had the upper hand, unless we kin counter 'em, we should jest pull our people out an' stay here," Ray laments.

The rest of the senior staff look stunned by Ray's comments.

"That ain't like you, Ray; walking away from a fight," Robert replies.

"Hell, son, ya know I'm always rarin' ta open a can o' whup ass. But let's face it; as long as they have our people, the Henoki and Bwentani, they got us by the short hairs."

"He does have a point, Bob," Ryan replies. "As long as our people are bein' held, there ain't a whole helluva lot we kin do 'bout it."

Robert pauses, and then taps the neural link behind his ear. "Z. What's our status on our fighters?"

"*Kemzeh* (father–in-law) our pilots have been fully trained on the WA-13s and Chief Pallia states that she has another four squadrons ready to be flight certified."

"Good work. Have the Senior Squadron Commanders report to the ready room in ten minutes. Also have Chief Pallia meet us and have her give us a status on the WA-13 that was zapped by the Cho'Kai base."

"Yes, *Kemzeh.*"

"Lyle and Ryan, do you mind joining us in the briefing room?"

"Of course not," says Lyle.

"Sure, son. On my way."

"Ray, you, Dave, Bat'ai and Rillius continue to analyze the Cho'Kai base and the Intel we got from the Empire. I have a feeling they have a part of our past we can use against them."

"Robert, I have confirmed that Talak'Vin is working with the Cho'Kai." Bat'ai states.

"I know, you already mentioned it."

"Need I remind you that all of our defenses are based on his theories of quantum and temporal mechanics?"

"I vaguely remember having a conversation about this, but I don't remember when."

Bat'ai looks surprised. "Robert, it was when you were the Special Ops Commander and the Empire first kidnapped Doctor Talak."

"You mean, I'm getting my memory back?"

Bat'ai stares at him and pauses. "I am not certain, but I may have a theory. Have Doctor Elizabeth scan you and see if having contact with the Cho'Kai environment altered you in any way."

47

Robert sighs. "Great, does this mean I'll grow a third eye or something?"

"No, Robert, but it may hold the key to unlocking the quantum amnesia you have about the other timeline."

"OK, I'll do it after I brief Rico and the others."

Robert, Lyle and Ryan leave the command center while the others continue to study the data they collected.

Linaiok and Ana walk to them.

Ana asks, "Bat'ai do you think something happened to my *Hu'Neh*?"

"Your father came in contact with the Cho'Kai native atmosphere for a brief time and it may have recovered some of his memories from our alternate history."

Ryan calls the command center.

"Ana, come in," he says with an urgent tone.

"Go ahead, sir," she replies.

"Darlin', git a medic here. Yer daddy collapsed an' he ain't lookin' so hot."

"What is your location?"

"East corridor, fifty meters from the command center."

"I'll have a medical team there right away."

"Thanks, darlin'."

Ana calls the medical center to get a team to her father's location, and is about to leave, when she realizes that she can't abandon her post.

"Go, I will cover the command center," Bat'ai tells her.

"Thank you."

She motions to her mother, who didn't hear Ryan's call. She relays what Ryan told her and they go to the medical center, which has nearly become a ritual after one of Robert's missions.

Medical Center – one hour later

Ana, Linaiok and the Senior Staff anxiously wait to hear why Robert suddenly collapsed.

Elizabeth enters the waiting area and goes to Bat'ai.

"Bat'ai I need your help."

"What is the matter, doctor?"

"His cellular structure is in a hyper-active state, and I can't determine the cause."

Bat'ai follows Elizabeth out of the waiting room.

Thirty minutes later, Elizabeth and Bat'ai enter the waiting area, motion to Linaiok and Ana and they speak to them off to one side.

A look of horror crosses their faces. They compose themselves, nod to Elizabeth and then enter the exam room.

Lyle and the rest of the staff walk over to Elizabeth.

"Doctor, what's happening?"

Elizabeth sighs, and then with a look of resignation states, "Colonel Tucker is dying."

Each of the senior staff is stunned into silence.

Lyle's voice quavers as he asks "W-w-what happened?"

"Bat'ai stated that the Colonel came into contact with the Cho'Kai's native environment while inside the station."

"Fer a split second," Ray replies.

"Wait a minute, Doc. We've done dozens of missions inside their environment during the war and it has never affected us," Dave states.

"We were in the Widow Maker with full shields an' usin' the zero g suits," Ray replies.

"You were never directly exposed to the environment, and it seems to have been modified to attack the Colonel's DNA," Elizabeth states.

"In what way?" Lyle asks.

"Bat'ai says that he found a virus designed to attack the human DNA at the quantum level."

"What's it doin' ta Bob? Reversin' what happened ta us?" Ray asks.

"It not only reversed the cellular regeneration, but it has speeded up the aging process. Chronologically he's two hundred and thirty-one, but with his enhanced DNA, he's still thirty-seven. In the last hour he has aged forty years. Bat'ai has him in stasis which has stopped the process."

"Can you treat him?" Lyle asks.

"We can't, and that's for the same reason we can't reverse what the vortex did to your DNA. It would kill him."

Ryan asks, "What would happen if ya take 'im outta the stasis chamber?"

"He will die almost immediately."

Dave becomes angry. "Dammit! We can't just give up trying to find a way to save him." He feels himself losing his composure and says, "He has saved everyone in this room at least once, for crying out loud, he's probably saved at least four different quantum realities. The universe owes him one."

"I agree, David," Rillius stoically replies. "Bat'ai stated that if we attempted to do a temporal incursion into the past, we could trigger a temporal shock wave bigger than the one that sent us through time. We could destroy our reality."

Dave is about to respond, when Bat'ai leaves the exam room.

"Bat'ai, Doctor Burke says that we can't save Bob."

"She is correct. I am sorry, David."

"What about going back in time?"

"The temporal balance..."

Dave yells, "I don't give a fuck about the temporal balance! I have fought side by side with this man for over two hundred years. I am not letting him go out like this."

He lets out a yell of fury, punches a hole in the wall and storms out of the medical center, yelling obscenities as objects are heard shattering and breaking in the hall.

Just as upset as Dave, Lyle says, "If I were twenty years younger, I'd be doing the same thing."

Ryan thinks of something. "Bat'ai, ya said somethin' awhile back 'bout alternate realities, mebbe one o' our doubles kin help."

Bat'ai nods. "We first acquired quantum technology from the Time Defense Force in a different reality. We have not had contact with them in the two years since the Empire altered our past. To be honest, the temporal wake could have affected them as well."

"Kin ya contact them?" Ray asks.

"I can try."

Ray looks in the room. He sees Robert in the stasis chamber, appearing to be twice as old as he was not more than two hours ago.

Linaiok and Ana sit next to Robert, each holding one of his hands. They both look extremely upset, but stoic, whispering Henoki prayers to *Ama'diok* to welcome him into the Divine Hall, even though he is human, they beseech the deity to welcome their loved one as one of their own.

Ray walks over to them. "Don't give up, girls. Bat'ai is gonna try ta git help."

Linaiok nods and whispers, "Thank you, Raymond."

Ana hugs her godfather and says "Please help him, *Hu'Neok*, I want my *Hu'Neh* to know his grandchild."

"We will do everythin' we can, darlin'."

Ana nods, gives him a kiss on the cheek, and then sits next to her father, holds his hand and continues the prayers to *Ama'diok*.

Ray puts his hand on Linaiok's shoulder and then leaves the room. He sees that Bat'ai and Rillius are not there.

"Lyle, where did Bat'ai an' Rillius git ta?"

"They went to the command center to try and contact that other reality."

"Lemme know if anythin' changes."

Ray leaves the medical center and jogs to the command center He sees Rillius and Bat'ai attempting to locate the TDF reality. He also sees Liaok and Dolquin, leader of the aquatic Taquan inhabitants focusing on telepathically locating the other realm.

Ray is about to speak, but Ricardo silences him and motions for him to step outside.

"How is he?" Ricardo asks, extremely upset.

"Don't look good, Hoss. This mebbe the only chance we got," Ray replies.

"Bat'ai says that it's too dangerous to go back in time. He said Dave is really pissed off."

"Yeah, I'd avoid 'im fer awhile. Lia an' Dolquin are helpin' 'em?"

"Yeah, Bat'ai said there is a lot of quantum interference and feels that they can help establish contact."

His statement is cut off by Liaok saying in a far off tone "Bat'ai, set the quantum matrix to a setting of 2-7-4-3-6-9."

Bat'ai sets the matrix to the prescribed setting and then opens a channel. "This is Bat'ai of the Special Operations Command to the Time Defense Force Command Center come in."

'Jackie Kensington's' voice is heard. "This is Colonel Kensington. We have been trying to reach you for two years. We recorded a temporal shock wave off the charts." She pauses and says in a tone of anger "We lost several of our Senior Staff, including Paul Foster, his wife, Miguel Herrera, Keith Sykes and Alberto Sanchez. General Tucker wants to speak to Commander Tucker immediately."

"Unfortunately, that is not possible. Colonel Tucker is dying," Bat'ai replies.

There is silence on the line, followed by TDF General 'Tucker' saying "I'm sorry. What happened?"

"It is a long story, General. To make it brief, the Terran Empire radically altered our history and caused a temporal event of such magnitude, our whole quantum reality is out of temporal balance, and the only way to save Commander Tucker is to go back and prevent an event from happening."

"And you want us to do that for you?"

"No sir. I have a possible solution, but it would require working with your Bat'ai or Pomar Zerellus."

'Tucker' says with a tone of sadness "Our Bat'ai died two years ago. We have been at war with the Celestians."

Bat'ai replies, "It appears that we have a common enemy. I will download our information and alternate reality along with a scan made of the Cho'Kai environment that poisoned Commander Tucker."

"Cho'Kai? We never encountered them," 'Tucker' replies.

"They are an extremely dangerous species, General. They found us through excessive temporal incursions."

'Tucker' sighs. "I warned Bob what would happen if you guys kept fucking with the temporal and quantum barriers."

"I assure you, General, it was not us. I will bring the scan of the event, along with information about how the Empire and Cho'Kai altered our history."

"You have permission to cross. We must warn you, we are under siege from the Celestians. They attacked us shortly after you supplied us with the defense technology and we have been unable to implement it because of losing Paul and our Chief Technician Mike Parnell."

"We lost our Chief, too. He was the one who helped me design the reverse polarity weapon that sent them back to their own dimension."

"I suggest you cross before the Celestians attack. They've been known to drop in unannounced."

"I will. Thank you, General."

Bat'ai closes the channel, downloads the scan along with the alternate history profile and research concerning the major temporal upheaval recorded by Allied Defense Radar just after the temporal shock wave was formed.

He opens a small quantum portal and steps through it.

CHAPTER 9

Time Defense Force Command Center- TDF City Ship *New Mexico*

Bat'ai emerges from the portal to the sound of alarms and chaos as the TDF is in the midst of an attack by the Celestian Forces using the WA-11 Snipers they confiscated from the TDF two years ago.

Bat'ai springs into action. He goes to a tactical station, and with hands moving quicker than the human eye can perceive, he enters a command that creates a quantum shield that surrounds the *New Mexico*, located near the Sandia Mountains on the outskirts of Albuquerque, which is now under the ocean that covered the Earth after the planet was struck by a meteor in 2035.

He then enters another command that overrides and disables the WA-11 defenses, allowing the weapons on the city ship to fire and destroy some of the Celestian forces, causing them to retreat.

Bat'ai turns from the station and sees the surviving TDF Senior Officers staring at him.

"I am sorry, if I overstepped my…"

He is interrupted by 'Tucker', 'Jackie', 'Ray', 'Carlos' and 'Zerellus' each warmly greeting him.

"Thank you, Bat'ai, you saved our ass," 'Tucker' tells him. The others also express their gratitude.

"I am glad to be of service, General. You were not under attack when we spoke."

'Tucker' replies, "The bastards are using the Kurai wormholes and they're able to penetrate our global shields."

"I can upgrade your defenses. All I ask is that you allow me to travel twelve hours back in time."

"Can't ya do it from yer own dimension?" 'Ray' asks.

"No, Raymond. As I told the General, our reality is out of temporal balance because of the Terran Empire. This is also why some of your people vanished. They went back in time and killed their parents before they were born. Since we are genetically linked, when they killed our people, your people and conversely their own people were affected."

Bat'ai goes to a console, downloads a comparative history of his reality and the tampering that led to two major upheavals in the timeline.

They stare in horrified silence as they watch the Special Ops Force reality disappearing in a blink of an eye, replaced by the Allied Defense Force and the Empire committing planet-wide genocide, leaving only a quarter of a million beings left alive.

They then witness the Covert Ops Force return and rescue the pilots and prevent the Empire from obtaining their defenses.

They watch a split second battle between the ADF and the Cho'Kai and Imperial forces, followed by a major distortion ending up on Bwentani Prime two years later in a span of thirty seconds.

"Shit! So the past two years in your reality somehow sped up because of the temporal shock wave?" 'Tucker' surmises.

"We were in a temporal vortex and it propelled us forward in time and apparently the rest of our reality was sped up as well."

"You are not able to undo this?" 'Zerellus' asks.

"It is a fixed point in time. The Triumvirate was killed and since they are the reason this occurred, it cannot be undone."

'Ray' has a puzzled look. "Then why do ya need ta go back twelve hours, son?"

"We went on a reconnaissance mission to the Cho'Kai Base. They had Talak'Vin working for them. He altered their atmosphere to affect human DNA. When Colonel Tucker came in contact with it, his DNA was affected and he aged forty years in less than an hour. We have him in stasis, but if we do not go back and prevent this mission, he will die."

Ray shakes his head. "So somethin' as simple as goin' back an' stopping a recon mission could completely fuck yer dimension up?"

"Yes, Colonel."

"Yer also fightin' the bastards that look like us, the Cho'Kai an' the Celestians? Damn son, sounds like we're both up shit's creek without a paddle or the boat," 'Ray' muses.

"That is an apt metaphor. I can help you upgrade your defenses and help you at least be on par with the Celestians here, and then I can go back and stop Colonel Tucker from going on this mission."

"Fair enough, but what about the Intel you gathered?"

"I have it saved in my device, which is protected from changes in the timeline. Truth be known, we could have gotten the same information with a quantum scan from our base. But now that we know that Talak'Vin is with them, he could trace our scan back to our base."

"Just to let you know, we lost a lot of our schematics in the initial Celestian attack and Bat'ai designed our systems." 'Tucker' manages a laugh and says "Looks like you're the only one who can retrieve it."

"Then I shall get started immediately."

A beep is heard at the communications console. 'Jackie' goes to the panel and listens to a message from Ana.

She acknowledges the message, and then walks to where 'Tucker' and Bat'ai are standing. Her voice quavers as she tells Bat'ai, "I just heard from Colonel Tucker's daughter. The stasis field did not help. He died five minutes ago, and it appears several of the other people that went on the mission have become ill as well. I'm sorry, Bat'ai."

"Thank you, Colonel," Bat'ai replies, visibly upset. He pauses and says, "I shall get to work immediately on upgrading your defenses."

"Bat'ai you should concentrate on saving your people," 'Tucker' states.

"General, to use a human cliché; I have all the time in the world. It is obvious your situation is of greater concern. What are your current offensive and defensive capabilities?"

"We still have the single squadron of WA-13s you provided. The quantum shields were never deployed, which allowed the Celestians to destroy the single duplication device, preventing us from producing more fighters or weapons and the schematics for everything are intact, but stuck inside Bat'ai computer."

"Then that is where I shall start."

Bat'ai walks to the data station, which shows signs of not being used in at least two years. He checks the damage and sees that several relays were destroyed, leaving the files locked in an encrypted server, with an access code known only to the other Bat'ai.

He closes his eyes, places his hand on the console, and then with his other hand punches in an access code, which brings the information to an alternate monitor.

"I was able to retrieve the data. If I can get three people who are mechanically proficient, we can have these vital systems operational in less than forty-eight hours."

"Ray, Zerellus and my son Quevok can help," 'Tucker' states.

Bat'ai laughs to himself and says, "Forgive me, but I am used to Robert having a daughter named Anamiok."

"That's Ricardo's daughter," 'Tucker' says with an uneasy tone.

"What is wrong?" Bat'ai asks.

He tells Bat'ai, "Ricardo was killed in a fire fight with a Zenaren raiding party. He sacrificed himself to save Ana and her sister Alejandra."

"I am sorry, General. We should not waste any more time."

"Folla me," 'Ray' says.

He leads Bat'ai and 'Zerellus' out of the command center and they walk to an elevator which leads them to the city ship's R&D facility, which is heavily fortified and ready for attack.

New Mexico Landing bay – 01.15.2222 TDF temporal time reference

Bat'ai and the senior staff look at the results of two day of non-stop construction by Bat'ai and the R&D staff: four more squadrons of the WA-13, renamed the Cobra in honor of 'Ricardo's' courageous sacrifice.

Several duplication devices ranging in size from a desk top to a hangar are in the Bay's repair shop.

They also constructed the quantum shields that not only surround the *New Mexico*, but the entire planet and which will protect the fifty remaining city ships.

He also upgraded the weapons, which are now able to destroy the old WA-11 fighters, even with their defenses fully deployed.

"We can't thank you enough, Bat'ai. We can now hold them off and may be able to turn the tide of the war," 'Tucker says.

"It is the least I could do. You have supplied me with the device which I can use to safely travel back in time and cross the barrier without causing a major temporal incursion. It may even help us restore the temporal balance."

"When Commander Tucker recovers, have him give me a call and we can reminisce about all the trouble he got me into," 'Tucker' teases.

Bat'ai replies, "He does not remember you, or this reality, General. The incursions have wiped out all memory of this reality."

"Then he can't get my ass in trouble anymore, and I'm not sure if that's a good thing or not," 'Tucker' jokes.

Bat'ai laughs and says, "I shall give him your regards in any case."

He shakes hands with Robert, and then the rest of the R&D and senior staff.

He sets the quantum and temporal coordinates, opens a portal and steps through it.

CHAPTER 10

Covert ops Command Center - temporal time index 01.13.2222. 0900

Robert is briefing the ops team on their mission to the Cho'Kai base. They are about to leave, when a temporal portal opens and Bat'ai steps out.

"Bat'ai, have you lost your fucking mind? You said any time travel would mess everything up," Robert admonishes.

"It was a risk I had to take," Bat'ai responds.

Robert eyes him. "That black hole better have opened up and swallowed us."

"No, but something just as catastrophic has occurred."

Robert appears skeptical. "What?"

"I had better show you."

Bat'ai goes to a console and plays the visual recording of the mission on the Cho'Kai base, the narrow escape and Robert, along with the rest of the human Covert Ops Team members getting sick and dying because of the Cho'Kai atmosphere.

"What the hell did they do ta us?" Ray asks, spooked at watching himself rapidly aging and dying.

"Talak'Vin altered the Cho'Kai atmosphere to attack your enhanced DNA, reverse the regeneration of your cells, which accelerated your aging process."

"Cal'vek and Rillius weren't affected?"

"No, but the Cho'Kai have the *Dev'Cha* Henoki on board, plus they have acquired our technology."

"So we're back to square one, shit three steps further back," Robert laments.

"No Robert, we obtained a quantum scan of the base, plus we found an abandoned Imperial base dating back almost two hundred years," Bat'ai states.

"They've been here that long?" Dave asks.

"Yes. From what we obtained from their database, they were drawn into our reality and thrown backwards in time the same way you were propelled forward. They did not possess our advanced technology and it took them almost two hundred years to fight their way to Earth and encountered our Allied Defense Force after we upgraded the weapons and defenses."

"Bat'ai, yer talkin' 'bout a closed causality loop," Mike says, intrigued.

Bat'ai nods, impressed. "Very observant, Michael. You must have taken Talak'Vin's "Quantum and Temporal" class at the Academy."

"Yep, two semesters."

"I think you found a new assistant, Bat'ai," Robert muses.

Mike has a panicked look on his face. "If it's all the same, Colonel, I'd rather stay in Special Forces."

Robert laughs." I wouldn't take you out of the field, but he can use a hand from time to time in R&D between missions."

"Be a good change o' pace."

"Robert, I also recovered the Time Defense Force technology we lost when they altered our history. It has the technology we can use to counter Talak'Vin."

"We always suspected that bastard would be a turncoat," Robert states. "You claimed he was first abducted by the Empire in the other reality. Our Intel said he was killed when our forces attacked the Empire. Now you're saying that Talak and the Triumvirate survived?"

"We detected four life signs with Imperial DNA. We did not have time to do a full genetic screen because we were caught in an immobilizer beam."

"Now that we don't need to go on the recon mission, what's our next step?" Dave asks.

"I will monitor the timeline to make sure there was no lasting impact. Michael, Raymond and Zerellus can go over the technology I acquired from the Time Defense Force."

"Whoa, son, that's a little outta my area o' expertise," Ray replies.

Bat'ai responds, "Understood. Zerellus, it is based on Bwentani equations from three hundred years ago. It was abandoned because they did not possess the technology."

Robert's eyes widen, "We may find more about it in the archives on Bwentani Prime."

"Bob, we ain't exactly welcome there," Ryan says.

Robert chuckles and is about to reply, when Ana calls him from the communications station.

"*Hu'Neh*. You may want to see this."

The senior staff walks over to where Ana is sitting. She is looking at a monitor with an angry, disgusted look on her face.

Robert is about to ask her about what is bothering her, when he sees Jen'Pway on the monitor with 'Robert Tucker'. Kn'Ri is standing next to them.

"What the fuck?" he says in disbelief.

Celestus Headquarters – Bwentani Prime

Jen'Pway stands at the podium, the 'exuberant crowd', encouraged by a contingent of Celestian soldiers aiming weapons at them, are chanting Jen'Pway's name. 'Tucker' stands beside him in his Imperial Triumvirate uniform and wearing dark glasses.

Jen'Pway raises his hand to silence the crowd. "It is a day that will be long remembered in Celestian Alliance history. An ally, long thought to have been massacred by Tucker's Traitors has been found by our benefactors, the

Cho'Kai and brought back to health. Here is Commander Robert Tucker of the Terran Defense Force. Our doctors have solved a long standing mystery as to how two genetically identical Terrans can exist without actually being related. We have confirmed that this Robert Tucker is the original and the renegade Terran Robert Tucker and his team are the result of a failed genetic experiment ..."

Covert Ops Command

Robert shuts off the feed and shakes his head. "What a fucking crock of shit!"

"An' this tick terd thinks people are gonna believe this?" Ray says with a sarcastic tone.

"Come on Ray, you remember politicians and the corporate media growing up? They took a page from the Nazi propaganda playbook; tell a lie, make it big, tell it often enough and people will take it for the truth."

"Joseph Goebbels," Lyle replies.

"Give the man a cigar," Robert quips, which causes confused looks from Rillius and Bat'ai. Robert laughs, "It's just a human figure of speech."

"If that bastard is alive, who knows what he'll do to our people in the detention camps," Dave says.

Robert shakes his head. "Something isn't adding up. If the Triumvirate survived, where have they been the last two years? And did you notice that he wasn't the one doing the talking. You know he wouldn't let a bureaucratic weasel like Jen'Pway have the stage; he's too much of a control freak to let anyone but himself be in charge. I'm no doctor, but he appeared drugged, almost catatonic."

"You think this was staged for our benefit?" Lyle asks.

"Yeah, they're trying to lure us into taking him out," Robert replies.

"How do we know that it's even him?" Lyle asks. The others look quizzically at him. "Remember when Jen'Pway had Kallaxians posing as Ryan and Palonius when they were supposedly executed. How do we know he isn't doing the same thing?"

"Shit, you're right, Lyle," Robert replies. He turns to Bat'ai. "Can you run a DNA analysis on Tucker from the footage we just got?"

"Yes, Robert."

Bat'ai downloads the footage and analyses 'Imperial Commander Tucker's' DNA.

After he gets the results, he turns to Robert and reports, "It is him."

"They know how much ya hate the sum'bitch. An' Ka'Nef's kid was jest standin' there. Betcha there's a shit load o' Chicken Chokers lurkin' around," Ray quips.

"Bat'ai, how safe would it be to do a quantum scan of Bwentani Prime?"

"If Talak'Vin has improved their technology, we may compromise the location of Taqua Four."

Robert nods in agreement. "Call up a chart of the systems surrounding Bwentani for five thousand light years in all directions."

Bat'ai nods and calls up a chart, which resembles a gigantic ball containing thousands of systems.

"All directions, Bob?" Lyle asks.

Robert chuckles and quips, "Ever notice in all the sci-fi shows and movies, the ships only move two dimensionally parallel to the planet and not go up or down away from the polar caps?"

"Limited human thinking, *binzah*," Rillius replies.

"Yup, now if we can find one of those abandoned Imperial Bases and use just enough technology to fool them into thinking it's our base; we can lure them into a firefight and get the Cho'Kai base to respond. Once we do that, we go in, take out the Celestians and reclaim Bwentani Prime."

"An' git the planet blown up," Ray snarks.

"That shield surrounding Bwentani Prime has kept them from attacking and if we get control of the shield and free our people, we'll have the planet back before the bastards know what hit them."

"This has to rate as one of the craziest plans you've come up with," Lyle retorts.

"Hey, no crazier than when we took out the Henoki Armada with six aircraft and an Obliterator filled with heat seeking missiles."

"Or Kabul," Dave snarks.

"Let's not go there, son," Ray replies, getting some laughs.

"Seriously, up until now we have only done small ops and a few sniper missions. They think we are just a small band of thugs with some automatic weapons and a single outdated fighter. We now have eight squadrons of WA-13s, a division of soldiers and three Special Forces teams. We divert the Cho'Kai base and we can take out the Celestians in one shot. But I will not commit us until we have good Intel."

Lyle nods. "Agreed. Ricardo, Ryan and I will devise a battle plan after you get the quantum scan of Bwentani Prime and get updated Intel of their troop and fighter compliments."

"Tel'Quan."

"Quennok's aide? Too risky," Lyle says, disagreeing with Robert's suggestion.

"He's the only one on Bwentani Prime that knows the truth."

Lyle replies, "If we tried to contact him, the *Dev'cha* would execute him."

"Bat'ai set up the security shield around their command center."

"Quennok removed it when the Celestians took over the colony and they have the *Dev'cha* probing them for disloyal citizens and attempting to locate you."

Dave sighs, "There goes that op. The second we go in to try and take out Jen'Pway and his goons, the *Dev'cha* goes after the Henoki people"

"Not necessarily," Robert replies. "The colony is an enclosed environment. If we use a sleep agent to take them out, we secure the colony, go after our people in the detention camps, take out the Celestian military facilities and then force Jen'Pway to surrender."

"There's a lot that go wrong in an op this complex," Dave replies.

"I know. We have to do this in stages. We get the Intel, at the same time we'll start probing their defense for weaknesses."

"Bob, the *Dev'cha* have been on us every time we've attempted to do that."

Robert has an enigmatic grin. "Mike, Bat'ai and I have been working on a solution to that. Follow me."

He leads them to the R&D lab, where they see a modified Pulse Beam Weapon mounted on a tripod."

Lyle starts to ask, "Is that…"

Robert interrupts him. "Yup, a portable pulse beam weapon."

"That damn thing looks like it weighs fifty pounds, not exactly Special Forces friendly," Dave observes.

"That's only half the surprise. Once perfected, it will change the way we carry out covert ops."

Robert motions to Bat'ai, who sits at a portable console and types in a command. Both the weapon and the stand vanish, and then reappear on the other side of the lab.

"Holy shit! Ya done an' went Star Trek on us!" Ryan exclaims.

"Not quite. Their system was based on breaking down matter, transporting it to a location, and then reassembling matter back into its original form. Mike and Bat'ai simply incorporated the immobilizer beam and the vortex activator to pick it up and move it to its destination."

Ray looks concerned.

"Don't ya think it's kinda dangerous using that thing, especially the slightest change in the timeline'll fuck us up six ways from Sunday?"

"It is using a whole new system from the one we now use, Raymond," Bat'ai replies. "It uses technology supplied to us from the Time Defense Force. We are replacing our quantum technology, because it is based on Talak'Vin's theories."

"What kind of range does it have?" Dave asks.

"We're still figgerin' that one out," Mike replies. "Doubt we'll be able ta transport ta Bwentani Prime from here, but we could probably use it from a WA- 13 in stealth mode."

Dave states, "The Cho'Kai can get past our shields."

Mike replies, "Not ennymore. We're replacin' the ole system with the one Bat'ai brought back."

"Great. What kind of time table are we looking at?" Lyle asks.

"To fully upgrade our fleet: seven to ten days."

"How about a squadron?" Robert asks.

"We will have them operational by the morning."

Robert nods. "Good, we'll test the system on our recon mission. What if Talak'Vin is still able to knock out our quantum vortex and shields?"

"I am installing a backup system that will use the Kurai wormhole without having to take our weapons off line." Bat'ai states.

Robert replies, "Good. Mike, you stay and work with Bat'ai."

"Understood."

Robert scans the room, "We do our recon in the morning. Until then, dismissed."

CHAPTER 11

Cho'Kai Base

Kn'Ri has returned to the base with 'Tucker', who has been placed back in stasis.

Jen'Pway appears uneasy at being summoned to the Cho'Kai command center.

Ka'Nef appears to be pleased with the day's events. "It was a truly cunning performance, Jen'Pway. Tucker's hatred for his genetic double will surely spur him into action."

"He may feel I am using one of my people to lure him into an ambush," Jen'Pway replies.

"Talak'Vin has stated they have technology to scan a being's genetic structure. Then he will realize that Imperial Commander Tucker is alive."

"Ka'Nef, we have searched every conceivable hiding place on Bwentani Prime, we have even conducted a scan using Doctor Talak's genetic device. We cannot locate him."

"Because, you *krupa* (fool), he is not on the planet," Ka'Nef replies with a tone of annoyance.

Jen'Pway blurts out, "Impossible, they could not get through the magnetic shield."

Talak'Vin walks over to them with a data pad. "I have detected the residual signature of their fighters near the Bwentani moon of Septimus. They have not been on Bwentani Prime for quite some time."

Jen'Pway stammers, trying to defend himself.

Ka'Nef holds his hand up "They possessed technology beyond your comprehension and ours as well, until Talak'Vin was found. We shall handle Tucker and his men, while you will continue presenting Imperial Commander Tucker as a friend of the people."

"Shall I execute some of his men to further entice him?"

"No! You would turn them into martyrs," Ka'Nef snaps. He walks to where Jen'Pway is standing. "You will do only what is required of you: pacify the people and ensure their continued cooperation."

"Yes, sir," Jen'Pway meekly replies.

Ka'Nef motions to Kn'Ri. "Go with him, *koba* (son) to make sure this fool does not undermine our long term plans. If he does, replace him with someone that will carry them out."

"Yes, *sabon*," Kn'Ri replies, as he motions his warriors and leaves the command center.

"Talak, have the facilities been constructed in the Henoki colony?"

"Yes, sir. We can transfer the Terrans there."

"Do so immediately, along with the Terran Doctor."

"Yes, sir," Talak'Vin replies and exits the command center.

Ka'Nef goes back to his quarters and kneels in front of several statues: his father Tor'Ka and his lineage go all the way back to his ancestors, who led the revolt against the YakinKai one hundred thousand years ago.

He bows his head and telepathically asks for guidance and forgiveness for not adhering to the Code of Battle, which has been handed down since Kul'Ta established their rule after the revolt.

He also 'explains' his other cardinal sin; cooperating with an enemy rather than destroying them, stating that they have improved their weapons which will help achieve their goal of recreating their plane of existence. This will provide their warriors with unlimited opportunities to fight, sharpening their skills, which have severely diminished since they conquered the last known race in their dimension ten thousand years ago.

He sits silently for a moment, and then stands up, feeling that his plea was well-received and approved of by his ancestors.

Henoki Colony

Talak'Vin, 'Burke' and several *Dev'cha* warriors bring the stasis chambers containing 'Tucker', 'Watson' and 'Colretti' into the medical bay.

'Burke' and Talak'Vin connect the chambers to the medical monitors and transfer the controls to the stations.

Dev'pok commands, "Bring in the blasphemous doctor."

Two *Dev'cha* guards bring in Henoki doctor Maiok (Quennok's mate) and then shove her towards Dev'pok, 'Burke' and Talak'Vin.

Dev'pok gives her a look of disgust, and then motions for the *Dev'cha* warriors to leave, posting two of them outside the door.

Talak'Vin says in a polite, respectful tone, "Doctor Maiok, I am Doctor Talak'Vin and my colleague, Doctor John Burke."

Though surprised at his civil tone, she asks, "Why have I been held against my will?"

"Forgive the *Dev'cha*, they can be … fanatical in carrying out their orders."

"I have been forbidden to treat my people since the *Dev'cha* have taken over the colony."

"Today is an exception," 'Burke' replies. "We have several of our people in a comatose state and we were informed you are the expert in treating such traumas."

"Yes." Maiok walks to the stasis chambers, looks inside the clear covers and sees 'Robert' 'Ray' and 'Colretti'. She gasps, before whispering prayer to *Ama'diok*. "We were told that Commander Tucker and Watson were wanted by the Celestus Council and shot on sight."

"Yes, and it still holds true. These three are the last remaining members of the Imperial Command who were savagely attacked by Tucker and his band of traitors."

She is about to argue that Robert and his men were not traitors, but thinks better of it. "What can you tell me about how they were injured?"

Talak'Vin states, "Our records were destroyed in the attack, but Commander Tucker and his men led the attack on the Imperial Headquarters, commandeered a Cho'Kai weapon and destroyed Earth. I was a witness to these events."

Maiok is conflicted on whether she is being told the truth, but casts this aside and decides to live up to her oath to treat the sick and injured, no matter what race or affiliation her patient happens to be.

She grabs a medical scanner off a tray, uses it on 'Robert', 'Ray' and 'Colretti'. She takes it to a console, downloads the data and then calls up a diagram of their bodies, which highlights the areas that suffered trauma.

She studies the monitor, "I can treat the affected areas, but bringing them out of a coma is beyond my ability to heal."

Talak'Vin hands her a device. "I have used this to bring a person out of a coma, but in a state where they cannot talk or react to stimuli. I am a theoretical temporal and quantum scientist. Perhaps with your medical knowledge you can bridge the gap."

Maiok studies the device and says with a tone of awe, "Doctor Talak, this would advance medicine one hundred years."

"Then I will assume we will have your cooperation?"

"Yes, but I could not do this alone. I would need my medical staff and an engineer to makes the modifications."

"I shall allow one engineer. Is Quevok here?"

Maiok replies, "He has been detained because of his affiliation with Commander Tucker and the Terran Alliance.

71

Do you know my son?"

Talak'Vin tells her, "He was one of my most brilliant students at the Academy. I shall seek authorization from the Cho'Kai leader and Dev'pok for him to work with us."

Talak'Vin walks out of the medical bay.

"Doctor, a question if I may. If you are a medical doctor, why would you need my assistance?"

'Burke' replies in no uncertain terms, "The Empire regrettably did not place emphasis on healing as much as coercing information and cooperation, which I would have done if you had not offered your services, and if you attempt to undermine our attempts to heal my Commanders, I will not hesitate to use my...expertise on you, Doctor. Don't mistake my civility for camaraderie. You are a means to an end and not the only doctor in this colony. I will have no problem in replacing you. Have I made my point clear?"

Maiok nods her head yes, feeling slightly intimidated, while at the same time suppressing her thoughts because of the *Dev'cha* posted outside the door.

Talak'Vin returns with the rest of the medical staff and Quevok, who shows signs of being physically abused by the *Dev'cha*.

Maiok is overjoyed to see him, but composes herself and says, "Quevok, it is pleasing to see you again."

"*Ki'Neh*, (Mother)" Quevok curtly replies.

"Your mentor has supplied us with a device that would help bring these men out of their coma."

She hands him the device and Quevok examines it. 'Burke' sees the look of contempt on Quevok's face and reiterates the warning he gave to Maiok.

Quevok composes himself takes the device from Maiok and runs a scan to retrieve the schematics. He states, "I cannot complete my work here, may I return to my lab?"

'Burke' replies while motioning to the *Dev'cha* and Cho'Kai warriors outside the medical facility, "Yes. Doctor Talak and Doctor Maiok will accompany you."

The three leave the lab surrounded by the security detail. 'Burke' has the stasis chambers hooked to the Henoki medical equipment, which is much superior to the Cho'Kai and Imperial equipment he is accustomed to working with.

The three go into the research lab. Talak and Quevok take the device and connect it to the diagnostic equipment.

"I am pleased to see you, Quevok. You were my brightest student," Talak'Vin tells him.

Quevok glances at the security detail posted at the lab entrance and then whispers "Why did you get involved with…them?"

He replies, "Simple, my boy: survival. You would be wise to cooperate."

Quevok does not respond.

Talak'Vin puts the schematics on the monitor. While he is occupied, Quevok types in a code and presses a button, which sends the information to Bat'ai.

CHAPTER 12

Covert Ops Command Center 1000 hours

Ana monitors a routine patrol of the system by a squadron of WA-13s, led by Jackie.

Ana contacts her. "Base to Patrol Leader. Anything to report?"

Jackie replies, "Other than some baby nebulas, all's quiet. Don't you miss the good old days when we had a fire fight to look forward to?"

Ana laughs, "Zerellus won't even argue with me anymore."

"I'll check back in thirty minutes, if I'm still awake."

Ana signs off, and is about to leave the comm station, when a light flashes and an encrypted message appears. She recognizes the code, and then contacts her father.

"*Hu'Neh*. I need you and Bat'ai in the command center."

"What's the matter, sweetheart?"

"I got an encrypted message, from Quevok."

"Be right there."

Robert and Bat'ai suddenly appear, startling Ana.

"*Hu'Neh*, how did you?" her voice trails off.

"That's just Bat'ai's latest invention. We now have the ability to move people and equipment without using the vortex. You said you had something from Quevok?"

"Yes," Ana replies, and then types in a command.

Schematics for an advanced device appears.

Bat'ai mutters somethin in his native language.

"What is it, B?" Robert asks.

"Robert, Doctor Talak invented a medical device that could theoretically reverse injury and even death."

"I thought the Cho'Kai self-healed?"

"They do."

Ana reads the message, written in the Henoki language and suddenly looks disturbed and angry.

Robert notices.

"Sweetheart, what's the matter?"

"According to Quevok, Your double, along with my *Hu'Neok's* and Black Ops Commander Colretti survived, but they are in a deep coma."

"Wait a minute, we saw Tucker at that bullshit news conference Jen'Pway had."

"Yes, Robert, but we both noticed that he did not move or talk, like he was drugged," Bat'ai tells him.

"They must've figured out a way to bring him around just long enough to make his appearance."

Ana pauses, before telling him, "*Hu'Neh*, it gets worse."

"What do you mean?"

"They claim to have evidence that you were the one that destroyed Earth."

"That's the same horseshit that Jen'Pway tried to shovel before."

Ana finds an encrypted file, opens it, watches the video feed and has a look of horror. "*Hu'Neh*."

Robert watches the monitor. His face turns red with outrage as he sees 'security footage' of the Cho'Kai command center and watches himself, Dave and Special Forces Operatives kill the Cho'Kai warriors, afterwards the Sub Atomic Disintegrator Weapon is activated. A blinding flash of light ends the video feed.

"This is why they issued the arrest warrant, *Hu'Neh*."

"Nobody's going to believe this. B, run a DNA analysis and authenticate this so called footage."

Bat'ai runs his analysis. He turns to Robert and tells him, "The footage is one hundred percent authentic. According to this, you and your team did destroy Earth."

Robert, clearly appalled, stammers, "That's impossible.

Other than a few days ago, we have never set foot on the Cho'Kai base."

"Actually, you have, Robert, when you, Raymond, David and Rillius rescued me from their base."

"That was in the other quantum reality, but we never activated the weapon."

"I have been postulating a theory and this may explain what happened. When we altered the timeline during our rescue of the pilots, we experienced the temporal wake that propelled us two years in time. The magnitude of it could have caused a quantum disruption that for a split second melded several realities together and in one of them your ops team did in fact destroy Earth."

"Bottom line, I may not have destroyed Earth, but our tampering may have been the catalyst, so I am guilty," Robert says, with an overwhelming feeling of remorse building inside of himself.

"What do we do, Robert?"

"Call the staff, let them know what's going on, then you, Mike and Ray take this footage, run a quantum DNA analysis on it. If it was me, I'll take responsibility for it, but if it was a different reality, we will investigate and get to the bottom of this."

Ana holds her father's hand to offer him moral support. She then contacts Ray and Mike to report to the briefing room.

Robert sighs and then taps his neural link to contact Dave, Lyle and Ryan to attend the briefing and if necessary, turn himself in for nearly eight BILLION counts of murder, making him the worst war criminal in Earth's history.

Briefing room

The assembled staff watches in horror as Bat'ai once again plays the footage of the ops team killing the Cho'Kai and Earth being destroyed.

"This has got to be some bullshit set up, Bob. We never attacked the base," Dave says, feeling as guilty as his friend at the destruction of their home world.

Bat'ai relays to him and the rest of the staff his theory on what happened.

"So ya think it was another version o' us?" Ray asks.

"It's possible, which would explain how we found the Imperial Base in the Kolromi sector." Robert replies.

"We may have another problem, Robert," Bat'ai states.

"What?"

"If Talak'Vin develops time travel for the Alliance or the Empire…"

"We're fucked six ways from Sunday," Dave replies.

"B. We're gonna have to risk exposing our location to warn Talak NOT to develop that technology," Robert warns.

"Why don't we jest warn 'im from that base we found?" Mike asks.

"Good idea. You guys download all the info we have on the temporal imbalance along with your theory about what happened."

"What makes you think Talak will listen?" Lyle asks.

"Kabrelians are survivalists by nature. He will listen." Bat'ai replies.

"Dave, you take the lead on this mission," Robert states.

"You're not gonna turn yourself over to those bastards. They'll execute you on the spot." Dave says after figuring out the reason for Robert's order for him to take command.

"No. I'll have Ana contact the Minarians, if they still exist. Even the Cho'Kai won't mess with them. At the very least I know I'll get a fair trial."

Dave sighs. "Then I should stand trial with you."

Robert shakes his head. "I was the mission commander, so the responsibility's mine."

"Let's figger out what happened first, Bob. We ain't gonna let ya martyr yerself," Ryan tells him.

He sighs, "I know. If it makes the Cho'Kai release our people, I'll fall on a sword."

Bat'ai looks confused.

Robert laughs. "In ancient times, Roman Generals would take a short sword, hold it against their gut and impale themselves if they dishonored the Empire."

"You humans do have strange ways."

"I know. Get the info and go with Dave's team. Ray, you and Mike run every kind of scan you can think of. Also document everything, even if it incriminates me."

"Ya got it, son," Ray replies.

Robert turns to Lyle. "I'm relieving myself of duty until this investigation's over. I am to have zero contact with anyone involved and do not brief me on what you found out, then turn the results over to the Minarians, so that they can determine whether I am to stand trial."

With a look of sadness Lyle nods and offers his hand and tells him, "I know you would never willingly commit genocide…"

"I almost wiped out the Henoki in the original timeline."

"You were at war."

Robert shakes his head "I also wanted payback for them killing my descendants. Sometimes I wonder what I'm truly capable of. This may be it."

"We'll stand by you, no matter what."

"All o' us, son," Ryan adds.

Robert nods, and then leaves the briefing room.

Ana and Linaiok are waiting for him.

"*A'nok.* What is going to happen?"

"I don't know, Lin. Can you stay married to a mass murderer?"

Ana replies "We do not know what actually happened, *Hu'Neh.* I cannot believe you would willingly do this."

"There's a chance I didn't do it, but, when we changed the past, we created the temporal wake that caused it to happen, so to some degree I am guilty."

"I am by your side always, *A'nok*."

"Me too."

Linaiok and Ana hug him. They can see the toll this latest revelation has taken on him and they take him back to their quarters so Robert can reconcile his emotions in private.

CHAPTER 13

WA-13 – Kolromi sector- 1300 hours

Ray and Bat'ai return to the abandoned Imperial base to establish contact with Talak'Vin.

A Special Forces team provides security around the old Imperial headquarters. A team of engineers sets up equipment in the old marshaling area.

"Ray ta Bravo Two."

"Go ahead," Morris replies.

"Son, I want ya ta keep yer eyeballs peeled. Enny sign o' Cho'Kai, Celestus or Imperial Forces, let us know right away."

"Yes, sir."

Bat'ai upgrades the antiquated communications equipment and incorporated special firewalls to prevent anyone but Talak'Vin from intercepting his broadcast.

"Raymond, we are quite safe, we are over five thousand light years from their space. It would take quite some time for them to reach us," Bat'ai assures him.

"I thought we wanted them ta find this base."

"We do, but after we have left. The automated defenses will make it appear this in an active base of operations."

"Jest the same, I'd like ta open a can o' whup ass on some o' them piss ants myself."

Bat'ai establishes a secure link. "Professor Talak, this is Bat'ai. Are you receiving this signal?"

"Bat'ai, my old apprentice. Are you surrendering?" Talak'Vin replies.

"No. I have some urgent information for you."

"Is it concerning the security footage your protégée sent to you?"

Bat'ai looks shocked "You know of this?"

"I supplied him with it."

"Is this a deception?"

"No, it is quite real. I warned you about being careful with your dealings with the Terrans."

"To use a human expression, the pot calling the kettle black," Bat'ai replies.

"These Terrans did not kill eight billion people."

"No, they destroyed over a dozen planets that we know of and at least fifty billion lives."

"That was another reality, *Tal'shul* (student)."

Bat'ai nods in agreement, remembering that Kabrelians share his ability to sense different realities.

"Yes, I am aware of this. *Pal'sha* (Professor), this is not why I contacted you, I have discovered…"

"This reality has a severe temporal imbalance. I detected it when your Commander Tucker altered time, and now several realities have melded together."

"Yes. Do you know how many?"

"At least six that I am aware of."

"I have scanned the quantum barrier. It is stable and there is no danger of another quantum black hole. But time travel is very dangerous and I am advising you not to develop time travel technology. We have already destroyed ours."

"I have no intention of doing so, my friend."

"Maybe we can work together and maybe we can find a solution."

"There is only one solution. Going back and changing the original event."

"I feared as much. I have already advised General Dickinson about this situation."

"I thought he was executed."

Bat'ai thinks quickly and replies, "His grandson. We have lost some personnel and he was the remaining senior officer."

Talak'Vin chuckles. "You have never been able to tell a convincing falsehood, old friend."

Bat'ai sighs and confesses, "This security footage has caused a great deal of distress among our senior officers. Vin, please do not relay this information to the Celestians or the Cho'Kai."

"My communicating with you would bring the most unpleasant form of punishment."

"Then we shall keep this between us."

"I fear that is not possible."

Bat'ai looks alarmed. "What do you mean?"

"I increased the range of our scanners and we detected your base in the Kolromi system. They are sending a task force equipped with my new hyper velocity drive. They will be there soon."

"How soon?"

"Soon enough. Good bye, my old friend," Talak'Vin says as he closes the channel.

Alarms go off in the Command Center and they pick up a wave of Celestian and Cho'Kai fighters.

Ray sees the blips on the screen. "Holy shit! They're sendin' everythin' but the kitchen sink!" He gets on the intercom. "Bravo Two, y'all better git back ta HQ pronto!"

"Yes, sir."

Seconds later, Morris and the team enter.

Two squads of modified Celestian WA-11s begin an attack run on the base. Ray activates the enhanced shields and sets the auto defenses to fire at the incoming craft.

The modified Pulse Beam Weapons easily penetrate the quantum shield and destroy half a dozen fighters.

Ray sees a squad of Cho'Kai fighters aligning themselves to fire on the modified Pulse Beam Weapon.

"Bat'ai, the Chicken Chokers are fixin' ta take out our guns! Time ta test that newfangled invention o' yers."

Bat'ai types in a command, activating the teleporter, causing it to disappear just before the Cho'Kai can fire on it. He then types in coordinates and a second command, causing the weapon reappear at a location to destroy the attacking Cho'Kai fighters, which it does an instant later.

"Raymond, I suggest we call for reinforcements. I detect another ten squadrons heading our way," Rillius tells him.

"Son, that is the understatement o' the millennium," Ray cracks before opening a secure channel to Ana.

Covert Ops Command

Ana, who is quite upset about the possible criminal charges facing her father, monitors the comm station, when Ray's urgent call comes in.

"Ops Three ta Base, Alpha One Priority, under attack by Celestus an' Cho'Kai fighters."

"Ops Three, sit rep."

"Two Celestus squadrons attackin', with ten more on an intercept course. ETA five minutes."

"Understood. Keep apprised. Out."

She presses the Alpha One Alert signal and says in a calm, but urgent tone, "Command to all squadrons, Alpha One Alert. Base in the Kolromi sector under attack, coordinates in nav computer, immediate scramble, I say again immediate scramble."

Robert quickly enters the command center, followed by Linaiok.

"Ana, what's going on?"

"*Hu'Neh*; *Hu'Neok's* team is being attacked."

"Dammit!" Robert exclaims, and then turns and starts towards the hangar.

"But *A'nok*, you were relieved of command…"

"I took myself off duty, and now I'm back on."

Ana immediately stands up, "I'm going, too."

He sternly replies, "You plant yourself in that chair, you're going anywhere."

"My *Hu'Neok* is out there, I'm going," Ana says, making it clear that she will not obey him.

Robert grunts, not wanting to waste time arguing with his stubborn daughter. "Fine. My ship, tactical station. Lin can you handle the comm center?"

"Yes. Be careful," she replies, with a look telling Robert that if something happens to their only daughter, don't bother coming back.

Ana telepathically tells her mother the situation. *"Ki'Neh, there are two squadrons of Celestian fighters attacking the base. Hu'Neok reports ten more will be there in five quells* (minutes)."

Linaiok acknowledges her and then sits at the control station, just as Lyle, Ryan and Palonius enter the Command center.

Linaiok relays to them what Ana told her. Ryan calls up the Kolromi system on screen and they see the nearly twelve dozen red blips on the screen bearing down on their new found base.

Lyle sees Robert, and is about to say something, but shakes his head and says, "Go!"

Robert motions to Ana and they run to the hangar. He sees Zerellus. "Our team is under attack in the Kolromi sector. I'm taking command of Alpha section. Ana's with me. You're on my six."

"Yes, *Kemzeh*."

He goes to his WA-13.

Robert does his preflight checks, gets a status check from his section commander and then calls Linaiok, "Ops One to Command, all units a go."

"Bob, this is Ryan. Y'all better haul ass, the Celestus

Alliance ships are 'bout five minutes from openin' a can o' whup ass."

"Feed us the coordinates, we'll hit 'em with a three prong attack."

"Ya got it, son."

"My squadrons will take the lead, Rico right flank, Jackie left flank."

Ryan states, "Calculatin' and sendin' coordinates now."

Ana sees the spatial coordinates appear on the navigational computer screen. "Coordinates received, sir."

"Ops One to Alpha and Bravo Squadrons, on my six. Charlie and Delta, with Colonel Pasqualle, Foxtrot and Golf, with Colonel Foster."

"ADF One, acknowledged," Ricardo replies.

"ADF Two, acknowledged," Jackie replies.

"Rico, your squadrons take off ten seconds after mine, Jackie ten seconds after that. We're gonna box 'em in, hit 'em hard and fast."

"Understood," they reply in unison.

"Ops One to command, we're Oscar Mike."

Ryan says, "Roger, go git 'em, son."

Robert nods to Ana, who opens a portal and two squadrons of WA-13s fly into it and disappear.

CHAPTER 14

Celestus Command Center – same time

Jen'Pway, Kn'Ri, and Talak'Vin observe the attack on the 'rebel base' in the Kolromi sector, which is now reachable thanks to Talak'Vin upgrading the Alliance's propulsion system. These improvements allow their fighters to reach speeds exponentially faster than the speed of light and the five thousand light year trip to the Hadar system can now be accomplished in a matter of hours.

"Very impressive, Doctor Talak," Kn'Ri says with a genuine tone of respect.

"You are too kind, sir."

"With this technology, we can now spread the influence of our alliance to the entire galaxy," Jen'Pway arrogantly states, receiving a dirty look from Kn'Ri.

"The propulsion technology is indeed impressive, but your fighter's tactics so far does not inspire confidence."

Jen'Pway goes to speak, but thinks better of it when two dozen white blips suddenly appear and their fighters begin 'disappearing', meaning they had been destroyed.

A short time later, a second group of white dots appear and begin attacking the Celestian attack force, followed seconds later by a third attacking the opposite flank, completely surrounding them.

"Sir, six squadron of enemy craft have—"

"I can see that, *krupa*! Where did they come from?" Kn'Ri screams.

"Unknown, sir, they…just appeared."

"That is impossible—"

"No it is not," Talak'Vin interrupts. "The Terrans at one time possessed extremely advanced fighters with stealth and quantum technology that can transport them anywhere in the galaxy in an instant. When the Empire altered time and eliminated several key members, the technology ceased to exist. My incursion into their database revealed one of the fighters survived and they were able to reproduce them."

"How advanced are they?" Kn'Ri asks.

"I fear far more advanced than the current capabilities of both Celestians and your fighters, and this is after I enhanced your technology."

"You stated..." Jen'Pway starts to admonish Talak'Vin.

Ka'Nef grabs him by the throat. "Your incompetence in allowing them to escape your custody allowed this to happen. Arrest him and confine him to the main detention camp...in general population."

Jen'Pway looks horrified and begins to beg for mercy as two Cho'Kai Warriors detain him. One hits him on the head, and he falls to the ground, unconscious. The warriors pick up his legs and drag him out of the Command Center.

"Recall the fighters," Kn'Ri commands.

"A retreat, sir?" asks a Celestian comm officer.

Kn'Ri is about to kill the Celestian for making such an insulting inquiry. He composes himself, and then replies "A tactical withdrawal. Doctor Talak, has the propulsion system to our base been upgraded?"

"Yes, sir. They have not been tested as of yet."

"I believe this will be a good initial trial. You will return with me to the base."

"Forgive me, sir. Who will be in command in your absence?' The Celestian comm officer asks.

"Summon the Henoki leader, Dev'pok. He is now the Celestus leader."

"Yes, sir."

"One more thing, Quennok and his people have been loyal to us. He is not to harm them in any way."

The Celestus comm officer nods in compliance and then contacts the *Dev'cha* leader to report to the Celestus command center, while a second comm officer orders the Celestus and Cho'Kai fleet to withdraw from the Kolromi sector, where they are facing a merciless onslaught from the ADF forces.

Space near Kolromi Prime - 1330 hours

The Celestus and Cho'Kai fighters have been driven off by the Alliance fleet.

Robert orders the fleet to return to Taqua Four, but remain on Alpha One Alert, ready to re-engage the enemy at a moment's notice.

Robert and Zerellus land their fighters and with Ana following close behind them, enter the Command Center.

Ray shakes Robert and Zerellus' hands, hugs Ana and says "Y'all really saved our bacon out there."

"Praise *Ama'diok* you're safe, *Hu'Neok*," Ana replies while continuing to hug him.

"I hear the new teleporter worked like a charm."

"Worked great, right up until they sent additional squadrons and blew the dad gum thing all ta hell."

"What concerns me, Robert was how fast they were able to send their fighters," Bat'ai states.

"They seemed to be coming in fast," Robert concurs.

"We did not detect any artificial wormholes or any spatial anomalies. What I did notice, however, is that they utilize a hyper velocity drive Talak'Vin had been postulating over the past decade."

"Faster than the speed of light?"

"Many times, upwards of a million times faster. I calculated they were able to travel from the Bwentani sector to here in only a few hours."

"Without an artificial wormhole?"

"Yes. Using your Star Trek vernacular, it was equivalent to travelling at Warp Twenty-one. This Terran, Roddenberry actually got some of the basic principles about faster than light travel correct, except they postulated that they could not travel faster than Warp Ten, which is inaccurate."

"Come on B, this was someone thinking this stuff up two hundred and fifty years ago, before we travelled in space," Robert says in his childhood hero's defense.

"Don't get me wrong, Robert, he was a genius who was ahead of his time, I can only imagine what he could theorize with today's technology."

All right, bottom line. Will they be able to detect and attack our headquarters?"

"The possibility is there, Robert. If Talak provides the Zenaren with updated technology," Rillius replies.

"That's what I thought. They are able to track our quantum drives, we may have left them bread crumbs to our front door."

Bat'ai has a momentary look of confusion, but then comprehends what Robert is saying, and then replies, "I resolved that problem, Robert."

"You did, how?"

"When I returned to the past, I travelled to the Time Defense Force Reality."

Robert nods. "I remember you telling us about them. This is where we got our quantum slipstream technology."

"Yes and the time travel technology. Their Bat'ai was dead and they could not access the technology we supplied to them, so I unlocked the encryption my counterpart entered." Bat'ai pauses, and then confesses "I...took the liberty of copying their database and found several programs which will aid us, including a component that will not only mask, but completely obliterate any quantum trail we leave, making it impossible for anyone, including the Zenaren to track."

"Does Talak have knowledge of this technology?"

"No. Talak'Vin was killed during one of the first attacks on the Celestians by your counterparts."

"They're at war with them in that dimension, too? Maybe we should compare notes."

"I shall make the arrangements…"

A shrill alarm stops Bat'ai's statement.

Ray checks the screen of the sector and discovers a massive distortion bearing down on them. "Bob, Bat'ai, we gotta huge ass object headin' our way."

"Can you identify it?"

"Nope, but the dad gum thing's 'bout as big as that Chicken Choker base. Two thousand light years and closin'. It's slowin' down, but it'll be on us in four hours."

"B, can you scan it?"

"Yes, Robert." Bat'ai sits at the tactical station, types in a set of calculations, which clears up the distortion."

"Holy shit!" Robert says in disbelief as they see the Cho'Kai Base coming at them travelling at a speed even Bat'ai cannot measure.

"Can we match their weaponry?"

"Not at this time."

"Shit. They'll probably see our escape and try to track us," Robert laments.

"What 'bout the program Bat'ai developed?" Ray asks.

"With the speed that thing is capable of, it would be on our ass every inch of the way," says Robert.

"He is correct," assures Bat'ai.

"How long can we hold them off?"

"That thing'll kick our dad gum asses an' take our lunch money," Ray quips.

"He is right, Robert. I fear our fighters would not last more than ten minutes."

"That's more than enough time."

"Fer what? Ta fill out our wills an' body bags?"

"No, to retake Bwentani Prime."

Everyone in the room says a collective "What?"

"*Hu'Neh*. The planet is heavily fortified," Ana states.

"By the Cho'Kai. We send in the Special Ops teams to capture the shield generator, communications center and free the main detention center," says Robert strongly.

"*Kemzeh*, they are mainly pilots being held in the camps," Zerellus tells him.

"We have a deep cover ops team in that facility. Darrel Henderson and his team have been laying low, gathering Intel and covertly sending us troop strengths," Dave replies.

Robert commands "Get on the horn and tell Darrel we are going ahead with Operation Valhalla and to wait for our signal."

"Understood," Dave replies and then goes to the WA-13 for the encrypted Special Ops transmitter.

"Valhalla, *Hu'Neh*?" Ana asks, confused.

"The Divine Hall for Vikings. Means we either free our people or die trying."

"I'm ready."

"Sorry, sweetheart, you better sit this one out. Z, bring your wife back to Command."

"Yes, *Kemzeh*."

"*Hu'Neh*," Ana replies in protest.

Robert takes her hand and tells her, "You're one of the bravest people I've ever known. If you weren't pregnant, I wouldn't hesitate to keep you here, but you're carrying the next generation of our family, and your mother would kill me if something happened to you and her unborn grandchild."

Ana chuckles slightly, knowing that her father isn't joking or exaggerating. She hugs and kisses him.

"I will obey your wishes, *Hu'Neh*."

"You are still needed. Your Uncle Ricardo says you are becoming a very good tactician. Work with him, Lyle and Uncle Ryan to formulate a strategy to deal with the *Dev'Cha* after we secure Bwentani Prime from the Celestians."

"I will."

She once again hugs and kisses her father and starts back to the WA-13 with Zerellus.

Robert stops him.

"Z, return with the ops team, we'll launch our counter attack from here."

Yes, *Kemzeh*."

Zerellus walk to the WA-13 and gets in just as Dave leaves it."

"Did Bob tell you to bring the teams here?"

Zerellus indicates yes.

"Gonna be a helluva trick getting past that base, but I guess he knows what he's doing."

"Indeed," Zerellus replies as he and Ana get into the Outlaw. "Ops Five to Ops One, ready to return to base."

"Acknowledged. Bat'ai has put up the quantum shield and will open a portal and scattering field to cover your exit. Return to these exact coordinates."

"Understood. Out."

A quantum vortex opens in the garrison hangar. Zerellus pilots the fighter into it and disappears.

Robert, Dave, Ray, Rillius and Bat'ai monitor the progress of the Cho'Kai base, now fifteen hundred light years away.

"They have slowed down even more, but they will still be here in three and a half hours," Bat'ai reports.

"Darrel and his team stand by.'

"Michael has sent the full-sized mounted Pulse Beam weapons."

Robert nods in approval. "Good. As soon as our teams get here, Mike will take charge and lead the assault on the comm center and wherever they house the shield generator. We're going on a different mission."

"Which is?" Dave asks.

"You, me, and Ray are going to infiltrate the Cho'Kai base and take out their weapons and propulsion systems."

"*Binzah*, that is not a good idea," Rillius replies. "Bat'ai said the last time we attempted a mission, they released some kind of compound that killed you and the rest of the Terran team."

"That is true, my friend, but we got a full scan of the base and I have located the environment controls and we can neutralize it," Bat'ai replies.

Rillius states, "I wish to join the mission."

"And I want you on the mission, *binzah*, if they have the *Dev'cha* on board, they can detect your presence."

"Bat'ai informed of what happened when you led the last mission onto their base."

"I want you to take charge of my team and lead the rescue of our people in the detention center on Bwentani Prime," Robert replies.

"I shall be honored." He grasps Robert's forearm.

"Good hunting," Robert replies.

Zerellus' WA-13 returns with the three Special Ops teams, Mike and Ryan.

"Ryan, what are you doing here?' Robert asks.

"Yer daughter told me 'bout this harebrained scheme ta take back Bwentani Prime an' take on the Cho'Kai base."

"It's a gamble, but it's the best shot we got. With the Cho'Kai here, we can take back Bwentani Prime, restore Quennok and Berellus' memories and free our people."

"Ya may have a point. But we're gonna be out manned and out gunned."

"I know, the WA-13s are mosquitoes compared to their fortress. We would need something like the old Bwentani battle cruisers, but Zerellus said they were destroyed when Jen'Pway seized control of the Council and allied themselves with the Cho'Kai."

"The Taquan Alliance in the Empire's home reality had battle cruisers that are comparable," Bat'ai replies.

"Hoss, they don't exist ennymore," Mike replies. "I was there when the temporal wake hit, enny traces of the old resistance vanished and the Empire controls their galaxy now."

"You also said they were benevolent. You think they would help us?"

"Possibly, but y'all said we only got 'bout a couple o' hours, an' it would probably take that long ta arrange a meetin'."

"Good point. Bat'ai said the Time Defense Force have their hands full with the Celestians in their reality. Guess we'll have to make do with what we got," Robert sighs.

'I may know where we kin git a couple o' battle cruisers," Mike replies.

"Where?"

"Remember the reality y'all were thrown inta when ya originally disappeared, with the Terran resistance Force."

"Mike, they had antiquated F-122s with a primitive electron shield," Robert replies.

"I know, but we went back ta that reality when the Empire attacked with the thermalitic weapon. The Bwentani sent their battle cruisers ta transport the Henoki an' their technology's equal ta our own. We kin go in an'…borrow a battle cruiser."

"Mike, you've been around Bob too long. You're just as fucking crazy as he is," Dave says, getting a laugh from the others.

"He may have something there," Robert replies.

"Shit, we're already fightin' the dad gum Celestians, *Dev'cha*, Chicken Chokers and possible the sum'bitches from the Empire. Enny one else ya wanna piss off?" Ray asks sarcastically.

"Well, now that you mention it, I've always wanted to have a go at the Borg and Cardassians," Robert snarks.

He gets dirty looks from Ray, Dave and Ryan.

"Ya remember Gibbs from NCIS?" Ryan asks.

"Yeah," Robert replies.

Ryan slaps him on the back of the head.

"OK, OK, I'm done. But seriously, if we can get a Bwentani battle cruiser, we can buy the time needed to make the op work. Mike, what are their defenses like?"

"Couldn't say, Colonel. We actually never dealt with 'em, only a passive scan ta track their location."

"Bat'ai can you locate their quantum reality and run a scan of their technological capabilities without being detected?" Robert asks.

"I can find their quantum coordinates, but it would be unwise to do a scan from our reality."

"Find them and we'll do the Intel from there. Dave, you and your team are with us. Ray, work with Ryan on our op inside the station. Z, have the squadron stand ready in case they send fighters to try and soften us up. Mike, Ryan will brief you on Operation Valhalla, you're leading the mission."

"Yes, sir.'

Rillius appears offended. "*Binzah...*"

"You're commanding the battle cruiser. You're the only one here who has experience with these ships."

"It has been awhile since I commanded a vessel."

"It's like riding a bike." Robert sees the puzzled look on Rillius' face. He chuckles. "Never mind."

"I have the quantum coordinates, Robert."

"You're with us B, just in case we screw up and all hell breaks loose, you gotta get us back."

Bat'ai laughs, nods in acknowledgement, and then follows Robert, Rillius, Dave and his Special Ops team to a WA-13.

Robert gets in the pilot's seat, Rillius mans the weapons station, Bat'ai sits at the tactical station, as Dave and his team get in the jump seat and check their weapons and equipment, as well as check Robert and Rillius' gear.

Bat'ai sets the quantum coordinates and says, "We are ready to proceed, Robert."

"Open a portal and engage the stealth shielding, we don't want to announce ourselves,' Robert replies.

Bat'ai opens the portal, engages the shields and Robert flies into the interdimensional vortex.

CHAPTER 15

Moon of Gaius – Bwentani Prime – Terran Resistance Force reality

The vortex opens and the WA-13 places itself in a fixed position behind the largest of the thirteen moons surrounding Bwentani Prime.

Robert has Bat'ai run a scan of the planet and Earth, which is approximately forty light years away.

"Bat'ai, report."

"According to my scan, Earth was destroyed approximately two years ago by a solar flare."

"Any signs of human lives on Bwentani Prime?"

"Negative, Robert."

"Those jackasses, we warned them to make peace with the Henoki. Throw Rug probably got them all killed."

Bat'ai corrects him. "It appears they have set aside their differences. The human colony is here on Gaius, and it contains approximately ten thousand humans."

"Should we contact them?"

"No, not a good idea, David. They do not possess the knowledge of alternate realities and their technology is still mid twenty-first century. I would advise not making our presence known"

Robert concurs. "I agree. Scan for the battle cruisers and find one that is unmanned or at least minimally staffed."

"Commencing scan."

Bat'ai scans the Imperium, which in this reality spans one thousand light years and includes two hundred planets. He locates a Bwentani battle cruiser garrison.

"I have located an outpost with battle cruisers. It is in the Celestus system."

"I love the poetic justice. How's the security?"

Rillius looks at the contingent at the facility. "It is standard for a Bwentani outpost, Robert. A half dozen crews, a company of Bremars, Ricars and the base Pomar."

"Can they detect us?"

"Their technology is more advanced, but we have the advantage of using our stealth technology."

"The invisibility vests?"

"Yes."

Robert checks his watch. "We better get moving. That Cho'Kai base will reach Kolromi in two hours."

Bat'ai chuckles and tells him, "To use a human cliché, we have all the time in the world. I will set the return coordinates to the exact time we left. My concern is that if we use these weapons in our reality, it could cause a quantum black hole."

"You said this was part of the reason our reality is out of balance, using technology that didn't belong there."

"Yes and no. The technology itself did not affect the quantum balance; it was the energy matrix of the weapons."

"So it's like mixing chlorine and bleach?" Dave asks.

"Exactly."

"Is there a way to adapt it to our reality?" Robert asks.

"I will know better once we acquire the battle cruiser."

"Feed me the coordinates and we'll recon the base."

Bat'ai sends the location of the Bwentani garrison.

Robert inputs them into the navigation computer and pilots the Outlaw to the edge of the Bwentani system and then opens a portal and flies into it.

Former TRF pilot John Adamson and his old son, Bob, named after Robert because he saved his life when Adamson was captured by the Henoki five years ago, are in the back yard of their home, looking through telescopes.

They both witness a slight flash and for a split second the stealth shield is disabled and they see the WA-13 enter the vortex and disappear."

"Daddy, daddy, a spaceship!"

"No, Bob that was a shooting star. Make a wish."

"I wish I was a pilot like you and could fly to the stars."

"You know, son, I believe you will."

"If the Bwennies let us leave our moon."

"They are Bwen-tah-ni, and they were very gracious to let us live here after Earth was destroyed."

"They won't let us do anything else."

"We can look at the stars."

"OK." Bob returns to looking at the constellations.

Adamson debates about whether to discuss what he really saw: A space craft that looked similar to the WA-01 Widow Maker flown by Captain Ray Watson when he encountered the Combined Defense Force.

Back then, an uneasy truce was reached between the humans and the Henoki, a member of the Imperium. The Henoki occupy a large lake similar to the one in the Special Ops force's home dimension, the humans are relegated to the Bwentani moon, where they were given materials to build homes, schools and commerce centers, but they are strictly forbidden to own any kind of weapons or maintain their military.

The TRF Council was outraged, but reluctantly agreed after given the ultimatum of either residing on the Bwentani moon, or returning to Earth.

Adamson now works as a pilot on the colony's transport shuttles. It's not as glamorous, but he likes the idea of being able to fly without worrying about being shot down.

He decides to keep this to himself, figuring that it would stir up old feelings of animosity towards the Henoki. On top of that, humans would most likely receive further sanctions from the Bwentani Council, which has them on twenty year 'probation', after which they would consider giving them the same rights as other citizens of the Imperium.

He goes back to looking at the stars with his son.

Bwentani garrison – Celestus Prime

The Outlaw takes up a stationary position outside of the Bwentani security perimeter. Bat'ai scans the security field, while Robert, Dave and Rillius study the layout of the Bwentani craft, which is roughly the size of an old style Terran aircraft carrier.

"*Binzah*, it appears we are both required to pilot the craft," Rillius states.

"Hell, other than the brief tour you gave me before the war, I have never stepped foot on the bridge," Robert complains.

"Rillius, I am well versed in the operations of your vessel," Bat'ai replies.

"OK, B, you're the co-pilot. We'll secure the landing bay and then you bring in the WA-13.Then we have to figure out how to get the hell out of here without half of their fleet starts coming after us.'

"We may have a bigger problem, Robert," Bat'ai says, motioning to the senior officers.

Robert, Rillius and Dave walk to the tactical console to see what Bat'ai has on screen. There is a security net surrounding the station with sensors, motion detectors and a device which appears similar to the Immobilizer Beam they've employed.

"Get a quantum level scan to see if there is a way around it," Robert commands.

"This is quantum level, Robert," Bat'ai replies.

"Shit. Does this technology look familiar, *Binzah*?"

"It seems similar to technology proposed by Imperium scientists a few centuries ago, but we did not possess the technology to make it practical."

"Looks like they did. Can we get past it?"

"We might be able to get past the net undetected using the teleporter, but we may not be able to return if our attempt fails," Bat'ai replies.

"Then we don't fail. How many can we teleport?"

"Up to four."

Robert nods, contemplates his next move and then says, "Me, Dave, Rillius and Sergeant Morris will cross. If we don't succeed or we are captured, don't wait, get your ass back to Kolromi and fend off the Cho'Kai the best you can, understood?"

"Understood, Robert," Bat'ai replies, and then hands Robert a device.

"What is it?"

"A quantum slipstream device. It will bring you back to our reality. It is the same as the failsafe we incorporated into the WA-13 in the event that the pilot is killed or injured."

"Never saw it this small."

"It was originally brought back by Raymond when my counterpart from the Time Defense Force discovered he was in a reality different from his own, I mean ours."

"I vaguely remember that scenario, the last time our reality was radically altered."

"Yes...by Rillius."

"I would never—"

"Forgive me, old friend, I should have clarified. It was a Rillius from a completely different reality. He was the one who brought the Terran Empire to our reality."

"Where did he come from?"

"We do not know. He had traces of at least ten different quantum realties in his DNA. We believe his moving between realities caused quantum psychosis and made him unpredictable and very dangerous."

"Is he still around?"

"He was killed by your counterpart four years ago, but if history has been altered–"

"He may still be around," Dave interrupts.

"Terrific. It's not like we don't already have enough maniacs to deal with—"

"And the enemy too," Dave snarks.

Robert laughs, and then suddenly becomes serious. "B, call up the schematics and tap into their medical database."

"Yes, Robert."

"Medical database, sir?" Morris asks.

Robert replies, "Yes, Sergeant. This is a non-lethal op. We discovered that if we kill someone in another dimension using our weapons, it can trigger a disturbance in the quantum barrier. On a large enough scale it can even cause a black hole...or a wave that can upset the quantum balance."

"Understood, sir."

"B, figure out which sleep agent we can use without adversely harming their physiology."

"Aprilozene works on my people, *binzah*," Rillius states.

But we don't know if your physiology is the same. Doctor Burke has discovered slight differences in our anatomy and those of our quantum doubles, besides the quantum markers," Robert informs him.

"Yes, if they are like our Bremar, they are honorable soldiers and I do not wish to permanently harm them."

"Neither do I *binzah*, besides we have enough enemies to deal with," Robert says with a slight chuckle.

"Robert, the Aprilozene will work without any lasting side effects," Bat'ai states.

"Good. Have you located a deserted battle cruiser?"

"No. They all have security patrols. I feel the one closest to the security field will be best. I can temporarily disable the field, but only for a few seconds."

"We'll trip the field and then all hell breaks loose."

"Essentially, Robert."

"Are you able to generate a quantum portal large enough to get the battle cruiser through?" Dave asks.

"Yes, David."

Robert asks, "Will the invisibility vests keep us from being detected?"

"That I cannot answer."

"Then we go straight to the environmental controls and flood the ship with the Aprilozene. We go in light, masks, sleep agent and the non-lethal weapons. B, tap into their comm system and figure out when is the best time to take the ship," Robert orders.

"Yes, Robert."

Bat'ai types in a series of commands and then accesses the comm link between the security garrison and the central command, all in the native Bwentani language.

"Bat'ai, run the translation matrix," Dave orders.

"Not advised, David. Their security would be able to pick up our intrusion."

Rillius listens to the comm traffic. "Other than a few differences in pronouns, their language is the same as mine. There is a shift change in ten minutes. Only four Bremars stay on board until the new shift arrives and they are relieved."

"Bridge?" Robert asks.

"Engineering section, near environmental control," Rillius replies.

"Well, that's gonna make it interesting," Dave snarks.

Robert sighs. "I would rather have an empty ship, but I would rather take on four than two dozen."

"Do not underestimate the fighting capabilities of an Imperium soldier," Rillius cautions.

"I know, *binzah*. I still feel it every once in a while from when I went through *Bahal'Zai* training.'

"*Bahal'Zai*, sir?" Morris asks.

"Bwentani Special Forces," Dave replies. "Where do you think the Colonel and I developed the training protocol for the Special Forces?"

"Quite frankly sir, from your sadistic minds."

"True to a point," Robert replies, laughing.

"They are changing the guard, Robert," Bat'ai states.

"We have about five of your minutes before the rest of the Bremars are on board. Now is the time to go."

Robert, Dave, Rillius and Morris stand next to the teleporter. Bat'ai types in the coordinates and then presses a button.

The teleporter glows, and then the ops team disappears.

CHAPTER 16

Engineering section – Bwentani battle cruiser

The team materializes and then immediately activates their invisibility vests. Robert gives Dave and Morris hand signals, telling them to secure the environmental control section while he and Rillius attempt to get some Intel from the inspection recently carried out by the station Commander, Lekar 'Septimus'.

Rillius is momentarily pleased to see his younger brother.

Robert notices this and whispers, "I know how glad you are to see your *binzah*. Your father told me he sacrificed himself to save him during an assassination attempt. Did they ever catch the guy?"

"No, but I was a suspect, five witnesses said I was the one who pulled the trigger."

"Yeah, and only the fact you were on Earth with me, Lyle and Berellus cleared you."

"Yes." He pauses for a moment, as he ponders before speaking, "Do you think this was the first attempt by my double to infiltrate our reality?"

"I think so. He probably had second thoughts when the Cho'Kai invaded."

"Or the one who sent them."

"Possibly." Robert pauses, straining to hear something, and then looks at Rillius and says, "My Bwentani is a little rusty, but if he said what I think he said, we're fucked.'

"I fear you have heard correctly. They have changed the security protocols on the ship. Computer control access restricted to Pomar or above access."

"You're a Pomar. Maybe your quantum double is one, too."

"I doubt it, Robert. If they hold true to Bwentani military tradition, a younger sibling may not outrank an older one. If 'Septimus' is a Lekar and I am a Pomar, it means that I have shamed my family," Rillius states sadly.

"Unless you still outrank him."

"Or I am dead in this reality."

"In either case, there's only one way we can do this–"

"We must abduct him and force him to access the central computer. But we better do it before he gets off the ship."

"He is ending the briefing."

Robert and Rillius move towards the Bwentani security detail, who receive their final orders; secure the battle cruiser until the morning, when they will test the upgraded operations system in the battle cruisers amid reports that the humans plan on stealing a craft with the aid of an underground Bwentani resistance movement.

'Septimus' finishes the briefing and then walks towards the loading dock, where he will brief the rest of the detail. The Two Ricars from the outgoing shift walk beside him, discussing the current unrest on the human colony.

They go into the tunnel leading to the dock, when the Ricars suddenly drop to the ground.

'Septimus' is stunned and suddenly realizes that he's being restrained by an unknown force. He suddenly collapses, but then is suspended in midair, and before disappearing.

The on duty Ricars hear a barely audible clanking sound that appears to come from walking on steel gravity plates. A moment later an elevator door opens and then closes.

The Ricars go to the elevator, access a monitor and look inside. It is empty, though it is going towards the main bridge.

One of the Ricars tries to stop the elevator, but his commands are overridden, while the other pulls out a comm device and calls for maintenance and reinforcements.

Dave and Morris see two dozen heavily armed Bwentani Bremars enter, followed by a couple of maintenance techs.

"Shit," Dave whispers. He presses the comm link behind his ear and says in a soft, but urgent tone, "Bob, Rillius, we have company. Two dozen unfriendlies. Mask up, we're gonna use the sleep agent and cut the comm channel."

"Understood. We're on the bridge. Out," Robert replies.

Dave turns to Morris, "Dan, get the comm channel, I'm activating the sleep agent."

"Yes, sir."

He uses a device to translate the Bwentani language and locates the central communications station. He looks over the console to figure out which panel will disable to ship's communications system. When he locates the panel and is about to disable it, he receives an electrical shock, which shorts out his invisibility vest, at the same time.

The ship's alarm goes off.

"Dan!" Dave shouts, as he turns his vest off and checks Morris' vitals.

He's alive but barely breathing.

Dave quickly uses the stasis device and then calls Robert on the comm link, shouting over the alarm. "Bob, man down. Dan received a shock while disabling the comm system. Obviously we have been compromised. Have the Bwentani General access the computer. I'll contact Bat'ai to see if he can get Morris out of here."

"Understood. Have him send the rest of the team."

"Negative. Just need the computer and I'll knock these mother fuckers out."

"Understood. Maintain radio silence until further notice and stay safe."

"Out." Dave pulls out the regular comm device. "Bat'ai, come in."

"Yes, David?"

"Morris is injured. Need to get him back to the ship."

"I shall attempt to teleport him."

Dave puts the comm device on Morris.

"Lock onto the comm signal. Have Pallia (Henoki team medic) stabilize him. Have the rest of the team ready to teleport at a moment's notice."

"Understood. Back away, attempting to teleport."

Dave backs away from Morris, who glows and then disappears.

Several Bwentani Bremars are heard as they advance towards the environmental control station.

"Shit," Dave curses to himself, while turning on his invisibility vest, hoping they don't have the technology to detect his presence.

A few seconds later, the Bremars approach the station, check the compromised area and then have one soldier to stand by while the rest of the team investigates the engineering section.

Bridge of the Bwentani battle cruiser

Robert and Rillius deactivate their vests, along with the one on 'Septimus' and then bring him towards the control panel.

He regains consciousness and then sees Rillius.

"*Binzah*?" he says with a tone of deep disappointment. He sees Robert, "You allied yourselves with the Terrans?"

"It's not what you think, Lekar Septimus," Robert says in Rillius' defense.

"I do not know you, Terran."

"Your brother is not a traitor. I wish we had time to explain, but to make a long story short, we are under attack by the Cho'Kai and the Imperium has the only weapons that can stop them."

"Do not attempt to deceive me, Terran."

"Have you ever known me to be deceptive, *binzah*?"

"No," 'Septimus' grudgingly answers.

"Read our thoughts, you will see we are telling the truth."

'Septimus' closes his eyes and then reads Rillius thoughts. He is stunned to the revelations about them being from an alternate reality and once again fighting their ancient enemy.

"Why did you not just come to us?"

"Forgive us, Lekar, our situation is desperate and time short. We only wish to borrow a battle cruiser and fully intended to return it," Robert truthfully states.

"I sense no deception. I will grant you a battle cruiser, but not this one. I shall allow you one that we are going to decommission with the condition that you never return to this reality or give aid or technology to the Terrans living on the colony."

"You have my word, *binzah*," Rillius states.

"You have my gratitude, Lekar. If we can ever return the favor, all you need to do is ask."

'Septimus' thinks for a moment and then says, "Maybe you can, Terran. The Terrans on the lunar colony no longer wish to adhere to our conditions for residing in the Imperium. Maybe they would be happier living with your people in your reality."

"The problem is our quantum signature is different, they would be able to stay for only seven Terran days before their quantum DNA breaks down and kills them," Robert states. "If you will allow, we can certainly transport them to a system outside of the Imperium."

"That sounds acceptable," 'Septimus' replies, extending his right arm.

Robert grasps the arm and notices the *Bahal'Zai* insignia burned into 'Septimus' bicep.

"Glad we reached a peaceful accord, I know better than to mess with a *Bahal'Zai*."

"You know of our elite forces?"

"Your *binzah* trained me, my shoulder still twinges with the *glemar* (rain)."

'Septimus' laughs, and then turns to Rillius.

"I know you are not my *binzah*, however your name has brought shame upon the family. He attempted an insurrection five Terran years ago. When he failed, he disappeared with an advanced scout ship and has not been seen since."

"Lekar, I believe we have seen him. He attempted to disrupt our reality as well and brought in the Terran Empire as well as the Cho'Kai to our universe."

"You said the Terran Empire?"

"Yes."

"Did they have a crest like this?"

'Septimus' shows him a knife with the crest of the Black Ops Force.

"Holy shit! Lekar, two years ago we had a major temporal incursion in our reality. Did your people experience something similar to an ion storm?"

"Yes, we thought it was the solar flare that destroyed the Terran home planet. It affected everything in a one hundred light year radius."

"Our Earth was the epicenter; we think several realities melded together in that instant. A Terran Empire garrison may have been shifted to your reality."

"Yes, these Terrans were more aggressive than the ones on the colony. They did die off within a week or we fear they could have done considerable damage to our reality."

"There is a possibility that your Rillius may still be alive, he has been to at least ten different realities and suffers from what is known as quantum psychosis."

"Unfortunately my brother was part of a research project for exploring alternate realities. I see your people have perfected the technology."

"Maybe we can arrange an exchange of technology."

"Our quantum scientists would welcome it."

"Actually it's based on our technology that we abandoned three centuries ago," Rillius states,

'Septimus' addresses him, "I shall make arrangement with Prime Minister Berellus."

"He is our prime minister and my brother-in-law. His son Zerellus is married to my daughter Anamiok," says Robert proudly.

"Your mate is Henoki?"

"Yes, her father is Quennok."

"A Terran named Tucker killed Quennok and his son."

Robert remains quiet and buries this memory using a Henoki exercise Linaiok taught him.

"I feel we should return. Until we meet again, *binzah*," Rillius says to 'Septimus'.

"We shall break bread then, *binzah*," 'Septimus' replies.

"Lekar, if we locate your brother, should we arrest him?"

"Attempt to return him. We may be able to reverse the effects of the quantum psychosis."

"We will do everything in our power, sir."

"I shall lead you to the battle cruiser."

"Lead the way, *binzah*."

'Septimus' contacts the Ricars in charge of the security detail to stand down.

Robert remains a few steps behind then taps his comm link. "Dave, stand down and return to the Outlaw. Lekar Septimus is giving us one of their outdated battle cruisers."

"OK, Bob. I was wondering what the hell was going on in there."

"Check on Morris."

"OK, out."

Robert closes the comm link and then catches up to Rillius and 'Septimus' who are having a conversation in their native language.

Robert takes out the regular comm device and then contacts Bat'ai. "Bat'ai, come in."

"Yes, Robert."

"We have made arrangements with Lekar Septimus for one of their retired battle cruisers. Meet us there and give him everything we have on our quantum technology. We suspect that the Rillius from this reality is responsible for the instability in ours and that he is suffering from quantum psychosis. Have our medical research available as well."

"Yes, Robert."

"Were you conversing with a quantum engineer named Bat'ai?" 'Septimus' asks.

"Yes, you know him?"

"He was the head of our Research and Development. Rillius abducted him before he disappeared."

"We found your Bat'ai in an abandoned shuttle five years ago. I'm sorry to say sir, but he was dead because he was in our reality too long. Our Bat'ai and Doctor Elizabeth Burke determined that he died of massive cellular degradation."

"If you could provide that research, we would be grateful."

"Consider it done."

They three of them leave the battle cruiser. 'Septimus' waves off the security detail and they boards a small shuttle craft to take them to an obsolete battle cruiser docked near a salvage yard near Pollux, one of the moons of Celestus.

CHAPTER 17

Battle cruiser *Glavius*

Bat'ai has piloted the WA-13 into the landing bay of the massive battle cruiser.

Imperium Commander 'Berellus' and members of the council are waiting their arrival.

"Septimus" steps out of the WA-13, followed by Robert, Bat'ai and Rillius.

The Bwentani delegation sees him, become outraged and demand that 'Berellus' has him arrested immediately.

"*Hemzeh (father)*, let me explain. Pomar Rillius is not from our reality," 'Septimus' states.

"Explain yourself."

"We are not from this quantum reality. My chief engineer, Bat'ai will provide you with a device that will allow you to compare my quantum DNA with yours."

"We have a similar device; no offense, but I trust our equipment more than yours."

"By all means."

A Ricar takes out a device, scans Robert, Bat'ai and Rillius, and then compares it with his own DNA."

"The Terran speaks the truth, Lekar."

"Forgive us, Pomar, but my son brought shame and dishonor to the Imperium and my family."

"We understand that he is been afflicted with quantum psychosis and we are working on a cure," Bat'ai states.

"Our researchers as well."

"Maybe an exchange of information may be mutually beneficial."

"One step at a time. For now we shall allow you the use our antiquated battle cruiser."

"We are grateful for your assistance, sir," Robert says.

Bat'ai hands a data pad with their research on quantum psychosis to 'Septimus', who brings it to his father.

"Thanks to you and your research, we are going to be able to treat the rest of our Bremars that have suffered quantum psychosis."

"I am pleased we are able to assist, Prasin," Rillius replies.

"Remarkable, how much you resemble our Rillius."

"Sir, they are identical, only their quantum DNA markers are different," Bat'ai responds.

"Do you feel that he is still a threat?"

"Before our reality was altered, your Rillius was killed by my quantum counterpart," Robert replies.

"Yes, the…Terran Empire?"

"Yes, sir."

"Are they still a threat?"

"That's uncertain, sir. Their home reality was altered and they progressed to a government similar to yours. The renegade Terran Commanders are in a coma and unfortunately we don't know the current whereabouts of your Rillius. We are concerned that the alteration of time may have resurrected him."

"That does concern me."

"I believe we can help, sir," Bat'ai replies.

"How?"

Robert states, "We have a device that can block us from returning without permission."

"What is this device?"

"A quantum barrier. I have already encoded our DNA, the Terran Empire's and if you wish we can encode yours, which will prevent Rillius from coming back."

"That would be most helpful," 'Berellus' states. He pauses and sighs, "I apologize if we do not supply you with our weapons, there is only so much generosity that we can extend."

"Sir, that is the best favor you can do for us," Robert replies, drawing a look of confusion from 'Berellus'. He chuckles and then tells him, "If we use your weapons in our reality it would further disrupt the quantum balance."

"I see, but what about the battle cruiser?"

"It is only the energy matrix from the weapons that disrupts the quantum balance," Bat'ai informs them.

"Again, sir we are indebted to you."

"Your debt has been paid–"

"You can call me Bob."

They grasp forearms. Robert then grasps 'Septimus' forearm before him and his father leave the battle cruiser.

Robert breathes a sigh of relief, as he wonders how these negotiations would have proceeded if they found out that while it was Ray who killed Quennok in this reality, he was the one responsible for killing his son, Quessok, and almost bombed the Henoki out of existence. He knows he has more than enough problems without being branded a war criminal in this reality, too.

"Let's get out of here," Robert says.

"I'll check on Dan," Dave says.

He walks towards the medical bay.

"Is this restricted access like the other battle cruiser?" Robert asks.

"No, Robert, Pomar Rillius and I will be able to fly the battle cruiser," Bat'ai states.

"Good, I guess I'll lead in the Outlaw and open a portal home." He checks his watch and says "Shit! We've been here twelve hours, they probably kicked our asses."

"I have preset the temporal coordinates to the exact moment we left. We will still have three hours before the base reaches the Hadar sector," Bat'ai replies.

"How long to integrate our weapons?" Robert asks.

"They left all the fire controls intact. Hour, two tops."

"Good, let's go home."

Robert goes to the WA-13, opens a portal and ends up one kilometer in front of the battle cruiser – which Rillius renames the 'Septimus'.

Rillius and Bat'ai go to the bridge. Bat'ai sits at the navigation console while Rillius sits at the pilot station.

Rillius activates the engines while Bat'ai plots a course out of the ship yard.

Rillius opens a channel to Robert, "We are ready to go, Binzah."

"Acknowledged. Opening the portal, come to heading one-seven-three. Event horizon in two minutes."

"One-seven-three, confirmed, Robert," Bat'ai replies.

"Pomar Rillius to command, permission to embark."

"Permission, granted, *binzah. Tul'haka* (success)." 'Septimus' replies.

"*Tul'haka.*"

'Berellus' and 'Septimus' watch the Terran craft and the battle cruiser leave the shipping yard.

They are also looking over the quantum barrier device Bat'ai supplied to them.

Pomar 'Renallius' enters with Terran Council President Elias Tolliver for a weekly briefing on the current status of the human colony.

"Forgive the intrusion, Prasin Berellus. Council President Tolliver is here for the weekly report."

"Councilman, you just missed a fellow Terran who supplied us quantum technology in exchange for one of our obsolete battle cruisers," 'Berellus' says.

"Really? Who is he?"

"Never got his full name. He only referred to himself as...Bob," 'Septimus' replies.

Tolliver sees the WA-13 approaching the quantum vortex. "Do you have footage of him?"

"Yes," 'Septimus' replies.

He accesses the archives and produces a recording of them on the bridge of the battle cruiser.

Tolliver is seething with anger and blurts out "That's him! That's Major Robert Tucker! He is the one responsible for the attack on the Henoki!"

"Summon the fleet and detain him," 'Berellus' orders.

"But they are about to enter the vortex, which will send them back to their own dimension," 'Septimus' replies. He sees the quantum barrier, finds the button to activate it and presses.

Robert's WA-13

He is about to enter the vortex, when a huge surge of polaron particles erupt from the opening, preventing him from entering.

"What the hell?" he wonders before running a scan and realizing the Bwentani have activated their quantum barrier, preventing them from leaving.

"Bwentani Command to Terran Craft.

"Terran space craft, over."

'Septimus' states, "Major Robert Tucker, you are under arrest for the attack on the Henoki; Terran Time reference June sixteenth in the year 2217. Stand down and prepare to be boarded."

Robert receives a signal on his neural comm link. "Bob, what the hell's going on?" Dave asks.

Robert sighs, "Apparently they found out about my attack on the Henoki."

"*Binzah*, I probed your mind, you did not reveal this information to them because Bwentani telepathy is very limited," Rillius states.

"They did not access our records, Robert," Bat'ai states.

"Well they somehow found out."

'Septimus' repeats his ultimatum.

Robert replies, "Robert Tucker to Bwentani command. My men were not part of this act. I request that you release them and I will surrender to your custody of my own free will."

There is a momentary pause.

"Permission granted. Prepare to be boarded."

"Returning to the Septimus."

Robert flies the WA-13 back to the loading dock and gets out. Dave and his Special Ops team are waiting for him.

"Bob, what are you doing? You can't surrender without a fight," Dave tells him.

"Dave, stand down. That's an order," Robert commands.

"Bob, this is bullshit. It was during war."

"We destroyed five city ships filled with Henoki. Ray may have detonated the explosives, but I gave the order. We established a new ally and we may need them to defeat the Cho'Kai, hell it's either face charges here...or face eight billion counts of murder back home."

"Rillius to Robert. *Binzah*, a Bwentani scout ship is preparing to dock."

"Understood. Bat'ai, pilot the WA-13. The second they drop the barrier, get the hell out of here, before they change their minds."

"Yes, Robert." Bat'ai says, while administering a shot.

"To stabilize your DNA, or else it will degrade within a year."

"Something tells me I won't be around in a year."

"I shall work on getting you back, Robert."

"Thanks, B. Dave, you're the MFIC in Ops. Get our people out of the camps and protect the Henoki from the *Dev'cha*. I'm not a priority and that's an order."

"Technically Bob, I have time in grade."

"Then it's a threat."

"Now that I will follow."

Robert sees the scout ship set down in the landing bay.

He commands, "As soon as you are able to access the

barrier, get the hell out and don't look back."

He takes off his weapons, hands them to Dave and then walks to the Bwentani Bremars, who search him and then bring him on the scout ship.

The loading dock opens, at the same time a shield is activated, keeping the bay pressurized. The ship passes through the shield and then the bay closes.

Dave is livid. He turns to Bat'ai "This is bullshit! We can't leave him here."

"I am not happy either, David. But the Bwentani will not mistreat him and he will receive a fair trial."

"Let me guess the Minarians are here, too?"

"No, David. The Bwentani are one of the oldest known civilizations. The Minarians based their legal system on the Bwentani's. He will be treated fairly."

"For their sake, he'd better be."

Bat'ai is about to respond when Rillius contacts him.

"Bat'ai. We have received clearance, prepare to return."

"I shall."

"Can Rillius pilot the battle cruiser by himself?"

"It will be difficult."

"I'll handle the WA-13. Bob's been training me."

"Actually David, I feel you would be able to help Rillius. I have to recalibrate the quantum and temporal coordinates." Bat'ai pauses before addressing him further. "David, I assure you that we will retrieve Robert unharmed. If he is able to clear his name on his own, it may work out for the best."

"And if he can't?"

"The injection I gave him included a tracking device."

"And the barrier?"

"Not a concern. You had better go, David."

"OK."

Dave jogs towards the bridge, while Bat'ai gets into the WA-13, opens a small portal and flies into it, ending up in front of the cruiser. He activates the quantum vortex and then radios Rillius. "Bat'ai to Rillius, quantum vortex activated, returning to our reality."

The Outlaw flies into the vortex, followed by the battle cruiser.

Kolromi Six – Covert Ops reality

After they return to their reality, Ray calls them on the comm unit. "Ops Three ta Ops One. I hope y'all hurry, the Chicken Chokers will be here in 'bout three hours."

Dave replies, "Ops Three, this is Ops Two. We're back, we had some complications, will explain later. Report to the sixth planet with Mike and every available tech and all the Pulse Beam Weapons on hand."

"Ya got it, son."

Rillius places the battle cruiser in stationary orbit to begin retrofitting their newest craft for the impending attack by the Cho'Kai and a possible rescue mission for their commander.

CHAPTER 18

Imperium Command Center – Bwentani Prime

Robert is escorted under heavy guard into the command center.

'Septimus' waves them off, "This Terran is to be treated with respect accorded to any senior officer in the Imperium."

The Bremars back away and leave.

"Talk about your past catching up to you," Robert quips.

"You admit to these atrocities?" 'Berellus' asks.

"Prasin, I led a mission against an enemy force that had hunted the human race to the brink of extinction. I have lived with the guilt and shame of what I did every day for the past two hundred years. If I could go back and reverse what had happened I would have. My people have the technology to do it, but how would your history have changed? Would the human race have been annihilated in the onslaught brought on by the Henoki Armada that was coming to attack? I don't know, and to be honest, maybe we should never find out."

"I sense no intended deception," 'Berellus' replies.

"What do you mean?"

"We uncovered new evidence that you may or may not be aware of. We discovered reports of civilians both on the city ships and on transports evacuating the area and they were attacked by your fighters."

Robert feels himself becoming furious at this obvious lie. He calms down and states, "Sir, we did not attack the civilians, in fact I ordered the commander of the Terran fleet, Captain Julio Sanchez to stand down."

"We have testimony to the contrary."

"From who?"

"Me," Tolliver says as he enters the command center with data discs.

Robert again holds back the urge to attack or insult Tolliver by uttering the nickname he gave him: Throw Rug.

"General Tolliver, nice to see you...sir," Robert says with the slightest hint of sarcasm.

"Tucker, you're finally going to face the music for your crimes," Tolliver replies with open hatred.

"I'd like to see this evidence."

"We will hold a tribunal to establish the facts and determine if a trial is warranted," 'Septimus' states.

"The Major already admitted his guilt. Under Bwentani law, he is to be executed," Tolliver counters.

'Septimus' replies, "Terran, you do not speak for the Bwentani. I do not know how you enforce your laws, but in the Imperium, a person is innocent until proven guilty beyond a shadow of a doubt."

'Berellus states', "We are obligated to investigate these allegations."

Robert replies, "Of course, Prasin. You will have my full cooperation."

"You will be detained in the Terran penal colony on the moon of Gaius with other Terrans accused of crimes against the Imperium."

'Septimus' motions to a Bremar, who walks up to Robert and escorts him towards the exit of the command center.

As he passes Tolliver, Robert notes the obnoxious smirk on his face.

"Gotcha," Tolliver says just loud enough for Robert to hear.

"Not if I get you first, Throw Rug," Robert replies.

Tolliver flushes with anger and is about to reply when 'Septimus' interrupts, "I will go with the Major to the Detention Camp to get his statement."

He leaves with Robert and the Bremar.

"Excuse me, Prime Minister, isn't it unusual for your Commanding General to escort a prisoner?"

'Berellus' has a look of disdain, "Major Tucker has more knowledge and respect for the Bwentani and our culture than you. Be advised, Terran, if find these charges are false, you will face the consequences."

He motions to two Bremar who bring Tolliver out, treating him more like a criminal than Robert.

Terran penal detention center – Bwentani moon of Gaius

Robert, now in a blue jumpsuit with the words, "Military Prisoner" on the back, is escorted to the yard after being stripped searched, decontaminated and having a discipline collar placed on his neck.

'Septimus' is about to turn Robert over to the human Corrections Officer. He exhales, disappointed. "Why were you not up front about who you are?

"I had a feeling that your reception would not have been as pleasant if you knew I was the one who attacked the Armada."

"We had conflicting reports. The Henoki were not the ones to lodge the complaint, they stated their warriors died with honor."

"Who filed the report about the civilians?'

"The Terran Council President."

"Tolliver. He was not part of the assault, he was at the Terran command center during our rescue mission."

"There was no mention of a rescue."

"Lieutenant John Adamson was captured and was going to be executed for a crime he didn't commit. They accused him of killing the Henoki leader, Quennok."

"The report stated you killed him."

"No, he was killed by one of my men during a fire fight."

"Then he died with honor."

"Yes, so did his son Quessok."

"The Terran filling charges tells quite a different story."

"Tolliver has a personal grudge against me."

"He is barely tolerated, only because he has kept the Terrans in check and helped us against the Bwentani Resistance Movement."

"Your brother headed a similar movement in our reality."

"How did he die?"

"He was betrayed by my counterpart, who was the leader of the Terran Empire. They destroyed my home world and according to Bat'ai, they attacked Earth in this reality, too."

"We were told it was a solar flare."

"They possessed a weapon that can rip away a planet's atmosphere." He pauses. "I vaguely remember being in this reality before the solar flare. I think here is a possibility that I was the one who sent the distress signal. The radical alteration of my native reality has tampered with my memory and I'm just now getting some of them back."

'Septimus' thinks for a moment and then replies, "If you could prove that you were the one who made contact; it would go a long way to proving that your attack was indeed an act of war and not terrorism, which is what Tolliver accused you of perpetrating. You will be informed of the time of your tribunal."

"*Tul'haka bal zin* (Success and long life)," says Robert.

"*Tul'haka bal zin.*"

'Septimus' hesitates, and then grasps Robert's forearm. He notices something on Robert's bicep. He is stunned, as he looks at Robert, and before leaving quickly.

Robert turns and sees other detainees in different colored jumpsuits, some blue like his, some red (Criminal) and orange (Terrorist). A number of detainees look at him with shock and disbelief registering on their faces.

He in turn, recognizes a good number of the detainees as former members of the Terran Resistance Force, including General Larry Kensington, Major Julio Sanchez and Captain John Adamson, who was just arrested and brought to the detention center for his 'part' in the attack.

Adamson was being held prisoner by the Henoki and rescued by Robert and the Combined Defense Force four years ago.

"Major?" Kensington says in disbelief.

He walks over to Robert, along with Julio and Adamson, each shaking his hand.

"General." He notices that Kensington is wearing a blue jumpsuit, like his, but Julio and Adamson are wearing orange. "Julio, what the hell is going on? And what is it with the different color jumpsuits?

"The General is considered a Military Prisoner, like you. Captain Adamson and I are suspected terrorists and in league with the Bwentani separatist movement," Julio replies.

"Major, what are you doing here?" Kensington asks.

"Long story, sir."

Kensington chuckles "I think we have time...life without parole here."

"I'm slated to be executed," Julio says with a tone of resignation.

"I was just brought in. A couple of goons that report to Tolliver grabbed me out of my house, in front of my wife and kid," Adamson says with a confused tone.

"That weasel Throw Rug accused me of being the master mind of the attack on the Henoki ships."

"It was a legitimate military op. Tragic, but they closed the book on it, stating it was an act of war and not punishable under Bwentani law," Kensington replies.

"They reopened the case after receiving a report that there were innocent civilians on board and my forces attacked the retreating civilian transports."

"Major, that's bull. You ordered us to stand down."

"I know, Julio. Why do you think Throw Rug wants you executed? You can dispute his accusations. John, you can collaborate that we were on a rescue mission and the civilians were evacuated before we even attacked."

"Sir, I haven't even been in the military for two years. As soon as we settled here, I resigned my commission and went to work for the transport company."

"Where's Admiral Foster?"

"Who?" Kensington asks.

"Admiral Walter Foster. He commanded the America?"

"We've never had an Admiral Foster. The America was commanded by Admiral Joaquin Pasqualle."

Robert suddenly remembers that Foster was a descendant of Paul Foster, who was erased out of existence by the Terran Empire shortly before history was altered.

"My bad, I was thinking of someone else."

"How did you end up here, Major?"

"Truth be known, I'm a Colonel in the Special Ops Force. I'm not from this reality. I command a specially trained team of operatives defending Earth and its allies from hostile forces both in our reality and others, like yours."

"You lied to us?" Kensington asks, disappointed.

"Yes and no. When I first disappeared, I was from Earth's past. It was later discovered I was thrown into your reality because my past was being altered."

"By the Henoki agent that killed your family?"

"Yes. I returned to commandeer a Bwentani battle cruiser to fight an old enemy of theirs, the Cho'Kai. I was literally seconds from returning when Throw Rug leveled his accusations against me." Robert takes a deep breath, and then asks, "How the fuck did this asshole get to be in charge?"

"He sold us down the river," Kensington replies.

"Who did he sell you out to, the Bwentani?"

"No, the Henoki residing on this planet, the *Dev'cha* caste, from what I understand," Julio says.

"The *Dev'cha* in my dimension are a fanatical cult. The Henoki follow the teachings of a deity named *Ama'diok*."

"For some weird reason I vaguely recall you having a Henoki wife and your daughter is half human and half Henoki."

"Yeah, before our history was altered, my team was here to stop a natural disaster. We couldn't prevent the solar flare from forming, but we did manage to contact the Bwentani, although I do remember you being…resistant to our help."

"Tolliver accused you of being a traitor."

"If he has us executed, there's no one left to dispute his claims," replies Julio.

"I just want to get back to my wife and son."

"You will, John."

Kensington is about to say something when a large, powerfully built man in a red jumpsuit walks towards Robert, with his fists curled.

"Colonel, look out!" Kensington yells.

The inmate, Yuri Yeshenko, a former MP working for Tolliver, rushes Robert and attempts to grab him.

With reflexes nearly faster than humanly possible, Robert ducks Yeshenko, at the same instant, he delivers three quick punches to the abdomen, knee and back, knocking him down.

Robert wags a finger at him and says, "I remember you, you're Admiral Yeshenko's son. You don't even like Throw Rug."

"I despise traitors even more," Yeshenko replies with a deep, gruff accented voice.

Robert turns to Kensington, Julio and Adamson. "Somebody actually believes Throw Rug's bullshit."

Yeshenko stands up, his face is a deep crimson as he

grunts in anger. He once again charges Robert, before he plants and then throws a punch.

Robert blocks the punch, grabs Yeshenko's wrist, twists it and forces him to one knee.

He out pulls a plastic knife, sharpened into a shiv and attempts to stab Robert in the right knee.

The knife shatters.

"Titanium knee, hard to penetrate," Robert says, while applying more pressure to Yeshenko's wrist.

Two human corrections officers rush over, ready to activate the discipline collars..

"What's goin on?" CO One asks.

Robert releases the wrist hold. "Nothing, I was just demonstrating the Russian martial art of *Systema Spetsnaz* to my friend, right *torvarich?*"

"*Da,*" Yeshenko replies.

"No fighting of any kind or next time you'll find yourself in solitary," CO Two says.

They walk away; surprised someone actually took down Yeshenko, who has spent more time in solitary for fighting than in general population.

Robert holds his hands up and says, "I know Tolliver put you up to this. Why?"

"He just tells me who to attack and I make sure they don't talk."

"Kill me?"

"No. Break your jaw so you can't testify." Yeshenko looks Robert squarely in the face. "How do you know of *Systema Spetsnaz.*"

"Old Earth American Special Forces. We learned the techniques of all of our adversaries, including the Russian Special Forces."

"My ancestor was *spetsnatz.*"

"*Сержант* (Sergeant), I have no argument with you, but why would you let Tolliver hang you out to dry like this?"

"He said he would have my family thrown in jail if I did not cooperate."

"It's time to take that son of a bitch down. Testify to what Tolliver put you up to and I will make sure your family is safe."

"You are prisoner. That is not possible."

"Right now according to Lekar Septimus, I have a lot more credibility than Tolliver. The Bwentani are telepathic and can sense when someone is telling the truth."

"Then why haven't they discovered that Tolliver is lying about everything?" Kensington asks.

"Because in his warped little mind, he's convinced that he's telling the truth, plus it appears that he's gotten rid of anyone who can expose him."

"Only ten thousand of us survived. Out of that mostly civilians, maybe a few hundred military," says Yeshenko sadly.

"Once I clear myself and the rest of you of these charges, Lekar Septimus will agree to let me relocate you."

"You sound confident that you can accomplish this," Julio says.

"Once they bring me to the tribunal, I'll prove Tolliver set this whole thing up just to save his cowardly ass."

"He has produced overwhelming evidence against us."

"The Henoki and the Bwentani value honor above everything, to act dishonorably is a grave insult to them."

"How will you do this?"

Robert is about to reply when 'Septimus' appears, and hands one of the corrections officers transfer orders.

"Major, the tribunal awaits."

"Yes, sir. Permission to bring Captain John Adamson, Major Julio Sanchez and Sergeant Yuri Yeshenko as my character witnesses?"

"Yes, you are entitled to anything that is relevant to your defense. Guard; make sure their names are added to the orders."

"Yes, sir."

"Thank you, Lekar. Also, permission to change into regular clothing, we do not want to bias the court in any manner."

"Yes."

"I have a recording of the actual encounter in my command archives. Permission to contact them and have the recording sent."

"How can you contact your command center?"

"They have the ability to pick up signals from any reality. Now that you have this technology you can, too."

The Corrections Officers flank the group.

"That will not be necessary, return to your post," 'Septimus' tells them.

The Corrections Officers salute and then return to their stations as 'Septimus' leads them out of the yard.

A short time later, the next shift of officers arrive and they are briefed on the day's activities, including the fact that a senior Bwentani officer took four prisoners, including two new detainees back to Bwentani Prime to be questioned by a tribunal. They are identifying the prisoners so they are not listed as missing or escaped custody.

The outgoing corrections officers leave the duty station overlooking the now deserted prison yard.

"I'm going to do a head count and get some coffee, want anything, Jake?' Corrections Officer Don Walton asks.

"Yeah, black, no sugar. I'll start the log," Jake Tolliver replies.

Walton leaves. Jake waits until he is gone, and then takes out a comm device.

"Dad, it's Jake, come in."

"What is it, son?"

"The Bwentani General just came in and he is bringing Tucker to the tribunal."

"Good, time to fry his ass."

"According to the transfer order, Julio Sanchez, John Adamson and Yuri Yeshenko are also going as material witnesses."

Tolliver curses then pauses for a moment, "I'll contact the Bwentani resistance and they'll attack the General's transport before it can reach the planet."

"Understood. What about Yeshenko's family?"

"Deal with them."

"Understood."

Jake ends the transmission, and then contacts a couple of Corrections Officers loyal to his father to grab Yeshenko's family and dispose of them.

CHAPTER 19

Bwentani Separatist Headquarters – Bwentani moon Rillius (Regulus)

The leadership of the separatist movement, represented by Bwentani, Human and Henoki representatives, discuss the latest outrage; the curtailing of the human's rights and the imposing of martial law by 'Berellus'.

"I told you Berellus can't be trusted. One minute they consider the matter with the Henoki closed and now they reopened the case and have taken more people into custody," former TRF Admiral Joaquin Pasqualle laments.

Pasqualle and the council don't realize they are being used by Tolliver to get rid of anyone who opposes him or a threat to his position on the Terran Council.

"There is a rumor they captured the man responsible for the attack and are having him stand trial," replies 'Clavius', a former Bwentani Pomar, who joined the movement.
"Not possible. Major Robert Tucker was brought to our time by a freak accident. He would be over two hundred years old."
"Then maybe Tolliver can fill us in," 'Clavius' states,
"Tolliver is not to be trusted. Because of him, several former TRF members have been executed, and my nephew, Julio Sanchez and former Captain John Adamson were arrested for being terrorists."
"Julio is a member of our movement."
"Yes, but he is not a terrorist. "

'Clavius' is about to speak, when the comm station beeps. Tolliver's voice is heard on the speaker.

"Tolliver to Clavius, respond."

"Yes, Tolliver, what information do you have?"

"Septimus is transporting Sanchez and a couple of other people to a special session of the Imperium Council. He is about to give the location of your headquarters in exchange for clemency."

"Tolliver, I will vouch for my nephew. He would not betray us," Pasqualle replies.

"I wouldn't be too sure of that."

The monitor flickers and a live feed from the corrections center landing strip clearly shows Julio being loaded onto a transport, followed by 'Septimus'.

"I will not condone my nephew being killed based solely on this."

"He will not. We will send a couple of fighters to capture the transport and bring them here. We can negotiate the release of Septimus for our brethren," 'Clavius' replies.

Tolliver ends the transmission without a response. because if Sanchez and Yeshenko are brought to the separatist headquarters, they will discover that he was one who sold out their members to the Imperium, thereby putting himself in a lose-lose situation.

He pauses, and then contacts *Dev'cha* leader 'Dev'pok'.

'Dev'pok' replies with a tone of disgust, "What do you want, Terran?"

"You may not like me, Henoki; but you despise Septimus more. Right now he is boarding a transport leaving the Terran penal colony on the way to their headquarters. From what I understand, the alignment of the moons makes for an ideal ambush."

"You may supply us with information, Terran, that does not mean we trust you. Anyone who would betray his own people is a *kava'dal* (coward)."

"But I keep the Imperium from attacking you by shifting the blame for your attacks on the separatists."

"That is the only reason you are marginally tolerated. Mark my words, Terran, betray us and I will personally feed you to my lord, *Dev'cha*."

'Dev'pok' ends his transmission.

Tolliver sits in his chair, nervous that if his plan backfires, he will suffer the wrath of all three factions, and he's not sure which fate would be worse, and decides not to stick around to find out.

He leaves his office to find the fastest transport out of the Bwentani system, but is met in the hall by two Bremar.

Bremar Octurist addresses him. "Terran, you have been summoned to testify at the tribunal, bring your evidence."

"Um, Ok," Tolliver replies.

He returns to his office and finds the altered discs from the battle between the Henoki Armada and the Combined Defense Force, the same ones that put Julio on death row. Then he returns to the Bremars, who bring him to a shuttle for transportation to the Tribunal at Bwentani Headquarters.

Transport shuttle – five hundred thousand kilometers from Bwentani Prime

A Bwentani Tarbon (Lieutenant) pilots the craft, while 'Septimus' is seated with a Bremar guarding the group that is going to testify.

Robert, Julio, Yeshenko and Adamson are in restraints.

'Septimus' states, "I apologize for the inconvenience. It is not that I cannot trust you, but I must adhere to our law."

"I wouldn't have it any other way, Lekar," Robert replies.

"You may refer to me as Septimus."

"After I clear myself and the others, Lekar."

"That is acceptable."

The pilot is about to establish orbit in order to land, when an alarm is heard, meaning hostile craft approaching.

"Lekar, Separatist fighters approaching, fifty thousand *halktars* (kilometers) and closing," Tarbon Callimus states.

"Evasive maneuvers. Signal for back up," 'Septimus' replies.

"I cannot. Communications—"

A Separatist craft fires at the transport, shorting out a panel, electrocuting Callimus, who slumps down to the floor unconscious.

"Bremar, attend to him."

He complies, and then pulls the unconscious pilot out of the pilot seat.

"Septimus, let me at the controls, I can fight them off," Robert says.

"Yes, release him."

The Bremar switches off the restraints. Robert jumps out of the seat and rushes to the cockpit, where he quickly studies the panels and finds the manual controls.

"Hang on to your asses!"

He executes a twisting dive to evade the enemy fighters. 'Septimus', the Bremar and Callimus are tossed around the cabin.

'Septimus' and the Bremar recover and take the unconscious pilot and put him in the seat Robert had occupied and activate the restraints to keep him secure.

"Secure yourself Bremar, this Terran has a reputation for…unorthodox flying."

"Yes, Lekar," Bremar Quintmus replies and straps himself in just as Robert performs a maneuver that causes the enemy fighters to miss.

'Septimus' makes his way to the cockpit and straps himself into the co-pilot seat.

"Is this thing armed?" Robert asks.

"Yes, in the event that the separatists attack us."

Robert observes the way the enemy aircraft are aligning to attack and says, "They're Henoki pilots."

"How can you tell?"

Robert executes a set of evasive maneuvers to gauge the way they respond.

"Watch their attack patterns. Same moves the Henoki used in their attacks when I was here five years ago."

"You are correct. Their fighters have the emblem of the separatist movement."

"We can figure that out later. Right now, let's get them off our asses."

He performs an inverted roll, dives straight down and then banks the transport, ending up behind one of the spacecraft.

'Septimus' targets the aircraft's engines and fires, destroying one of them. The other craft begins to withdraw.

'Septimus' activates an Immobilizer beam, stopping the enemy aircraft from escaping. Almost instantly the separatist fighter self-destructs. The beam contains the explosion, but still causes a shock wave to impact the transport.

"You were right, Robert. They are *Dev'cha* Henoki. They will kill themselves, rather than be taken prisoner.

"Good to know."

The communications channel clears up.

"Transport craft, this is Glenarius Tower. Confirmed enemy activity. Do you require assistance?"

'Septimus' replies, "Negative. Enemy aircraft destroyed. Have a squadron standing by. We shall be landing shortly. We need a medical team."

"Medical team standing by. Clear for landing."

"Thank you, Robert. I feel it would be best if you return to your seat."

"Of course."

He sets the controls to auto pilot, gets out of the cockpit and goes to an empty seat. The Bremar nods out of respect, and then activates the restraints.

The transport lands at the central command air strip. A squad of Bremars and a medical team are waiting. The hatch opens and 'Septimus' steps out.

"Tarbon Callimus was injured in the attack. Get him in stasis and contact Doctor Cal'vek immediately."

"Yes, Lekar."

The medical team goes in and brings Callimus out, places him on a stretcher with advanced life support controls, put him in a medically induced coma, and bring him to the medical center.

Bremar Quintus exits the transport, followed by Robert, Julio, Adamson and Yeshenko, now in hand and leg restraints.

The remaining Bremars point their weapons at them, but 'Septimus' holds his hand up. "These prisoners are in my custody. Lower your weapons and return to your stations."

The Bremars salute and then leave. Quintus waits until they leave before releasing the restraints.

"Thank you for what you did. The Lekar and I did not wish for you to be treated like criminals. If you left the transport without restraints they would have shot on sight and even Lekar Septimus could not stop them."

"I understand, Bremar. Hope your friend makes it."

"He is my *binzah*."

"Tend to your brother. I shall take it from here," commands Septimus respectfully.

Quintus salutes 'Septimus' and then leaves.

Robert asks, "Lekar, don't you feel it would break your security protocol if we are seen walking unguarded?"

"Everyone is at the Tribunal, waiting for our arrival."

"Who knew we were being transported?"

"Only the council and the security detail that met us."

"Obviously the information got to whoever launched the attack. I don't think you were the target."

"The separatists attack our transports quite frequently."

"And the *Dev'cha* associate with the separatists?"

"No, they despise Terrans and my people. War broke out three hundred years ago and we fought to a stalemate. An agreement was reached and we conceded land in a remote, isolated region with a large inland sea and have left them to their own affairs."

"Apparently someone pissed them off."

"Pissed them off?"

"Human expression."

"Maybe they heard you were captured and wanted retaliation for attacking the Henoki." Julio suggests.

"The Henoki we fought were followers of *Ama'diok* and in my reality the two factions hate each other. The *Dev'cha* would have considered what happened as a favor to them."

'Septimus' replies, "It is the same here."

"The only other person who would arrange this is …"

"Who, Robert?"

"I have a sneaking suspicion about who is behind this, but I don't want to throw around accusations. Does the council know what happened?"

"I shall ask the tower." 'Septimus' takes out a comm device. "Lekar Septimus to Glenarius tower."

"This is Glenarius tower. Ricar Augustus, how may I be of assistance, Lekar?"

"Has the council been informed of these events?"

"I was about to inform them."

Robert shakes his head no.

"Do not inform them. I shall do so myself. Instruct Pomar Sekarus to launch patrols for separatist craft until further notice on my orders."

"Yes, Lekar."

"The tribunal is set to begin. I regret we do not have time to secure your evidence."

"Will they proceed without us?"

"Yes."

"We should go ahead with contacting my people. I have a feeling that whoever's behind this will play their hand and when we show up, he will lose their shit."

"You Terrans speak strangely."

"Sir, we don't understand him either," Julio quips.

'Septimus' laughs, his opinion of Terrans doing a near one-eighty reversal of his former position in twelve hours.

They proceed to the command center. A lone communications officer, 'Kalla' is on duty.

She stands, salutes 'Septimus', "Lekar."

'Septimus' tells her in their native language that he is temporarily relieving her and dismisses her.

Kalla bows her head and leaves.

Robert studies the comm panel, which is very similar to the set up the Covert Ops Force uses. He uses the quantum slipstream device, scans for his home reality, gets the setting, inputs the quantum coordinates, and opens a frequency.

Covert Ops Command Center

Ana monitors the situation in the Kolromi Sector. A monitor beeps and then Robert appears, slightly distorted.

"Colonel Tucker to Special Ops Command. Come in."

Ana sees her father and smiles, becoming emotional, having heard he was taken prisoner and feared the worse.

"*Hu'Neh*! Praise Ama'diok."

"I'm all right, sweetheart. I need you, your mother and Bat'ai to come here. I need help clearing my name."

"Bat'ai is helping Zerellus and my *Hu'Neok* fight the Cho'Kai base. It's not going well, *Hu'Neh*."

Robert sighs. "Have them fall back and return to base on my orders. Then have Bat'ai contact me when he gets back."

"They were unable to execute the rescue plan."

"We'll try again later."

Ana looks confused.

Robert laughs. "I'll explain everything when you get here."

"Yes, *Hu'Neh*. I love you.'

"I love you, too, sweetheart."

Robert ends the transmission.

Ana relays the orders and then has her aunt contact the Taquan leader to help enhance the security net surrounding Taqua Four.

Moments later, Ray, Dave, and Bat'ai enter the command center. Ana relays the information to them what her father has requested.

Bat'ai finds Robert's frequency and opens a channel.

"B. Good, you're back."

"The plan did not succeed, Robert. The battle cruiser was not enough. I fear we lost Rillius in the attack along with his crew."

"Dammit. We'll try again, this time I'll request more ships."

"You have cleared your name?"

"Not yet. I need you to access the Covert Defense Force archives for time index 0-6-1-7-2-2-1-7.'

"Covert Defense Force?" Bat'ai asks, confused.

"Lemme at it son. Ya need the attack on the Armada, Bob?"

"Yeah, Throw Rug said we committed war crimes by attacking innocent civilians on the transports and the city ships."

"That's horse shit." Ray sees Julio, Adamson and Yeshenko standing with 'Septimus'. "Hey Bob isn't that—"

"Lekar Septimus. He is the commander that allowed us to use their battleship and he is allowing us to get the evidence to clear us."

"Much obliged, sir. I kin also testify that we're innocent o' these charges."

"Ray, stay there and monitor the situation. I need the archives. Have Bat'ai Ana, Lin and Zerellus report here."

Ray has an uncharacteristic look of sorrow. "We…lost Zerellus in the fight. Ricardo an' Jackie, too."

Ana turns to Ray, becoming hysterical. *"Hu'Neok—"*

"I'm sorry, darlin'. I was gonna tell ya in private."

Ana breaks down and hugs Ray.

Robert closes his eyes, trying to contain his grief.

"Sweetheart, I'm sorry. I swear we'll make this right. Ray, have Bat'ai report here."

"Ya got it, Bob."

Ray shows Bat'ai where the archives are located, and then brings his hysterical goddaughter towards her quarters. She suddenly gasps in pain.

"The baby?"

"Yes, it's time."

"I'll git ya ta medical." Ray taps the neural link. "Doc, I'm bringin' Ana ta ya. She may be goin' inta labor."

"I'll be waiting," Elizabeth replies.

Bat'ai downloads the original footage from the battle, which from a chronological standpoint is less than five years ago, but after everything this group has gone through, it seems like an eternity.

He secures the information on a data pad, takes out his personal quantum slipstream device, sets the coordinates for the reality Robert is in and presses a button.

A small vortex appears and he steps into it.

Ana is in medical, fully in the middle of labor. She gives birth to a son, who she names Zerellus Robert in honor of her late husband and her father, who she hopes is acquitted and able to return home soon.

CHAPTER 20

Bwentani amphitheater

The Tribunal, after waiting the prescribed amount of time for 'Septimus' and the 'war criminal' Major Robert Tucker to appear and after receiving a report of the transport being attacked and apparently destroyed, have decided to allow Tolliver to present his evidence so they are able to officially convict Robert of being a war criminal and close the books on this dark chapter of Imperium history.

Tolliver shows the recently obtained 'archived footage' of the attack, allegedly taken from TRF Commander Julio Sanchez' F-122J along with communications between Robert, Julio and General Larry Kensington.

The footage is pixilated, blurry and somewhat degraded, but shows the Combined Defense Force pilots and TRF pilots attacking the civilian craft and then the Armada, destroying the city ships and transports that were caught in the wake of the explosions.

At the end there are whispers and cursing in Henoki, Bwentani and several other Imperium languages.

"I was appalled at discovering this travesty while decommissioning our fighter craft to turn over to the Imperium," Tolliver says with feigned outrage.

"Our experts could not authenticate this footage due to the poor quality," 'Berellus' replies.

"Yes, it is unfortunate. Captain Sanchez's fighter suffered damage during the battle and failed to report the incident."

"Captain Sanchez was to appear to either confess or dispute your claims. We received a report that the transport was attacked and we do not know what their status. We fear all aboard were killed in the attack, including my son," 'Berellus' states.

"My sincerest condolences on your loss, sir."

"Thank you, Council Leader Tolliver. If there is no more evidence or testimony in this matter, we shall reclose the case and move on to the matter of the attack on the transport by the Separatists—"

"Prasin Berellus, I think we can shed some light on that as well as the fantasy presented by former General Tolliver," Robert says as 'Septimus' leads the group, joined by Bat'ai into the amphitheater.

There are shouts of outrage, so 'Berellus' bangs his gavel. "Silence!"

The crowd quiets down. 'Berellus' pauses and then asks "You dispute the claims made by Tolliver? Are you saying he is lying to the council?"

"Not at all. I'm sure if you have read his thoughts, he sincerely believes these events occurred, but how can one report on an event they were not there to witness?"

"I was in the command center, Tucker. I heard the conversation between yourself and that other criminal, Captain Sanchez."

"General, unless you were able to break the encryption on my fighter's comm unit, you could not hear the conversation. It was not on any TRF frequencies."

"I found that footage on Captain Sanchez' fighter."

"I saw it. It seemed strangely degraded. Fortunately I also have footage from the fight with the Armada which is in much better condition, and is authenticated by an expert, Chief Temporal and Quantum engineer Bat'ai. Go ahead, B."

Bat'ai begins to play the footage.

Tolliver blurts out, "I object! This man is a war criminal and a mass murderer. His word is not to be trusted."

Robert's demeanor suddenly changes. He snarls, "You dare question the integrity of a member of the *Bahal'Zai* and the Quennok Warrior caste?"

"It is true, *Hemzeh*," 'Septimus' replies. He motions to Robert, who shows the mark of the *Bahal'Zai* burned into one bicep and the mark of the Quennok caste on the underside of his fore arm.

Tolliver sputters, "He…he … he could have gotten them just before he came here to steal one of your ships."

"The General is correct. I originally came here to use one of your old ships in a fight against an ancient enemy. Prasin, in my reality the penalty for one who falsely wears the mark of the *Bahal'Zai* is death. Is it true here as well?"

"Yes."

"Is *Kia'mok* Quevok present?"

"I am, Terran."

"I did not kill your *Hu'Neh*, Quennok. I confess to killing your brother, Quessok in armed combat. He died honorably in battle. It is five years too late, but I offer a salute to a fallen warrior."

Robert begins a Henoki death chant. He is joined by 'Quevok' and other Henoki present.

"You honor us by offering praise to an enemy."

"At the time I had anger in my heart because an assassin was sent to kill my family. Bat'ai has uncovered evidence that the assassin was not Henoki, but a Kallaxian, a species that has the ability to change their appearance. We also uncovered evidence that it was another Kallaxian that set off the explosives that not only killed your mother Maiok, but your sisters Linaiok and Liaok. The bomb also killed my son Robert Tucker the second and my daughter Sarah when they tried to negotiate a peaceful cohabitation of the planet."

"You have such evidence?"

"Yes. If the council wishes, I will turn over all material recorded during my time in your reality."

Tolliver turns pale as the realization that Robert possesses material that will not only clear his name, but implicate him of wrongfully convicting members of the TRF. He looks around desperately and sees a Bremar with a weapon slung over his shoulder. He shoves the Bremar, grabs the weapon and aims it at Robert.

"These fools may not see you for who you are, but I do! And I will do what they are too weak to."

The Bremar tackles Tolliver and confiscates the weapon and then stand him up to place him under arrest.

Robert turns to the Tribunal. "It appears I have been challenged. I invoke the *Kuli'tah* to prove my innocence."

The Henoki whisper among themselves because an 'outsider' knows about the ancient ritual of combat to the death.

"Release him," 'Berellus' orders.

The Bremar releases Tolliver and then backs away, because he is also familiar with the pending fight.

Robert claps his hands, arms and legs to show he is unarmed. He taunts Tolliver. "Here you go, Throw Rug, this is your chance to kill me and get away with it." He takes up a martial arts stance.

"What is the meaning of this?"

'Quevok' replies, "When you insulted his honor and brandished a weapon to kill him, you relinquished the right to examine him at a trial and agreed to the ancient Henoki ritual to prove innocence or guilt in combat to the death."

"I ... I did no such thing," Tolliver stammers.

Robert smiles. "It appears you know nothing about Henoki or Bwentani law." He pauses and then asks in a tone of ridicule, "Or are you too much of a *kava'dal* to go through with it?" causing the Henoki and Bwentani to laugh.

Tolliver turns to 'Berellus', who tells him, "He just called you a coward."

"I am no coward, but how is a test of strength proof of who is right or wrong?"

Robert shrugs, "OK, then we'll do it the way we did it on Earth two centuries ago, I will answer the accusations against me."

He motions to Bat'ai, who puts in a disc. He enters a command and a video play back of the battle in the open waters fifty miles from the Henoki Armada.

Open Waters near the Henoki City Ships

The Combined Defense Force pilots are nearing the city ships to deliver the Obliterator back to the Henoki. Ray is still flying close to the ocean's surface with the Obliterator following just below sea level.

Robert suddenly detects numerous vessels leaving the city ships heading in the opposite direction. He starts to inform the TRF but he detects no weapons signature and determines that these are unarmed vessels.

Ray suddenly picks up communications from the ships, which carry messages from many who sound scared and confused. He realizes that there are women and children on board the vessels being evacuated.

"Bob, those transports that are leavin' the city ships have civilians on board. Women and children."

"Copy that, Ray," Robert replies, as he detects some TRF F-122 Js going after them. He radios Julio, "Joker One to TRF One break off pursuit, they are unarmed. I say again they are unarmed."

"How can you be sure, Joker One?" Julio replies.

"Ray Watson says there are women and children on board," Robert replies.

"I am under orders to destroy all Henoki vessels—"

"TRF One, break off pursuit now, or I'll personally come after you and put a Sidewinder straight up your ass."

"Joker One, this is Anvil—"

"With all due respect, Anvil, I will not condone the slaughter of innocent women and children."

"I know, Joker One. I was about to give the order to TRF One to terminate pursuit. Is that understood, TRF One?" Kensington orders.

"Yes, sir," Julio replies.

Robert sighs in relief as he sees the F-122 break off pursuit.

When the file ends there are murmurs in the crowd.

"Captain Sanchez will authenticate the transmission, along with Bat'ai."

"I sense no deception from the Terran," 'Quevok' states, "I will also offer testimony that our city ships were evacuated of all civilians before the Terran attack, an ...error submitted by the Terran named Tolliver.

"In light of this new evidence, all charges against Major Robert Tucker, Captain Julio Sanchez and all members of the Terran Resistance Force that have been falsely accused of war crimes are hereby dropped."

Robert sighs in relief, and then shakes hands with Julio, Adamson and Yeshenko.

Tolliver becomes furious and begins cursing, stomping and ranting incoherently.

'Septimus' asks Robert, "Is this what you refer to as losing his shit?"

Robert starts laughing, "Yeah."

Two Bremars grab Tolliver who resists and yells, "Unhand me you alien filth."

'Berellus' appears angry momentarily, and then composes himself, "For your crimes against the Imperium, Henoki Citadel and the surviving Terrans, Elias Tolliver, you are hereby stripped of your authority on the Terran Council and placed under arrest for false testimony leading to the unjust convictions against a dozen men, resulting in the wrongful execution of six men, inciting an insurrection by the Bwentani Separatists, and consorting with the *Dev'cha*, you are remanded for trial on the penal colony on Kurai

Three. The Separatists and the *Dev'cha* will be informed and given a chance to testify that the actions they have taken are a result of your deception."

Tolliver turns pale with an expression of horror as he is led out of the amphitheater.

CHAPTER 21

Bwentani Command Center – 1900 hours Imperium time index

Robert, Joaquin Pasqualle, representing the Separatists and 'Dev'pok' meet with 'Berellus' and 'Septimus' under a flag of truce.

"It appears we have all been deceived by the Terran named Tolliver," 'Berellus' states.

"I understand the separatist movement started out as a rebellion against your government. We now only wish to live peacefully, either by co-existing with the Imperium, or finding a home world where we can rebuild our civilization," Pasqualle states.

Robert replies, "I discussed with Lekar Septimus the possibility of transporting you and whoever wants to go with you to a system that is not a part of the Imperium," He turns to 'Dev'pok'. "We extend our offer to you and your caste as well."

'Dev'pok' bluntly responds, "We require nothing, but to be left in peace, as it has been for the past three hundred years."

'Berellus' states, "We shall honor the agreement set forth by our ancestors."

Robert hands 'Dev'pok' a device. "It's an electronic barrier so that no one will be able to enter your territory."

He grunts before leaving with his bodyguards.

"Likable fellow," Robert muses.

"For him, that was pleasant conversation," 'Septimus' quips, causing Robert to laugh.

'Berellus' states, "Our Imperium extends for one thousand of your light-years in all directions. It would take decades to reach a planet that is not a part of the Imperium."

"We have technology that allows us to travel vast distances in a short amount of time. What uninhabited systems lie outside the Imperium that can support life?"

"The Hadar system. The Imperium had planned to colonize the fourth planet. The Terrans and anyone who wishes to leave the Imperium may settle there. However, since it is out of the Imperium's jurisdiction, we shall provide no assistance or means of support."

"We accept," Pasqualle says.

"Major, we will provide you with five of our battle cruisers to transport the Terrans. Each ship will hold up to three thousand people and three months' worth of supplies. Shelter and other creature comforts are up to you."

"Thank you. Sir."

"Thank you, Prasin. I will return them when we are finished," Robert replies.

"Accept them as a gift of the Imperium as a gesture of good will."

"*Tul'haka*, Prasin," Robert turns to 'Septimus'. "Until we meet again, *binzah*."

"We shall break bread, *binzah*.'

Robert and 'Septimus' grasp forearms.

Robert offers his hand to 'Berellus' who shakes it.

"Septimus told me about the death of your Zerellus, I understand he was mated to your daughter."

"Yes, she is about to give birth to their child."

"Terran, Henoki and Bwentani, it will be the Prophecy child."

"It will also be a grandchild about to be spoiled by his grandfather. Maybe we can arrange visits."

"I would be honored to welcome you and your daughter into my home."

Thank you, Prasin. B, Admiral, we have a lot of work ahead of us. We better get started."

Robert, Bat'ai and Pasqualle are about to leave when a transmission from Kurai three comes in.

Their leader 'Kaleel' appears on the monitor.

"Kaleel to Prasin Berellus."

"Greetings, *shuvag* (friend). What can I do for you."

"I am informing you that the Terran prisoner Tolliver was found dead in his cell. He was found hanging from a ceiling rafter. Our doctor states it was self-inflicted and we are closing the case.

"We shall too. *Tul'haka*"

"*Tul'haka*," 'Kaleel' replies and ends the transmission.

'Berellus' bluntly states, "I guess he took the *kava'dal* way out."

"He had you, the separatists and the *Dev'cha* wanting a piece of him, figured this was the least painful option."

"Very true. Good journey."

Robert, Pasqualle and Bat'ai leave.

Hadar Four - a week later

The people from the separatist movement, the human survivors, and several Bwentani dissidents are settling into domed living quarters, made from material similar to what the Henoki use in their underwater settlements.

Robert and Bat'ai returned to their reality and brought back duplication technology, defensive satellites placed in orbit around the planet and stripped down WA-01s with basic weapons and shields, but no time travel or quantum technology.

Rillius and four Bwentani pilots are piloting the battle cruisers in orbit around the planet.

Kensington, the newly elected head of the new Hadar

Council talks with Robert and Ray.

"Once again, Colonel, you saved our lives."

"You can call me Bob."

"Fair enough. Thank you for your help, Captain."

"Jest call me Ray."

"Word is Tolliver hung himself in prison."

"He got himself in a world of hurt double crossing not only the Bwentani, but the separatists and the *Dev'cha*."

"Can't say I'm sorry."

Ray quips, "I can't speak ill o' the dead, so I won't say shit."

Robert and Kensington laugh.

Bat'ai walks over to them. "Sir, we have set up duplication devices to provide food, clothing and comfort items. However these devices will not duplicate or produce weapons."

"Excellent, thank you…Bat'ai," Kensington replies.

Adamson, his wife and son walk over.

"Major, once again I owe you my life. This is my wife, Tonya and our son Robert."

"Nice to meet you, ma'am." Robert kneels next to his namesake and says "Your dad named you after me."

"He told me you saved his life. Thank you." He hugs Robert.

"You're welcome. Word is you want to be an astronaut and explore the stars."

"Yes, just like my Dad."

"You're now an astronaut, John?"

"Now that we are independent, I want to explore the systems around us. There are several within reach of our current technology."

"Good luck." Robert shakes his hand.

Tonya gives Robert a hug and a peck on the cheek, "Thank you for clearing my husband's name."

"Glad to do it." He turns to Ray and says "I guess it's time to head back."

"Yeah, time fer some payback."

Ray and Bat'ai follow Robert back towards the WA-01.

Yeshenko, his wife and daughter stop Robert. "I wanted to thank you for stopping Tolliver from hurting my family, *torvarich.*"

He shakes Robert's hand.

"I asked 'Septimus' to send his Bremars to make sure no one hurt them."

Yeshenko's wife, Irena says "Спасибо (Thank you)" and gives Robert a peck on each cheek.

Yeshenko's daughter, Nadia tells Robert, "Thank you, sir," and gives him a hug.

"You're welcome." He says to Yeshenko, "You've got a beautiful family, Yuri. What are your plans?"

"Council Leader Kensington asked me to head the security force."

"Good luck then."

"Good bye."

Robert, Ray and Bat'ai return to the WA-01. Robert gets in the pilot's seat, Ray copilot's chair and Bat'ai sits at the tactical station. Robert takes off from the planet and joins the Battle cruisers in orbit.

"Ops One to Ops Three, come in."

"Yes, Robert," Rillius replies.

"As much as I enjoy reminiscing about the past, I say it's time to get back to get back to our reality."

"I agree *binzah.*"

"Open a portal, B."

"I am setting coordinates to a minute after we left."

"Will anything happen if we set it back a day or two?"

"I would not recommend it, Robert."

"Understood. Let's go home."

Bat'ai opens a portal. Ray resets the stealth shields returning the 'WA-01' back to the WA-13 Outlaw and they enter the quantum vortex, followed by the battle cruisers.

CHAPTER 22

Kolromi Four - 01.13.2222. 1345 hours

Zerellus and the task force are about to launch their offensive against the oncoming Celestus and Cho'Kai when Robert's WA-13 and the five battle cruisers arrive back in their reality.

He radios Zerellus. "Ops One to Ops Four. Z. return with the fleet and our battle cruisers to Taqua Four."

Zerellus sounds confused, but replies, "Yes, *Kemzeh*."

A portal opens and the entire fleet returns to their home system. Robert pilots the WA -13 into the hangar and then goes to the command center with Ray and Bat'ai.

"Ray, let me know how far out they are."

"Five thousand light years an' closing. ETA on the base, two hours."

"First wave of fighters?"

"ETA, ten minutes."

"B. Teleport the Pulse Beam Weapons into position and disperse them in a pattern that will do the most damage until the base arrives."

Bat'ai types a command and presses a button. "In position, Robert."

"One question, Bob. Why did ya have everyone skin out like that?"

"First attack, they kicked our asses and took our lunch money. We lost half the fleet, including Rico, Jackie, Rillius and Z."

"Weren't ya successful in what y'all did?"

"Somewhat. We only brought back one battle cruiser. Apparently that wasn't enough. Either not enough firepower or we needed more ships."

"We need time ta fully upgrade the battle cruisers."

"Yeah, the whole nine yards, weapons, shields, stealth technology and the ability to open a portal on its own."

"That will take time, Robert, at least a week."

"Then we'll make the time. If they think they destroyed our base of operations, it will buy us that time."

"Ops Two to Ops Three. Ray, any sign of Bob yet?" Dave asks.

"I'm back, Dave. I cleared my name and got us a fleet of ships."

"Helluva coup, Bob."

"How's Dan?"

"Stable. He's out of commission, but he'll be back on duty in a week."

"Just in time for Valhalla."

"We're not going through with it?"

"Not yet. I'll explain when we get back."

"Understood. Out."

Robert realizes something and then asks, "B, what affect would destroying the planet have on the quantum balance?"

"I was thinking the same thing, Robert. It could trigger a catastrophic shock wave."

"Thought as much. We gotta scale back a little, put up a fight at first, and then let them destroy the base before the Cho'Kai gets here."

Ray asks, "Ya wanna deploy the decoy fighters?"

"No time. They'll be in weapons range in less than a minute. We'll just have to take 'em out with what we got."

Ray enters a command. "Weapons ready ta go."

"We'll stay as long as possible, transfer the controls to the Outlaw, and then we'll control the guns for the first wave. After that we'll set the auto guns for the second and then cover our exit."

Bat'ai transfers the weapons control to the WA-13. Then sets the auto destruct to go off when an enemy fighter attacks the command center and then goes to the WA-13. He sits at the tactical station just as the first group of Celestus fighters begin their attack run.

Robert and Ray watch in amazement as they observe him control several portable Pulse Beam Weapons at the same time, picking off the Celestians with the same efficiency as a squadron of WA-13s.

"Imagine what kinda score he woulda had on an arcade game?" Ray whispers.

Robert laughs, and then comes up with an idea for upgrading the WA-13. "Ray, do you know what a Multi Vector Attack Weapon is?"

"Lemme guess, somethin' outta Star Trek?"

"You know me so well. We mount several portable Pulse Beam Weapons on the Outlaw, programmed to fire individually or on a single target with a concentrated blast."

"Damn ambitious, but somethin' with that kinda fire power could destroy a planet...or a Chicken Choker base."

"That's the drawback. Hell it was just a thought."

"I like yer idea, but we gotta do it the smart way."

Bat'ai lets out a sigh of relief, turns to them and says," First wave destroyed, Robert."

"Good job, B."

An alarm goes off and Bat'ai checks the monitor. "Second wave approaching, Robert. Ten Squadron, Cho'Kai fighters."

"Set the guns, B. Ray, put us in orbit and use the destroying the base as cover."

"Ya got it."

Robert opens a portal and Ray flies into it.

Kolromi moon

The WA-13 emerges from the artificial wormhole and then immediate engages the stealth shields, now designed to evade Talak'Vin's quantum technology.

Bat'ai enters a command and a large virtual reality monitor appears outside the Outlaw, enhancing the battle currently taking place on the planet's surface.

"This is new," Robert muses.

"Courtesy of my other self in the Time Defense Force reality," says Bat'ai.

Ray asks, "Ya said I was in that reality, son?"

"For quite some time, Raymond."

"I remember bits an' pieces. They live on big ass ships."

"Yes, city ships. In that reality the Earth was hit by a meteor in Terran calendar year 2035."

"We stopped it from occurring in our reality."

"It was caused by the Rillius that escaped from the Imperium reality. In their dimension, it was a natural disaster so they could not go back and prevent it."

"So when the temporal shock wave hit, it altered history so that the Imperium Rillius didn't show here and our Rillius wasn't killed."

"Yes, but it was when the Triumvirate eliminated our people."

"Son, ya said this was a fixed point 'n time, but since them sum'bitches are still alive, we can undo this."

"As tempting as it is, we screwed things up enough, who knows what the hell would happen if we did anything else."

"Bob, eight billion people died."

"And how more will die if we fuck things up, and this time it will be our fault."

"Yer right, Bob."

Bat'ai sees that several Cho'Kai fighters have gotten past the automated defenses and begin a strafing attack on the command center.

"Robert."

Robert sees what's going on and enters a command. "Get ready to haul ass, Ray."

"Ya got it, son."

The Cho'Kai fighters fire their upgraded Sub Atomic Disintegrator Weapon at the command center, causing the structure to lose molecular cohesion, at the same time triggering the self-destruct sequence.

Thirty seconds later a blinding explosion destroys the command center and in its wake the entire Cho'Kai attack force.

On Board the base, Ka'Nef witnesses this and bows his head to the gallant warriors who died in the fight that has destroyed the Terran's base of operation.

"Return to Bwentani Prime, the captive Terrans may use our absence to attempt to retake the planet. Inform Dev'pok to prepare for any potential attack."

"Yes, *sabon*," Kn'Ri replies.

He issues a command to return to the Bwentani system.

CHAPTER 23

Covert Ops Command Center – 1600 hours

Robert and Ray enter the command center.

Ana sees her father, goes to him, smiling and teary eyed and hugs him. "Praise to *Ama'diok* you're safe."

"Thank you, sweetheart."

"I'm gonna help Bat'ai an' Mike git started on outfittin' the battle cruisers," says Ray, excusing himself.

"Keep me informed."

Ray pats Robert on the back, touches Ana's shoulder and then leaves the command center.

Lyle and Ryan enter.

"Good to have you back," Lyle says while shaking Robert's hand followed by Ryan.

"So yer off the hook there?" asks Ryan.

"Yeah, and with a new ally if we need them."

"Your mission was a success?"

"Yeah, I think we convinced them that they got one of our bases of operations."

"One?"

"Yeah, we set in motion a plan to feed them false information on the location of another base."

"Who's the bait?"

"Rico. He wants payback for Alejandra."

Lyle changes the subject by asking, "Ana, any word from Bwentani Prime?"

"We received a message out that the *Dev'cha* increased patrols outside the camps."

"I thought as much. Good thing we called off the op."

"We intercepted a communiqué that Jen'Pway is no longer in command. The leader of the *Dev'cha*, Dev'pok; is now in charge of the Celestus Council," Lyle adds.

Ana becomes upset. "The *Dev'cha* leader hates my *Hu'che'Neh*."

"Don't worry about your grandfather. The message stated that the Henoki not to be harmed," Lyle assures her,

"We're working as fast as we can to get them out."

"I know *Hu'Neh*, but ..." she lets out a gasp of pain. "*Hu'Neh*, it's time."

"Lyle get a hold of Elizabeth, my wife and Zerellus. Ana's going into labor."

"OK."

"I'll help ya, Bob," Ryan says.

They each put their arms around Ana, who is breathing heavily, and walk her towards the corridor leading to medical.

A Henoki medical team, led by Cal'vek, arrive with a gurney at the entrance. They help Ana onto the stretcher.

"Cal, her contractions just started, if they're anything like her mother's, this baby is gonna get here quickly."

Cal'vek motions to the team and they bring Ana to the medical bay.

"Go, I'll git the cigars."

Robert laughs. "Thanks, Ryan."

He walks towards the medical bay while Ryan returns to the command center.

Medial Bay

Robert, Linaiok, Zerellus, Ray, Rillius and Jackie are in the waiting room. Everyone but Robert appears to be nervous about Ana's labor.

Ray quips, "I wish I could be as calm as ya, Bob. Hell, I'm a nervous as a June bug."

"Helps to have gone through it already," he replies. The others give him a look. He laughs and then tells them, "Ana went into labor around this time while I was in the other reality."

"My *binzah* helped to clear your name, Robert?"

"Yes, Rillius. Some prick with a grudge set me and everyone else up to save his own sorry ass."

"An' got want he deserved."

"I could have killed him myself, but he wasn't worth it."

"I am pleased you restored your honor, *A 'nok*."

"Not quite out of the woods yet, Lin. I have to get to the bottom of what the hell happened here."

"I know you will."

Linaiok holds his hand.

Elizabeth walks into the waiting room.

"Congratulations, Zerellus. You have a son...and a daughter."

"Twins?" Robert says with a look of surprise. He is about to comment about Ana only having one child, but remembers he probably altered this reality slightly by time travelling.

"Twins are very rare for the Bwentani." says Zerellus happily.

"For the Henoki as well," Linaiok replies.

"Guess it runs in my family."

"Henoki tradition holds that a child receives one *Hu'Neok*. Ana asked that Rillius and Jacqueline be present," Linaiok states. She turns to Ray, "Raymond, Ana wanted to name you, but since you are already her *Hu'Neok*—"

"I understand, Lin. As long as I git ta spoil 'em."

Robert quips, "You gotta wait in line for that one, pal."

"May I see my wife?" Zerellus asks.

"Of course. She can have visitors," answers Elizabeth.

The group goes in and congratulates Ana, who is already sitting in a chair, holding her son and daughter. She smiles, and when she sees Ray is about to speak.

"It's all right, darlin'. I understand."

"Thanks, *Hu'Neok*."

"What are their names?" Jackie asks.

"That's the godparent's responsibility," Robert replies.

"Jackie, you are *Ki'Neok* (godmother) to my daughter, you have the honor of naming her."

"Alejandra, in honor of your cousin."

Ana becomes emotional and mouths, "Thank you." She composes herself and then says to Rillius, "You, my son's *Hu'Neok*, you have the honor of naming him."

"I shall name him Robert Septimus, for my *binzahs*, both in spirit and in flesh."

"As *Hu'che'Neh*, I guess the first round of drinks are on me," Robert says smiling proudly.

"I shall supply the *Kalnem* (Bwentani liquor)," Zerellus proclaims.

"I'll bring the Texas Hell Fire fer everyone–" Ray is given a hostile glare by Ana. "Everyone...but Zerellus,"

Everyone laughs.

Ana smiles, but then becomes upset, "I wish my *Hu'che'Neh* and *Kemzeh* could see them."

Robert says, "We'll get them out, sweetheart, and we'll even hold the *Buk'tah* (blessing) on Bwentani Prime, I promise."

Ryan changes the subject and addresses to Rillius and Jackie, "I guess y'all bein' godparents kind makes ya married."

"I guess now...using the Terran phrase; the cat is out of the bag. Jacqueline and I are betrothed."

The group is surprised and congratulates them.

Robert asks, "Why didn't you say anything?"

"We wanted to wait—"

Lyle calls Robert on the comm unit.

"Bob, this is Lyle. You had better get to the command center."

"On my way." He replies. "Z, stay with Ana, rest of you, follow me."

He kisses his wife and daughter and then returns to the command center.

Lyle is monitoring a Celestus Communications Network broadcast.

"What's going on, Lyle?"

"Our mission may have just gone down the tubes."

He enters a command. The broadcast is replayed from the beginning.

Podium outside of central government building - Bwentani Prime

Dev'pok stands at the podium with Berellus. There are no cheering crowds, only multiple battalions of *Dev'cha* and Cho'Kai warriors.

"The days of soft leadership are over. By order of Ka'Nef, leader of the Cho'Kai Alliance I have been appointed as leader of the Celestus Council. Disobedience will not be tolerated. Any attempts at protest, rebellion or aggression by the Terrans, Bwentani or blasphemous Henoki will result in immediate termination. The false god *Ama'diok* will no longer be worshipped in public or in private. Any Henoki who renounces the false prophet as their deity will be welcome to live free in our domain. Those who refuse shall be re-educated, or purified. Our people once were genetically pure, and under my rule shall be pure again. Any Henoki who has dishonored *Dev'cha* by mating, producing a *kor'tul* (mixed breed) offspring, or allow this to happen shall be tried as traitors to the Henoki and suffer the consequences."

He walks off without saying another word.

Covert Ops Command

Lyle, Robert, Ryan, Ray, Rillius and Dave are seething

with anger after they've heard what Dev'pok has said. They are also upset because they chose not to go through with Operation Valhalla.

"That bigoted sum'bitch," Ray mutters.

"Where the hell is Quennok?" Robert asks. "You don't think he–" his voice trailing off because he fears the worst has happened to his father-in-law.

"Bob, Ka'Nef gave specific orders he is not to harm Quennok."

A radio transmission comes in on the Special Forces secure channel.

"Listening post Alpha two-seven-nine to base."

"Two-Seven-Nine, this is Ops One," Robert replies.

"Colonel, this is Sergeant Quan."

"What do you got, Quan?"

"Just heard from SF Two. They just brought the Henoki leader into the camp. Looks pretty roughed up."

"Tell SF Two slight delay in Valhalla and to keep a man on Quennok at all times. Will message when the op is a go."

"Understood. Two-Seven-Nine out."

Robert sighs. "Wouldn't put it past these bastards to try and off him in the camp and then blame us."

"I think we played our hand when they destroyed the base. They think we have been eliminated," says Lyle.

"After our last escapade, they'll be wary of any diversions." Dave adds.

"And it's too dangerous to take them on head on, now that the *Dev'cha* are running the show. Because of them, it'll be that much more difficult to storm the camps."

"Once we upgrade the battle cruisers and the WA-13s, we will be able to match their firepower and get our people out of the camps."

"I think you better fill us in on what you have in mind, Bob." says Lyle.

"Better yet, I'll show you."

They follow Robert out of the command center.

Covert Ops hangar – surface of Taqua Four

They enter the massive cavern that is on the surface of the planet. A shield protects them from the toxic atmosphere, providing a perfect line of defense against attack.

They see one of the massive battle cruisers going through an upgrade by Bat'ai, Ray, Mike and the entire R&D personnel.

"Holy shit," Lyle gasps.

"Beauty, ain't she?" Robert replies.

"And we have six of them?"

"Yes. The one we originally brought back and five that Septimus allowed us to keep."

"They didn't supply the weaponry?"

"No, it would be too risky. According to Bat'ai, their technology is compatible with ours. He said we got a lot of our technology from them in the first place."

Having heard his name, Bat'ai walks over to them. "The upgrades are under way, Robert."

"What kind of time frame are we looking at? The *Dev'cha* are running the place and our people may be in deep shit."

"This battle cruiser is almost ready. I feel within three days we can equip the rest of the fleet."

"B. I know you're going all out, but Quennok and our people may not have three days. I will get everyone but Ana down here and work around the clock."

"I shall have Raymond organize them into three shifts."

"The Special Forces teams know the weapons system. So I'll assign a team to each shift. Rillius knows the time travel and quantum technology. Lyle and Ryan know the shield technology," Robert adds.

"Then the remainder of this ship's upgrades can be achieved in orbit." Bat'ai replies.

"All right, I'll get a crew and they can switch them out."

"That will not be necessary, Robert."

Bat'ai goes to a console, enters a command and presses a button. A blinding light engulfs the battle cruiser. It disappears and a split second later another battle cruiser appears.

Robert is flabbergasted.

"Holy shit! You just transported that ship like it was nothing!"

"If we had a generator powerful enough we could transport the entire colony."

"How about a Cho'Kai Base?"

"Impractical, Robert. It would require a device the size of a battle cruiser." He pauses before adding. "We would be able to teleport our people out of the prisons and the colony."

"How many ships would it require?"

"Just the ones we now have."

"How would we ensure that only our people teleport?"

"We would isolate the human, Bwentani and non *Dev'cha* Henoki."

"I'd say go now, but if we went up against the Cho'Kai base again, we would get our heads handed to us."

"I concur."

"Ryan and I will get started on the shields."

Lyle walks over to the battle cruiser, marveling at the size of the vessel.

The Special Forces teams arrive. Robert calls up the schematics for the battle cruiser: the placement of the Pulse Beam Weapons, the fire controls in the engineering and tactical station on the bridge.

"We are assisting the techs to install the weapons system. Alpha Team, you will assist the installation of the weapons. Bravo Team you will assist in engineering. Colonel Walsh and myself will be on the bridge. Any questions?" No one responds. "Move out!"

The teams move to their assigned areas. Robert and Bat'ai walk to where Dave is standing.

"When was the last time we did anything like this?" Robert asks.

"When the Terran Empire attacked us."

"And how many realities ago was this?"

"I lost track a long time ago, " Dave says laughing.

The three enter the battle cruiser and make their way to the bridge to install the fire controls for the weapons.

CHAPTER 24

Detention Center – Bwentani Prime

Quennok, who shows signs of being abused physically, walks among the military prisoners.

The Henoki warriors bow in reverence to their Kia'mok. He is also shown respect by the Bwentani and human detainees. He acknowledges the Bwentani prisoners, but distances himself from the humans because his memory is still altered.

Special Forces Operative Darrel Henderson walks over to Quennok to inform him of the pending rescue plan.

"*Kia'mok—*"

"Stay away from me, Terran," Quennok replies tersely.

"Sir, I'm part of Colonel Tucker's team…"

"The traitors that destroyed the planet."

"Traitor? Sir I'm only here to warn you—"

"And I shall warn you. Keep your distance or I will turn you over to the *Dev'cha* and you get the punishment you deserve," Quennok commands. He looks disgustingly at Darrel and walks away.

"What the fuck?" Darrel whispers to himself. Then he looks around, walks to an isolated spot near a wall and taps a spot behind his ear. "SF Two to Alpha two-seven-nine."

"This is two-seven-nine."

"Quan, get a message to command. Made contact with Henoki leader. Attempted to inform him of Valhalla, but he threatened to turn me over to the *Dev'cha*. Advise on next move, over."

"Wait one, SF Two."

A moment later Quan tells him, "Henoki leader had memory altered. Advise no further contact. Implement plan Bravo. Will advise on change of plan. Over."

"Understood. Out."

Dave taps the spot to close the neural link, and then presses a spot below the link to initiate an implanted neural inhibitor that blocks the specific memory of Operation Valhalla from all of the Special Forces.

He sees a Henoki Special Forces Operative, Tal'Shen, and whispers to him about keeping Quennok safe against a possible assassination attempt. Then he walks over to where a group of ADF detainees are playing football and joins the game.

During the game, Darrel notices a Henoki holding a knife hidden from view, walking towards Quennok, who has his back turned.

He motions to the quarterback, SF Operative Ken Harris to throw the ball towards Quennok.

Harris throws the ball. Darrel pretends to be watching it as he runs, discreetly angling towards the would-be assassin.

Just as the assassin is about to make his move by hiding the knife by his abdomen as he closes in on Quennok, Darrel hits him and they both fall, with him landing hard on the Henoki.

Two guards come running over to the apparent fight.

Darrel picks up the football and says, "Sorry guys, errant pass." He then says to the assassin, "Didn't mean to run into you, dude, sorry."

The guards motion for him to leave. He jogs back to the group playing football, tossing the ball back to Harris. They continue playing as if nothing happened.

The guards turn the assassin over. He has a knife sticking in his abdomen and has bled to death. They question people in the area and they all confirm what Darrel said: the Terrans were playing their strange game and the ball was thrown in the area and Darrel was trying to catch the ball and then ran into the other person by accident.

The guards grab the assassin's arms and drag him out of the compound.

The Dev'cha warriors guarding the perimeter see that the assassination attempt failed and they telepathically inform Dev'pok. His response is to lock down the camp and to question the Terran responsible and substantiate the claim of it being an accident.

Two *Dev'cha* warriors enter the camp, and walk to where the ADF detainees are playing football.

Dev'cha warrior Kul'pok demands, "Who is responsible for killing the other inmate?"

"What killing? I ran into the guy while playing football. It was an accident," Darrel replies.

"Come with us."

The *Dev'cha* warriors roughly grab him and lead him out of the compound.

An hour later he is returned, showing signs of abuse, but otherwise fine he walks back to the group.

"What happened, sir?' Harris asked.

"They weren't happy that I killed their guy and tried to get me to confess."

"Did they probe your mind?"

"They tried. Luckily the Colonel taught us the mental block the Henoki use."

"What now?"

"Tal'Shen and his guys will keep an eye on Quennok. Weird thing, he don't remember me and thinks the Colonel is a traitor."

"I think I can shed some light on that," Ricardo says as he walks over towards Darrel.

"Sir, when did they capture you?" Darrel asks.

"They just brought me in. We tried to set a diversion to

draw the Cho'Kai to our base and–"

"Sir you better keep that to yourself. The Dev'cha have ways of extracting that information."

"That's what we're counting on."

"You mean?"

"Yeah."

"You were saying that you knew why Quennok is acting like we're the enemy."

"His memory was altered to convince the Celestians and the Cho'Kai that the Henoki consider the Colonel a war criminal. They also altered Berellus, the Bwentani leader."

"As long as Quennok thinks we're the enemy, there's no way in hell I can protect him."

"Bat'ai gave me this," he shows Darrel a neural inhibitor. "I have it set to alter my memory and implant information for the Cho'Kai and Dev'cha. I need you to use it on me."

"OK."

"After that it will automatically set to restore Quennok's memory."

They see two Dev'cha warriors flanking Dev'pok.

"They're here for me. Do it."

Darrel presses a button and alters Ricardo's memory.

The *Dev'cha* approach and then aim their weapons at Darrel and the rest of the ADF detainees.

"Stand aside, Terran. The Colonel is to be questioned," Dev'pok demands.

"I have rights under the Celestus Charter of 2090."

"You have no rights, Terran. The Celestians are no longer in charge, the *Dev'cha* are in charge now."

"I was under the impression that the Cho'Kai were."

Dev'pok gives him an angry stare, and then motions for his guards to grab Ricardo. "Cooperate and I shall let you live, that is the only right you have."

The Dev'cha bring Ricardo out of the compound.

CHAPTER 25

Covert Ops Command Center – 1800 hours

The senior command is listening to Ricardo being interrogated via the neural link. He is following the plan, which is not to give up the information too easily, but not resist to the point where he would be killed by the *Dev'cha*.

"I sure as hell hope this don't blow up in our faces," Ryan says as he listens to Ricardo being tortured.

"Dev'pok said that if he cooperated he would live."

"How do we know that sum'bitch will keep his word?"

"They're like the Henoki I fought when I first disappeared. They're brutal, but in their warped way do adhere to a code of honor," Robert tells them.

They hear Ricardo gasp in pain again.

"How long do we stand by and do nothing?"

"Lyle, I would never ask Rico to do anything I wouldn't do myself. Hell I would have gone, but they'd probably torture and then publicly execute me."

"I know, Bob. How long did you endure it in Kabul?"

He replies, "About a week; but I don't think Dev'pok is that patient."

They hear Ricardo let out an agonizing yell.

"That's long enough, send the signal," Lyle says.

Robert sends an encoded signal to Ricardo's neural link.

Interrogation room – Bwentani prime

Ricardo is slumped in a chair, breathing heavily, having endured almost an hour of interrogation using a device which

Talak'Vin discovered the schematics for in the Special Ops Force archives: the Neural Shock Device originally developed by the Terran Defense Force.

Dev'pok is impressed by Ricardo's tenacity. "You are to be commended for your strength. Our test subjects died within minutes of being in this device. I however, am growing weary of your resistance. Cooperate, or I shall have you terminated."

Ricardo is about to hurl another insult in Spanish, when a beep that can only be heard by him goes off, signaling him to 'cooperate'.

"OK, I'll talk," Ricardo says, though still in pain.

"We destroyed the base in the Kolromi sector. Is there another base?"

Ricardo pauses, appearing to be hesitant about answering. He sighs and then replies, "There is a garrison in the Celestus system."

"That is impossible. That system was cleansed by the Cho'Kai."

They destroyed Celestus Prime, but Celestus Two has a moon that is habitable."

"If you are deceiving us, Terran–"

"You have the ability to probe my mind. Do it."

Dev'pok concentrates and then places his hands on Ricardo's head. A moment later he stops.

"I sense no deception. What are the Terrans planning?"

"We were going to launch an attack from the Kolromi system to draw the Cho'Kai base to engage our fighters. While they were fighting our fleet, we were to launch an attack from the Celestus system and free our detainees."

"Are they still going to attack?"

"The Cho'Kai took out our main fleet. We don't have the personnel to go through with it."

"I will take you at your word, Terran. If I find this to be a deception—"

"Look, I'm a dead man already. I sold out my people and when word gets out; I doubt I'll live out the day."

Dev'pok responds, "Consider your actions as saving your fellow Terrans…as long as they cooperate."

"Yeah, I'll have them put it on my tombstone."

Dev'pok appears confused at the reference made by Ricardo. He motions to the guards to return Ricardo to the compound.

Covert ops command

Robert closes the comm channel.

Lyle muses, "Pretty damn convincing. Maybe we should have gone with Ricardo's plan."

"The only thing is we don't actually have a base on Celestus Two. Just a handful of Pulse Beam Weapons and just enough technology to fool the Cho'Kai." He pauses and then asks, "Lyle, what do the Celestians do with people that die in the detention center?"

Lyle looks disgusted. "They throw them in a pit and when it gets full, plow it over."

"They're taking a page from our history. What if we give them a show and get Rico out at the same time?"

Ryan eyes him. "What are ya plannin', Bob?"

"Make it look like Rico committed suicide."

"You told us about the guy in the other reality that hung himself; but I don't think that will work."

"No, but we can make it look like he took poison."

"How in the cornbread hell do we pull that off?"

"Have Elizabeth make up a compound to simulate death, enough to fool their doctors and then get him out of there."

"How?"

"How would you guys like to do a little covert ops?"

Ryan grins. "Son, I thought ya'd never ask."

"What's the plan?"

"Let's get the compound. I'll tell you on the way."

Liaok enters the command center, worried about her husband.

"Robert, is Ricardo well?"

"We're going to get him, Lia. He'll be fine, I give you my word." Liaok nods in appreciation. "Lia, I know it's been rough since Alejandra was killed…"

"She is in the Divine Hall with *Ama'diok.*"

"Ana's daughter is named Alejandra in her honor.'

"Yes, she told me. Ana said I may consider her to be my *Ke'che'Neh* (grandchild)."

"We're on our way to get him."

"Thank you. All of you. I shall stay here and monitor the command center."

She gives the three of them a hug in appreciation and then sits at the communications station.

They leave the command center. Robert briefs them on what he has planned on the way to the medical bay to converse with Elizabeth and allow Ryan and Lyle to congratulate Ana and Zerellus.

Ricardo's cell- later in the evening

Ricardo is lying on a bunk with a thin mattress, still feeling the effects of the Neural Shock Device.

A whispered voice suddenly speaks to him.

"Rico." Ricardo sits up in bed, looks around and then lays back down, thinking the NSD has affected his mind. Once again the whispered voice says, "Rico, it's Bob. You're not hallucinating. I'm using an invisibility vest. If I deactivate it, they'll pick up my bio signature."

"Yeah, You're high on their shit list. Speaking of shit lists, thanks for having the guys threaten me; real fun."

"Sorry I had to put you through this, Rico, but it looks like you bought our people some time."

"Something tells me that now they think I'm being

175

cooperative, they're gonna try and pump me for more information. To be honest I don't know how long I can take that fucking thing. Now I know what you went through when we were captured by the TDF."

"They only tortured me for half an hour. You now hold the record, *hermano*."

"Gee, I'm honored."

"We're getting you out of here."

"How?" Ricardo is caught off guard by two small pills, one purple and one red float in front of him. "What the hell are they?"

"One's a pill to simulate death by poisoning. The other is fake blood to sell the effect. When do they make their rounds?"

"Every hour. They're due in about five minutes."

"Go ahead and take it. It'll put you in a deep coma and should fool their doctors."

"If they try and do an autopsy on me, I'm coming back and haunting your sorry ass."

Robert chuckles. "I'll be right here, Rico. If something goes wrong, I'll knock them out and get you out of here."

Ricardo sighs. "OK."

He takes the purple pill and then places the red pill between his teeth, bites down and then lets the blood fill his mouth and spill out.

A minute later he becomes very limp and falls to the floor, appearing to be dead.

A short time later, two guards walk up to the bars, doing a bed check. They see Ricardo lying on the floor. They go in with weapons drawn. One points his weapon at Ricardo, while the other checks his breathing and heartbeat, or lack thereof.

"The Terran's dead."

"This was the one who cooperated and was threatened by the other Terrans."

"They could not have gotten in to kill him. He must killed himself somehow."

The other guard notices a pill lying next to him.

"He must have taken poison. How did he get them?"

"I hear rumors that Terrans will sometimes carry poison on them and would rather kill themselves before allowing themselves to be captured."

"He must have been captured before he could take them. He must have taken them because he cooperated and the other Terrans threatened to kill him."

"We will take the pills to the doctor to verify that it is poison and then dump him."

"He is dead. We will just dump him."

"The pit is full; we will dump him and then cover it and start a new one."

They pick up Ricardo's body and then leave the cell.

WA-13 – ten minutes later

A light flashes and then Ricardo, who is still under the effects of the pill and covered in dirt appears on the floor of the main compartment. A cough is heard, and then Robert appears, also covered in dirt.

"Mission accomplished," Robert says, with a haunted look.

Lyle asks, "Bob, what's the matter?"

"Remember those pictures of the mass graves from Nazi Germany? Now I know what it was like."

"How's Ricardo?"

"Probably grateful he's in a coma. His vitals are stable. Let's get him back to medical, so Elizabeth can give him the compound to bring him out of this."

Lyle opens a portal and then Ryan pilots the Outlaw into the portal and disappears.

CHAPTER 26

Covert ops progress report:

It's been two days since we pulled off the operation inside the detention center.

We received a report from deep cover Special Forces Operative, Major Darrel Henderson, that since Colonel Ricardo Pasqualle 'cooperated' with the Dev'cha, conditions at the facility have improved. They ruled his "death" a suicide and have not perused the matter.

Henoki Special Forces Operative Tal'Shen was able to successfully restore Quennok's memories and has secretly rallied the Henoki detainees. There have been no other attempts on his life.

Colonel Pasqualle has fully recovered from the compound given to him and has been cleared for limited duty.

Bat'ai reports that all six of the battle cruisers have been fully upgraded along with two squadrons of fighters upgraded with Colonel Robert Tucker's idea of a Multi-Vector Attack Weapon, designated MVAW.

The new craft has been designated the WA-14 Septimus. They have also included verbal and neural interfaces that were incorporated into the original WA-13 before the temporal upheaval.

Rillius and a squadron of Bwentani pilots have the distinction of flying the new fighter. Colonel Ray Watson, filling in for Colonel Pasqualle, will lead the other squadron.

Six crews of human and Bwentani have been trained to pilot the battle cruisers, which can hold a squadron of WA-13 fighters and transports for the Special Forces.

Tomorrow we commence the liberation of Bwentani Prime – code name Operation Valhalla.

Report filed by General Lyle Kensington Terran time index 01.15.2218.2230

CHAPTER 27

Covert Ops Command Center – 01.16.2222 - 0700 hours

Robert, Ryan, Lyle, Dave, Ray, Bat'ai and Rillius are meeting to go over the final details of Operation Valhalla.

"Since we played our hand with the original plan of attack, we have to figure out a whole new approach," states Lyle.

"Lyle, do you remember what Bat'ai and I discussed as a possible scenario?" Robert asks.

"Refresh my memory."

"Since we know that we can teleport people, we can simultaneously get our people out of the detention camps and send in our Special Forces and ground troops."

"What about the Henoki? I don't think we can teleport all six million of them," Lyle says skeptically.

"We can flood the colony with Aprilozene."

"What do we do with the *Dev'cha*?"

"We relocate them to an isolated providence on the other side of the planet, in an environment that can support them indefinitely. We can put a shield around them and keep their sorry asses there as long as we want."

"I say jest kill the sum'bitches," Ray quips.

"Then we'd be the butchers we've been accused of being. We hit them hard and fast, we can pull this off with a minimum loss of life on either side."

"You do remember that the Cho'Kai base is lurking somewhere in the Bwentani system and I doubt they will fall for any diversions," Lyle counters.

"I know. Five of the battle cruisers are heavily armed and can easily match their weaponry. The sixth one is a transport for the sick and wounded."

"Sounds like we're ready ta go," declares Ryan.

"We have Darrel's team in position. They're waiting for our cue."

"Rico, Lia, you have the command center's yours, keep us posted on any changes.

"We will. Good luck, *hermano*."

"May *Ama'diok* be with you."

"Thanks, Lia."

They leave the command center to say their farewells to their families and significant others, while others go to pray to their deities for strength and a successful mission.

Orbit around Taqua Four – 0755 hours

The task force prepares for their most dangerous mission to date.

Five of the battle cruisers hold two squadrons of the WA-13s, while the command battle cruiser carries the WA-14s, the Special Forces and four battalions of ADF troops, along with medical personnel.

The Command ship, the *Septimus* leads the Armada away from Taqua Four. On the bridge, Lyle, Ryan and Robert make final preparations.

"We move out in five minutes, Bob. You better join your teams," says Lyle.

"I will. If we're not successful, get everyone you can out of there and settle on Taqua Four."

"I am ready to open the vortex," Bat'ai says from the tactical station.

"Thanks, B. Good hunting, sirs."

"Good hunting, Bob."

"Go git 'em son."

Robert shakes hands with Lyle and Ryan, then walks over to Bat'ai and does the same before getting into the elevator and going to the landing bay where the Special Forces, WA-14 pilots and the medical team have assembled.

Dave addresses Robert, "We're ready. Just point us at something, and we'll kill it."

Robert laughs, "Darrel and his people?"

"Ready, they're waiting on our command."

"As soon as we're in position, give the signal."

Bat'ai's voice is heard over the ship's comm system. "One minute to event horizon. All personnel prepare for hyper velocity."

"You heard him. Go to your assigned ships and wait for General Kensington's command to commence Operation Valhalla," Dave shouts.

The pilots get into their assigned fighters, while the Special Forces get into the WA-13 transports.

Jackie gets into the pilot's seat and Robert takes the co-pilot's chair."

"Ready to do this, Jackie?"

"Just like old times."

"When I give the signal, teleport us down along with the equipment we have for Major Henderson's team. Be careful, I don't want your *Balshon* (Fiancé) kicking my ass."

"You be careful, too, Bob. I want my goddaughter to have her father around," she says laughing.

Robert puts his hand on her shoulder.

Bat'ai states over the comm system. "Event horizon occurring in ten seconds. Five seconds. Three. Two. One."

A massive portal opens and the battle cruisers enter.

Space above Bwentani Prime

A portal opens behind Gaius, the largest of the thirteen moons, obstructing their entry from the *Dev'cha* and

Cho'Kai. The battle cruisers appear and instantly engage their stealth shields.

From the bridge of the *Septimus*, Lyle addresses the fleet. "General Kensington to fleet. Battle cruisers execute attack pattern Epsilon seven–four–one. Commanders, deploy the fleet. Special Forces teams, prepare to begin Operation Valhalla."

The ship commanders radio their compliance.

Lyle checks the status of the Cho'Kai, *Dev'cha* and Celestus forces. He sees that conditions are optimal for deployment and announces, "Commence Valhalla."

All six of the battle cruisers open their landing bays and twelve squadrons of ADF fighters deploy and engage their shields.

Robert orders Jackie, "Go to grid coordinates Alpha one-seven-six and stand by to teleport us."

"Yes, sir."

Robert goes to the cabin, puts on his invisibility vest, body armor and collects his weapon; a combination energy, conventional and sniper rifle. "Ops one to Ops Two. We're ready. Have SF Two begin diversion."

"Fuckin' A," Dave replies. he taps his neural link and sends a coded message to begin their part: Causing a riot to draw out the Celestus and *Dev'cha*.

"Ops One to command; Bat'ai, ground team ready to create diversion. Prepare to teleport our people."

"Yes, Robert."

"Team one. Stand by to teleport."

The team readies their weapons and prepare for battle.

Detention center

Darrel and his team mull around, strategically placing themselves close to the Celestus camp guards, who observe the detainees doing nothing out of the ordinary.

A beep goes off in each of the team's neural links. The team springs into action, grabbing the guard nearest them, snapping their necks and taking their weapons.

"Charlie Team, form a perimeter. Everyone inside the circle. We are getting the fuck out of here!" orders Darrel.

The detainees make their way inside the circle formed by the Special Forces team.

Celestus guards run out of their barracks and are instantly cut down. A guard in the tower sees the insurrection and sends a signal to the *Dev'cha* that there is a riot in progress in the main detention center.

"I have called for the *Dev'cha*, you will return to your cells immediately!" The Celestian tower guard calls out.

Darrel is about to shoot the guard, chuckles, and then lowers the rifle and yells, "Good! Let the fuckers come! I'll even give you a head start before I shoot your ass out of the tower!"

The guard pulls out a rifle and shoots at Darrel, missing him.

"Had your chance." Darrel aims and shoots the guard who falls out of the tower.

The body nearly lands on Dev'pok, who leads a battalion of warriors to the perimeter of the camp. He issues a command. "*Chor'ka* (deploy)."

The warriors fan out and block every exit to the detention center.

Dev'pok pauses and says in galactic standard, "We have you surrounded. Surrender and you will die mercifully. Resist and we will feed you all to *Dev'cha* and he will feast on your carcasses."

"Fuck you and your piece of shit god!" Dave yells back, at the same time the team fires at the *Dev'cha*, killing some and wounding others.

"Kill them!" orders Dev'pok.

Darrel taps his neural link. "Bob, now!"

A blinding light engulfs the detainees and a split second later, Robert, Dave and Mike's Special Forces team appear. Robert presses a button and a shield surrounds the facility.

The three teams cover Darrel's people as they get inside the new perimeter and put on their combat gear.

The *Dev'cha* fire their weapons and nothing happens.

"We're inside a dampening field. Energy weapons will not work. We have conventional weapons and could kill you right now. But I think we would rather kill you with our bare hands. Darrel, the leader's yours," Robert yells.

"Much obliged. Let's fucking kill something!" Darrel shouts.

The four Special Forces teams let out an unearthly howl and charge the *Dev'cha*, who are momentarily caught off guard, but then pull out knives and prepare to fight the Terrans running towards them.

A large scale melee breaks out, with Darrel's team leading the charge, letting out pent up anger from two years of captivity, abuse and the death of a couple of the operatives who were killed for no other reason than to "set an example."

Dev'pok manages to retreat to the relative safety of a guard tower and then calls Ka'Nef.

"Ka'Nef, this is Dev'pok. The Terrans have mounted an insurrection. We request assistance–"

Ka'Nef tersely replies, "You are more incompetent than Jen'Pway. At least he maintained order. This planet is forfeit, we shall cleanse the planet and seek our needs elsewhere."

Dev'pok lets out a Henoki curse and is about to summon reinforcements, when Robert and a couple of operatives appear.

"Hello, asshole. Your claims to being superior to us have just proven to be bullshit. Your men gave up pretty much without a fight. You're no better than the terrorists I fought two hundred years ago. They thought they were all big and bad going up against unarmed civilians, but when they faced someone equally armed, they ran and hid like fucking cowards. I'm a sporting man and I'll give you a chance. The *Kuli'tah*; if you win, you and your warriors go free."

"If I lose?"

"You die and your men still go free." Dev'pok does not respond. Robert lets out a disgusted grunt. "*Kava'dal*. Arrest him."

"I will face you."

"You won't be facing me. Him," Robert says pointing to Darrel, who is standing ten feet away.

Darrel clenches and unclenches his fists showing his readiness to take Dev'pok on..

"Who is the *kava'dal* now?" snarks Dev'pok.

Robert scoffs and shows him the *Bahal'Zai* mark. "He will only kill you. I will make you wish you were dead."

Dev'pok knows the reputation of the *Bahal'Zai* and for Robert to have survived the training means he is not one to be trifled with.

"I accept."

Robert and the Special Forces Operatives lead Dev'pok to the center of the detention center.

"*Dev'cha* Warriors, you have fought with honor. Your leader has agreed to the *Kuli'tah*. Win or lose, you are free to go, if your leader wins, he will join you. If he loses, you may take his body and feed him to *Dev'cha* to honor his dedication to your deity."

The *Dev'cha* are surprised that a Terran would know their burial rituals, until some of them realize he is the mate of the daughter of the Henoki leader.

"As the challenged party, I claim the right to choose how we fight," Dev'pok states.

"That is your right. Name your weapon."

"I choose the Cho'Kai *mok'to*."

Robert quips, "I have a couple as trophies off the last Cho'Kai I killed," He takes out his comm device. "Bat'ai, have Major Foster send down the Cho'Kai weapons I have hanging in my fighter."

"Yes, Robert."

The *Dev'cha* thinks that Robert is bluffing because there has been no record of a Terran or anyone defeating a Cho'Kai Warrior in hand to hand combat, but are stunned when two staffs, with a rounded mace on one side and a curved blade on the other, appear in the middle of the compound.

"Fuck them up and I will fuck you up. Or perhaps I'll just have to kill a couple of more Cho'Kai to replace them," Robert says.

His comment receives a laugh from Darrel and the Special Forces operatives which intimidates the *Dev'cha*.

Dev'pok and Darrel pick up their *mok'to*.

Dev'pok regains some of his swagger and begins to twirl the weapon in a display of skill.

Darrel also twirls the *mok'to*, matching him move for move, but faster and more skillfully.

Robert shouts "*Quen'Te*! (begin)."

Darrel and Dev'pok advance towards each other, looking for an opening to attack. They suddenly begin trading blows and countering each other's moves.

"Gotta admit, he's pretty good," Dave quips.

"Seeing that Darrel's our hand to hand combat instructor, this may take a while," Robert retorts. He receives a call on his comm unit.

"Ops One, this is Command One."

"Go ahead, Lyle."

"Bob, we've taken the Henoki colony. Zero casualties. Henoki leader Quennok is pointing out the *Dev'cha*. What should we do with them?"

"Have Bat'ai transport them to the detention center."

"Will do. Out."

"What do you have in mind, Bob?"

"Possible peace accord."

They go back to watching the fight between Dev'pok and Darrel. The fight has grown in intensity as the *Dev'cha* and the Special Forces cheer them on.

Dev'pok lads a very hard shot to Darrel's midsection, knocking the wind out of him. He sees his opportunity and then goes to deliver the killing blow, using the sickle end to slice Darrel in half.

Darrel sees the strike coming, and manages to dive out of the way. Then he sweeps his legs knocking Dev'pok down. Then he grabs his staff, and holds the mace end to smash Dev'pok in the face. Before striking he pauses, "Yield."

"Never! Kill me."

Darrel is about to oblige, when Robert steps in.

"Stop!"

Darrel looks at him, and then steps away.

Robert walks to Dev'pok, "You have proven yourself in combat and have restored your honor. If we can come to an accord, we will call an end to the hostilities."

"The *Dev'cha* will never bow to the false god!"

"Nor should you. My people almost wiped themselves out of existence battling over their beliefs. The irony is that they all worship the same deity, only by a different name."

"Dev'cha and the false god are not the same."

"Yes, I know the story of *Ama'diok* and *Dev'cha*. I'm sure each side has an account of what happened. That was ten thousand Terran years ago and what actually occurred may never be known. What I propose is to give you a choice; you can either relocate to a planet that is habitable for you or there is a land mass on Bwentani Prime that has submerged, with the exception of sharp impassable rock walls. There you can live in peace."

"Your offer intrigues me, Terran. Where is this planet?"

"That I can't divulge just yet. But it is very isolated and I guarantee you that no one would interfere with you."

"I wish to inspect the—"

Dev'pok is cut off by Lyle's voice on the comm device. "Cho'Kai base moving into range. ETA twenty minutes."

"Acknowledged."

"Colonel, Ka'Nef plans to cleanse the planet."

It takes a couple of seconds for Robert to realize that the Cho'Kai plan to destroy the planet. "Shit. If these assholes do that, they'll cause a quantum shock wave and destroy us all."

"I offer the services of the *Dev'cha*."

"We accept. Your pilots can join our fleet."

Dev'pok issues an order in the Henoki language. The warriors comply and then leave the detention center.

Robert lowers the barrier.

Dave asks, "Can we trust these fuckers?"

"Bat'ai intercepted a transmission from Ka'Nef, pretty much telling Dev'pok A-A-YO-YO (Adios Asshole, You're On Your Own)," Robert replies.

"We have to disable their weapons and a Special Forces raid is pretty much out of the question after what Bat'ai told us what happened the last time we tried it."

"We now have the layout of the base, the invisibility vests and the individual shield to protect us."

"Teams, on me," Dave commands.

The four teams assemble in front of Dave and Robert.

"We just intercepted a transmission that the Cho'Kai are about to attack the planet. Two teams will secure the facility housing the planetary shield. The objective is to repair and reactivate it. Mike and Darrel, your teams will handle that," Robert orders.

"Yes, sir," They reply and then lead their teams out of the detention center.

"Alpha and Bravo will enter the base, disable their environment controls and then destroy their main weapons.

If we are successful, we will also attempt to capture their leadership."

"My team will go after the main weapon."

"Agreed. Ops one to Major Foster."

Jackie replies, "Go ahead, Ops One."

"Beam us up." Dave look at him with one eyebrow cocked. "I've always wanted to say that," Robert laughs.

Dave shakes his head and rolls his eyes as they teleport back to the WA-13.

CHAPTER 28

Bridge of the *Septimus*

Lyle and Ryan watch as the Cho'Kai base slowly establishes a position in orbit around Bwentani Prime.

"Let's get their attention. Bat'ai adjust our shields and let them see us," Lyle orders.

"Yes, sir."

Bat'ai adjusts the stealth shields so the battle cruisers are visible to the Cho'Kai.

"Deploy the WA-14s to draw out their fighters, and then commit the rest of the fleet."

"Command Two ta fleet. WA-14s deploy and engage the base ta draw out their fighters. Cruisers decloak an' prepare ta engage the base. Squadron Commanders, take charge of yer sections an' whup some ass," Ryan orders.

The commanders comply.

Ray and Rillius lead the WA-14s on an attack run on the base. They identify several weapons platforms attempting to track them."

Ops Three Ta Ops Four. Ya ready ta see what these sum'bitches can do?"

"I am with you, *binzah*."

"Ops Three ta Alpha Squadron. Deploy MVAW. Target the weapons platforms. Attack Pattern Cobra Two. Engage!"

"Ops Four to Bravo Squadron attack pattern Rillius Three, deploy MVAW and engage the enemy."

The squadrons activate their weapons which detach from the frame of the WA-14. They hover ten meters, surround the fighter, target several weapons platforms, and fire all five

Pulse Beam Weapons at once. This destroys numerous platforms and causes damage to the surface of the base.

"Hot damn! Now that's what I'm talkin' bout!" Ray gleefully says as he destroys three platforms with a single volley.

Lyle contacts Ray and Rillius, "Base to Ops Three and Four. Cho'Kai fighters deploying from hangars located on the southern hemisphere. Alex's squadrons can take on the fighters; we need you and Rillius to take out the bays."

"Understood, Lyle," Rillius replies.

"Ya got it, son. Ops Three ta Squadron break off attack, regroup and proceed ta the landin' bay. Bearin' three – four two. Disengage MVAW."

"Bravo Squadron, new target. Grid coordinates three-four – two. Disengage MVAW and proceed to target area," orders Rillius.

The two squadrons break off their attack on the annihilated weapons platform, and fly towards the hangars on the opposite side of the base.

Cho'Kai command center

Ka'Nef is furious at how easily their first line of defenses was rendered useless in a matter of minutes.

He turns to Talak'Vin, "Why did you not tell us the Terrans possessed such weaponry?"

"Sir, I was not aware this technology existed."

"You have access to their weapons and schematics. We based our defenses on defeating them."

"This is from a quantum reality different from ours."

Ka'Nef grabs him. "I thought you said they did not possess this technology."

"Sir, they fear using it, because any altering of this reality would cause a catastrophic quantum shockwave that would obliterate everything in this universe."

"And yet they acquire technology that is able to destroy us." He squeezes Talak'Vin's neck. "I should kill you, but you are the only one who can counter it. Analyze it and come up with a defense, immediately!"

He telepathically commands Kn'Ri to take Talak'Vin to the engineering section to come up with a solution and ready the Sub Atomic Disintegrator Weapon for deployment.

Special Forces WA-13

Jackie pilots the fighter towards the base, using the stealth shields to conceal their approach.

Robert's been listening to the reports. "Looks like the WA-14 is a hit," he quips,

"Don't be surprised if the bastards start priming their main weapon," says Dave.

"Good Point. Ops One to Delta One."

"Go ahead, sir," Mike replies.

"Mike, ETA on getting the shield online?"

"Fraid we did a little too good o' a job, sir," answers Mike. "Repairs are a no go."

"Shit! Stand by for extract. Ops One to Ops Command."

"Go ahead, Bob," says Ricardo.

"Rico I need Zerellus to load up a WA-13 with Global Defensive Satellites and get here PFQ (Pretty Fucking Quick)." Robert replies,

"I'll have him there pronto."

"When he arrives, have him contact SF Two. Charlie and Delta teams will help with the deployment."

"Say again, Ops One."

"They're gonna deploy the satellites on the Bwentani moons and secondary deployment around the planet."

"Understood. Out."

Robert turns to Jackie, "There's a small service dock at the southern axis. Bring us there and we'll teleport in."

"Yes, sir."

She pilots the WA-13 towards the dock.

The fighter is rocked by distortions, meaning the Cho'Kai main weapon is starting to build for deployment.

"Hang on, I'll adjust the shields," says Robert. He sits down at the tactical station, and quickly enters a command and a few seconds later the distortions stop.

"We have less than fifteen minutes, Bob. Fuck the environmental controls; we need to sabotage that fucking thing ASAP," yells Dave.

"Agreed. Suit up, hostile environment gear and engage the portable shield on your vests. Their environment has a virus designed to attack our DNA. Contact, even for a second, will kill you in a matter of minutes. Check your vests, anyone with less than a fully functional vest do not deploy."

One of the Operatives, Intel Specialist Jim Henning has a damaged control mechanism on his vest.

"Sir," he says and shows Robert.

"Sorry Jim, you gotta sit this one out. Assist Major Foster by manning the tactical station. Sweep for Cho'Kai and alert us if we are about to encounter then. We need a clear route and don't have time for any fire fights.'

"Understood, sir. *Operor vel intereo* (Do or Die)."

He shakes Robert's hand and then sits at the tactical station.

Dave's team loads up on smoke and flash bang grenades as Robert enters the main compartment.

He addresses Dave, "Jim's vest is down, he'll man the tactical station and steer us clear of the Cho'Kai."

"And if we're discovered?"

"I'll pull a Kabul and lead them away."

"Uh, Bob, running though the station naked is not exactly a good idea."

Robert laughs. "No, shithead, my team will lead them away and try to take out the environmental and any other system that we can."

"OK," Dave says as his team hands the smoke and flash/bangs to Robert's team. His team grabs satchels of high explosives and slings them onto their backs.

Jackie calls over the intercom, "We're in position."

"Acknowledged. Jim, sweep for any kind of detection equipment," Robert replies.

"Dock clear, sir."

"Acknowledged. Jackie, go ahead and teleport us."

They engage their invisibility vests and shields to protect them from the Cho'Kai environment.

A light engulfs the teams and they are instantly teleported inside the service dock. The teams leave the dock and begin their advancement towards the engineering section and their objective.

Bridge of the *Septimus*

Jackie radios Lyle. "ADF Two to base."

"Go ahead."

"Sir, Alpha and Bravo teams are in the station to disable the Cho'Kai weapon."

"Understood. Command to Ops Five."

"Ops Five."

"Zerellus, what is your status?"

"Michael and Darrel's teams are deploying the satellites on the moons. I am dispersing additional satellites. We shall accomplish our mission in fifteen minutes."

"Bat'ai to Zerellus. The Cho'Kai weapon will reach full deployment in seven minutes."

"We shall quicken our pace."

"The ops team is in the base, attempting to disable the weapon. We'll also try to buy you some time."

"Acknowledged. Out."

"Ryan, order the battle cruisers to destroy the weapons port."

"The dad-gum thing is too well protected," argues Ryan.

Lyle sighs. "If Bob and Dave's teams fail and Zerellus can't get the satellites operational in time; we may have only one option left."

Ryan nods, understanding. "I'll git the ship ready."

He motions to Bat'ai and tells him to prepare the ship to ram the Cho'Kai base as a final measure against it destroying the planet. He has everyone but the bridge crew evacuate to the *Kensington*, commanded by Major John Randall.

Cho'Kai Base

Lyle radios Robert and tells him about the fail safe plan and how they have less than five minutes to disable the weapon.

"We're two minutes to target," Robert replies.

"Good Hunting."

"*Operor vel intereo.*" Robert ends the transmission. Looking though his modified visor, he sees Dave's team ahead of him spread out in tactical formation. He whispers, "Ops One to Ops Two. We have three minutes before the weapon is beyond the point where we can destroy it."

"Understood. Target in range."

"Acknowledged. Ops One to ADF Two."

"Go ahead, sir."

"Lock onto our signal Jackie; we are one minute to target and three minutes to fail safe point. If we don't succeed, Command One is going to ram the weapons port. Be ready to teleport. If you can't, get the hell out of here. That is an order."

"Yes, sir. Good luck."

Robert ends the transmission, and readies his weapon. "Ops One to Alpha and Bravo teams, switch to conventional weapons and shielding. Bravo team, Target the primary fire control station. Alpha team will provide diversion and cover fire."

"Acknowledged. Ops Two. Out," Dave responds.

"Ops One to Alpha team. Smoke and flash-bang on my mark." Robert pulls out a smoke and flash-bang, pops the pins, rolls the smoke and then throws the flash-bang at the Cho'Kai manning the fire control station. "Now!"

Robert's team throws grenades and fires at the Cho'Kai, catching them completely off guard.

One of the warriors manages to activate an alarm.

Dave yells, "Plant the charges!" His team quickly set the satchels next to the station. "Thirty second charge. Let's get the fuck out of here!"

"Jackie, now!" yells Robert.

"The signal's jammed."

"Move the fuck out!"

The teams quickly leave the engineering section. Robert sees a panel for the thick double doors set up in the event of an explosion to contain it. He hits the button and two one foot thick metal doors close with a loud thud. Robert and his team run towards the service dock.

Ten seconds later the entire station shakes violently as the high explosives destroy not only the fire control station, but the Sub Atomic Disintegrator Weapon itself.

"Command One to Ops One. Bat'ai reports the main weapon is off line. Congratulations."

"We're Oscar Mike. We might need a hard extract–"

The station begins shaking violently.

"Secondary explosion?" Dave asks.

"No, feels like we're moving. Command One, feels like the base is rotating. Can you confirm?" Robert answers.

"Affirmative. Bat'ai states they have a secondary weapon. It is fully charged and will be in range in five minutes," states Lyle.

"Will Zerellus have the satellites deployed in time?"

"Wait One," Lyle replies. A moment later he informs Robert, "Uncertain. We are preparing to ram the base."

"We will try to disable it from their command center. Give us four minutes and then go through with it."

"Good luck."

"Out." He addresses to teams, "They have a secondary weapon primed. We can't take it out. So our only option is to disable it from their command center. We have four minutes. Stealth mode and haul ass."

"We'll split up and double our chances."

"Agreed. Ops One to Bat'ai."

"Yes, Robert?"

"B. We need to locate two elevators to get us to their command center."

"Sending specs to your visor."

A schematic of the base appears on their visors.

"Got it, thanks B. Dave your team takes the west lift, we'll take the east. First one to the command center gets to kill Ka'Nef."

"You're on. Move out!"

The two teams reengage their stealth personal shields and quickly proceed to the elevators in order to reach their objective before it's too late.

Cho'Kai Command center

Ka'Nef paces, agitated that the primary Sub Atomic Disintegrator Weapon was destroyed and he now has to use a smaller, less powerful version to destroy the Terran fleet. The secondary weapon is not powerful enough to destroy a planet, but will annihilate the enemy armada.

"Tu'Klat, increase the rotational speed."

"Sir, maximum rotation. Terran fleet will be in range in one *kel* (minute)."

"Set weapon to activate the instant they are in range."

"Yes, Ka'Nef."

The tactical officer, Ta'Rin notices a single battle cruiser advancing rapidly towards them. "Sir, the Terran ship is on a collision course. Less than one *kel* to impact."

Tu'Klat states, "Sir, it is in weapons range."

Ka'Nef is about to give the command to fire, when both elevators open and a split second later a shot rings out, killing him.

The Special Forces teams rush into the command center.

Ta'Rin is about to activate the weapon, but Robert sees him and shoots him in the head. He falls forward, his body landing on the button activating their weapon.

At the same instant, the *Septimus* impacts with the base and the shields activate around Bwentani Prime.

A blinding light engulfs the Bwentani system.

CHAPTER 29

Command Center

The Special Forces teams are still in the base command center, but instead of Cho'Kai Warriors, the Imperial Triumvirate and their Shock Troopers are manning the station. The base is no longer orbiting Bwentani Prime, instead they are orbiting Earth, preparing to attack using a Particle Laser Weapon designed by Imperial technology developer Talak'Vin.

The Special Forces teams experience a few seconds of dizziness, and then recover. They hear Imperial Commander 'Robert Tucker' giving an order.

"Dammit, I said fire!"

"Sir, the weapon is offline," Commander 'Keith Sykes' replies.

Robert exclaims "What the fuck!?"

'Tucker' turns and sees him. "It's Tucker's team! Seize them!"

The Shock troopers draw their weapons and start to close in on the Special Forces team.

Robert and Dave throw a couple of smoke and flash-bang grenades, fire at the troopers and then return to the lift.

"Bob, what the hell happened?" Dave asks.

"Looks like we screwed the pooch."

"You mean the whole fucking kennel!"

"No shit." He taps the neural link "Ops One to ADF Two."

"ADF Two, go ahead, Bob," a male voice answers.

Robert and Dave look at each other with totally confused expressions.

"Stand by." He turns off the link. "Who the hell is that?"

"Not a clue, man." The elevator stops. "Shit they have us trapped."

"ADF Two. Can you lock on to us and teleport us back to the ship?"

"Teleporting now."

A light engulfs them. A few seconds later the door opens and a squad of Shock Troopers has their weapons pointed into the compartment.

To their shock and dismay, the compartment is empty.

Black Ops Commander 'Dave Walsh' contacts 'Tucker'.

"Black Ops One to Commander Tucker."

"Go ahead, Walsh."

"Bob, somehow these mother fuckers got away."

"Impossible, they may have climbed out. Have every Black Ops soldier and Shock Trooper comb this place from top to bottom. We are returning to the Bwentani system."

"What do you want with them when we find them?"

"Bring them to the labyrinth, of course."

"Acknowledged. Black Ops One to Black Ops Two."

"This is Black Ops Two," 'Vince Colretti' replies.

"Colretti, the ADF Special Forces somehow got on the station, disabled our weapon and are now somewhere in the base. Your teams search the upper half of the station. My teams will start at the bottom and we will meet in the middle.'

"Acknowledged. Out."

'Walsh' motions for his team to move out and to search every conceivable hiding place on the station.

WA-13

The Special Forces teams materialize onto the Outlaw. They stare at the pilot, who according to Bat'ai, ceased to exist: Commander Keith Sykes.

"Everything all right, Bob?" Keith asks. "Looks like you succeeded in stopping them from destroying Earth."

"Yeah. We had a moment of vertigo for some reason. We better have Doctor Burke check us."

Lyle calls him on the radio. "Command One to Ops One."

Robert replies, "Go ahead."

"Return to the Kensington."

"We're Oscar Mike."

"OK, take us back, Colonel."

"The Kensington?"

"I think I better fly."

Keith gets out of the pilot's seat and looks at Robert, wondering why one of his oldest friends is treating him like a stranger.

Robert gets in and then sets a course to the camouflaged battle cruiser.

ADF battle cruiser *Kensington*

Robert sends the fighter down on the flight deck. The Special Forces teams emerge, followed by Keith.

Lyle, Ryan, Rillius and Bat'ai are waiting for them.

Keith is stunned to see Lyle, then notices Rillius and draws his weapon. "Hold it right there you bastard!"

Rillius is shocked.

Robert disarms Keith and then knocks him down and points Keith's weapon at him.

"All right, asshole, what the fuck are you doing drawing downing down on a senior officer?"

"Senior officer? What the hell are you talking about? This son of a bitch is on the Alliance Council's most wanted list."

Bat'ai concentrates. He looks momentarily confused before he speaks. "Robert, this is Commander Keith Sykes."

Robert lets go of Keith and lets him stand up. "B. Didn't you say the Triumvirate eliminated his parents before he was born?"

"Yes, that is correct, Robert."

"Commander. What's the time index?"

"Zero one sixteen, twenty- two-twenty-two."

"Something weird is going on. The last thing I remember is being on the bridge of the Cho'Kai station. There was a flash and then the place is crawling with Imperial Troopers."

Dave pauses a moment to take everything in. "Oh, fuck me, I think we altered history again!"

"We better get back to Bwentani Prime and figure out what's going on."

Keith replies, "You don't want to go there. That's an Imperial stronghold."

"I can scan to determine if we have been transported to another reality," Bat'ai suggests.

"Well that probably explains why you don't know me."

"No offense, Commander, up until now you didn't exist," says Robert.

"We have served together since 2021."

Robert exhales deeply. "Cue the Twilight Zone music."

The bay opens and a squadron of WA-14s land. Ray and his squadron disembark.

"Y'all are dismissed." The pilots salute Ray and then leave. He walks towards them, rubbing the back of his neck. "Guys, there's somethin' strange goin' on?" He notices Keith. "Who the hell are you?"

Keith sarcastically replies, "Well, nice to see you, too, pal."

"Ray, this is Keith Sykes. And for the nine billionth time, either history got altered, or we've been thrown into another reality," Robert informs him,

"What the hell happened?"

"Bat'ai is gonna run an alternate history profile."

"Follow me," says Bat'ai.

The group leaves the loading dock and makes their way to the bridge.

Ryan and the crew of the *Kensington* are still reeling from the events of the past few minutes.

Lyle and the senior officers enter the bridge. Ryan sees Keith. "Who is he?"

"Ryan this is Commander Keith Sykes. Before you ask, I think we screwed the pooch and changed history." Robert says, getting tired of repeating what happened.

"Ya ain't jokin', son. Look."

The group turns and sees Earth.

"B. Run a quantum DNA scan and figure out where the hell we are."

Bat'ai runs the scan. "This is our reality. Keith Sykes and everyone the Triumvirate eliminated have returned." He runs the historical profile, thinks for a moment and then runs the footage they had from when Robert was accused of destroying the Earth and plays it.

Robert and Dave have a disturbed feeling of déjà vu.

"B. is this what I think it is? A closed causality loop?"

"Yes, Robert, he replies, "And I believe it has reached its conclusion."

"You mind filling me in on what you're talking about?" Keith asks.

"Two years ago, when we were thrown forward in time, it was due to a major quantum shock wave hitting us and several realities interacted. When Robert was accused of destroying Earth, we were shown footage of the Special Forces teams on the bridge of the Cho'Kai station when they used their weapon. We assumed it was used to destroy the Earth," Bat'ai answers.

"B. We were in a reality where the Empire and Cho'Kai nearly wiped us out of existence. I don't remember Commander Sykes."

"I am aware of that, Robert," he replies, "The Empire triggered a major quantum disturbance when they went back in time and eliminated the parents of Commander Sykes, Commander Miguel Herrera, Commander Paul Foster, Major Allison Foster and Chief ground technician Mike Parnell." He turns to Keith and says "Keith, are these names familiar to you?"

"Yeah, and my descendant, Rebecca." He pauses looking sadly at Ray, "Your wife."

Robert starts laughing loudly. "Ray, married?" He covers his mouth and laughs even harder.

"Yeah, and he has kids, too," adds Keith.

This makes Robert nearly double over laughing. He calms himself down suddenly becoming serious. "Do I have a wife?"

"Yeah, Linaiok and a daughter, Ana. Her and Zerellus just became parents to twins."

"OK, that's consistent with the reality we were just in."

A call comes in from Alliance Defense Force Headquarters.

"Base to Ops One," says Allison Foster.

"Until we figure out what's going on, would you mind … Keith?" Robert asks.

"Sure. Base, this is Commander Sykes."

"Sir, will you inform Commander Tucker that the Empire base has withdrawn and are on their way back to Bwentani Prime?"

"Affirmative. We are discussing our next course of action. Will advise. Over."

"Acknowledged. Out."

"Thanks. I hope you can bear with me; I don't have any memory of you, but my gut tells me we have known each other for a long time," Robert says hoping to trigger a memory.

"We served together until you and Commander Walsh formed the Special Forces teams about a decade ago."

"Lyle is overall commander. Why didn't they ask for him or Ryan? He's second in command."

"Lyle was murdered by Black Ops bastard Dave Walsh, and Ryan was killed on Bwentani Prime. Quite frankly until Bat'ai confirmed your DNA, I thought you were from a different reality." Looking at the massive battle cruiser, Keith adds, "We have nothing like this in our arsenal."

"But you do remember the WA-13?"

"Yeah, Bat'ai, Ray and Paul Foster developed it almost three years ago."

"I remember Ray and Bat'ai, but I don't remember Paul Foster."

"He's Jackie's brother."

"She never mentioned a brother," says Robert.

"She died saving my life."

Bat'ai speaks up. "Robert, you and the entire task force are suffering from quantum amnesia."

"How is it that you remember Commander Sykes, Bat'ai?"

"My people travel between quantum realities and we can sense changes in history and differentiate between our own and the ones we visit."

"Can you restore our memories?"

"This is a unique situation. I sense that three realities have folded into one with events from each and these changes have created a whole new reality." Bat'ai exhales deeply.

"So we totally fucked the quantum balance?"

"Actually, Robert, the balance has been restored."

"Getting back to our situation, what can we do?"

"I can load the neural inhibitor with the history of this reality and it should help you to remember and adjust to this new quantum setting."

"I hate to spoil this family reunion," Keith interrupts, "but Pomar Rillius is wanted by the Alliance Council for betraying the Bwentani and selling them out to the Empire by handing over the access codes to their defenses."

Lyle says, "I will vouch for Pomar Rillius. It was his

quantum double from a different reality that originally killed him and took his place to allow the Terran Empire to enter this reality."

"Respectfully speaking Lyle; I hope you can provide hard evidence. Standing council order is to either arrest or shoot on sight. Anyone helping him will be considered an accessory to his crimes and extradited to the Minarians for trial. The council may not take the word of–"

"A dead person?" asks Lyle.

"Unfortunately, no, but it is good to see you and Ryan. It's been too long."

"It may take a while to obtain that evidence," Robert states.

Keith sighs. "Then I'm sorry, Bob, I'm obliged to report this to the Alliance council."

Robert discreetly motions to Ray, who takes out a hypodermic needle filled with Aprilozene and injects it into Keith's neck. He falls to the ground, unconscious.

"He seems OK, but really has to take that stick out of his ass," Robert quips.

"What are we gonna do 'bout Rillius ?" Ryan asks.

"B, is our base on Taqua Four still there?"

Bat'ai scans the Taqua system. "Yes, but it is currently uninhabited."

Robert addresses Rillius, "I'm sorry, *binzah*, but until we figure out how to clear your name, we need to keep you out of sight."

"I understand, *binzah*."

"I think both squadrons of WA-14s should be based there. I think your men are probably the only ones who won't try to turn you over to the Council. I would also advise against contacting Zerellus, his father and your father until we get the whole story."

"I agree." He grasps Robert's forearm. "Until we meet again, *binzah*."

"We shall break bread, *binzah*."

Rillius repeats this farewell to the rest of the senior staff. Then he contacts his squadron to meet in the bay and to prepare to return to Taqua Four.

"Ray, see if Jackie is still…with us. If she is, have her take the rest of the WA-14s to Taqua Four. If not, Rillius will take charge. We'll keep him on ice until then. Another thing, I have this feeling that he isn't telling us the whole truth. Lyle you take the task force and return to Taqua Four. Ray, Dave and I will stick around with Keith and find out what the hell is going on."

"B, we better get started on restoring our memories. Ray will alter his so he doesn't remember coming onto the ship or seeing anyone here. The four of us will go back to Earth."

"And if it's some sort of trap?"

"Ray and I will grab our families, haul ass back to Taqua Four and go into deep covert op. All communications through the neural link on frequency Alpha seven –four."

The senior commanders comply.

Ray locates Jackie, who is now a squadron commander. After he verifies that she remembers the previous reality, he explains the situation involving her fiancé and gives her orders to lead the other squadron of WA-14s back to their base.

Robert has every member of the task force gather in the landing bay of the *Kensington*.

Bat'ai utilizes a neural inhibitor hastily installed into the ceiling of the bay and uses it to integrate the history of this reality with the memories of the previous one. He then alters Keith's memory, joins the team on the WA-13 that they flew into the landing bay, and opens a portal.

Robert flies into it.

The five remaining battle cruisers enter a quantum vortex opened behind Earth's moon, obscuring the ADF scanners from detecting it and return to the Taqua system.

CHAPTER 30

WA-13 – In orbit above Earth's atmosphere – Covert Ops Time index 01.16.2222.1200

Robert sets the WA-13 adrift, gets out of the pilot's seat, puts Keith back into it and then has Bat'ai set the delay to wake him, while the rest lay on the floor of the cabin pretending to be unconscious.

Bat'ai presses the delay on the inhibitor, and then joins the others in their ruse.

Keith groans and regains consciousness. "What happened?" He sees the rest of the team knocked out. "Bob."

Robert groans and pretends to regain consciousness. "What happened?"

"I think we got hit by an Imperial weapon before they withdrew." Keith responds.

"I remember calling Allison and telling her we were going over our options. Maybe one of the bastards ambushed us in a Reaper before hightailing it out of here."

"I think we better head back and have Doc check us."

"You better check in with Allison."

"OK. Ops One to Base."

"Go ahead sir," Allison responds.

"We were just ambushed by an Imperial Reaper. Can you have Doctor Burke meet us in the landing bay?"

"He'll be waiting for you."

"Thanks, Allison. Out."

"Take us home, Keith."

"You bet. I can use some down time."

"Ain't that the truth?"

Keith pilots the WA-13 towards Earth.

Robert and the rest of the team feel a collective lump in their throats upon seeing their beloved home planet, which was originally destroyed by an Imperial attack in the year 2218.

Alliance Defense Force Hangar – ADF Base Kensington – Albuquerque, New Mexico

Keith lands the Outlaw at the airstrip that houses the WA-13s of the Alliance Defense Force's Joker Squadron.

Above the hangar, the emblem of the squadron: A playing card with a skull wearing clown's makeup and a hat.
At the bottom of the card the Units' motto:

THE JOKE'S ON YOU

The group gets out of the fighter and they are met on the tarmac by Doctor James Burke and Alliance Commander Quennok.

Burke says, "Major Foster stated that you require medical attention."

"We were knocked out by some kind of energy source. Type and origin uncertain," Robert replies.

"What do you mean uncertain?" Quennok asks.

"An Imperial base was in orbit."

"Yes, for peace negotiations, Robert. You were briefed on their arrival under a flag of truce."

"Well, then something's going on, because this happened as they left." Robert tells him.

"There was no report of any weapon fire; however, there was a solar flare detected ten million miles from Earth."

"That could have been it."

Quennok looks at Robert and then asks "Are you, well, *Ke'tul'Neh* (son-in-law)? I sense there is something different with you."

"It could have been effects of the flare, *Hu'tul'Neh* (father-in-law). My memory is scrambled."

"I will give you a thorough exam," Dr. Burke replies.

The group follows Burke and Quennok to the base medical facility.

ADF medical – 1300 hours

Quennok observes Burke finishing his exam on the final member of the group – Robert. He looks at the results.

"With the exception of Commander Sykes, you were all exposed to a massive surge of unknown type energy."

Robert responds, "Just remember Doc, we were drawn through a vortex and exposed to some kind of temporal flux that affected our DNA."

"Yes, Commander, I have taken that into account. This is more recent however, my guess is it occurred somewhere within the past couple of hours. And it is not from a solar flare."

"Then what was it?"

"I'll tell you what it was," a voice is heard from the entrance to the medical bay.

The group turns and sees ADF Council Member Todd Meyers, flanked by two ADF MPs (Military Police).

"Councilman Meyers," Quennok states.

Meyers looks at Quennok and scoffs. He turns to Robert with an expression of disgust. "You really screwed up this time, Tucker."

"What the hell you talking about?"

"What am I talking about? You went on an unauthorized

mission inside the Imperial flagship and messed up months of delicate negotiations." Meyers is clearly livid.

"Negotiate, with the Empire?"

Meyers addresses him in a condescending tone, "Yes, you insubordinate barbarian. They were here under a flag of truce to negotiate terms of their withdrawal from Bwentani Prime. Because of your sabotaging their station, they have backed out of the agreement."

"They had no intention of withdrawing from Bwentani Prime, you ignorant jack ass–"

Meyers glares at Robert. "What did you call me?"

"Ignorant jackass, though personally, I think that fucking idiot is a better assessment. Imperial Commander Tucker was ordering his Weapons Officer to fire on Earth."

"Our defense grid recorded no such thing."

"No shit. Commander Walsh, Commander Watson and myself took it offline before they had a chance. By the way, you're welcome."

"You tell that to the fifty million Bwentani citizens that are still under Imperial rule."

"I'd rather tell the eight billion lives I just saved."

"The Imperial Triumvirate has just submitted a formal complaint, charging you with undermining the peace process," states Meyers, triumphantly.

"So you're taking the word of a lying, murdering bastard over mine?"

"You were the one caught on their station without authorization." He turns to Quennok. "You are just as liable for not keeping Tucker and his thugs on a short leash."

"Commander Tucker has proven himself to be a valuable asset in the defense of the Alliance. If he states the Empire was less than honorable in their intentions, I shall take him at his word."

"Yeah, and the fact that you are his father-in-law."

"Councilman, if you check the Commander's file, if he has overstepped his authority, he has been dealt with."

"Well he overstepped it, and a reprimand will not do."

"You wish to convene a court-martial?"

"Either that or Tucker, Watson, Walsh and Sykes can resign their commissions."

"Commander Sykes was acting under orders and under protest," Robert states, getting progressively angry.

"Is that true, Commander Sykes?"

Keith hesitates, and then replies, "Yes, Councilman. When I learned the nature of Commander Tucker's mission, I refused to pilot the transport."

Robert states, "I threatened to throw him in the brig for insubordination."

"If that was the case, why didn't you report the incident earlier?"

"Because as I said earlier, we were knocked unconscious until about an hour ago."

"All right, my apologies, Commander. You have an exemplary record and Tucker's criminal act should not be held against you."

"Commander Tucker's actions were ill advised, but not criminal."

"Such as trespassing on Imperial property and damaging equipment," Meyers retorts.

"Did we kill anyone?" Robert asks sarcastically.

"No," Meyers concedes.

"Then Commander Tucker and his team will receive a formal reprimand, a reduction in rank, forfeiture of two month's pay and thirty days confinement. That is standard punishment for this infraction under the Terran Uniform Code of Military Justice," Quennok replies.

"Not good enough. The Imperial Triumvirate did state that they are willing to resume negotiations if Tucker and his men either resign or face a court-martial."

"I'll save you the trouble, Meyers." Robert says, fighting the desire to bury his fist in Meyers' face. "Take my commission and shove it up your ass."

"Sideways," Dave adds.

"With a cactus," Ray quips.

Meyers' face turns so red that it looks like he's going to explode from the neck up. "Take them into custody!"

"On what grounds?" Quennok asks.

"Insubordination to a member of the Alliance Council."

"You can't do shit to us, Meyers. We're civilians, although we should give a proper military send off. Right Ray?" Robert chuckles.

In his best Drill Sergeant voice, Ray commands, "Team, attention!" Robert, Ray and Dave stand attention. "About face!" They turn facing away from Meyers. "Present cheeks!"

They unbuckle their belts, unbutton their BDU (Battle Dress Uniform) trousers, grab the waist, bend over and moon Meyers.

The shock of seeing their exposed behinds sends Myers into a rage. When he turns to the MPs, he can clearly see that they are desperately trying to keep from laughing. After a few moments, he finally calms down, "Sykes, you're now in charge of ADF Operations. Escort these three to the command center, delete their access codes and throw them off this base. After fourteen hundred hours they will be trespassing on government property and be placed under arrest. They are also to turn in their uniforms and personal side arms."

"This stuff is ours, paid for out of our own pockets."

"Go ahead, keep it, Tucker. Let it serve as a reminder of who you used to be," Meyers scoffs.

"Two time Congressional Medal of Honor recipient, saved this planet more times than you can count, which is more than I can say about your weasely, pathetic ass." He pauses for emphasis. "Todd."

"Get them out of here!"

The ADF MPs escort Robert, Ray and Dave out, followed by Meyers and Quennok.

ADF Command Center

Keith enters the command center, followed by the MPs escorting Robert, Ray and Dave. They receive a standing ovation from the personnel, who also high five and fist bump them.

"I'll take it from here," Keith says to the MPs.

The MPs reply, "Yes, sir," and then leave.

"Bob, did you guys really moon that *pendejo*?" Miguel Herrera asks.

"Yeah, an' Bob sang 'im a four lettered aria," Ray replies.

"Word is that Meyers was going to have you guys court-martialed." wonders Paul Foster.

"We didn't give him the satisfaction. We resigned our commissions," Dave scoffs.

"Who's in charge?"

"Keith, so you guys are in good hands."

The staff congratulates Keith.

"You know I didn't want this, Bob?"

"I know. That asshole's been after me for a long time. He saw the opportunity and capitalized on it."

"Bob, the station's weapons weren't active. We would have picked up on it," Keith says trying to reason with Robert,

"No offense Keith, but you weren't there. My quantum double, Imperial Commander Tucker gave the order to attack. If we hadn't disabled their weapon, this place would be a hole in the ground."

"They would need more than your word."

Robert pulls a disc out of his shirt pocket and puts in into a slot next to a monitor. "From my visor," he replies and pushes a button.

The command crew sit in shock as they hear 'Tucker' yelling for 'Sykes' to fire the Particle Laser Weapon and his replying the weapon is offline. They hear Robert mutter something and then the Shock troops advancing and the smoke and flash-bang grenades going off. The sound of the elevator doors closing ends the transmission.

Keith says with sincere regret, "Bob, I'm sorry I doubted you. Why didn't you show this to Meyers?"

"It's obvious that Meyers wants us out of the way. Whether he's in cahoots with the Empire or a blind fucking idiot, it didn't matter what evidence I presented. He wasn't going to change his point of view."

"What are you going to do?" Allison asks.

"First things first; I'm going to spoil my new grandkids."

The command staff laughs and congratulates him.

Miguel asks, "Do you think Ana and Zerellus will also resign?"

"I don't know. The Empire is up to something and you need to stay vigilant and watch your asses with them, and Meyers."

"I'm sorry to do this, Bob, but I need the three of you to delete your access codes and then I'll escort you off base."

"Yeah, I don't want you to get reamed on your first day," Robert chuckles.

He places his hand on a sensor pad. A message appears:

Tucker, Robert Steven, Commander Alliance Defense Force, Alpha One Clearance

Keith lets out a loud sigh, and hesitates before speaking. "Delete access, Commander Robert Tucker, authorization Sykes seven –seven – two."

The pad beeps and then a new message appears:

Access deleted

Keith repeats the process with Dave and Ray.

Then they say their goodbyes to the staff and then walk out of the central command building with Keith escorting them.

"Hell, why don't we jest take the Outlaw?" Ray asks,

"Sorry Ray, it's Alliance property."

Ray is about to protest, but Robert quiets him down by giving him a discreet hand signal.

"Yer right, son," Ray sighs while at the same time, pressing a button on his sleeve, activating the shield around the WA-13, which prevents anyone from entering it.

They get into an electric powered military vehicle and Keith drives them to the front gate.

Robert chuckles then asks, "I don't suppose you can call us a cab?"

"No," Keith laughs. "But I can bring you to the hospital. Linaiok said that Ana and the babies can go home."

"OK, Appreciate it."

Keith drives off the base to the military hospital located a mile down the road. At the entrance he stops and the three former ADF Commanders get out. "Good luck guys. Maybe Quennok can get you reinstated."

"With Meyers around, I doubt it. I hope I'm wrong, but I don't trust him or the Empire as far as I can throw them."

"Give them hell, Keith," Dave says while shaking his hand.

"If them tick terds do act up, open a can o' whup ass fer me," Ray quips.

Keith smiles. "I will. You can definitely count on that."

He drives off.

Robert shrugs, "I don't think I could have planned it better myself."

Ray and Dave laugh in agreement and then enter the hospital to visit Robert's daughter and new grandchildren.

CHAPTER 31

Imperial Base – Orbiting Bwentani Prime

'Tucker' is in his office, furious about not only being denied the perfect opportunity to eliminate the Alliance Central Command by his counterpart, but them escaping the base despite their air tight security.

The remaining members of the Triumvirate, Imperial Commanders 'Ray Watson' and 'Ricardo Pasqualle' along with 'Walsh' enters his office.

"Well?"

"Bob, those sum'bitches up 'n disappeared," 'Watson' replies.

"How? We have every fucking entry and exit point under surveillance. A fucking ant can't get past. Talak even has the system set to detect their fucking stealth shielding on the vests they stole from us."

"We had every vent, shaft, nook and cranny flooded with poison gas. We should have at least found their bodies," 'Walsh' adds.

Robert is about to speak, when 'Allison Parker' calls them.

"Ops to Commander Tucker."

"What is it, Allison?"

"The Alliance Councilman requests to speak to you."

'Tucker' closes his eyes and exhales nosily. "Put him through."

Meyers appears on a monitor. "Commander Tucker."

"Councilman."

"First of all, I wish to apologize on behalf of the Alliance Council. In no way did we or the ADF Command authorize or condone Commander Tucker on his actions in your station. We are fully prepared to make full restitution for any damages his team has done."

"That is mighty gracious of you Councilman. We're still assessing the extent of the damages. So far we estimate about one hundred million Alliance credits." 'Tucker' replies,

"You give us a final figure and I personally guarantee it will come out of Tucker's pension for the next one hundred years."

"Seeing him behind bars is gratification enough for me."

"Um, that is a problem. Tucker resigned his commission and is no longer under military jurisdiction."

"So? You can still throw him in jail."

"Unfortunately, our charter prevents it. However he is a private civilian and if he takes further action against you, he has no protection from your laws."

"He no longer has access to military equipment?"

"Yes, all of his security clearances have been revoked and he no longer has access to our bases or any piece of military hardware."

"Now that you have taken care of this matter to my satisfaction, I feel that we can resume negotiations."

"We will make arrangements for our next meeting,"

"We will contact you when we are ready."

Meyers ends the transmission.

The four of them laugh at the gullibility of the Council representative.

"Can ya believe that shit? Not only will we blast 'em straight ta hell, that idiot's gonna pay us, too," 'Watson' says, shaking his head in disbelief.

'Not only that," 'Walsh' adds, "But Tucker's now a sitting duck. I can send my Black Ops team to take him out."

"No, have him brought here. I think he'll enjoy running our gauntlet. Contact Talak and find out how long repairs will take." 'Tucker' wears a sadistic grin.

"Right away Bob," 'Watson' says before he leaves followed by the other Imperial senior officers.

"Too bad they didn't incarcerate you, Tucker, that fool of a Councilman has just signed his own death warrant…and yours." 'Tucker' says loudly to the walls of his empty office.

Robert's residence – Albuquerque 2200 hours

A Black Ops team approaches Robert's home, which is a modest residence on the South East side close to the base.

'Walsh' observes the house through night vision goggles. He sees Robert and his wife sitting in their living room, talking with their daughter and son-in-law, laughing and drinking what appears to be alcohol, apparently toasting the birth of Robert's grandchildren.

An hour later, the celebration appears to be ending as Ana and Zerellus leave the house with the babies in carriers, go to their electric vehicle, and leave the property.

Robert takes Linaiok by the hand and they walk to the bedroom.

"Black Ops One to team, target appears to be turning in for the evening. It's 2300 local time, we move in thirty minutes. Black Ops Two, cut the power to the home and put in electronic dampener to prevent communications."

"Black Ops two, acknowledged," 'Colretti' replies.

"Black Ops Three. Administer sleep agent through the heating duct. This is a non-lethal op. I repeat a non-lethal op. Team confirm."

'Walsh' receives confirmation from all six members of the team who have completely surrounded the house, covering every door, window as well as every other possible means of entry or escape.

'Colretti' goes to the master bedroom window and places a device in the corner just below the window sill to block all forms of communication. He moves to his designated spot near the circuit panel and then whispers "Black Ops One, device set. Waiting to cut power."

"Acknowledged."

Black Ops member 'John Randall' stands by with the sleep agent he will set inside the heating system. "Black Ops Three in position."

"Wait for my signal."

"Acknowledged."

"Black Ops One to Triumvirate One. Team in position. Will move in thirty minutes."

"Black Ops One, you will wait for target to be fully asleep before approaching," 'Tucker' commands.

"Understood. Out. Black Ops One to team. New orders. We wait until target is asleep. Confirm."

The team confirm the orders from 'Tucker'.

'Walsh' kneels next to a wall obscuring himself from passing traffic and tries to stay warm in the thirty degree winter evening.

Around 0100 hours the lights in the bedroom flicker and then go off, signaling that Robert and his wife have finally ended their intimate evening.

'Walsh' who is half awake and shivering from the weather, which has dipped into the teens tries to move. Though the temperature has affected his reflexes, he signals 'Randall' to administer the sleep agent.

'Randall' pops the lid on the canister and sets it inside the heating duct.

'Walsh waits one minute before speaking, "Black Ops team, move in. Soft entry and by pass security system.

Black Ops members 'Andres Atencio' and 'Jorge Montoya' go to the front door, pick the electronic lock, don their gas masks, quietly open the door, and proceed to the security panel.

'Atencio' holds an electronic panel, which deciphers the security code.

'Montoya' enters the panel.

'Atencio' states, "Security deactivated."

"Power cut," 'Colretti' reports.

"All Units, move in to secure house and take target into custody."

"The wife?" 'Colretti' asks.

"Party time."

The team chuckles and then the four remaining members make their entry through the front door, proceeding through the smoke filled home to the bedroom door and line up on either side of it.

'Walsh' tries the door handle, which is unlocked, turns the handle and opens the door, slowly and quietly.

They see two bodies lying in the bed, unconscious from the sleep agent.

'Walsh' motions for the team to surround the bed and pulls back the covers revealing pillows arranged to look like Robert and Linaiok's bodies.

Robert's Special Forces team, who are also wearing masks, slip in behind the Black Ops team, and put weapons to their heads."

"Surprise, asshole," Robert says through his mask.

'Walsh' is stunned. "How did they get in here? We have been surveilling the house all afternoon and evening. There was no one in or out except your daughter and son-in-law."

"That's for me to know, and for you to never find out," Robert replies, while pulling 'Walsh's' mask off followed by his team removing the Black Ops team's masks.

Suddenly they all become drowsy and fall to the ground.

"Ops One to Ops Four."

Rillius answers, "Yes, *binzah*?"

"Black Ops team secure. Teleport us up."

"Commencing teleport."

Both the Special Forces and Black Ops teams are teleported to the camouflaged WA-13.

They off their masks and then set the Black Ops team in

a seated position and then tie them together.

"I think they'll make a nice gift for Keith," jokes Dave.

Robert grins slyly. "I have a better idea."

The team busts out laughing when Robert tells them what he has in mind to humiliate the 'elite Imperial forces'.

Meyer's home 0300 hours

Meyers and his wife Jillian are fast asleep. An extremely loud pounding on their front door wakes them up. Meyers and his wife see multiple flashing lights on their property, so he puts on his robe, tells his wife to remain calm, and goes to the front door.

"Who is it?" he asks, annoyed at being disturbed.

"Albuquerque Police. We have a report of an attempted kidnapping. Are you all right, sir?"

"Yes." He opens the door and a dozen APD SWAT officers enter with weapons drawn and immediately begin to check the house.

Meyer's wife screams as she is brought down the stairs by the SWAT officers.

"House is clear," The SWAT states.

"What is the meaning of this?" Meyers demands.

"Step outside, sir."

Meyers, his wife and the SWAT officers step onto the front porch. He is stunned to see the Black Ops team tied up on his porch.

On 'Walsh's' lap is a white cardboard sign, which reads:

We are Imperial Black Ops Soldiers. We were very naughty. We tried to kidnap Commander Tucker and his wife. We have recorded it so you see how naughty we were. Call the Minarian Magistrate to come get us.

Meyers is flabbergasted by what he has seen.

A news reporter walks up to Meyers and asks, "Councilman Meyers. You are leading the negotiations with the Imperial Commanders who are occupying Bwentani Prime. You reported that Commander Tucker overstepped his authority when he entered the Imperial station and disabled their weapons. He submitted combat footage to back up his report that the Imperial Commander was going to attack, as well as the footage of the Black Ops Soldiers breaking into the Tucker's home. Do you have any comments?"

Meyers stammers and then blurts out, "I will have an official statement in the morning." He retreats back into his home, followed by his wife and slams the door.

WA-13

"Mission accomplished," Dave says as the other ops members join him in laughing at the embarrassing situation they set up for Meyers.

"Not quite. We have to get our fighter back. *Binzah*, put us over the base, I'll teleport down. The second I take off, put one of their own fighters in their place."

"Yes, Robert," Rillius replies."

He pilots the WA-13 to the base and then hovers above the Outlaw that is being guarded by two MPs because they can't get past the shields.

Robert is teleported into the cockpit where he sits in the pilot's seat, quick starts the engine and then engages the shields and lifts off, causing the snow falling on the ground to swirl distracting the MPs long enough for them not to notice that another WA-13 belonging to the ADF is teleported into position.

"What the hell was that?" one of the MPs asks.

"The wind around here does this shit all the time," the other MP, who is an Albuquerque native, replies.

"Commander Sykes is going to contact Commander Tucker in the morning to lower the shield."

"Then why are we guarding it?"

"Orders from Councilman Meyers."

"You have to admit what Tucker and his team did to Meyers was priceless. My girlfriend recorded it; I'll show you in the morning. "

"Cool."

They continue to guard the WA-13, unaware of the switch that just took place.

The two WA-13s enter a quantum vortex and return to their base on Taqua Four.

CHAPTER 32

ADF Command center – 01.17.2222.0700

Keith and the command staff are laughing at the news coverage of the Black Ops soldiers and the embarrassing half- hearted explanation made by Meyers as he tenders his resignation as ADF Council representative.

A call comes into the Command Center and Robert appears on a monitor.

"Ops One to ADF Command."

"Go ahead Ops One," Allison replies.

"You forget that I'm Ops One now, Bob," Keith chuckles.

"You're ADF Ops One; I'm Covert Ops One," Robert quips. "Thanks for the heads up, Paul."

"Commander Quennok had his suspicions about Meyers, so he had me monitor his communications," he responds,

"Bob, Zerellus and your daughter have requested a transfer to your unit. I'll approve it."

"Thanks, Keith. Officially we're not sanctioned, so they'll have to resign their commissions or retire."

"I'll draw up the paperwork."

"Keith, I would recommend that you put the base on high alert and keep the Global Defense Shields active, 'cause you know that once 'Tucker' finds out, the shit's gonna hit the fan."

"You know he'll go after the Bwentani in retaliation. Especially since he knows that Berellus is your brother-in-law, he's going to want revenge."

"We already have an op planned."

"We can deploy in two hours."

"Keith you have to stay neutral. Besides, with their main weapon offline, they'll have to attack with fighters and then we'll have the advantage."

"Bob, that thing carries fifty squadrons of their Reapers, which are comparable to the WA-13."

"Now don't forget it was taken from our database by Talak'Vin. We made upgrades they don't know about. We'll secure Bwentani Prime and then give you the schematics. We're commencing operations within the hour."

"Good hunting."

Robert signs off.

Keith turns to Paul and Miguel. "Paul, I want continual surveillance on Bwentani Prime. If that damn base hiccups, I want to know."

"I'm on it," Paul replies as he activates the quantum scanners on a continual sweep on Bwentani Prime.

"Miguel, contact the Bwentani underground and get a sit/rep. Any kind of Imperial action, have Allison contact Bob on the secure channel he just provided us."

"No *problema*."

Quennok enters the command center. "I am sure you have heard about former Councilman Meyers?"

"Damn entertaining piece of television," Keith quips.

"I concur," Quennok laughs. "Unfortunately I fear for our brethren; the Bwentani will incur the wrath of the Empire. I am now the Council representative. Keith, you are now Commander in Chief of the ADF. I recommend you contact Robert and his team and reinstate their commission."

"Bob and his team are already on it. Covert ops."

"I thought as much."

"You think Bob intentionally did this to make the Empire think he was no longer in the military."

"Robert has been married to my daughter for thirty years and I have known him for over a hundred. I still do not understand how his mind works."

"I served with him for two hundred and I don't understand him either and I gave up trying long ago." Keith laughs.

Quennok chuckles, "Maybe that is why you still have a little of your sanity left."

"Not that much."

Quennok changes the subject. "I must now convince the Council that the Empire is not to be trusted and we may have to prepare for the possibility of renewed aggression."

"We're already on it and so is Bob, he has a covert op ready to go."

"The council may not sanction it."

"He won't wait."

"If he fails, he could be branded a war criminal."

"Quennok, some of Earth's biggest war criminals defended themselves by saying they were just following orders."

"I will pray to *Ama'diok* that he is successful."

"He says they're running their op within the hour. I'll keep you informed."

"I shall stay here and monitor the battle. Have our forces on standby and alert Mars Defense Force Command of the situation and have them activate the Meteor Belt defenses.

"Right away."

Keith contacts Mars Defense Force Commander Edward Kensington and updates him on the events of the past twenty-four hours and puts them on Alert Two status and to have MDF pilots ready to deploy at a moment's notice.

Rick concurs, and then signs off.

Bridge of the *Kensington* – in orbit around Taqua Four - 0700 Taquan local time

For the second time in twenty-four hours, the senior staff plans out Operation Valhalla.

"OK, I guess we can consider yesterday a dry run," Robert jokes, receiving a few laughs.

"There are differences between fighting the Cho'Kai and the Empire," Lyle says in all seriousness.

"Bat'ai tapped into their database and we got the specs on their Reapers, which are compatible with our WA-13s, minus the quantum and temporal technology."

"Talak'Vin didn't develop it for them?"

"No, he is a weapons engineer, they possess none of this technology. That battle station is Talak's brainchild." Bat'ai informs him, "That is why we have upgraded another eight squadrons of WA-14s, bringing us up to ten."

"That pretty much eliminates their five to one advantage," Lyle states.

"They also carry a division of Shock Troops and three Black Ops teams...well, now they're down to two," Robert jests, getting a few laughs about the transmission from Earth.

"What's the situation with the *Dev'cha?*"

"We showed 'em the ocean on Taqua Three. They loved it an' settled right in," Ryan informs him,

"Maybe we can hold them in reserve, especially with the number of Henoki forces we have here."

"Commander Herrera supplied us with the Intel they have on the Bwentani detention camps. They're similar to what the Celestians were using to hold our forces," Ricardo reports.

"Glad to see you're back in the pink, Rico."

"Considering we've changed realities four times in the past two years, I'm just glad to find my ass with both hands," he retorts.

"True. What kind of security?" asks Robert.

"They're using the Bwentani security shields, so teleporting in is a no-go. However our WA-13s can get in using the quantum vortex"

"We'll have Darrel and Mike's teams go after the facility."

"What's our troop strength?"

"We have two battalions of ADF and Henoki troops. They have a battalion of Shock troops guarding their lone detention facility, which is where the Imperium leadership, the division on the station and another battalion stationed in garrisons in each of the providences being occupied. This will not be a swift operation. We have to be prepared for a long, drawn out conflict," Lyle states realistically. "The key is to free their leadership and the Bwentani forces being held captive."

"If we attack the station's hangars and prevent them from sending reinforcements, we might stand a chance," Ricardo states.

"So it's pretty much like stormin' the beaches on D-Day", Ryan adds.

Robert nods. "That's not too far from the truth. We are gonna get real bloody and if the Empire gets their weapon online, we'll be screwed six ways from Sunday."

"I tapped into their comm system. Their weapon will be offline for another forty-eight hours," Bat'ai informs them.

"If we concentrate the battle cruisers on their station, we can take them out in a matter of hours."

"According to ADF Intelligence, they also have battle cruisers comparable to ours. The closest ones are in the Venpari system, which is twelve hours at their top speed. We have to hit their communications and make sure they can't call for reinforcements."

"I doubt we can get away with another stroll inside their station," Dave says sarcastically.

Robert has Bat'ai call up a schematic of the base. Using a laser pointer, he highlights the northern axis of the station, "If we have a squadron of WA-14s attack and take out the defense surrounding their transmitter and destroy it, while the remaining ones take out the four landing bays, we can effect rescue on Berellus and the government and then liberate the providences one at a time."

"If we have the ADF join forces with us, we can overwhelm them before they know what hit them."

"Tempting, but I get a feeling they had better just stick to defending Earth," adds Dave. "After the way we stung them, 'Tucker's' probably spitting nails."

Bat'ai intercepts a transmission.

He reports, "Robert, Commander Tucker' has ordered one village with Bwentani women, children and old men rounded up to be executed."

"Contact the fleet, we're Oscar Mike," Lyle commands,

"B. get a location, Dave and I are going in with a hard insert. Have Mike and Darrel's team take out the shield facility. We're going now, feed us the coordinates to the WA-13," Robert orders.

"I shall have them momentarily, Robert."

"Rico, feel up to piloting our transport?"

"Let's go stop those *cabrones*."

Robert taps his neural link. "Ops One to all teams, report to your assigned transports. Hot ops, gear up, we go in one minute."

Without waiting for a reply, Robert, Dave and Ricardo leave the bridge.

"We're right on your heels, Bob," Lyle states.

"Give 'em hell Lyle," Robert yells as the elevator closes to bring them to the landing bay."

Two WA-13 transports are ready to lift off; all four teams are in the main compartment.

Ricardo gets in the cockpit, the transport has already been prepped by Chief Ground Technician, Mike Parnell.

Robert gives Parnell the thumbs up as he steps out. He secures the door and then backs away as a quantum vortex opens and the two WA-13s fly to prevent a malicious act of revenge by the Imperial Triumvirate.

CHAPTER 33

Bwentani village- Glenarius Providence -0600 hours local time

Two squads of Shock Troopers lead Bwentani women, children, along with the men too old for military service, from the neighboring village to the square.

The rest of the citizens are being forced to watch as these innocent people are being paraded in front of them to be executed.

Other than the children, no other Bwentani shows any sign of fear. They walk with their heads held high and with their dignity intact, which clearly angers the Shock Troops.

One Shock Troop leader notices one woman who is particularly defiant and then hits her on the side of the head with the butt of their energy pistol.

She falls to the ground, then turns and looks at him with no expression whatsoever. Then she picks herself up, gets back in line and continues walking as if nothing happened.

This further angers the Shock Troop Leader, who at the same time realizes that executing the Bwentani will not have the desired affect since the populace may believe that they are becoming martyrs.

They reach the square and have them line up in rows. The Bwentani facing execution have a collective look of joy on their faces. Even the children join them in singing praises to their gods for allowing them to be selected to join them in the afterlife. They are joined by the villagers being forced to watch 'Imperial discipline'.

The Shock Troop leader is perplexed and unsure of what to do, so he takes out his comm device.

"Trooper Jensen to Commander Tucker."

"Have you rounded up the villagers?"

"Yes. Sir, they…appear happy to be executed."

"Then oblige them."

"Sir, I don't think it will intimidate the others."

"I don't give a fuck. If they want to meet their maker, then let them. And then execute the rest of the village."

'Jensen' replies, "Yes, sir." He puts the comm device away and instead of the prepared speech he was going to give about this being the price for disobeying the Empire; he has one squad form a perimeter and the other one line up as a firing squad.

He is about to give the order to fire when Robert and Dave's Ops teams appear and take down the Shock Troopers with non-lethal weapons.

Robert turns to the villagers. "Everyone OK?"

The village leader, Kallavus laughs. "These *badruls* (morons) actually thought they could incite fear by killing us."

"These Terrans have no concept of Bwentani culture. We're going to liberate Bwentani Prime. I will leave these *kava'dals* in your custody," Robert replies respectfully.

Kallavus sees the *Bahal'Zai* marks on Robert and Dave. Showing his own mark, he says "*Binzah*. I am Kallavus, Pomar, Glavius Regiment, retired." He grasps their forearms, "It has been many *trinweis* (years) since I have heard the call to battle. I will be honored to fight at your side."

"And I at yours. Do you know where the Shock Troop garrison is located?"

"At Glenarius, the providence capital."

"Troop strength?" Dave asks.

"There are two Battalions. These *kava'dals* are part of that detachment." Kallavus reports,

"Gather everyone who has military training and we'll secure the providence."

"Commander Tucker to First Trooper Jensen."

Robert hears the transmission, picks it up and is about to say something sarcastic in nature, but instead taps his neural link. "Ops one to Command One."

"Go ahead, Bob."

"Lyle, situation neutralized. Sit rep on the base."

"Two docks destroyed."

"Their communications."

"Long range down. Total comm black out imminent."

"That's all I need to know. Out."

'Tucker' again calls. "Triumvirate One to Jensen respond.

Robert puts the comm device up to 'Jensen', while Dave holds a weapon to his head.

"This is First Trooper Jensen."

"Have you killed them?"

"I was about to give the order."

"Good. Record it for me."

"Yes, sir."

Robert pulls away the com unit. A sadistic grin appears on his face.

Dave notices and asks, "What you got planned now, Bob?"

"I'd say it's time to send him another gift package."

Dave starts laughing and then motions for the team to tie the troopers up.

Imperial Command Center

The Triumvirate directs the battle against the Covert Ops Force, who caught the Empire off guard with the blitz attack using a battle cruiser, and WA-13s and the WA-14, which have already decimated fifty percent of the Imperial Forces.

"Launch the dag-gum fighters," 'Watson' commands.

"Sir, all of our docks are under attack. Unable to launch," Black Ops First Trooper 'Albert Sanchez' replies.

'Tucker' yells, "Talak, where is my fucking weapon?"

"We only have partial power."

"I don't give a shit. Fire now!"

"Yes, sir."

A moment later the station recoils from the Particle Laser Weapon as it fires at a battle cruiser, causing major damage.

"About fucking time! Keep firing."

"One minute recharge."

'Tucker' growls in anger. "When it does, target their command ship's bridge and blast that fucker to smithereens!'

"Yes, sir," 'Sykes' replies.

A message from Bwentani Prime comes in. "First Trooper Jensen to Commander Tucker."

"You get it done?"

"Yes, sir. Ready to transmit."

"Good, open a channel to their commander."

"Yes, sir," 'Allison responds. She finds the battleship's communications frequency. "Channel open."

He sneers, stands with his hands on his hips and announces, "This is Imperial Commander Tucker to ADF Commander. While I am impressed with the fire power you now possess, it will not prevent the massacre of every man, women and child on the planet. Withdraw now, or every village will meet the fate of the people in the Glenarius providence." He motions to 'Allison' to close the audio channel. "Have First Trooper 'Jensen' play the recording and play it on their visual channels both here and on Earth."

"Yes, sir."

'Allison' presses a button to play the recorded account of the massacre of over one hundred Bwentani villagers.

'Tucker' screams "What the fuck!?" as once again his Imperial Forces have been humiliated by being tied together, with Bwentani villagers surrounding them and laughing.

A cardboard sign rests on 'Jensen's' lap:

We are Imperial Shock Troopers that have been captured by Bwentani citizens. We were very naughty and tried to kill them, but they took our weapons, laughed and made fun of us. Please contact the Minarians and let us join the other naughty Imperial soldiers in their custody.

The two ops teams appear on screen.

"Just kidding, Robert jests, "We actually captured them without firing a single shot or a causing single casualty, just like your so called elite Black Ops team." His face dominates the screen. "So much for the master race, dickhead."

He stands back and along with the rest of the Covert Ops teams and Bwentani citizens. They all salute 'Tucker' with their middle fingers.

A violent explosion knocks out the signal.

'Tucker' flies into a violent tantrum, grabbing command personnel and slamming them into control panels.

The senior officers quickly leave the command center.

After a moment, 'Tucker' calms down slightly. He turns to 'Parker', breathing heavily and commands, "Parker, I want every available battle cruiser, Shock Troop division and Black Ops team in the vicinity to get here immediately!"

She tentatively replies, "Yes, sir." Then down sits at the comm panel and attempts to contact the Garrison Commander at Venpari Prime. She can't get a signal and runs a diagnostic. She look afraid, but summons the courage to speak. "S-S-Sir, all communications are offline."

'Tucker' growls an incomprehensible curse, and then turns to 'Sykes'. "Target that village and turn it into a fucking crater!"

"Yes, sir." He enters a command and manipulates the controls to line up the center of the Glenarius providence. "Thirty seconds to target acquisition. Ninety percent charge."

"When it gets to one hundred, open fire."
"Yes, sir."

Bwentani village

The ops teams, along with Kallavus and two dozen villagers with combat training are prepared to assault the Imperial garrison.

An urgent call comes in.

"Command to Ops one."

"Go ahead."

"Bob, the Empire got their primary weapon online and they are targeting you. We can't intercept in time," Lyle reports.

"Planetary shield status?"

"Charlie and Delta team have secured the station."

"Have them raise the shields."

"It won't be enough to contain it."

"Can you teleport?"

"Systems damage and the rest of the battleships are out of range. Calculating fifteen seconds to deployment."

"Understood. Out." Robert replies. "Rico come in."

"Yeah, Bob?"

"We need a teleport PFQ."

"Ship can't hold you all."

"Site to site. Get us clear of the village."

A blinding light appears in the sky as the Imperial base fires on the village. At the same instant everyone in the village is teleported as the Particle Laser Weapon destroys the village and everything in a mile radius, leaving a fifty foot deep crater and triggering a massive seismic event.

The villagers are teleported to the providence capital, where the ops teams, Kallavus and the armed Bwentani citizens capture the garrison.

"I'm sorry about your village, Pomar."

"*Binzah*, I am retired."

"Once a *Bahal'Zai*, always a *Bahal'Zai*."

Kallavus grasps Robert's forearm. "We shall handle this from here."

"Lock these guys up, we'll contact the Minarians and when we liberate the planet they'll stand trial."

"Once that traitorous *dach* (swine) Rillius is in custody, he shall incur the wrath of the people he betrayed."

Robert and Dave remain quiet.

Robert changes the subject by saying, "Our next op is to liberate your leaders and military. I shall inform Berellus of your actions. He may reinstate you and place you in command of a Regiment."

"Thank you, *binzah*, my health is fading but you allowed me one to take part in last battle so I may rejoin the gods as a Warrior."

"I shall rejoice at your funeral."

"My final wish is to live long enough to send Rillius to the pits of *Kul'dahl* (Bwentani hell)."

"Ops One to Alpha One."

"Go ahead, Bob."

"Ready to teleport."

The ops teams get into position. A light engulfs them and they are teleported back to the WA-13.

Bridge of the *Kensington*

Lyle sits in shock because of the devastation caused by the Imperial weapon. The crater caused by the impact is visible from space, and he hasn't heard from the ops team to know if everything went as planned.

"Ops One to Command."

"Thank God," Lyle says to himself. "Go ahead, Ops One."

"Zero casualties, I say again, zero casualties from the weapon. Over."

"Understood. Proceed to the camp, liberate leadership."

"Send Charlie and Delta Teams. We're going after their central command."

"Too risky."

"We have to stop that fucking maniac before he tries to destroy the planet."

"Agreed. Take him alive, if possible; but I won't lose any sleep if he accidentally steps in front of a bullet."

"I was thinking of wrapping the fucker in razor wire and dipping him in a vat of rubbing alcohol."

"Remind me to never piss you off," Lyle chuckles.

"Out."

WA-13

Robert gets grenades and close quarter weapons from the ship's armory while Dave stands next to him.

"If we go after the fire controls," Dave says in a whispered tone, "We're going to get bloody."

"We're not going after the weapon. We're going into the hornet's nest."

Dave looks at him. "Storm the command center. That's insane, even for you."

"Dave we don't have a choice. That weapon is going to recharge in less than five minutes. After our last escapade, it'll be heavily guarded. They're probably going to target the Capitol. Besides, he thinks we're dead."

"Bob, Ray reports they've knocked out communications and their monitoring equipment," Ricardo informs him, "So they're essentially blind and deaf."

"Take us within range of the command center and prepare to teleport."

"We'll be in range in ten seconds."

The teams get into a staggered formation, with their weapons pointing outward with a three hundred and sixty range of coverage.

Ricardo pilots the WA-13 parallel to the Imperial command center and then activates the teleporter.

Imperial Command Center

The ops teams materialize and immediately secure the command center before the Triumvirate and the Shock Troopers can react.

'Tucker displays a look of pure hatred. "You."

"Surprise asshole, we're not dead. Imperial Commander Tucker, by order of the Minarian magistrate, you are under arrest for crimes against the Alliance Council and the Bwentani Imperium. Will you come peacefully or will I have to beat the shit out of you?"

"Please resist," Dave jests.

'Tucker' is about to respond, when the entire Imperial command staff disappears.

"What the fuck? Ops One to Command One.

"Command One. Go ahead, Bob."

"Lyle, did you teleport Tucker and his people?"

"Negative. None of our ships have him."

"Rico?"

"Negative."

"We'll figure it out later. Secure the command center and get that weapon offline.

Tactical Specialist Denton Miller goes to the weapons station, powers down the Particle Laser Weapon and disables the control.

"Weapon secure."

Dave instructs Sergeant Morris, "Dan, flood all areas but the command center with Aprilozene."

"On it."

Morris accesses the environmental controls and releases the sleep agent.

Within seconds, as the gas makes its way through the ventilation system, Shock Troopers throughout the station fall to the ground unconscious.

Robert contacts Lyle, "Ops One to Command One."

"Go ahead Ops One."

"Imperial Base secure."

"Excellent work. The Triumvirate?"

"Status unknown."

Bat'ai interrupts. "Robert, I have just detected a Reaper leaving the station using an artificial wormhole."

"Talak. I think the son of a bitch developed something like your teleporter to get them out of the command center."

"Very likely."

"Can you contact Alliance Command? Let them know we have secured the station, but that we need help taking back Bwentani Prime."

"They have been contacted. Alliance forces on the way."

"The troopers on this station ain't going anywhere. We're returning to the surface," states Robert.

"Acknowledged. Looks like a third CMH for you, Bob."

"Team effort, Lyle."

"Command One out."

"Seal off the command center, disable the weapons and pump in enough Aprilozene until Alliance forces can take custody of the station.

The teams carry out Robert's orders and then teleport back to the WA-13.

Imperial Reaper

The Triumvirate and Imperial command staff are feeling disoriented by the teleportation device recently developed by Talak'Vin. 'Tucker' sees Talak piloting the Reaper.

"Not that I'm ungrateful; but what the fuck did you just do?"

"The Alliance was about the capture or destroy the station. My apologies for the side effects of the teleportation device, because I have not had a chance to refine it."

"No shit, I feel like my head has been scrambled; but you did get us out of there before Tucker could take me into custody. Kudos, Talak."

"I live to serve the Empire."

"Talak, I hate ta burst yer bubble, but them sum'bitches took down yer station like it was nothin', Hoss," 'Watson' quips.

"Very true, Commander."

"Care ta explain yer screw up?"

"It was through no fault of mine, Commander. I had a chance to analyze their technology. It is not of this reality."

"What the hell are ya talking about?"

"He means alternate realities," 'Tucker' replies.

"Yes, Commander. The Empire originated in a reality different than this one. A massive quantum event brought you into this reality and somehow adapted your DNA to exist here."

"OK, that's all well and good, but what the fuck does that have to do with them humiliating us?"

"Their technology comes from a reality that is hundreds of years more advanced than ours."

"Can't you steal their technology," 'Pasqualle' asks, "Like you did to develop the Reaper."

"I fear it is not possible. They have developed a way to keep us from stealing their technology."

"So you are saying we're screwed?"

"Not at all, Commander. My people have been working on a new weapon."

"What kinda weapon?" 'Watson' asks.

"I shall demonstrate."

He enters a command and an artificial wormhole appears. He pilots the Reaper in and they are transported five thousand light years to an abandoned Imperial base.

'Tucker' recognizes the star system. "This is the Kolromi system. It's about five thousand light years from Bwentani Prime. It took us almost two hundred years to get to that part of the galaxy and you got here in a second."

"Yes, this is an artificial wormhole that was developed by the Bwentani's allies, the Kurai."

"How far can we go?"

"We have travelled its maximum range. My people have developed a shield to prevent the alliance from detecting us."

"So we have a new base of operations. Now all we need are weapons to counter what those bastards are packing."

"We are developing them, Commander, along with a new station with better weapons and defenses, including a new primary weapon that will start a thermalitic chain reaction that will vaporize a planet's atmosphere and render the planet uninhabitable in one planetary cycle. Once the weapon has deployed, the effects are irreversible."

"Now this, I'd like to see."

"Select a planet, Commander."

"You're shitting? It works now?"

"I had one installed on the Reaper. It will not be a planetary reaction, but it will vaporize a small section and make that part of the planet unsuitable for living."

'Tucker' is excited. "I wanna see this. Where's the nearest inhabited planet?"

Talak'Vin replies, "There is a populated planet in the nearby Moravin system."

"Well, what are you waiting for?"

Talak'Vin pilots the Reaper to the neighboring Moravin system, places the Reaper in a high orbit above a densely populated region, calibrates it, and then fires the Thermalitic weapon.

It impacts with the Thermosphere, obliterating a one thousand square mile section and works its way down to the lower most part, the Troposphere in a matter of minutes, allowing deadly radiation and unfiltered sunlight, heating the surface instantly to five hundred degrees, killing the entire population, including wild life, and plants, and devastating structures within the affected area.

"Holy shit! How much longer until you can do this on a planetary scale?"

"I am sorry, but it may take a few months before we can achieve it."

'Tucker' replies, "If we can fry those bastards, I'm willing to wait."

Talak'Vin nods, "I shall also work on upgrading our weapons and perfecting the teleportation device."

"Take us to the base and get to work."

"Yes, sir."

Talak'Vin pilots the Reaper to the Kolromi system and sets it down near the main garrison.

The command staff gets out at the recently renovated command building.

"Not bad," 'Watson' quips. "Too bad there ain't a place ta brew my Imperial Hellfire."

"That need has been anticipated. And there's also a labyrinth for your entertainment, Commander."

'Tucker' laughs, "Talak. Ass kissing will get you everywhere. Find someone to christen the place."

"We have already selected someone."

A Black Ops team brings Meyers to the Triumvirate.

'Tucker' walks to where Meyers is standing. "Your little stunt got my best Black ops team incarcerated."

"I swear it wasn't me. It was Tucker."

"I know, but you did nothing to prevent it. So you will take his place."

He motions to the Black ops soldiers to bring him to the entrance of the labyrinth, which is full of booby traps, deadly pitfalls and wild beasts.

"Let's go watch the fun, gentlemen."

The Imperial senior officers go to a balcony overlooking the one acre maze to witness Meyers as he is pushed into the labyrinth to try and make it to the center safe zone, where if he is able to make it unscathed, he will be set free.

They whoop and cheer when Meyers springs a bear trap, catching his leg. Wild dogs tear him apart and make a meal of him, leaving nothing for his poor wife to bury.

"Now that's entertainment," 'Watson' snarks.

They leave the balcony and go to the command center and begin planning their revenge on the Alliance, the Bwentani and especially Robert Tucker and his ops teams.

CHAPTER 34

Bwentani Prime – Covert Ops temporal time index 03.01.2222

After a month of heavy fighting, the last of the Imperial garrisons has been defeated and Bwentani Prime is liberated.

The Shock Troop Commanders have been arrested and await trial by the Minarian Magistrate along with the Troopers captured in the Glenarius providence, the Imperial station, and the Black Ops team captured during the attempted kidnapping of Robert and Linaiok.

Berellus is once again the Prime Minister and has brought the Special Forces commanders to present them with the latest in a series of unit commendations: The Glavius Commendation of Valor, the highest reward a soldier can receive from the Imperium.

Robert, Dave and Ray have just arrived from Earth after attending a ceremony by the ADF Council. Robert received his third Congressional Medal of Honor, while Dave and Ray each receiving their second.

They are standing on the podium behind Berellus.

"Any more dag-gum medals an' we're gonna rust when it rains," Ray jokes, getting a slight chuckle from Robert and Dave.

"You ever think we'll get back to...ya know, just being soldiers?" Robert shoots back.

Dave is about to speak. He stops when Berellus turns to Robert and hands him a placard with the silhouette of the most decorated Bwentani soldier in Imperium history.

"Thank you, Prime Minister. On behalf of the Special Forces, I accept this honor."

He shakes hands with Berellus, and then the three of them leave the stage. Linaiok, Ana and Zerellus, hold their one month old children wait for Robert. While Ray's wife, Rebecca and their ten year old son, Robert- Keith and four year old twins Reba and Garth wait for him. Dave's girlfriend, Bwentani weapons technician Kalla, is at the bottom of the stairs as they step down from the platform ready to congratulate him.

Lyle and Ryan walk towards them.

"Oh shit, don't tell me; you want to give us another medal?" Robert says with sarcasm.

"No, if you guys remember that you're paid to be soldiers and not talk show celebrities, we actually have work to do. ADF Intelligence reports they have a solid lead on the Triumvirate's whereabouts."

"They're slipperier 'n electric eel," Ray quips. "The last three leads we had, we missed 'em by a few hours."

"Their main base is in the Kolromi sector. We have a recon team on the ground outside of their headquarters and report the Triumvirate is there at this time."

"How old is this Intel?"

"Less than ten minutes."

"Let's haul ass."

"Your team is on the transport, along with your equipment."

"Who's our pilot?"

"Rillius," Ryan whispers.

"Ops one to Ops Five. Ready for teleport. Out."

The three of them are teleported to the WA-13. The teams razz Robert, Ray, and Dave with whistles and cat calls because of being in formal uniforms, each with rows of medals.

"Turn your heads, perverts," Robert snarks as they change into the black Covert Ops uniforms.

"Did Lyle fill you in on our destination?"

"Yes, David," Rillius replies.

Robert sits in the co-pilots seat. He knows that Rillius is depressed because even though Bwentani Prime has been liberated, the Imperium still considers him a traitor.

"*Binzah*, you are just as deserving of this citation."

"I know, Robert. I am also aware that you have tried to clear my name. I fear nothing less than producing the Rillius that was responsible for betraying my people will exonerate me."

Ray opens a quantum portal and the WA-13 enters it and transports to Hadar Prime.

Kolromi Prime

The ops team makes their way to a makeshift command post a mile from the Imperial Headquarters. There are two ADF soldiers at the entrance to the cave. They are about to stop the approaching teams, but stop and stand at attention when Robert, Dave and Ray approach.

"At ease, men," Robert commands, "We just got word that the Triumvirate is still in their headquarters."

"Yes, sir. Commander Sykes is waiting for you.

They walk inside and see Keith, Paul, Miguel and Allison studying a monitor.

"Guys," Keith says, as Robert, Ray and Dave walk over and exchange greetings with the ADF senior staff.

"What you got?"

"I've been monitoring their comm traffic," Allison reports. "It's mainly troop movements and a possible build up in the Venpari sector."

"We haven't heard a peep from them since we took their station. We dealt them a pretty big blow when we captured a good chunk of their forces. So they may be ready to make their move."

"Thanks to the stealth vests you provided for us," Paul adds. "We were able to get eyes and ears inside."

"Do you have a live feed?"

"Yeah."

Paul enters a command. They watch the senior staff, with their backs to the hidden camera, study a monitor of the ceremonial gathering on Bwentani Prime."

"Our battle cruisers are in position," 'Pasqualle' reports.

"Signal the fleet. Order the attack," 'Tucker' replies.

Keith exclaims, "Shit! Allison block that transmission and signal General Kensington to have the Bwentani activate their shields." He turns to say something to the Ops team, but they are already out of the cave and being teleported to the command center to stop the Triumvirate from ordering the attack.

Imperial command center

The Ops teams finish the teleport and surround the command staff with weapons drawn.

"One more fucking word and it'll be your last, asshole!" Robert snarls as he reaches over, grabs the shoulder of his counterpart and turns him around. "What the fuck?" he says as he realizes that the person in front of him is not 'Tucker' but a Kolromi native dressed in 'Tucker's' uniform, shaking and extremely frightened.

The team examines the rest of the people who are supposedly the senior staff and realize that they are also local citizens, equally frightened.

Robert motions for the Ops team to lower their weapons and "Do you speak standard?"

The Kolromi man indicates no.

"Let me take care of that, Bob" 'Tucker' says in a voice dripping with sarcasm.

His voice emanates from a speaker on the control panel.

Robert retorts, "Gee, Bob, you send me an invitation and you didn't want to play?"

"Oh, play time is over ... pal. All the shit you did to humiliate us? We are paying it back … in spades."

"The Bwentani are ready for you."

"Who said anything about the Bwentani? While your friends in the cave have been keeping tabs on us, we've been keeping tabs on them. And you should tell Commander Sykes the encryption sequence he uses was developed by Talak'Vin before he went to work for the Empire, which by the way is how we were able to secure the Bwentani codes."

"With help from Rillius' quantum double," Robert says, finishing his counter part's statement.

"My, my, my. You are a bright boy. Say hello, Rillius."

'Rillius' appears on screen.

"General Psychopath," Ray quips.

'Rillius' looks furious and is about to reply, but 'Tucker' holds his hand up to stop him.

"Witty remarks won't help you save Earth."

"Our battle cruisers are better armed and have more advanced defenses. They'll cut through yours like butter."

"Who said anything about battle cruisers? Turn your attention to the main monitor." Robert and the rest of the ops team turn to the monitor and see a brightly lit moon.

"Kolromi's moon? Did you move your base there?"

'Tucker' sighs. "I guess you're just not as bright as I thought you were. Kolromi has no moon. Oh, if you have anyone you want to say good bye to on Earth, you had better say it now."

Before Robert can answer, a giant vortex opens and the 'moon' propels forward and enters it.

"Shit! We've been played. Rillius beam us up. The Empire developed a new battle station and they're going after Earth."

The teams are teleported to the WA-13.

Robert sits at the tactical and accesses the priority One channel which broadcasts to all Alliance members.

"This is Commander Robert Tucker. The Empire has developed a space station disguised as a moon. It is on the way to Earth. Acknowledge."

Lyle appears on the screen, his face pale with a haunted, traumatized expression. His voice trembles as he speaks, "The Empire has just attacked Earth with some kind of new weapon."

"What kind of weapon?"

Bat'ai appears, and he too looks extremely shaken up. "Robert, it appears that the Empire has developed a weapon that destroys the atmosphere."

Robert thinks for a second, "You mean like the hole in Moravian's atmosphere?"

"Yes, but on a planetary scale."

"Can we stop it?"

"No, the effects are irreversible. Mars was totally destroyed. Lyle's son, Ed, his brother-in-law, Harry Benson and daughter-in law, Samantha Kensington were all lost along with the entire Mars Defense Force."

Robert feels himself becoming extremely emotional. He takes deep breaths to try and maintain his composure and clear his head. "Was Earth also destroyed?"

"The initial attack resulted in earthquakes, tsunamis and volcanic eruptions, along with the devastation of the Thermosphere. We calculate over ninety-nine percent of Earth's population has been lost."

"Is the Empire still there?"

"No, they deployed the weapon and disappeared. They are using a form of the Kurai wormhole so they do not have infinite range, but calculate they have a five thousand light year range."

"Which is pretty much the range from Kolromi Prime to Earth," says Robert. "So using three hundred and sixty degree navigation they can be—"

"Anywhere in an area encompassing one million eight hundred thousand light years."

"Is there any good news?"

"The Henoki were protected by Earth's oceans. They are safe for a few days before Earth's oceans boil away."

"And how long for Earth's survivors … if there are any?" Robert asks,

"Twenty-four hours before the Troposphere is stripped away and they die from exposure to solar radiation and eight hundred degree heat from the sun."

"Get every battle cruiser, transport and space vehicle that can carry passengers to Earth. Then contact Berellus and ask him to send his fleet."

"He is already sending every available spacecraft and medical personnel."

"Let me speak to Lyle."

Ryan appears on the monitor.

"Bob, Lyle's been taken ta the infirmary. We think his heart gave out."

"Is he—"

"Elizabeth says he's in bad shape."

"We'll get Keith's team and rendezvous with you in orbit around Earth."

"Yer first an' only mission is ta find that sum'bitch."

"He can wait, Ryan. People on Earth can't."

"Yer right, son. Ya know my boy Tom was a part o' the Mars Defense Force."

"I know, Ryan. I'm sorry. Do you want me to tell Mike?"

"He already knows."

"We're headin' ta Earth."

"See you there."

Robert has Ray lock onto the ADF team on the planet surface and teleport them to the WA-13.

The ADF team appears. Allison is hysterical, because her descendant, Samantha and her father were reported to be among the MDF casualties.

"Keith—"

"We heard everything."

"We'll bring you to Bwentani Prime," Robert says. "I'm assuming they're going to need help with getting the survivors situated."

"They reported a handful of our battle cruisers survived and they have already begun evacuations.

Keith suddenly notices Rillius in the pilot's seat. "What the hell is he doing here?"

"Keith, this is not the Rillius that sold out the Bwentani. Here, listen to this."

He plays the recording of 'Tucker' confessing to the truth about how they got the access code, which also shows the quantum double of Rillius.

"I'm sorry," Keith says after he realizes he's snapped at the wrong Rillius.

"I understand. This situation may stir up old feelings and even with this new evidence, I shall be as you Terrans say *persona non grata*."

"You may have a point, contact Ops Command, make sure they send every available craft and maybe you should coordinate rescue efforts from there. Don't worry, *binzah*, I will make it my priority to clear your name and spearhead the search for the Triumvirate."

Rillius contacts Liaok at Ops Command and a WA-13 appears. Rillius teleports to the other fighter and they return to Taqua Four.

Robert gets in the pilot's seat and opens a portal.

CHAPTER 35

Orbit above Albuquerque – Covert Ops time index 03.02.2218. 1900 hours Terran Mountain Time

The WA-13 arrives and goes into a stationary orbit. Everyone is shocked and sickened at the appearance of their once beautiful planet: fires, volcanic eruptions and vast areas of land covered by the massive tsunamis that hit the coastlines of every continent fill the screen.

Keith and his team insisted on staying and helping with search and rescue efforts. The team medic, Cal'vek hands them trauma kits and a handheld Immobilizer designed to put injured personnel into a stasis field.

Ray is at the tactical station, running a sweep to detect bio signatures of surviving human or other species on Earth at the time of the attack.

He picks up life signs, some human, but one of them has a greenish/blue color, indicating half human, half Henoki.

"Bob."

Robert sees the bio signature and a look of horror appears. "Oh my God. Ana!"

"We don't know that fer sure."

"Let's get down there and find out." He goes into the main compartment, anxious, while maintaining his military bearing."

"We have a hot op. Search and rescue, load on med kits and triage. Keith, you have the helm."

Allison responds, "Sir, I have pilot training. Commander Sykes and my husband are search and rescue certified,"

"Very well, Major. You have the helm."

"Sir, I'm not familiar with your teleporter."

"Sir, I shall work the teleporter," states Cal'vek.

"We can use you on the surface, Cal.'

"I will be able to stabilize them better in here. Send up the worst cases and I shall put them in stasis pods."

"Good plan, Cal. We're ready to teleport."

The Ops team and ADF senior officers arrive in one of the ADF Command buildings which were devastated by a massive earthquake.

They spread out and search the building for survivors. Ray and Robert key in on the bio signature, as Robert says silent prayers that if it is his daughter, she is still alive. They track the signal to an office. They go inside and hear the moan of a female in pain.

"Ana?" Robert says as he lifts a part of a wall that collapsed. To his surprise, he sees Samantha, who is barely conscious.

She sees him and says, "Uncle Bob?"

"I'm here, Sam. Is your father here?"

"Yes, he was sitting next to me."

"I found 'im. Checkin' 'im now," Ray says as he checks Harry, the ADF /MDF Liaison Officer.

"Daddy?"

"He's unconscious, but he'll be all right, darlin'."

"Ops One to Cal'vek."

"Cal'vek here, sir."

"Cal, I have two to teleport. One in serious condition. Harry Benson and his daughter."

Harry and Samantha are teleported out of the office.

Robert and Ray hear creaking noises, "Let's get the hell out of here."

They leave the office and the unstable part of the Central Command building. The office collapses as they exit the building.

The ops team spends the night and the early part of the morning searching for survivors and then teleporting them to the Outlaw, where they are stabilized and they are sent to one of fifty battle cruisers, each designed to carry up to twenty-five thousand people.

After an exhaustive search and working to the last possible minute, the Alliance managed to rescue over ten million people, accounting for every single person that survived the worst disaster in Earth's history.

They were also able to rescue a number of animals, wild and domesticated. The giant Bwentani ship that transports the animals was dubbed "The Ark."

The armada returned to Earth and teleported the Henoki's one million inhabitants and many species of marine life in specially modified Henoki transports. They were brought to the Bwentani Glenarius providence where Lake Glenarius has been designated as the new Henoki colony.

Robert, Ray and Dave made one last trip to Earth and watched as the sun rose and incinerated the planet. They felt that the planet should not have met its doom without witnesses.

CHAPTER 36

Imperial space station

The senior officers sit in a small theater, where they usually watch fights to the death between two condemned prisoners or watch captured soldiers traverse the labyrinth. Since they didn't take any prisoners from their attacks on Earth or Mars, they have to settle for watching the recording made of their attack on Earth.

They let out whoops and high five 'Sykes' because he was the one that deployed the weapon, which struck the Thermosphere, spread across the Earth, triggering the natural disasters.

'Tucker' exhales sigh of satisfaction. "I could watch this all night."

"We have son," 'Watson' replies. "We have."

"The only thing that is more satisfying than this is that Tucker fell for our diversion, and there was nothing he could have done to prevent it. And the best part; he has to live with the fact that I beat him."

"We beat him," 'Pasqualle' chimes in.

"Yeah, whatever."

"What's next?" 'Sykes asks.

"We get our people back from the bastards that are holding them the Minihahas."

"Minarians," 'Parker' corrects him.

"Whatever. We need to find their home world, give them two minutes to hand them over and if they don't, fry them."

"But you know if you do, Walsh, Colretti and the rest of our people will get fried as well," 'Pasqualle' points out.

"Well I guess that serves them right for getting their dumb asses caught in the first place. Besides, it ain't about them. I could care less if we get them back. The point is that if people don't fall in line, we have the means to fuck them up."

"The only drawback is that once we use the weapon, we have to wait twenty-four hours to fully recharge it, so we only have one shot." 'Sykes' notes.

"According to Talak the ADF defenses are useless against his weapon," 'Tucker' states,

"That's what he said about the Particle Laser Weapons," 'Pasqualle' retorts.

"But he also said their weapons and defenses are from a more advanced dimension. So maybe they are, too," mentions 'Sykes.'

"You may have a point. They could have been thrust into this reality the way we were."

"Since Talak can't steal the technology, we have to capture one of their fighters and dissect it. Then we can let Burke dissect the pilot."

"They're probably no different than we are."

"I know, but he should be allowed to have fun once in a while," 'Tucker' shrugs.

The senior staff laughs.

'Tucker' gets a call 'Donna Sheridan'

"Stellar Cartography to Commander Tucker."

"Go ahead."

"Sir, I have located the Minarian home world."

"Sheridan, send the coordinates to navigation and have Montoya prepare to open a wormhole to the Minarian system." 'Tucker' commands. He says to 'Sykes', "Keith, status on the weapon?"

"Fully charged and ready to deploy."

"Good. Let's either get our people back or roast another planet. Personally I hope they don't return them." 'Tucker' nods.

They leave the theater, leaving the recording of the Earth being destroyed on a continuous loop.

Minarian Prime

An artificial wormhole opens and the space station appears, establishing an orbit above the planet's Capitol.

'Tucker' sits in a high-backed chair contemplating whether he should try being diplomatic or just threaten total annihilation to get his people released. A moment goes, by and he laughs to himself, having reached the obvious decision.

He scoffs, "Who am I kidding? Allison contact their representative."

"Yes, sir."

"Keith, have the weapon ready to fire if they don't give us the right answer."

"Weapon ready," 'Sykes' states.

"Minarian magistrate Kaslo standing by," 'Parker' replies.

'Tucker' pauses as he decides to have some fun and see if he can pass himself off as his counterpart.

He stands up and says in a cordial manner, "Magistrate Kaslo, Commander Tucker, Allied Defense Force—"

"Imperial Commander Tucker, the Minarian Magistrate is well aware of your identity as well as the offenses your Empire has committed since you were brought into this reality one hundred ninety seven years ago," Kaslo counters.

"Nice to see my reputation precedes me. Since you are aware of who I am and what I am capable of, I'm going to cut to the chase. You are holding a great number of my people, some of whom are members of my senior staff."

"They have been tried according to their offenses. Most of the convicted are soldiers, who under duress followed your commands. They will be incarcerated and after they are rehabilitated, they be released to the custody of the Alliance to be integrated into society."

"Fine, I don't give a shit about them. I want Black Ops Commander Dave Walsh, First Trooper Vince Colretti and the rest of my Black Ops team released immediately."

"They are being held on charges of rape, attempted kidnapping, and genocide of several species across the galaxy."

Kaslo stares at 'Tucker' and continues, "Their crimes pale in comparison to the atrocities you have committed as a Black Ops soldier, and when you assassinated Imperial Commander Kensington to seize control of your Empire sixty years ago."

"Murder? He fell—"

"On a knife thirty times," 'Watson' retorts.

"What can I say? He was a klutz."

"We have amended the charges to include the recent attempted genocide of the Earth."

"Attempted? No, no, no. We didn't attempt anything. We wiped them out of fucking existence. Hey we even have it recorded, come on up and take a look, it was a real blast." This prompts groans from his senior officers.

"I have already read your thoughts—"

"Then you know I am not bluffing when I say you have sixty seconds to turn our people over or we'll add you to the list of my offenses."

"The Minarian Magistrate does not yield to threats from petty terrorists." Kaslo states simply states.

"Petty? I'm through dealing with this fucking clown. Keith, blast them."

"With pleasure."

'Sykes' activates and then presses the fire controls for the Thermalitic Weapon. The weapon discharges, shaking the command center from the recoil.

A few seconds later the weapon impacts with the atmosphere. The weapon dissipates with no affect.

"What the fuck?!"

"Your primitive weapons are insignificant. For we have existed and evolved since before the rise of the Bwentani Imperium. We are the galactic guardians—"

"Some guardians. Why haven't you done anything to stop us? 'Tucker scoffs.

"We cannot interfere."

"Is that a fact? Well, in that case, get ready to amend your charges against me, 'cause I'm just getting started."

'Allison' ends the transmission.

"Well that totally sucked." 'Watson' snarks.

"Get us out of here before they decide to lock our asses up too," 'Tucker' commands.

Navigator 'Carlos Montoya' opens a wormhole and navigates the station into it.

They arrive in an uncharted system two thousand light years away and enter a nebula.

Talak'Vin enters the command center.

"Talak. Why the fuck didn't you warn us our weapons were useless against the Minarians?" 'Pasqualle' asks.

"I was not aware of your order to encounter them."

"They are holding our people. You honestly think I was going to let them get away with it?"

"Of course not. I should have informed you that in their history, there has only been one successful escape from a Minarian prison."

"When?"

"Twenty years ago. The Zenaren broke their leader out when he tried to kill a group of Bwentani cadets during their war with the Imperium."

"Not that it don't sound like fun; but why in the hell would he bother with a group o' snot nosed kids?" 'Watson' scoffs.

The Zenaren used a viral weapon and it depleted the Bwentani military. They had to use cadets to fill their ranks."

"Hmm, then why didn't we know about this?"

"Sir, you were a hundred light years from here and did not arrive into Imperium space until five years ago."

"The Zenaren. Did we wipe them out?" 'Tucker' asks,

"No. They hire themselves out as mercenaries and bounty hunters. And you sir, have quite a considerable price on your head." Talak'Vin answers.

"Yeah, how much?" 'Watson' jokes.

"Don't even think about it, shit head."

"Geez, Bob what kinda o' friend do ya think I am? I would at least wait 'til yer dead 'fore I turned ya in ta collect." 'Watson' looks hurt.

"Yeah, and I would do the same for you guys," 'Tucker' shrugs.

"I hate to break up this tender moment, but before we go up against the Zenaren, the weapon has to recharge," 'Sykes' adds.

"I have reduced the recharge time to twenty minutes."

"Yeah, but if we run into this problem again, for those twenty minutes, we are vulnerable," 'Sykes' notes.

"The secondary weapons systems are online. I have analyzed their weapons and designed a shield to protect the hangars and our weapons ports."

"Montoya, plot a course to the Zenaren home world." 'Tucker' commands.

Talak'Vin speaks up. "Sir, if I may interject. The Zenaren have been in hiding since they broke their leader out. The best we can do is to locate one and force him to reveal their location." He calls up a program. "My former student Paul Foster invented this device to scan for genetic profiles."

"Send the program to Watson's Reaper. Then take Sanchez and his Black Ops team."

"Ya got it, son."

'Watson' motions to 'Sanchez' and they leave the command center.

"Tucker knows where our base of operations is, so we need to lay low until we get the Zenaren to give up where they're hiding, and find out more about this viral bomb, it could be useful in conjunction with the thermalitic weapon. According to the Minarians, there were survivors. If word gets out about this or the fact that the Minarians have a defense against the thermalitic weapon, we're screwed," 'Pasqualle' points out.

"Good point, Rico. Montoya, find an inhabited planet."

"Any one in particular?"

"The Bwentani think they're done with us. Let's show them they're wrong."

"Sir, the Bwentani and Minarian shield technologies are similar," Talak'Vin interrupts.

"I thought you said the Thermalitic weapon could penetrate any defensive system," 'Tucker' says angrily.

"Sir, I did explain it to you—"

"Probably when we were shit-faced. Point is, when we lost Bwentani Prime, we were made out to be weak, pathetic fools. Destroying Earth got their attention, but I think we had better show them we mean business. What is the nearest system?"

"The Celestus system. It's five light years away, bearing two-seven-zero due South." 'Montoya' replies.

"Set a course. As soon as we arrive, blast the fuckers without a warning."

"Weapon primed."

"Open a portal."

"Yes, sir."

'Montoya' sets navigation for the Celestus system, opens a portal and the stations enters.

Upon arrival at Celestus Prime, 'Sykes' locates the central communications center, destroys it and then fires the thermalitic weapon.

The Celestians are unable to call for assistance and by the time the Alliance is alerted, all life on the planet ceases to exist.

This wanton act of genocide is repeated on four other planets in a two hour period.

CHAPTER 37

Covert Ops time index 03.08. 2222

Commander Robert Tucker reporting:

It has been one week since the attack on Earth. The Covert Ops Force, Alliance Defense Force and the Imperium government have been working tirelessly to treat and provide temporary housing to the survivors of the Thermalitic attack.

Alliance Central Command has been overwhelmed with reports of attacks by the Empire in five different planetary systems. In each case, the attacks came without warning and their central communications were disabled beforehand. The attacks were reported by civilian transports too late for the Alliance to rescue the handful of survivors.

It wasn't until the fifth and final attack that the Empire contacted the Alliance, only to taunt them and state that any planet that did not unconditionally surrender to the Empire would be destroyed.

Berellus was about to hold a vote in the Imperium Council, when I informed him that my team delivered Kabrelian scientists for questioning, Magistrate Kaslo informed him that the Empire attempted to attack, but were stopped by their planetary defenses.

This prompted the Bwentani to refuse the ultimatum, but the remaining members of the Alliance were urged to decide for themselves.

A majority of the Alliance decided to surrender after receiving assurances that they would be 'treated fairly', a statement which no one believed for one moment.

One of the few species that refused, the Kurai, were promptly attacked.

Only the fact that the Alliance evacuated the planet's six hundred thousand inhabitants before defying the Empire saved them from extinction.

After this attack, the remaining planets surrendered and their military was given a simple choice: pledge their loyalty to the Empire or their families would die.

With our combat effectiveness down to twenty percent, even after the merging of Alliance, Imperium and Kurai forces, the Empire outnumbers our forces one hundred to one.

With Earth's military practically wiped out, I had Commander Keith Sykes and Earth's ADF senior command relocated to Taqua Four and integrated into the Covert Ops Force.

On a sad note, General Lyle Kensington died from complications of a massive heart attack shortly after learning about the death of his son, Mars Defense Force Commander Edward Kensington.

Services were held yesterday and Lyle was buried with full Military honors. He was buried beside a marker for his son and all of the murdered Alliance Defense Force personnel. Pomar Kallavus was also buried with full honors.

We have renamed the WA-14 from the Septimus to the Anvil to honor his memory.

General Ryan Dickinson has taken over as Commanding officer. Rillius has been cleared of all charges by the Alliance and Imperium has been reinstated. He is now the Executive Officer and promoted to the rank of Lekar.

While technically I have time in grade over Rillius, I preferred to stay in the position that I currently hold: Commander of the Special Forces and a team leader.

Major Samantha Benson-Kensington and Harry Benson recovered from their injuries. Samantha has been placed in charge of a WA-13 Squadron and Harry is the liaison between the Alliance / Imperium Council and the Kurai.

Officially the Covert Ops Force does not exist and we have been given ourselves the cover unit as the Joker Squadron, carrying on the legacy started by Lyle when the Unit was formed in Earth calendar year 2015.

Our primary mission is to infiltrate the Imperial held planets, organize a resistance movement and gather Intel on Empire activities and find an effective counter for the Thermalitic weapon developed by Talak'Vin, former mentor to new Covert Ops Intelligence Operative Paul Foster.

Ryan has called a meeting in the morning to delegate command responsibilities and begin planning our counter insurgencies and make sure at the very least the Alliance citizens are not treated brutally.

Report filed on 03.08.2222.1800
Robert Steven Tucker

CHAPTER 38

Covert Ops Command Center – Taqua Four time index 03.09.2222 - 0700 hours

Ryan addresses the existing and newly integrated senior officers their main mission: to track down and arrest the Imperial Command of the Terran Empire, also render their forces combat ineffective.

He is also formally introducing Rillius as the new Executive Officer. There are whispers among some of the officer who did not know that he is innocent of the charges of treason leveled against him.

"I'm sure he appears ta be the same as the sum'bitch that sold out the Bwentani, but Bat'ai has verified that Lekar Rillius is from our reality an' the one who sold out to the Empire is from an alternate dimension," Ryan notes.

"But the problem is they look the same," Keith points out.

"They are the same. The only difference is a genetic marker at the quantum level that is unique to each of their home realities," Bat'ai informs him.

"Plus that Rillius suffers from quantum psychosis because of jumping between at least ten different realities."

"An' our Rillius has been dealin' with us fer the last twenty years. So he's sufferin' the same thing," Ray cracks.

"Wait 'til he has to deal with you as long as I have," Keith snarks, prompting laughter.

"To be fair, Keith, we're not sure how long we have been in this reality or if you dealt with an earlier version of us. I'm sure Bat'ai can figure it out," adds Robert.

"I fear I cannot, Robert. By my estimate at least three different realities have intertwined to form this one.'

"Not that I'm complaining, but why wasn't the quantum balance screwed up like it was the last time?" Ricardo asks.

Ray adds, "Or us bein' churned inta galactic butter?"

"The last large scale incursion was caused by the Empire when they eliminated members of the Special Ops Force," Bat'ai responds. "The last incursion restored things to the way they were and restored the temporal balance."

"OK, so what does this mean?" Paul asks.

"We're back at square one and the Terran Empire is more dangerous than the last time we faced them. It looks like they acquired technology from when the Cho'Kai were here," Robert replies.

"Cho'Kai, who are they?" Colonel Albert Sanchez asks.

"To be honest, I lost track in which realities we fought them and which ones we haven't," Robert jokes. He pauses before adding, "They are an extremely violent and dangerous race. They have a weapon similar to the one the Empire uses and their station is based on the Cho'Kai design."

"Maybe Talak'Vin acquired the schematics from the Cho'Kai. The Kabrelians are similar to my people in the fact they are able to sense different realities and they are one of the most technologically advanced races in our galaxy."

"So bottom line B, is the Empire unstoppable?"

"At this time I do not have the technology to completely counter their thermalitic weapon, Robert."

"I thought ya said that the Minarians and Bwentani shields are effective. Can't we duplicate them?" Ray wonders.

"That piece of technology was developed several millennia ago and the means of reproducing it has been lost."

"Bwentani Prime is safe as long as the shield remains operational. And Berellus says that it will be activated at all times." Robert states. "Our quantum vortex is the only known way to penetrate it and Bat'ai has stated that Talak'Vin can't access our database. As a safety precaution the quantum technology has a failsafe that will automatically wipe it out if an attempt to scan the system is made by anyone one, even by the Alliance or the Kurai."

"What happens if it does, *Kemzeh*?" Zerellus asks.

"The technology will release a fatal virus to only the quantum system on our craft and it will also wipe out the entire system of whoever does the scanning. Nice piece of work coming up with that one by Ray, Paul, Bat'ai and Chief Parnell."

They nod in acknowledgement.

"Ain't that goin' a li'l overboard, Bob?"

"Ryan, we can't afford to trust anyone outside of the Covert Ops Force."

"If this happens while we're on a mission, how do we return?" Keith asks,

"Bat'ai has programmed a one-time quantum jump that will bring the fighter, battle cruiser or Special Forces transport back to Taqua Four and a scattering field to prevent anyone, including the the Zenaren, from tracking us," Paul states.

"One more thing; Ryan, Rillius and I have been working on revitalizing the *Bahal'Zai*."

"*Bahal'Zai*?" Keith asks.

"Bwentani elite forces. I relinquish my role as Executive Officer to concentrate on training our warriors."

"Good idea. Keith yer my XO and Ricardo is now our Chief Tactical Officer an' head o' the fleet."

Keith and Ricardo nod in appreciation for their new assignments.

"Bob, who will train the *Bahal'Zai*?" Keith asks.

"Myself, Commander Walsh, Commander Watson and Pomar Rillius are all certified as instructors in their fighting and covert operational skills. All Special Forces members will receive mandatory training to retain their status as operatives. Rillius will be in command of the *Bahal'Zai*, which will operate as a separate entity from the Special Forces. Zerellus and my daughter, Major Ana Tucker are trained *Bahal'Zai* operatives and will each lead a team. They will recruit and train Bwentani and Henoki volunteers after they are given a thorough security background check."

"Why are the *Bahal'Zai* and the Special Forces separate units?" Keith asks,

"They will blend in better with other races from the Alliance. Unless they possess the technology to scan our quantum DNA, our Special Forces operatives will be able to infiltrate the Imperial forces. We will need Intelligence operatives to work with the teams. I have gone over the ADF personnel files and Majors Foster and Herrera have extensive experience in gathering Intel. You will work with our teams. We will need to recruit five more operatives, two for my teams and three for the *Bahal'Zai*."

"Zerellus and I shall screen applicants," Rillius states.

"Dave and I will do the same."

"Count me in, Bob." Ricardo says.

"We need you to be in charge of the fighter squadrons. We're taking Colonel Jackie Foster, Colonel Alberto Sanchez, Pomar Renallius and Major Samantha Kensington as Special Forces pilots."

"Bob, they're our most experienced pilots. Shoot, Jackie and Alberto have been with us from the beginning," Keith replies.

"I know. We're gonna be flying into some white knuckle situations and we need pilots that have been there, done that and won't buckle under pressure."

"I understand, Bob. Ricardo says with slight hint of disappointment.

"Oh, don't worry, Rico, you and Keith are probably going to get about as much shit as you can handle. Besides you get the big toys."

"Battle cruisers?" Ricardo asks.

"Yup," Ryan says. "You, me an' Keith will each head up a battle group."

"I thought we weren't going to take them on directly?"

"For the time being, we're not. Until Bat'ai and our R&D can figure out how to fully defend against their weapon, including that thing that fucking destroyed six planets, we'll stay low key."

"What do we do in the mean time?"

"We are upgrading the entire fleet to the WA-14 Anvil."

"The Anvil?" Keith asks,

"Lyle's call sign when he was a pilot," Ryan replies, still grieving the loss of his long time friend and former squadron commander.

"The space docks orbiting Taqua Four are upgrading the battle cruisers. R&D are installing stealth shields and the MVAW on each battle cruiser."

"MVAW?" Keith asks.

"Multi Vector Attack Weapon; they're basically a module with four Pulse Beam Weapons on each and four MVAWs attached to each cruiser, quadrupling the offensive capability. They report we will be combat ready within a week."

"Until then we're gonna train our butts off in the simulators, recruitin' operatives an' sendin' our teams ta start gatherin' Intel."

"Ryan, I shall speak with the leader of the Kurai, Kaleel. He informed me that the Empire is interested in locating the Zenaren." Zerellus states.

"Rumor is they're the best trackers in the Imperium. They got in trouble with the Minarians for breaking their leader Traxis out of their penal colony."

"The Zenaren can't be trusted, the *pendejos* used a bio agent and nearly wiped out both the Bwentani and our own forces. There's no way in hell they'll ally with us," Miguel adds.

"I am aware of that. The Kurai and Bwentani have an

alliance. The Kurai and Zenaren have a nonaggression pact and Kaleel is a friend," Zerellus states,

"You trust Kaleel?"

"I saved his life, *Kemzeh.* He has a life debt to me. He is honor bound to never betray me or the Bwentani."

"Also the sum'bitches jest tried ta kill 'em."

"OK Z, work that angle. If the Empire contacts the Zenaren, have them fully cooperate, but feed us the Intel."

"Double agents," Ryan nods.

"Exactly, we're gonna get boots on the ground. B, I need to know where the Empire established their garrisons and who is willing to set up an underground Intel network."

"Right away, Robert."

"Z, set up a meet with Kaleel. Take Ana with you.'

"Yes, *Kemzeh.*"

"Dave, have the teams muster in the hangar at 1400 hours. Until then, dismissed." Ryan says,

The senior officers leave the command center to start on their assigned tasks.

CHAPTER 39

Kurai settlement – Bwentani Prime

The Kurai leader, Kaleel, oversees the construction of the capital of the Kurai Providence.

They have been given complete autonomy and once the Empire has been defeated, they will be allowed to resettle on the planet of their choice, either inside or outside of the Imperium, and maintain their status as a sovereign species.

With an escort of two warriors, Zerellus and Ana walk over to Kaleel.

"Greetings, *shuvag* (friend)," Kaleel says warmly as he gives them both a handshake and a hug. "Blessings to your new children. Your grandfather Quennok feels they are the children prophesized to lead the galaxy into a new era of peace and prosperity."

"Zerellus and I would rather do that ourselves," Ana replies.

"*Ama'diok* himself would not tangle with her," Zerellus chuckles. His comment is rewarded with a slap to the arm from his wife.

Kaleel laughs. "Tell your father the Kurai are in his debt for helping us evacuate our planet before the *kulswas* (bastards) destroyed it. Name it and it will be done."

"Are you still in contact with Traxis?"

"The Zenaren leader? Yes. I do not wish to offend you, *shuvag*, but the Zenaren will not ally themselves with the Terrans, Henoki or Bwentani."

"But he will ally himself with you."

"Yes."

"We received word that the Empire is looking for the Zenaren because they were able to liberate Traxis. We feel they are going to attempt to free their Black Ops team."

"I have heard similar rumors."

"Convince Traxis to cooperate."

"He may sense we are setting them up, especially after what the Empire has done."

"Agreed. Do you have any contacts that would act as a go-between?"

Kaleel thinks for a moment. "I do have a contact with the Rokari."

"Rokari?" Ana asks, confused.

"They are Information brokers," Zerellus tells her. "If you wish to know what is happening inside or outside the Imperium, they are the ones to go to."

"Is your contact trustworthy?"

"If he knows what is good for him, he will not betray me," Kaleel replies.

Zerellus thinks for a moment. "*Binzah*, this may work even better."

"What do you mean?"

"We can use your contact to leak information–"

Kaleel looks offended. "Our trust works both ways; I will not betray my contact."

"I would never ask you to do otherwise. But other Rokari are notorious *hol'dens* (eavesdroppers)."

"Yes, if you ever want to remember a secret, tell it around a Rokari," Kaleel quips.

Zerellus and Ana laugh.

"What information do you wish to divulge?"

"I want you to contact the Zenaren to put a bounty of ten million galactic credits on the head of the Imperial leader Robert Tucker, with a ten percent finder's fee to your contact."

"What is the actual purpose of this?" asks Kaleel.

"What I have stated. They will either take the bounty or cooperate with the Empire."

"I do not understand."

"The Zenaren are the best trackers in the galaxy. One way or the other they will find the Empire. Truth be known, we would rather they ally with them."

"You do not make sense to me, *shuvag*."

"They use ships and technology stolen from the Bwentani during the war," Zerellus states. "So we have the ability to track them."

"Yes, very clever. I see you have not lost the ways of the *Bahal'Zai*."

"My *Kemzet* trained me well."

"Relay to your father and Commander Tucker the Kurai wish to do more than just pass messages, we are ready to take revenge."

"We would be honored to fight alongside of you, "Ana replies. "The Empire thinks your people were all killed when they attacked. Until we are able to defend ourselves, we are... how did my father put it? Flying under the radar."

"Yes, a wise precaution. This would present a dilemma. How will I put the information out without revealing that the Kurai survived?"

"You were on Bwentani Prime and you are the sole remaining Kurai."

"I shall start immediately."

Zerellus and Ana say their farewells and leave the settlement.

Kaleel assigns the task of overseeing the construction to his second in command, Parull.

He goes to Central Command and after speaking to Berellus, goes to the field where the Kurai fighters are based, has the controller open a gap in the shield for him to fly through and then proceeds to a planetoid which is used as a place for spaceship repairs, pilots and travelers to refuel their ships and get food and drink.

Commerce Planetoid – Rokarian system

Kaleel, in clothing resembling a tradesman, enters the establishment. It is a clean, modern place of business. He visually scans the room for his contact, a Rokarian information broker named Klax.

He sees him sitting at a dimly lit booth in the corner, and walks over to him, sits down and discreetly takes out a DNA tester and scans the Rokarian.

"Friend, I am hurt. Do you not trust me?"

"You know the drill, Klax. The information I have is for you and for you only."

"I am intrigued."

"After what I have to offer, you will be more than intrigued."

"What information do you require?"

"I need to find Traxis."

"The Zenaren leader?"

"Yes, I want to place a bounty on someone."

"The Leader of the Terran Empire I presume. I am saddened at what they have done to your people, my friend."

"I know you are full of *schlug* (shit), but thank you for the sentiment."

"You remember that we are incapable of emotions," Klax chuckles. "But what they have done was a travesty. Why do you not help the Alliance and the Imperium?"

"They are *kava'dals* and afraid to go against the Empire and I am the last of the Kurai. When I die, my people die with me, but I want to have the satisfaction of killing the *kulswa* before I die."

"The Zenaren are not easy to locate."

Kaleel hands him a disc. "Here are one million galactic credits. Locate the Zenaren and I will give you another million. If Traxis brings Tucker to me, he will get ten million and I will give you another three million."

"Five million credits just for locating the Zenaren and passing a message?"

"He killed my people and destroyed my planet. If I had more, I would give it."

"I believe you would."

"Contact me when you contact him."

Kaleel starts to stand.

"Wait," says Klax. He motions to someone at the bar and Traxis walks to the table. "I anticipated that you would seek the Zenaren to avenge your people."

Kaleel hands him another disc. "That is why I have always depended on you."

"Then my business is done. I shall stay in touch if you require my services."

"*Siywaolao* (Good bye)." Kaleel turns to Traxis. "I am sure you heard."

"Yes, I have warned you that Terrans are not to be trusted, no matter what universe they are from."

"You know what I want."

"Yes, but the Terran space station is a fortress."

"This coming from the person who escaped from the Minarians. Have your people lost their touch?"

"Not at all," Traxis scoffs, "We are smart enough not to go against the most dangerous species in the galaxy."

"If I am able to acquire the defenses for the station, get you technology to infiltrate the station undetected and offer you ten million credits for bringing Tucker to me alive, will that change your mind?"

"For that much I would throw in the *kulswa* that fired the weapon. His name is Sykes."

"I would be satisfied with the leader; if you want to sell the other Terran to the Yonkari for their *Kuli'tah* events. I may even leave enough of Tucker for you to sell him as well."

"You drive quite a bargain, *shuvag*," Traxis chuckles.

"Just be careful. If the Terrans find out that you are after him, they will go after your people."

"If the Minarians have not found my people, I do not fear the Terrans finding us."

"I shall get you the information on the Terran station. Here are five million credits." Kaleel hands him a disc. "You will get the other five when I have my hands around that *kava'dal's* neck."

Traxis grunts in approval.

Kaleel stands up and leaves the booth.

Traxis stands to go to the bar, when he is grabbed by two men and brought out the back door to an Imperial Reaper.

'Alberto' and First Trooper 'Alex Pasqualle' drag him into the fighter/transport which lifts off, opens a wormhole, and disappears.

CHAPTER 40

Imperial space station torture chamber

Ready to question him, 'Tucker' stands in front of Traxis, who is strapped into a neural shock device, while Doctor 'James Burke' is at the controls.

"So you thought you could profit by handing me over to the Kurai leader for destroying his planet?"

"I am a bounty hunter. That is what I do."

"You're honest. I like that but, that is the wrong answer."

He motions to 'Burke', who turns up the intensity control, giving Traxis a moderate shock.

He grimaces, but refuses to cry out.

"Impressive. That'll be all doctor."

"Yes, sir," 'Burke' replies, and then leaves.

'Tucker' motions to the Shock Troopers, who release Traxis from the restraints.

Traxis appears to be unimpressed. "That was not much of an interrogation."

"It wasn't an interrogation. In fact, I wish to retain your services."

"To go after the Alliance."

"What Alliance? Except for the Bwentani, the entire Alliance and Imperium are under my rule. And as soon as we discover how to penetrate their shield, the Bwentani will become a shining example of what happens if you defy the Empire."

"Then who do you wish my people to hunt?"

"The Minarians are holding several key Imperial officers in their custody. I want you to break them out."

Traxis suddenly pulls out a device, pushes a button and surrounds himself and 'Tucker' with a shield. He pulls out a weapon. "With a push of the button I can transport us to my ship and disappear and even your best technology will be not able to trace me. I was offered ten million to bring you back alive."

"There are two problems with your scenario. One, you have no means off this station. Two, even if you did, my Black Ops team has put a tracking device on you fighter. We will hunt your people down and with one button I will wipe your fucking people out of existence." 'Tucker' smiles.

Traxis sighs, lowers the shield and then hands the devices to the Shock Troopers. "I suppose you are going to kill me now."

"On the contrary, you are fearless and inventive. The Kurai leader offered you ten million galactic credits to bring me in. I will offer you one hundred million to retrieve my team and employ you as our bounty hunters."

"On the condition that I do not have to go after my friend Kaleel."

"The Kurai leader?" 'Tucker' laughs. "His species dies with him, so he is of no concern of mine. As a token of good will, I will even let you have first crack at going after my counterpart. Wasn't he the one who arrested you and brought you to the Minarians?"

"Yes."

"Of course, he will not be an easy target."

Traxis nods. "He is *Bahal'Zai*. He could kill a battalion of your Shock Troops with nothing more than a knife."

"I am aware of his combat record which as you know, is similar to mine. I am not sure if I could take him one-on-one, but I would not be stupid enough to go against anyone with less than an energy weapon, unless I have an advantage."

Traxis keeps his thoughts about 'Tucker's' cowardice to himself. "We have not been able to locate Tucker since the attack on Terra."

"He was last seen on Bwentani Prime."

"His people are no longer there. They used a scattering field, to prevent our scanning equipment from determining the location of their new base of operations," Traxis states.

"They also haven't reacted about the planets we destroyed," 'Tucker' states. "So we must have dealt a bigger blow to them than they are willing to let on. For all we know, they could be rebuilding their forces and possibly improving their technology to counter ours. So that's is your first assignment; locate where Tucker and his people are operating out and send that information to me."

"What about your people?"

"They can wait. If we eliminate the remaining Alliance Forces and the Bwentani, there will be no one left to resist."

"Tucker and his people have an annoying habit of showing up when you least expect them."

"Where have they been for the last five planets we destroyed?"

"You attacked without warning and by the time they responded, it was too late to save anyone."

"You may have a point. We will draw them out and if we destroy them great, if not you track them back to their base and we'll take it from there."

"I will be waiting for your signal. What planet will you attack next?"

"I'll let you know." 'Tucker' addresses a Shock Trooper, "Have Sanchez and his team return Traxis to his ship in the Rokari system."

"Yes, sir."

The Shock Troopers bring Traxis out of the torture chamber. Then motion to 'Sanchez', who brings Klax over to him.

"Well done, Klax."

"Thank you, sir. I knew that the Kurai leader would seek out the Zenaren. The device you confiscated is what they used to bypass the shield to rescue Traxis."

"Will it work on the Bwentani shield?"

"No. The Zenaren tried to use the device during their war, but they were unsuccessful."

"So the Zenaren was setting me up?"

"Yes, he was going to double-cross you by setting up an ambush and then supply your counterpart with these devices to attack and cripple the station."

"Funny, I heard the Zenaren hate the Alliance."

"They are not choosy who they deal with if the price is right."

"The same can be said about yourself."

"It is well known that the Rokari have no allegiances and information has no bias."

"Speaking of which, do you have the information about where the Zenaren are hiding?"

"They change locations on a regular basis. I do not want to give you outdated information."

"I see you heard about the last information broker that gave us a bad lead. When you have the information, contact us immediately."

Klax bows his head and is escorted out by two Black Ops soldiers.

'Sanchez' starts to leave, but 'Tucker' stops him. "Have the Rokarian followed."

"You think he is feeding us bad Intel?"

"Rokarians are incapable of lying, but he more than likely got this information from the Kurai leader, who is friends with the Bwentani."

"I'll have one team follow the Zenaren and another at the Rokarian Commerce Center."

"If we play our cards right, we may solve both problems at once and no one will dare defy us," 'Tucker' surmises, "Dismissed, Commander."

"I live to serve the Empire."

'Sanchez' leaves the chamber.

'Tucker' returns to the command center.

"Montoya, stand by for location of our target."

"Who's the target, Bob?" 'Montoya' asks.

"Either the Zenaren or the Rokari; depends on who tries to screw us over first."

"Commander, Black Ops team returned the Zenaren to the Rokari planetoid, tracking device activated and they are now tailing the Rokarian inside the outpost," 'Parker' announces.

"The moment you get info on the Zenaren whereabouts, give the coordinates to Montoya and proceed immediately to their base."

"Yes, sir," both 'Parker' and 'Montoya' reply.

Rokarian Commerce center

Klax enters the establishment and proceeds to his usual place of business. Two silhouetted figures watch him as he walks past them. He walks around a large support beam and proceeds to his table.

The two figures, 'Alex' and Black Ops soldier 'Mike Dickinson' walk to an adjacent table and order drinks as Klax sits and talks to his next client:

Another Rokarian, resembling Klax puts a hood over his head, takes a last look at Klax and the Black Ops soldiers and then walks out of the establishment. He walks to a dimly lit section of the landing bay. A hatch opens up and he slips inside.

Robert, Dave and Alberto are waiting inside.

'Klax' takes off his hood and then transforms into a female Kallaxian metamorph named Ky'Holl.

"Mission accomplished."

Robert turns to Traxis who is tied up in a jump seat.

"Like it or not we saved your ass, too."

Traxis grunts, angrily but concedes the point.

"Ryan's waiting for our report," Dave says.

"Yeah, Al, take us back to the Kensington."

"We're Oscar Mike."

Robert sits at tactical, opens a quantum vortex, engages the scattering field as Alberto pilots the WA-13 into the opening and returns to the Covert Ops flagship.

CHAPTER 41

Conference room – battlecruiser *Kensington* Covert Ops time index - 03.10.2222 – 0800 hours

Robert, Dave, Ky'Holl and a reluctant Traxis are with Ryan, reporting on their mixed results.

"So far all attempts to establish a resistance movement has been unsuccessful," Dave states. "People are too afraid to defy the Empire."

"Why do you think my people have stayed out of it," Traxis snorts.

"Well, like it or not, you're now involved," Robert counters. He pauses before continuing, "Imperial Commander Tucker was using you to free his people before getting rid of you."

"And now I suppose you're going to return me to the Minarians."

"No. We may not like other, but we need each other. Your people are the best trackers and the Kallaxians are the best spies and assassins. We've also had our differences with Ky'Holl's people—"

"Correction, Commander Tucker," she interrupts. "You had problems with Jen'Pway. Most Kallaxians do not seek the political spotlight."

"You would rather kill for sport," Traxis quips.

"This coming from someone who kills for the highest bidder and used a—"

"All right, that's dad-gum enough!" Ryan commands. "In case y'all fergot we have a common enemy an' we need ta werk together."

Ky'Holl and Traxis nod, conceding the point.

"We have safely relocated your people. Traxis, I know the last place your people want to be is on Bwentani Prime, but for right now that is the only place safe from the Empire's thermalitic weapon," Robert states.

"Yeah, I am sure Berellus will greet my people with unholstered weapons."

"He doesn't know your people are there. They're on an isolated continent, with plenty of provisions, comfortable living arrangements, plus a shield to prevent them from being discovered."

"Double cross your own brother-in-law?" Traxis scoffs. "I am beginning to like you, Terran."

"Don't. I'm not that pleasant, especially when someone tries to screw me over."

Traxis eyes the *Bahal'Zai* mark on Robert's arm and decides to stop trying to push his buttons.

Robert turns to address Ky'Holl. "Ky, I regret we weren't able to save more of your people."

"It was not your fault, Commander. That arrogant *kavak* Jen'Pway thought he could dictate the terms to the Empire."

"I hate ta say it, but we gotta give 'em credit fer not mistreatin' ennyone so far."

"That also makes it more difficult to recruit help, Ryan," Robert replies. "They figure as long as they got the threat of destroying anyone who resists them, they can go about their business of exploiting them as slave labor and building their war machines. We have to not only take out that station, but somehow prevent Talak'Vin from expanding their arsenal. The rest of the Kabrelians are in Minarian custody"

"Yeah, one station will be tough, but if they build ten of them motherfuckers, we're screwed," Dave quips.

"Tucker's too much of a control freak to let anyone but himself have that much power."

"Along with the rest o' the Triumvirate, Bob."

"Calling themselves a triumvirate is a fucking joke." Robert scoffs. "Watson and Pasqualle are lap dogs with no real power. Tucker is smart enough to know he can't control the Empire without them or the Black Ops Force, so he gives them just enough authority to appease them. But, he holds all the cards."

"Some have said the same about you, Terran," Traxis rebuts.

"You're probably right. That's why I know this bastard so well, the only difference is that I surround myself with people better than me and I can take orders as well as give them."

"Most o' the time, Bob," Ryan quips.

"Good point. Bottom line is that before we can make any move to start liberating these people, we have to neutralize the station and Talak'Vin."

"Bat'ai's heard from our contact inside o' the station. He got a schematic o' the improvements they've made. Their dad gum weapon kin recharge in twenty minutes an' fortified their defenses with improved Particle Laser Weapons an' better shieldin'."

"How did our contact manage to do that?"

"Helps ta be in a position ta git that Intel."

"Good going," Robert replies, "But we should keep contact to a minimum."

"Yer right, cuz nothin' short o' an all-out attack will work this time."

"I suppose you are going to recruit my people to participate in your suicide mission?" Traxis snarks.

"Not at all. You've done your part. I secured a pardon from the Minarians and once we take out that station you and your people can settle wherever you want. In fact, we even have a nice section of the galaxy where you can live alongside the *Dev'cha*. Because," Robert looks him dead in the eye, "You're going to forget all about this meeting."

Before Traxis can reply, Dave takes the neural inhibitor and erases Traxis' memory of the meeting and has him taken to the WA-13 to be returned to the Zenaren colony.

"We could have used them as trackers, Bob."

"Too unreliable, Dave."

"Then why did he get the pardon?"

"The last thing we need is a bunch of bounty hunters looking for the Zenaren and finding the Kurai and Kallaxis survivors."

"They can conceivably escape the colony and sell out the Bwentani to the Empire," Dave says.

Robert replies, "That's why they're on their way to the Palayas system."

"Where the hell is that?"

"About twenty light years from Taqua Four. We have confiscated their weapons and their ships. We set up a colony and turned them into farmers. They will not bother anyone for a long time."

"Jest what we needed, a fruit stand fer Taqua Four."

The others laugh.

"Everything is in place. All we need is their Black Ops team to track the drone ship ta the Hadar system and get them to commit their thermalitic weapon."

"Bob, that dad-gum thing only takes twenty minutes ta recharge an' we don't have the firepower ta take 'em down."

"Let me handle that Ryan. I still have a few aces up my sleeve."

"Bob, I sure as hell hope ya have more 'n aces up yer sleeve, like a dag-gum armada."

"You'll be pleasantly surprised."

"We better git everyone inta position."

"See you on the other side."

Robert, Dave and Ky'Holl walk towards the WA-13.

"I am honored you have allowed me to become a part of your team."

"We didn't give you anything, Ky. You earned it. My daughter is the only other female to pass the Special Forces training course."

"You've been assigned to my team for your probationary period." Dave tells her. "You'll be in the command center with my Intel specialist, Commander Herrera."

"You've already proven yourself to be an expert at infiltrating enemy positions and gathering Intel, now you need to know how to decipher it in the field."

"After this phase of the operation we are going to be spending a lot of time on occupied planets setting up Intel networks and sabotaging enemy positions. We are going to witness a lot of atrocities and until the time is right, we won't be in a position to do anything but to stand by and allow it. Commander Tucker and I have been doing this for over two hundred years and it still gets to us and it has broken even the hardest of operatives. Will you be able to handle this assignment?"

"You ask this because I am Kallaxian and female?"

"No, we ask this because you are a sentient being with a soul and a conscience." Robert replies, "We have looked evil in the eye and the bastards we are facing are twisted, soulless sociopaths. The universe they came from their behavior is considered the norm. In order to beat them we have to think like them and do the unexpected."

"The Kallaxians are an empathic species, but we have mastered suppressing our feelings to do unpleasant things."

"If we didn't think you could do the job, we would not have recruited you."

Robert gets a call on his neural link.

"Ops Three ta Ops One."

"Go ahead, Ray."

"Bob we jest landed the drone on Hadar Prime. Looks like the Black Ops team they had bird doggin' it fell fer it. They jest radioed the position ta the space station."

"Understood. Out. Ops One to Command One. Bait has been set time to spring the trap. Is Bat'ai ready?"

"Raymond, Michael and I are standing by on Hadar Prime."

"We're rolling hot – ETA thirty seconds."

"All Units in position, Bob." Keith says.

"Understood. Out. Rico take us to Hadar Prime."

"On the way."

Ricardo opens a portal and they enter the vortex.

CHAPTER 42

Imperial Space Station

'Parker' receives the coordinates from 'Alex'. She immediately sends them to 'Montoya', who sets the coordinates and opens a vortex and the station moves forward and enters. Then she contacts 'Tucker'. "Sir coordinates received, proceeding to target."

The Triumvirate enters the command center.

"Excellent," 'Tucker' states. "Weapons?"

"Charged and ready, Bob," 'Sykes' replies. "We will be able to fire immediately upon entering orbit."

"No, our objective is to draw Tucker and his people into a fight. We will wait until they appear, fire on the base and take out the battle cruisers with the Particle Laser Weapon. Talak was able to modify it to penetrate their shields, plus he constructed five more to give us three hundred sixty degrees of coverage."

"Sir will be in position in one minute," Montoya' mentions.

"Have Black Ops personnel in the command center and two battalions defending the weapons control center. If I know Tucker, he'll go after these targets. Also have Curazide ready; he may try to flood the station with sleep agent again."

'Parker' contacts 'Sanchez' and relays Robert's orders.

'Montoya' reports, "Approaching Hadar Prime."

The vortex opens and the battle station appears two thousand kilometers from the Capitol city, which is near the equator.

'Tucker' commands, "Open a channel."

"Channel opened."

"Traxis, this is your old buddy, Bob." 'Tucker' says in a cordial tone. "Have you considered my offer and decided to come to work for us?"

Traxis and Robert appear on screen.

"I would never align myself with a *kava'dal* like you."

"But he would lead you here into our trap and collect the two cent reward, which to me is still overpaying, but I'm willing to splurge." Robert states. "Ryan, now."

Five battleships emerge from the stealth shields, deploy the MVAW and all weapons are aimed at the station.

'Tucker' yells furiously, "Fry that mother fucker!"

'Sykes' presses the fire control for the thermalitic weapon, which quickly builds to deployment and fires at the planet.

Hadar Prime suddenly shimmers and disappears, revealing another fifty battleships belonging to the Imperium forces commanded by 'Septimus'.

'Tucker' stammers, "What the—"

"Surprised, Bob? Well once again you've been played like a violin. The Bwentani upgraded our battle cruisers and we in turn upgraded their weapons. We have the combined fire power of ten of your stations and will cut you to shreds long before you weapon can recharge. You have three options, you can fight and get your sorry ass blown straight to hell. Two, you can run, but we can track your every move, or three, surrender, where you'll receive a fair trial and a first class execution."

"I choose option…one. Fire everything!"

The station erupts as all of the Particle Laser Weapons fire at once, aimed at the combined fleet. The Particle Laser Weapons impact with the ADF battle cruisers, but pass through the Bwentani, revealing them to be holographic.

"They're fakes! 'Tucker' exclaims. "Concentrate on the ADF battle cruisers and find that fucking planet!"

Talak'Vin scans space to the quantum level. "Sir, it is not registering."

"The whole planet was fake, too?"

The planet phases back into normal space.

"No." Robert tells him. "My protégée Bat'ai was working on a device that has the ability to take an object and phase it in between dimensional realities."

'Tucker' motions to 'Parker' to mute the transmission. "Can you get the schematics?" He asks Talak'Vin.

"Bat'ai keeps his inventions committed to memory."

"We'll settle up with them later. Focus on the battle cruisers and blast anything that comes close—" 'Tucker' is knocked to the ground from the impact of multiple weapons. "What the fuck was that?!" he exclaims as he stands up.

"Sir," 'Parker' says as she points to the monitor, which shows a half dozen ADF battle cruisers, each armed with the MVAW as well as enhanced primary weapons.

Robert's face appears on the communications monitor.

"I'm sorry, Bob, I lied. We only have the firepower to kill you twice over…but once more than is enough. Surrender. Now."

"Never!" 'Tucker' yells. "Find that son of a bitch and destroy him!"

'Sykes' targets the base, but the planet once again disappears.

"Bob—"

"Take out their battle cruisers!"

'Sykes' enters a command and the Particle Laser Weapons begin to fire in a precise pattern, hitting each battle cruiser, doing minimal damage, but weakening the shields.

On board the Kensington, Ryan receives reports of damage. "Back us off, git us outta range," he commands.

"Bat'ai tell the fleet back off to one hundred thousand kilometers." The battleships comply. "General, one cruiser, the Seattle has sustained heavy damage. Commander Sykes has been injured. Major Kyle Sheridan has assumed command."

"Can they continue?" asks Robert.

"Their weapons and shields are offline."

"Git 'em back ta Taqua Four. We'll cover their exit."

"Message relayed."

"Command One ta fleet, pattern Delta two-two. Launch all available fighters an' try ta knock out their defenses."

The battle cruisers disperse followed by twelve squadrons of WA-14s launch, each taking a different approach and deploying their MVAW. They begin attacking the weapons tower.

The modified shielding protects the weapons and they begin targeting the WA-14, destroying three and damaging several others.

Major John Randall radios Ryan. "Alpha One to Command One. Weapons ineffective, I say again weapons ineffective."

"Break off attack an' regroup."

"Yes—" Randall is cut off after his fighter is hit and destroyed by the Imperial weapon.

The remaining WA-14s engage their stealth shields and retreat from the station. Despite being cloaked, several more are destroyed, bringing their losses to two squadrons.

"Command one, they are able to track us even though we are cloaked," Henoki Squadron commander Pelok.

"We'll cover yer exit."

The five remaining battleships move in from all sides and begin firing at the stations, more as a distraction than attacking, realizing their weapons are ineffective against the station.

'Tucker' realizes they now have the advantage, thanks to Talak'Vin's adapting their weapons to the ADF shield harmonics.

"Launch the Reapers. Target their landing bays."

"Yes, sir." 'Parker' contacts the Imperial Squadron Commander, 'Kyle Sheridan'. "Command to First Trooper Sheridan."

"This is Sheridan. Go ahead."

"Launch fighter, target the battle cruiser landing bays."

"Proceeding at once."

Twenty squadrons of Imperial Reapers leave the station landing bays and begin flying towards the battle cruisers.

A call comes into the command center.

"Venpari garrison to Command."

"Go ahead."

"We are entering the Hadar system. ETA ten minutes."

"What is your compliment?"

"Ten battle cruisers and twenty Reaper squadrons."

"You can have whatever is left over," 'Tucker' replies.

He sits in his command chair with a slight smirk, seeing how quickly the tables have been turned on his quantum double.

The *Kensington* and the remaining battle cruisers are under attack by the Reapers, who are immune from the ADF weapons, including the MVAW. They are receiving reports of heavy damage to the landing bays and the WA-14s that are damaged are unable to land.

Robert calls in, "Ops One to Command One. We had the advantage; what the hell happened?"

"They figured out our dad-gum shield an' weapons. We can't hold 'em off."

"They have a shitload of backup coming in. This is a no-go. Break off and return to headquarters."

"We can't open a vortex with these dad-gum things attackin' us," Ryan replies.

"Then we'll have to give them a new target."

Hadar Prime shimmers back into view and a mounted Pulse Beam Weapon fires at the space station, hitting and destroying a weapons tower.

Robert slaps Paul on the back and says, "Send an encrypted message to the fleet to drop their shields for a split second so you can program the defenses with the multiphasic chip you installed and set the weapons on a rotating frequency."

"Will do."

Paul sends the message and then reprograms the fleet's shield and weapons systems.

"Ops One to Command One," Robert contacts Ryan. "Commander Foster reprogrammed the shields and weapons."

"We lost half our fighters and three battle cruisers are too damaged ta fight."

"Bob, they're about to fire the thermalitic weapon."

"Gotta go. Paul, engage the slipstream as soon as they fire, then return and resume attack, all weapons."

Hadar Prime once again shimmers and disappears just as the thermalitic weapon fires. Paul enters a command and adjusts the planet's orbit twenty thousand kilometers east of its previous position and rematerializes, firing ten mounted weapons, hitting and damaging the station.

"Continue firing," Robert commands.

The Imperial command center severely rocked by the new assault from the planet.

"You can't hit a fucking planet that is fucking right in fucking front of you?" 'Tucker' screams furiously at 'Sykes' "Are you blind or just completely fucking incompetent?"

"Bob, they're—"

'Tucker pulls out a pistol and shoots 'Sykes' between the eyes, killing him instantly. The rest of the senior staff is stunned.

'Tucker' points his weapon at 'Parker'.

"Take over weapons."

"Sir, I—"

He shoots her in the shoulder.

'Foster' grabs 'Tucker' from behind and tries to subdue him. 'Tucker' breaks free, elbows 'Foster' in the gut, then kicks him in the stomach and aims his pistol at him. He is about to pull the trigger, when a gun is placed to his head. He turns and sees 'Rillius' with the weapon and the rest of the senior staff have their weapons trained on him.

'Tucker puts his hands up, gives 'Rillius' his weapon and then backs away, all traces of his sanity gone. "I knew you fuckers would eventually turn on me."

"We let ya git away with a lotta shit, but killin' Keith stepped over the line, hoss," 'Watson snarls.

"Let me? I'm the head of the fucking Empire; I will do whatever the fuck I want. If I want to kill you, it's my right and you can't stop me."

"We jest did."

"We'll see."

'Tucker' takes out the device he took from Traxis pushes a button, which activates a shield. He then pushes a second button and disappears.

'Foster' checks 'Parker', who is in pain.

"I'm all right, Paul, he just grazed me."

"I'll get you a medic, Allison." 'Foster' motions to a Black Ops medic, who checks on her.

"I knew that sum'bitch would go off the deep end." The station is suddenly rocked by an explosion. "An' picked a helluva time ta do it."

"We are in position awaiting orders," Venpari Commander 'Delhan' signals.

"The planetary weapons are your priority. The Alliance fleet is retreating," 'Rillius' answers. "Let them."

"Yes, sir."

"I am temporarily assuming command." 'Rillius' states. "Does anyone have a problem with this?"

None of the senior staff objects.

"What is our status?"

"Besides the obvious, missin' a weapons officer, defenses damaged, but holdin', thermalitic weapon fifteen minutes ta bein' fully charged, secondary weapons an' shields down twenty percent," 'Watson answers.

"Commander, you are in charge of weapons." 'Rillius' responds. "Commander Pasqualle, recommendations?"

"Proceed as planned. Planet is obvious main threat."

"Formulate a secondary strategy. I have observed you, Commander. Tucker has wasted your talents as a tactical officer."

"Pasqualle to fleet, status."

'Sheridan' replies, "Commander, the ADF fleet has broken off their attack and have retreated. They have lost two battle cruisers and their fighters have been rendered combat ineffective."

"Join the fleet and concentrate on planetary defenses. They are using a device that enables them to phase out of our dimension. Attempt to locate and destroy it. The thermalitic weapon will be ready in less than ten minutes."

"Yes, sir."

"Chief Parker, will you require further medical assistance?"

"I'll be all right," she replies as the medic finishes bandaging her shoulder.

"Delhan to Command. Fleet in position surrounding Hadar Prime, awaiting orders."

"Stand by. Chief Parker, open a channel to Commander Tucker."

"Channel open."

Robert appears on screen.

"Commander Tucker, I'm sure you know who I am?"

"Lekar Rillius. Your *binzah* and *hemzeh* would like you to return to the Imperium."

"Why would I want to do that? I have a death sentence for attempting to overthrow my father."

"Lekar, we know you have a condition from the number of quantum leaps you have made. Septimus wants to help."

"My brother has always been a sentimental fool. Besides I know I have quantum psychosis. I found a doctor that cured me. Perhaps I can refer him to you?"

"Another time. I see Tucker is no longer in charge."

"The *kava'dal* used a device and escaped before we could arrest him."

"You've come to your senses?"

"He killed a senior officer."

"I thought that's how the Empire operates."

"Not anymore. It will be run the way the Imperium should have been governed."

"By you?"

'Rillius' shrugs, "If the senior command allows me to lead. Unlike their narcissistic former leader, I know to surround myself with quality commanders and not lap dogs."

"Spoken like a *Bahal'Zai*."

"Yes, I heard rumors you have been trained in our ways. Unfortunately, Commander, it will not help you; I have learned ways to counter whatever training you have received from my people."

"So I assume we won't reach a peaceful accord?"

"I think we can…as long as you withdraw and do not interfere with Imperial rule."

"Sorry, *binzah*, you know I can't do that. I swore an oath to defend the Imperium and the Alliance."

"I respect that, Commander." 'Rillius' nods. "It will be a shame to destroy you. But do not take it personally; after we are done with you, we are going to track down former

Imperial Commander Tucker to try him for crimes against the Empire."

"Wait, did he use the device he took from the Zenaren, Traxis?"

'Watson' replies "Yeah, why?"

Robert laughs.

'Watson' whispers, "The cheese done slipped off the dadgum cracker."

Robert stops laughing. "I'm sorry, but you don't have to worry about that fucking lunatic. You see, before we gave the device to him, our engineer reprogrammed it to send him directly to the Minarians. No offense guys, I was hoping you would all be a part of his escape plan."

"Sorry ta disappoint ya," 'Watson' quips.

"Maybe we'll do better the next time."

"You do not grasp the situation," 'Rillius' responds. "We have you surrounded and with superior firepower. Surrender is your only option."

"Are you sure?"

Mike presses a button. Once again Hadar Prime disappears and the fifty Bwentani battle cruisers reappear.

"Does he think we're stupid, they're not real—"

One of the Bwentani battle cruisers fires, destroying an Imperial battle cruiser."

'Septimus' appears on the screen.

"This is Lekar 'Septimus' of the Bwentani Imp—"

"Greetings, *binzah*." 'Rillius' replies.

"*Binzah*, I do not wish to fight you, but I shall if you do not return with me. I have secured a pardon now that we know that you were afflicted."

"Commander Tucker offered a similar proposition. I will quote an old Terran proverb. "It is better to rule in hell than to serve in heaven."

"We have you surrounded and you have no means of escape," 'Septimus' states.

"You seem to forget the first rule of the *Bahal'Zai*, there is always a means to escape to fight another day."

Talak'Vin enters a command, which releases a massive scattering beam, temporarily blinding the Bwentani fleet. He then opens a vortex, the station and the entire Imperial fleet enters and disappears.

Hadar Prime shimmers and reappears.

"Commander Tucker to Septimus. Thanks for saving my ass, *binzah*."

"My debt to you is paid. We are now even."

"Now we know where your brother is. He claims to be cured of his quantum psychosis."

"I sense he has regained his faculties, but still refuses to return to the Imperium."

"As he said, why serve as a prince when you can live as an emperor?"

"My brother has always felt he would make a better leader than our father."

"And with the weapons he has in his possession, he has made the Empire that much more dangerous."

"If my brother has indeed regained his former identity, he will not command with brutality. However, he will expect total obedience and will not tolerate insurrection."

"The Empire has a weapon that can devastate a planet by targeting its atmosphere and leave it vulnerable to cosmic radiation and solar flares. A *Bahal'Zai* would never resort to that kind of weapon. Do you feel he'll live up to the code?"

"I cannot say. Part of his personality has always been to acquire more power. This may be a temptation he may not be able to resist."

"That means we'll have to go after the station."

"I must return to my reality. If he still possesses the quantum slipstream device he may try to complete what he set out to accomplish."

"Understood. The quantum barrier will keep him out."

"It shall keep you from returning as well, *binzah*."

"I feel until both the Empire and your brother are stopped, this is the way it has to be, Septimus."

"You stated that you would attempt to apprehend my brother and return him to my people unharmed."

"I will do everything in my power. Until we meet again, *binzah*."

"I shall look forward to that day, *binzah*."

"I'll bring the *Kalnem*."

"*Kulhuka* ."

"Septimus, wait. One last question. Do you have a species called the Kallaxians in your reality? Their home planet would be on the border of the Imperium."

"I have never heard of their species. Who are they?"

"The key to defeating that Imperial station."

"I do not understand."

"Rule two. The best way to defeat an opponent who knows you as well as you knows yourself -"

"Do what is unexpected," 'Septimus' finishes.

"Exactly. I have to return to my headquarters. We lost a lot of good people and I have to notify their families."

"May the gods welcome them as warriors."

"Thank you, *binzah*. My respect to your father."

"*Kulhuka*." 'Septimus' ends the transmission.

"I'm sorry, Bob. I guess our modifications weren't enough," Paul says with a tone of guilt.

"We were up against one of the most brilliant minds in the galaxy…and your mentor."

Mike asks, "Back ta base, sir?"

"Yeah, Bat'ai said we could keep Hadar Prime in the slipstream indefinitely. We're gonna need a secondary op headquarters."

"Yes, sir." Mike sets the quantum slipstream device, causing the planet to disappear once again. "Guess we screwed the pooch."

"Not entirely, Mike. At least one good thing came out of this."

Minarian Prime

Two Magistrate soldiers bring 'Tucker' to a maximum security holding cell. He is struggling, cursing and hurling threats at them.

"You had better fucking let go of me before I rip your fucking lungs out!"

The soldiers ignore him and put him in a cell with clear walls, a bunk, sink and a toilet. One of the soldiers punches a security code and an electronic force field secures the cell.

'Tucker' spots 'Walsh' and the Black Ops team, who await trial for their crimes.

"Tucker got you, too, Bob?" 'Walsh asks.

"No, I was sold out by our own people and that fucking traitor Rillius."

"I knew he couldn't be trusted."

"Then why didn't you say something?"

"I did, and as usual you didn't listen."

"Shut the fuck up."

"That's what you told me."

"Then keep it shut, I don't want to hear it."

"You have up until your execution to think about it."

"They're not gonna execute me."

"Gonna slit your own throat?"

"I did not become the head of the Empire by giving up when things seemed impossible. We're Black Ops soldiers, we can get out of any situation or have you forgotten?"

"We forgot nothing. We're just waiting for the perfect opportunity. The Minarians don't follow a pattern and the discipline collars are set to incapacitate if we try to escape."

"They haven't fitted me for one."

"They will after your arraignment."

"When do they do that?"

"After they compile charges against you; it took them about a week for me and Colretti."

"Then that should take a few years for me." 'Tucker' chuckles.

"Did they search you?"

"They took my weapon and communications, but didn't find the other compartments."

"Hide them. We're a couple of components short of building a device to neutralize their security system."

"Who has it?"

"I do sir," 'Colretti' replies.

"What do you need?"

"A couple of processing chips and an additional power source," 'Colretti' answers.

"I have a -" The device suddenly disappears.

"How the fuck did you do that?"

"I stole the mini teleporting device Talak invented," 'Colretti' answers. "That's how I've been assembling the device."

"Why didn't you use it to escape?"

"Not enough power to teleport a person, only small objects."

"How about a mini grenade?"

"Yeah, but we had ours confiscated," 'Colretti' replies, "They didn't find yours?"

"They didn't look hard enough."

"You mean—"

"If I fart, I'm fucked."

This gets a laugh from the Black Ops team.

"When 'Colretti' finishes the component he'll send it to you and when they take you in for arraignment, you'll be led past the detention center control room. From there you'll be able to neutralize the collars and the cells," 'Walsh' says. "We managed to keep a few small arms, but we'll need more firepower."

"If someone managed to hide their minicomputer, I may be able to tap into their system and locate the armory. Talak was able to break the encryption and gave the code to me."

A mini-computer appears in 'Tucker's' cell.

"When do they do security checks?"

"They don't. Between the collars and the cells they figure we are under control."

"That arrogance will do them in. Colretti, do you think the teleporter can retrieve a Minarian weapon?"

"If I know the location."

'Tucker' sits on his bunk and using the encryption code hacks into the Minarian database, where he gets the layout of the central security complex, locates the armory and then has 'Colretti' teleport the computer back to begin their escape plan.

CHAPTER 43

Covert Ops Command 1430 hours 03.12.2222

The senior staff meets to go over the casualty figures from their mission: Three battle cruisers destroyed, all hands lost, including Commander Quevok of the battle cruiser *Quennok*, Commander Mercellus of the *Glavius* and Commander Carlos Montoya of the *Tigre*.

Also lost were six squadrons of WA-14 fighters, including Commander John Randall.

Keith is in the medical bay in serious, but stable condition, additional casualties were referred to the Henoki medical center in the Glenarius providence.

We fucked up, Ryan. We underestimated them," Robert says with guilt in his voice.

"We knew who we were goin' up against, Bob. Hell we were lucky ta survive at all."

"Dumb luck. We had the advantage and we should have capitalized on it."

"Talak'Vin countered our shields and weapons. If we went ahead and launched a full scale attack, we would have lost our entire fleet."

"Paul and Septimus saved our asses."

"What did ya do ta our shields an' weapons?" Ryan asks.

"It was a concept Ray, Bat'ai, your grandson and I came up with," Paul answers, "Multiphasic shielding designed to adapt to any form of energy attack. The Pulse Beam Weapons were modified to do the opposite; find the shield's operating frequency and adapt to pass through the shield. It was highly experimental and quite frankly we were surprised it worked."

"We need ta perfect it, Ryan," Ray insists.

"Y'all git ta it. We are suspendin' any further operations 'til we can avoid ennymore blood baths like this."

Ray, Bat'ai, Mike and Paul leave the command center to go to R&D.

"Fucking waste, almost two thousand of our people and still no closer to neutralizing that damn thing," Dave says, disgusted.

"We knew it was a risk, Dave. It's my fault."

"Bob, I gave the order," Ryan retorts.

"OK, now we've played the blame game, what the hell do we do now?" Dave says sarcastically.

"I said we're suspendin' operations, an' I mean it. If y'all disobey me an' try somethin' stupid, I'll personally put my foot up yer asses an' then throw ya in the stockade."

"I want one more crack at it," Robert says, drawing a menacing stare from Ryan. "Hear me out, Ryan. Tucker was a wild card, and Rillius has been trained to think and act as a *Bahal'Zai*."

"But he's nutty as a June bug."

"Septimus and I confirmed that he's been cured of the quantum psychosis. Don't get me wrong, the Empire is probably more dangerous than ever, but Rillius will not tolerate wonton violence on civilians."

"But he'll come after us with gun's blazin' an' we saw what that dad-gum station can do with Talak's upgrades."

Robert nods in agreement, "Exactly. We need to infiltrate the station and destroy it."

"If he is *Bahal'Zai*, he'll know our doctrine inside and out. Shit, the son of a bitch probably wrote the book."

"Actually it was my grandfather four hundred years ago," Rillius replies. "But David is correct, if we share the same experiences, my counterpart will be extra vigilant against any attempt to infiltrate him operations, including if we were to use our stealth vests."

"I know of one contingency he will not expect, at the same time motioning to Ky'Holl. She walks towards them.

"You wish to speak to me, Commander?"

"Yes, Ky. Gentlemen, I'm not sure if you all have met Lieutenant Ky'Holl, our newest member of the Covert Ops Force."

"Commander Tucker has told me all 'bout ya, I'm General Ryan Dickinson."

She bows her head, "I am honored, general. I have trained with your grandson, Michael."

"Ky is a Kallaxian metamorph. It was her posing as Klax, the Rokarian that laid the ground work for Tucker ending up in Minarian custody, which is about the only thing positive that came out of this mess."

"Well done, Lieutenant," says Ryan.

"Thank you, sir."

"Bob, are ya plannin' on sendin' her ta that station all by herself?"

"No, we'll go with a four person team."

"I'm sure she can fool 'em, but you'll stick out like a sore thumb."

"Not necessarily Ryan."

"I don't suppose ya learned how ta shape shift."

"In a way I have."

"Care ta run that by me agin, son?"

"Would you care to explain, Ky?"

"Yes, Commander. Not all Kallaxians have the ability to naturally change their appearances. They rely on a device that can rearrange their molecular structure."

"The Kallaxian assassin that killed Marcus Holloman used one."

"Only a few of my people still retain the ability to do this naturally. I am one of them."

"An' this device'll work on humans?"

"Elizabeth and Bat'ai were able to adapt it to work on us, thanks to our unique DNA."

"I don't know 'bout this, Bob."

"I'm not Bob." Robert and Dave each hit a button and they transform back to themselves.

"All right, ya convinced me, but ya better have this op worked ta my satisfaction or it's a no-go."

"We're gonna run it through the simulator and we're going to have Rico throw every scenario he can think of at us," Robert replies.

"Who's yer fourth?"

"I am," Rillius replies.

"Figures," Ryan mutters. "Yer 'bout the only other one crazy enough ta try it. Might as well take Ray an' complete the dad-gum nut-fecta."

"We would, but Ray's needed to upgrade the weapons and shields."

"I don't know how much o' a window you'll have, they think they whupped our asses six ways from Sunday an' won't be hearin' from us enny time soon."

"They did, and we're gonna give them bastards some payback and you know what they say about that?"

"Revenge's a bitch but payback's a motherfucker."

Ky'Holl looks confused, so Rillius translates everything to her in Kallaxian. She nods in understanding and laughs.

They walk towards the training room. Linaiok sees Robert, goes to him and hugs him.

"Praise *Ama'diok*. I saw your name on the casualty list."

"Show me."

Linaiok brings him to a monitor with the official ADF casualty list and shows him his name.

Robert sees his name listed as Robert Tucker, the Sixth and then below his name Roberta Tucker.

"Lin, they're—" He becomes upset. "My descendants that served on the Mars Defense Force."

"I am sorry, *A'nok*."

"I never really got a chance to know them…at least in this reality."

"Ana said we lost a lot of people."

"Yeah, including some old friends, and we still didn't destroy the station."

"I will ask *Ama'diok* to guide them to their deities."

"I feel like I failed them, Lin."

"You cannot fail them unless you give up fighting."

Robert manages a chuckle. "You know me better than that. I just need to get it out of my system and go in with a clear head."

"You are going back?"

"We have to. Someone more dangerous is now leading the Empire; Rillius' quantum double."

"*A'nok*, he is *tul'shal* (insane)."

"Claims he's been cured of the quantum psychosis, but he'll run the Empire like the *Bahal'Zai* before Berellus reformed them."

"My *Hu'Neh* told me told me of the brutality of the Bahal'Zai before the Alliance, when the Henoki were at war with the Bwentani."

"Yeah, in fact it was your father and Berellus who saw the futility of war and ended it three hundred fifty years ago."

"I see in your eyes that you have also witnessed death and destruction."

"I've seen my world destroyed too many times to count. This time I fear there is no way to reverse it."

"You stated Bat'ai has knowledge of temporal technology," Linaiok replies.

"I already spoke with him. He said it's a fixed point in time and the only way to reverse this is to go back to the point of origin and stop the event that triggered it. If I did that, I wouldn't have been pulled into the future, my DNA rewritten to extend my life, met you and had our beautiful daughter and now grandchildren."

"Could you," she pauses briefly. "Go through with it if you had to?"

"Only it the universe was unraveling at the seams."

"It may, if Rillius is not stopped."

"Thanks for putting it in perspective, Lin."

"Besides I will need assistance with our new child," Linaiok smiles.

"*Sel'quay?*"

"Yes, Doctor Elizabeth just confirmed it."

Robert laughs, then hugs and kisses his wife. "How far along?"

"A month."

"We'll celebrate tonight."

Dave calls Robert on the neural link. "Ops Two to Ops One. We're all set, waiting on you."

"Be there in two."

Robert kisses Linaiok and then goes to the training center, focused and determined to succeed on their latest mission.

CHAPTER 44

Imperial Station – Moravin Nebula

'Rillius' has ordered the station into the nebula to avoid detection and to determine the extent of damages inflicted by the assault from both the Bwentani fleet and the base at Hadar Prime.

He also assesses the tactics used by his command staff along with the effectiveness of their weapons.

"While I am pleased overall as to the outcome of the battle, my contact states we destroyed three of their battle cruisers and six squadrons of their latest fighters; I feel there were tactical errors which prevented total victory."

'Pasqualle' is slightly defensive. "Such as?"

"Commander, your battle strategy was nearly flawless; it was the cunning deception by Commander Tucker that turned the tide. It was your Commander Tucker's actions that kept you from destroying the Alliance fleet. Nevertheless, you have dealt a serious blow to the Alliance and it may be several months before they are in any condition to mount an offensive, which is why we are going to tighten security."

"What do ya mean?" 'Watson' asks.

"Commander Tucker is a trained *Bahal'Zai* operative, which means he is unpredictable and will use this defeat to launch a counter offensive against Imperial targets, most likely this station, if he is not already aboard."

"We have run security scans and I have Black Ops patrols on every deck," 'Sanchez' replies.

"Do not misunderstand me, Commander Sanchez, I am sure your methods are more than effective in fighting a conventional enemy, but a *Bahal'Zai* operative has the skill to infiltrate any enemy position and overcome their tightest defenses. If you allow me, I will train your Black Ops teams in the ways of the ancient *Bahal'Zai*; before my father made them weak. I must warn you it is demanding and not everyone who undergoes it will survive; but rest assured by the time they are trained, they will be able to take on Commander Tucker's forces and emerge victoriously."

"I will notify my men."

"Volunteers, Commander."

"Of course."

'Sanchez' leaves to brief his Black Ops teams.

"Look like yer takin' charge, I like yer style, but where does that leave me?" 'Watson asks.

"Commander, do not mistake my reorganizing as an attempt to undermine your authority. I am merely working to make the Empire more secure and efficient."

"Tucker kept a tight leash, if he hadn't vanished he probably would've fallen on a dagger forty times."

"Promotion by assassination. I have studied your history, Commander. Ambitious, but in the end jealousy and paranoia have brought down many a civilization."

"Don't knock it, son. We've been 'round fer 'bout five thousand years."

"And my ways has kept the Bwentani secure for over twenty five thousand of your years."

"Guess ya got us there."

"If you do not wish my assistance, we shall part company and I will continue my search for beings that are willing to share my vision of building an empire that will endure the ages."

"And you can achieve this without the use of force?" 'Pasqualle' asks.

"There is a difference between ruling with discipline and ruling by intimidation."

"Well, if ya instill the fear o' death a lotta them will toe the line."

"There are species that do not fear death, it also breeds contempt and encourages insurrection. Eventually they come to understand that no matter how powerful your weapons are or how many of them are put to death; they outnumber you and will eventually overthrow you."

"You make good points, but in the here and now, we have the advantage, this station being one of them, how do you propose we maintain order?"

"Allow certain freedoms, and make sure your people understand that obedience brings rewards and disobedience brings punishment."

"Like 'em up an' shoot 'em?"

"No. They are tried according to law and if they are guilty, they serve the community by doing what is deemed unworthy by their own standards."

"Sounds kinda candy ass ta me."

"As I said, Commander, if you do not wish my services, I shall leave."

"I, for one am willing to give it a go," 'Pasqualle' says.

"What the hell? Worse comes ta worse, we can always open a can o' whup ass."

'Rillius' nods, "I am pleased you are in accord. Contact your regimental commanders and ensure they follow the new guidelines. Punishment for infractions will be severe, just as the rewards for adhering to them will be bountiful."

"I'm sure the Alliance will be upgrading their weapons to match ours. Their technology is more advanced."

"Yes, they acquired it from the reality where I originated. I will provide your chief weapons builder with plans to our ships, weapons and scanning technology."

"So those ships that attacked us came from your reality?" 'Pasqualle' asks.

"Yes, commanded by my brother."

"An' if he decides ta help Tucker fulltime?"

"He cannot. My people's quantum DNA will degrade if we are outside of our native dimension for more than seven Terran days, in the same way, we cannot exist in another dimension for the same period of time."

"Seems ta me yer well-adjusted, an' we've been her fer 'bout two hunnred years."

"I have the ability to adjust my quantum DNA to any reality I visit, and your DNA somehow was adapted by a rather massive quantum event."

"We have one problem. The Kabrelian engineers who were working with Talak'Vin are now in Minarian custody."

"I am sure there are engineers among the planets that are part of the Empire."

"I don't think they'll be keen on helpin' us build weapons ta use against 'em."

"Each species will only build one component, that way they are not fully responsible for what is created. Also remember: reward and punishment."

"Ta be honest, this is gonna take some gittin' used ta."

"I understand, Commander. It took my people almost one thousand of your years to embrace the change. It will be difficult, but I am sure you will be pleased with the result."

"An' what are yer long term goals, Rillius?"

"Quite simple, commander. In my extensive travels through at least two dozen different quantum realities, I have experienced nothing but pure chaos, mayhem and disorder."

"Sounds like my idea o' fun," 'Watson' quips.

"After enduring a decade of quantum psychosis, I find harmony and tranquility rewarding. Your reality is the closest I have come to experiencing this feeling. If it means eliminating the Alliance or anyone who impedes my search for perfection, I will do so. Do not mistake my benevolence for weakness; if someone interferes with my attaining that perfection, they will be eliminated. That is why I ask that you accept my offer of your own volition. Once you make an agreement with a *Bahal'Zai*, it is to be honored at all times."

"Don't 'spect me ta change overnight, son."

"I do not; in fact, I sense you will have the most difficulty because of your upbringing in the Imperial Republic of Texas. I am not expecting total obedience; all I ask is that you do not betray me."

"Don't screw me over, an' I won't screw you over."

"That is fair. Besides weapons, do you have any other skills that can be utilized?"

"I know a thing or two 'bout that computer. Did my share o' hackin' in my day; pretty much the reason why I got sent ta the Imperial Academy."

"With *Bahal'Zai* training, you can become an accomplished code breaker."

"What the hell is that?"

"Someone who can decipher enemy codes and infiltrate their systems; the way ours have been infiltrated."

"Them sum'bitches broke in?"

"No, we have a spy in our midst," 'Rillius' replies. "He turns to 'Alex', and points his weapon at 'Alex's' head. "Here is your spy." He is too stunned to speak.

"One damn minute! That is my son!" 'Pasqualle' says with a tone of outrage.

"He is not your son, Commander. Have Talak'Vin perform a quantum DNA scan, you will see that despite having your son's memories, they have been artificially implanted. I sense he has been here for several months and the Alliance is holding your actual son prisoner. Of course, where he is, I am not certain."

"How can you tell?"

"My training has refined my sensory perception, so that I am able to distinguish fact from falsehood and how to identify beings from different realities, an art lost upon the modern *Bahal'Zai*. What do you feel we should do?"

"Verify his identity, torture him for information and where they are holding my son and then execute him."

"I concur."

"Well hell, I can git behind that."

Two Black ops soldiers apprehend 'Alex' and bring him out of the command center.

'Rillius' types a message and then sends it.

Covert Ops Command center

Allison monitors the data that is being transmitted from the Imperial database via the ghost program developed by Paul.

Data stops transmitting and a message appears:

Notify Commander Tucker to prepare for one more funeral. Commander Pasqualle's son.

Allison cuts the feed from the Empire, and uses a virus to erase any attempt to trace the signal before allowing her emotions to take over. "Oh my God." She tries to calm herself and then contacts Robert.

"Command to Ops One.'

"Go ahead."

"Sir, we have a major problem. Captain Pasqualle's cover has been compromised."

Robert is heard cursing before he replies, "Notify Commander Pasqualle and Liaok."

"Yes, sir."

Ricardo and Liaok enter the command center, followed by Ryan, Robert and the ops team.

"Allison, what happened?"

"Sir, I was monitoring the ghost program, reviewing their daily reports, when I got this message." She points to the monitor.

"Something major must be happening if he broke cover," Robert says.

"I do not think that is the case," Rillius replies.

"What do you mean *binzah?*"

"Robert, my quantum double stated he wanted to rule the Empire using the ways of the ancient *Bahal'Zai.*"

"Yeah, that's what Septimus said was the reason he tried to throw over their father."

"The ancient *Bahal'Zai* developed a refined sense of sensory perception. He may have discovered Captain Pasqualle's identity."

"Not possible, we altered his memory. Shit he didn't even know he was working for us, everything he did was subconscious."

"Enough of his original identity remained for 'Rillius' to discover. Even though he appears fully human, Captain Pasqualle is also half Henoki and 'Rillius' may have sensed it. Only one who attained the level of *Bahal'Dai* is able to accomplish this."

"A *Bahal'Zai* master; shit; that's way above my pay grade."

"Maybe not, Robert. Linaiok taught you the Henoki technique of forming a mental filter?"

"Yeah."

"That's no different than the methods used by my ancestors."

"Well then, you, me and Dave are good to go. What about Ray and Ky'Holl?"

"Kallaxians have mastered the technique. I cannot say whether or not Raymond can accomplish this."

"Bob, I'd normally raise six kinds o' hell fer bein' left behind on a mission, but Alex's life is more important."

"You'll man tactical and if we run into trouble teleport us out in a minute's notice."

"I'm going too, Bob."

"I you frosty on this one, Rico. You're no good to us if you let your emotions cloud your judgment."

Ricardo composes himself. "I'm good to go."

"The ghost program has been compromised. Ray, we're gonna need fresh Intel, including personnel who are guarding Alex so that we can access the central core."

"This'll be my biggest hack since breaking inta the congressional payroll system."

"You got caught doing that."

"Only 'cause I reduced their pay ta minimum wage."

"Still overpaid," which gets a few chuckles.

Robert exhales deeply before speaking. "This has to be a virgin operation, no fuck ups." He turns to address Allison. "Allison, did that program also have the personnel roster?"

"Yes, sir."

"Send the information to my WA-14."

"The Anvil ain't a transport," Ryan says.

"Mine is and it already has the multiphasic shielding and weapons. Let's roll."

"Y'all could use a diversion, but we jest don't have the man power."

"Don't worry, Ryan, we'll come up with something."

Dave threatens, "If you even think about saying Kabul, I'm gonna kick your scrawny ass across that fucking station."

'What is Kabul?" Ky'Holl asks.

"Trust me, darlin' ya don't wanna know," Ray replies.

She has a confused look on her face while the rest of the team laughs.

Liaok watches her husband and the rest of the team leave as Ryan and Allison try and reassure her.

Linaiok and Ana enter the command center, having heard the news. They join Liaok in praying to *Ama'diok* to deliver Alex safely back to them or to welcome him into the Divine Hall to serve the Henoki people in the afterlife.

CHAPTER 45

Cloaked WA-14 – Moravin nebula

Ricardo pilots the WA-14 to within one hundred thousand kilometers of the station, having maneuvered the fighter/transport inside of a large asteroid to prevent it from being detected.

Robert observes, "Now I know why these bastards are in the nebula, it wreaks havoc on the shields."

Ray says with a tinge of guilt, "My bad. I shoulda scanned fer polaron particles."

"Any kind of scan would give us away. This reminds me of the gravitation flux we encountered against the Cho'Kai."

Ky'Holl asks, "Cho'Kai, sir?"

He tells her, "Extremely violent and dangerous race. Their environment is similar to this. We developed a program called "Hell's Gate" to learn how to navigate it. Ray, do we still have that program?"

"Not sure if the main frame has it," he replies, "But my minicomputer does."

"Patch it in."

"Ya got it."

He takes out his palm sized computer, puts in a command and downloads into the WA-14 database. He then uses the minicomputer to do a scan of the nebula on a frequency too low to be detected and then inputs a command into the tactical station.

"Yer all set."

Ricardo adjusts the shields and the WA-14 blends into the background, appearing to be nothing more than spatial disruption. "We're invisible, Bob."

"Good work. Now tap into their system and see if he has been scheduled for interrogation or execution?"

This comment puts a look of anxiety, mixed with anger on Ricardo's face.

Ky'Holl puts her hand on his. "I care very much for your son. He befriended me when the others in our training class wouldn't. I will lay down my life to bring him back."

He manages a smile. "He spoke of you, his feelings are mutual. No matter what happens, thank you."

Robert tells him, "I should have been more careful with how I phrased it. Sorry, Rico."

"We know what they're planning, Bob. Denying it makes it worse."

Ray changes the subject.

"Bob, I found it. They're bringin' 'im ta interrogation chamber two an'." He pauses. "Dadgummit, Rillius is gonna be doin' the interrogatin'."

"Son of a bitch, even with changing our appearances, he'll be on us. Ky, you're the only one who can pull it off."

She appears apprehensive.

"Commander Tucker, Rillius and I will be in the station, but we can't get too close him," Dave assures her,

"I am able, David," Rillius replies.

She takes a couple of deep breaths, goes into a meditative state and then opens her eyes. "I am ready."

"Change of plans, You'll go to the chamber and make sure Alex is OK. Rillius will be your backup. Commander Walsh and I will tap into the environmental systems and use the Aprilozene to knock everyone out. Unfortunately you won't be able to mask because it will tip the other Rillius."

"Sir, I am immune to Aprilozene."

"Good," Robert nods. "You and Rillius will bring Alex out, we'll sabotage the core, trigger the evacuation alarm and then get the hell out."

"I say let the fuckers die," replies Ricardo, vainly trying to control his emotions.

"Then we're no better than they are. As soon as Ray gets the files on the personnel we're replacing we're going in," says Robert.

Ray accesses the files of four Imperial personnel that will put them in a position to carry out their assignments: Ky'Holl and Rillius will be Shock Troopers stationed outside of the torture chamber. Robert and Dave will take over personnel on the surface of the space station doing maintenance on the weapons array.

Robert grins, "Always enjoy doing a spacewalk."

"Speak for yourself," Dave grumbles.

"Sir?" Ky'Holl asks.

"He had a bad experience the last time we did a space borne insert," Robert chuckles. "To be fair, we were breaching a Cho'Kai base."

"Time ta change yer faces and fer some that'll be an improvement," Ray snarks.

"And for others, a broken nose will be an improvement," Dave retorts.

Ray grunts, and then studies the picture of the personnel that Rillius, Robert and Dave are replacing, while Ky'Holl concentrates and then transforms into Shock Trooper Jake Miller.

As soon as Ray finishes Robert, who now looks and sounds like maintenance tech Sean Evans says, "Rico, we're ready, take us to within teleporter range."

Ricardo is confused by the change in Robert's voice, turns and sees a short, hefty person where Robert used to be.

"Whoa—".

Robert sees his new appearance and comments, "Nice work, Ray, but could you at least make me thirty pounds lighter and six inches taller?"

"No can do."

"Guess PT isn't a requirement for maintenance techs."

"I'll take the thirty pounds, I look like a bean pole," Dave whose appearance resembles maintenance tech Joseph

Collins, quips. He says with a serious tone, "If we run into trouble, we're fucked."

"As soon as we finish and flood the station with Aprilozene, we can change back."

"OK. Anytime you're ready, Ray."

Ray advises him, "Dave, teleportin' won't be a good idea."

"Why not?"

"Talak'Vin has their scanners tweaked ta detect our teleporter signal."

"That sucks."

"The good news is there's a maintenance hatch near the array. Ricardo can set 'er down, y'all grab the techs, bring 'em in here an' when we're done, take 'em ta the Minarians."

"They're civilians. I doubt they committed any crime, other than associating with the Empire."

"And that's probably not by choice."

Ray finishes transforming Rillius, who now looks like Shock Trooper Kent Williams.

He tells Ricardo, "I sent ya the coordinates ta the array, you kin set 'er down an' they'll never see us."

"OK into the environmental suits, Dave and I will slip them the sleep agent, commandeer their suits and then we go in through the hatch."

Ricardo pilots the camouflaged WA-14 to the main weapons array located near the equator of the station, which is currently facing away from the sun. He lands one hundred feet away from the panel where the two techs are performing routine maintenance.

Collins and Evans are checking the readings on the array, making sure the equipment is within normal operating parameters. They both feel a tap on the shoulder They turn are stunned to see themselves smiling and waving at them. Robert and Dave quickly administer the Aprilozene through the hose, causing Collins and Evans to fall to the ground, unconscious.

They bring the techs back to the WA-14 and put them in the depressurized cabin. Dave pressurizes the cabin, and they strip the environmental suits off, and put on the Imperial suits, first making sure the Aprilozene has been purged from them.

Collins and Evans are brought to the front and tied up in chairs in front of the tactical station.

Rillius and Ky'Holl are already in their environmental suits. They bring an environmental suit for Alex, hoping they'll be able to pull this off and get off the station before the explosives, which will have a sixty minute delay.

Ray motions for the device the techs were using. He reads it and tells them, "There's a slight variation in the targetin' computer."

"Gee that's too bad, why are you telling us?"

"Ya hafta go inside an' git a calibration device. They may have a door sensor an' ask what yer doin'."

"Good point." Robert checks his chronometer. "I have 0932; we'll have fifty minutes to get Alex out. Any later than that, lock onto us and pull us out."

"Ya got it, son."

"We're Oscar Mike."

Robert and Dave leave the cockpit and Ray seals the cabin. The rest of the team gets into their environmental suits while Robert depressurizes the cabin and shuts off the interior lights. Then they exit the Anvil and move to the maintenance hatch.

When Robert turns the wheel it makes hissing then the hatch opens.

Robert and Dave hear 'Parker's' voice. "Command to Techs Collins and Evans. I have an unsecure exit near your position. Report."

"The targeting computer is out of calibration, I sent Collins to get the equipment to get it back to specifications."

"Proceed. In the future notify me before opening the hatch."

"Yes, ma'am."

Rillius, Ky'Holl and Dave enter the decompression area, close the hatch, pressurize the compartment and when a light flashes, they open the door leading into the maintenance tunnel.

Dave pulls out a minicomputer, calls up the schematic for the station and then shows Ky'Holl and Rillius the location of the torture chamber.

He then locates Williams and Miller, who are in their crew quarters, alone. Rillius and Ky'Holl check the Aprilozene injectors, synchronize their chronometers and then proceed to the quarters.

Dave finds the storage locker for the maintenance equipment, locates a diagnostic scanner, opens it and loads it with high explosives that will trigger a cascade failure in the system, leading to an overload.

"Maintenance tech Collins to command; exiting hatch to complete repairs."

"Received, thank you."

Dave opens the hatch, depressurizes the compartment and waits for the light to flash. When it is lit, he opens the hatch and returns to the console.

"About time you got back, Collins."

"Well, next time you can get it yourself."

"Clear the channel," 'Parker' admonishes.

Robert and Dave nod, confirming their suspicions that the communications channel are being monitored.

They appear to be calibrating the targeting computer, when in fact they are setting the explosives to disable it.

After a few moments they walk back to the hatch.

"Repairs complete, reentering the base."

"Acknowledged. Collins, report to environmental control, they are reporting a bad sensor in the main panel. Evans report to engineering for central core maintenance."

"Collins, acknowledged."

"Evans acknowledged."

They return to the hatch, enter, pressurize and then enter the station. They walk over to a rack where other environmental suits are located. They take theirs off, put them on the rack, and then walk down the hall.

"They're making this too easy," Dave whispers.

"You know what that means?" Robert replies.

"Things are going to get totally fucked up," they reply in unison.

They discreetly check their minicomputers for where they are supposed to report, and then send a text coordinating their next move. Dave will go to environmental control and discreetly release the Aprilozene into the central air system, while Robert will go to the central core and cause an irreversible core breach.

Dave gives Robert the hand signal for ten minutes and then they go their separate ways.

Door outside torture chamber

Rillius and Ky'Holl approach the Shock Troopers who are standing watch while Alex cries out in pain from the torture he is receiving.

"We are here to relieve you," Rillius says.

"It's about time, that guy's screaming is beginning to give me a headache," Shock Trooper Wallace says.

"Invest in earplugs," Ky'Holl quips.

"And a cold one at the mess hall."

"You are to relieve us in four hours," Rillius states.

"If he's still around, Rillius is working him hard. He showed us different ways the *Bahal'Zai* gets information. I look forward to his next demonstration, but I feel sorry for the next bastard he uses."

The two Shock Troopers walk away, arguing about what was the most effective technique Rillius demonstrated.

An excruciating cry of pain emanates from the chamber. Ky'Holl has a split second look of empathy, but quickly suppresses it.

"Troopers, front and center," 'Rillius' commands.

Rillius and Ky'Holl enter the room and see 'Alex' restrained in a chair showing signs of inhumane abuse: he's covered in cuts and burns, along with bruising and bleeding from his eyes, nose and ears.

"Troopers Miller and Williams reporting as ordered, sir," Rillius states.

"Excellent, who is Miller?"

Ky'Holl steps forward.

"You are new to serving the Empire?"

"Six months out of the Academy, sir."

"Good, new conscripts are easier to train than older ones. I am sure you studied interrogation techniques as part of your training. What is the first rule?"

"Sir, the first rule is to gather Intelligence by methods using physical or psychological force designed in inflict maximum pain, without killing the prisoner until Intelligence can be verified."

"Very good," 'Rillius', replies. "That is the same basic concept as the *Bahal'Zai*. According to your file you have never tortured a prisoner or been present at an interrogation."

"No sir. I was on garrison duty until recently."

"Well, here is your first opportunity. Your knife."

Without hesitation Ky'Holl takes out a sharp pointed knife.

"Impressive. Now in order to inflict pain you have to know your enemy's vulnerable area. This prisoner, for example is half Terran and half Henoki. He has sensitive membranes in his arms, chest and neck to help with absorbing oxygen out of aquatic environments. Normally we would use the Neural Shock Beam devised by Doctor Burke to gain information from him, but the Henoki physiology is sensitive to neural stimulation and would kill him. So we will use the old fashioned technique of small cuts to areas where pain receptors are prevalent." He looks at Ky'Holl, and then says "Make tiny incisions on the tips of his fingers."

Ky'Holl puts the tip of the knife to a finger. "Here?" she asks.

"Perfect."

She flicks the knife causing 'Alex' to cry out in pain.

"Another finger."

Ky'Holl complies, producing another cry of pain.

"Another."

She complies, and then asks, "Sir what information am I extracting?"

"This test was more for you, Trooper. The other purpose of torture is to filter out your enemy. Any hesitation on your part would have led me to believe you were a spy sent to rescue the prisoner. Congratulations, you pass."

Ky'Holl stands at attention. "May I finish, sir?"

"Return to your post." 'Rillius' chuckles.

She salutes 'Rillius' and then returns outside. She stands at attention, appearing stoic, but her eyes reflect pain and guilt. She once again suppresses her emotions and stands at her post where she hears 'Rillius' giving the same speech to his counterpart, suppressing the urge to kill him.

Environmental control

Dave is under a control panel, using a scanner to locate the malfunctioning sensor, at the same time finding the central ventilation shaft. He reaches into his pouch, slips out a concentrated canister of Aprilozene, attaches it to the back of the sensor, and then sets the timer for five minutes.

He replaces the malfunctioning sensor and then slides out of the tube.

"Problem corrected, sir," he says to Environmental Chief Kevin Lassiter.

"Dismissed."

Dave picks up the maintenance pouch, leaves the Environmental Control Center and begins walking to the maintenance hatch to rendezvous with the rest of the team.

"Too easy ... shit," he mutters to himself as he picks up the pace to retrieve weapons in the event of a hard extract.

Engineering section outside of the Central Core

Robert approaches the entrance to the core, wearing a hazard suit and carrying a pouch filled with diagnostic tools.

Two Black Ops soldiers stop him.

"Identification." Black Ops Soldier One states.

"Sean Evans, Maintenance Technician," Robert replies as he hands them an identification card.

The Black Ops soldiers compare the picture to Robert. Black Ops Soldier Two takes out a device.

"Prepare to verify identity." Robert holds out his thumb.

"Retinal scan, dumbass."

"Rillius just instituted the check, so the dumbass probably wasn't briefed," Black Ops Soldier One rebuts.

Robert feels anxious for a moment, certain that his cover is blown and mentally begins to go over options.

"Hold still," Black Ops Soldier Two says as he places the retinal scanner to Robert's eye.

The computer checks its personnel database, beeps and then a message appears on the screen:

Evans, Sean: Maintenance Technician First Class, Imperial Clearance Level Ten.

Black Ops Soldier Two says, "OK, you are cleared. You

are doing a routine check; you do not need anything other than your maintenance scanner. You are to do a visual scan and do not touch any equipment unless there is a problem and verified by us. Failure to follow procedure and you will be executed on the spot. Do you understand these instructions?"

"Eyes open, hands off, got it."

"You may want to stow that flippant attitude, we have been known to accidentally shoot smart asses."

"Yes sir, my apologies, sir."

"We're enlisted, we work for a living," Black Ops Soldier One states, "You may want to refresh yourself on protocol when dealing with the military."

"Understood."

"We will be watching."

Robert nods and enters the core, goes to the central panel and visually checks the readings. "Slight variance on constrictor number two."

Black Ops Soldier One walks up to the panel, checks it and then replies, "Within tolerance, carry on."

Robert takes out the maintenance scanner, walks around the central core, and continues to check readings.

A moment later a light blips on the scanner, meaning the Aprilozene has been released into the ventilation.

He sees the two Black Ops soldiers collapse, quickly takes a small explosive, sets it on the constrictor and leaves the central core.

He takes out a device, presses a button and then returns to his normal appearance. He taps his neural link.

"Charge set, twenty minutes to detonation, status."

"Ops Two standing by at hatch."

Rillius reports, "We have secured Captain Pasqualle. My counterpart is unconscious. Should we detain him as well?"

"Use your best judgment. The effects of the Aprilozene will wear off in ten minutes. Can you reach the hatch?"

"Affirmative."

"Do It. I will rendezvous with you at the tunnel leading to the hatch in five minutes."

"Acknowledged."

Robert ends the transmission and leaves the core, going to the central computer, finds the evacuation alarm, and sets it to go off in ten minutes.

He exits engineering, cursing to himself about the bulky suit, at the same time being thankful the filter was enough to keep him from inhaling the sleep agent.

Hall leading to the maintenance hatch

Robert arrives at the rendezvous point. Dave is already standing by with a couple of Special Forces Weapons.

The Aprilozene has been purged and they have five minutes before the Imperial forces regain consciousness.

"Any problems?" Dave asks as Robert takes a weapon.

"None. You?"

"No, same with Rillius and Ky and it even went smoother than expected, which means the shit's gonna hit the fan any second."

They see Ky'Holl helping 'Alex' and Rillius dragging his counterpart approaching their position, one hundred meters away.

They pass a corridor, where 'Alberto' and another Black Ops Soldiers are lying unconscious.

The Black Ops soldier stands, brandishing a weapon and shoots Ky'Holl in the back, near the thoracic cavity.

The soldier takes out a device, points it at himself and presses a button and transforms into Jen'Pway.

"Greetings, Commander Tucker."

"Jen'Pway. We heard you tried to get greedy and got your sorry ass blown away."

"Do not believe everything you hear. I am impressed you were able to fool Rillius."

"Metamorphs don't exist in his reality."

"True metamorphs like Ky'Holl are extremely rare. It was a shame to kill her." He aims his weapon at 'Alex' and says "I should finish what Rillius started and make your mission for naught."

"Not quite. This stations gonna blow in about fifteen minutes from an irreversible core breach. I have no qualms standing here and going up with it."

"I know you would, Commander. That is why I propose a deal."

"What kind of deal?"

"I escape, you do not pursue me and I take Rillius' identity and control the Empire."

"Always the power hungry son of a bitch."

Jen'Pway becomes angry and pulls out a small grenade. "I throw this and kill everyone within ten meters, namely your team and hostage."

Robert and Dave aim their rifles at him.

"And we drop you before you can even pull the pin."

"Is this is what you would refer to as a Terran stand-off?" Rillius asks.

"Mexican, but close enough," Robert replies. "He sees 'Sanchez' stirring and asks "Why don't you kill Rillius and take his place?"

"Commander, use that tactical logic you are well known for. I am a small time crook compared to Rillius, I know the Minarians have a large reward for him and it would go a long way to rebuilding the Alliance fleet."

"Leaving you in charge of the Empire?"

"Of course. We would even negotiate a truce."

"And the planets under Imperial control?"

"I am willing to trade a number of systems for the return of Commander Tucker and his Black Ops Force."

"What about the senior staff he betrayed?"

333

"They will be easy enough to dispose of, once this station blows–"

Jen'Pway is shot in the back and falls.

'Sanchez' gets to his feet, motions to Rillius to back away, grabs the other 'Rillius' and drags him to safety and demands, "You sabotaged the station. Fix it."

"Core breach in ten minutes, irreversible, Commander Sanchez." The evacuation alarm goes off. "I suggest you get your people out of here."

"You could have killed us."

"Not my way, Commander. We'll defeat you on the battlefield; we're just making things even."

"You're taking Commander Pasqualle's son."

"He's our Alex Pasqualle. Yours is in our medical bay kept in a stasis field. Let us go and I'll return him unharmed; you have my word."

"Fair enough. But I keep Jen'Pway."

Rillius states, "He is all yours. My quantum double can demonstrate enhanced *Bahal'Zai* interrogation techniques."

"Deal. You may bury your dead."

"Another time, Commander Sanchez."

"Another time."

'Sanchez', picks 'Rillius' up in a fireman's carry, grabs Jen'Pway by the leg and drags him away.

Robert picks up Ky'Holl, Rillius and Dave helps 'Alex' to his feet and they proceed to the hatch, put on the environmental suits open the hatches, go to the waiting WA-14, and get in.

Robert pressurizes the main compartment, grabs a med kit and uses a device to put 'Alex' in an induced coma.

Dave checks Ky'Holl's vitals and shakes his head.

"Damn," Robert whispers.

Ray and Ricardo enter the cabin. Ricardo sees his son and becomes shaken up.

"He's gonna be OK, Rico."

"What about Ky'Holl?"

"She was shot in the back and killed by Jen'Pway."

"They said that bastard was dead."

"He will be, once Rillius gets a hold of him."

Rillius states, "Robert, she performed her duty worthy of a *Bahal'Zai.*"

"Then she will receive a memorial worthy of one."

An explosion at the targeting array signifies that the station is about to fully self-destruct.

"Let's get the hell out of here," Robert yells. "Rico, stay with Alex, I'll fly."

Ricardo nods and then kneels next to 'Alex'.

"Hang in there, son." He turns to Ky'Holl. "I will always remember the sacrifice you made to save my son." He grabs hold of her hand.

She suddenly lets out a sharp gasp for air, startling him.

"She's breathing! Ray, get her into stasis!"

"Ya got it."

Ray grabs a medical device and places her into stasis.

Robert starts the engines of the Anvil, pilots the craft away from the station and out of the nebula. Once clear of the polaron distortions, he activates a scattering field, opens a portal and returns to Taqua Four.

Imperial craft of all shapes and sizes are evacuating their personnel and leaving the station and setting a course for their base in the Venpari system.

Ten minutes later the central core ruptures, causing a massive explosion and the imperial space station is shattered into billions of tiny particles that spread throughout the Moravin nebula.

CHAPTER 46

Covert Ops Medical Bay

The Ops team sits with Alex and Ky'Holl, who are both unconscious.

Elizabeth enters the ward. "Commander Pasqualle, your son's memories have been restored and he will make a full recovery."

Ricardo mutters a prayer of gratitude in Spanish and crosses himself.

"Liz," Robert says to Elizabeth. "Ky'Holl was dead for a full ten minutes."

"She was never dead, Commander. Her physiology is similar to the Kurai. If they are mortally wounded, they have the ability to shut their bodies down and heal themselves, with the appearance of death, even the lack of vital signs."

"Didn't know the Kallaxians can do that."

"Only ones that have the metamorphic gene."

"So Jen'Pway is in deep shit," Dave chuckles.

"Maybe Rillius will send us a tape," Robert quips,

"If not, I know Sanchez will."

The team laughs.

Ryan enters the ward. "I don't know how you crazy sum'bitches pulled it off, but ya did it."

"It ain't over, Ryan, not by a long shot."

"At least y'all can start the counter insurgency."

"After we're trained in the ancient *Bahal'Zai* ways.

"I thought y'all did that?"

"In the ways developed by my grandfather, Glavius, the ancient *Bahal'Zai* developed their minds to the point here they could channel their psychic energy and kill someone."

"Like a Sith Lord," Robert jokes.

Rillius appears confused.

"Long story, son." Ryan smiles.

"Why did the *Bahal'Zai* abandon this?"

"A corrupt Lekar named Draconius misused the power to kill the Bwentani Emperor, Quintus. Then he seized control and ruled the Imperium for three hundred Terran years until Glavius defeated him and restored order. He declared the ancient ways will no longer be taught or used, and if a *Bahal'Zai* attempts to use this power, he will be put to death."

"Is this law still on the books?"

"Yes, Robert."

"How did Glavius defeat him?"

"By the training we now go by, *binzah*. He was also a *Bahal'Dai* master."

"According to Alex, He's training the Black Ops team in their techniques, but humans won't be able to develop the mental discipline."

Allison calls the senior command on their neural links. "Sirs, we just got a report from Bwentani Prime. They've been attacked."

"We're on the way, darlin'," Ryan replies.

Ricardo stands up.

"Stay with your son and Ky." Robert orders.

They leave the medical bay. Liaok, Linaiok and Ana walk towards the bay.

"Alexander?" Liaok asks.

"He's going to be fine, Lia."

She sighs, relieved, "Praise to *Ama'diok*." She hugs Robert and the ops team. "Thank you."

"It was a brave young woman named Ky'Holl who saved his life. They're recovering in the medical bay. Elizabeth said you can sit with him."

Liaok nods, and then goes into the medical bay. Linaiok and Ana start to follow, but Robert stops his daughter.

"There's a situation on Bwentani Prime. We may have a

priority op. Get a hold of Z."

"Yes, *Hu'Neh*."

She taps her neural link to call Zerellus.

"*A'nok* report to the command center."

"I am there."

"Acknowledged."

Ana ends the transmission and follows the ops team to the command center.

Allison, Paul, Zerellus and Bat'ai are hard at work examining data and a monitor that is broadcasting a terrorist attack on the Bwentani Capital.

"Report," Ryan says as the team enters.

Allison replies, "We don't have all the information. Bwentani Intelligence reported that a group attacked the Imperium ministry. Prime Minister Berellus was assassinated and Henoki leader Quennok is in critical condition."

"The Empire?" Robert asks.

"No, a group calling themselves the Order of Draconius have claimed responsibility. They destroyed the Bwentani protective shield, stole a squadron of fighters and a couple of battlecruisers."

"Shit. *Binzah*, you know what this means?"

"Yes, my namesake is re-establishing the Order."

"Allison, contact Bwentani Prime," Ryan commands.

Allison establishes contact with Bwentani Prime. Assistant Prime Minister Marilla appears on screen.

"Marilla. It's been too long," Robert says.

"Yes, Since Palonius' funeral."

"Ya had my condolences on yer loss, Ma'am. Berellus was a good man," Ryan states.

"Thank you, General."

Robert states, "Marilla, According to your report, the Order of Draconius was responsible for the attack."

"Yes. They infiltrated our military using what you Terrans call sleeper agents and that *kava'dal* Rillius killed Berellus using the *hom'dahl*—"

"The death touch." Robert says as if in a trance.

Marilla sees Rillius, feels her anger rise within her, but then composes herself. "I know it was not you, Lekar, but if you will forgive me–"

"I understand. I shall leave your presence." Rillius bows his head and leaves the command center.

"Marilla, you know we will need Rillius in order to defeat his quantum double, especially now that the Order has the military backing of the Terran Empire."

"I know Robert. It will take some time."

"What did the other Rillius do?"

"He made me watch him kill Berellus and the senior advisors, and then torture Quennok. He had me in his grasp and was about to use the *hom'dahl*, but instead he threw me to the ground and said since I was a mere woman, I was not worth killing."

"Takin' on the Order has jest become our number one priority," Ryan assures her.

"The Order is more than just regular soldiers, they are *Bahal'Zai*."

"Myself, Commander Walsh, Commander Watson, Zerellus and Rillius are also *Bahal'Zai*," Robert states.

"Yes, Robert, I know, but the Order has begun recruiting Bwentani that are dissatisfied with the Imperium, mainly our youth, you may be facing a legion."

"We'll deal with that when it comes. Right now we have to get your security shield online. The Empire's station was destroyed, but they may look to Bwentani Prime to consolidate their power."

"Yes, we have already begun repairs and have begun questioning our Imperium troops."

"Tread lightly, Marilla, if you push too hard, you may turn a few that are on the fence."

"Your Terran history has taught us how to deal with terrorism," she replies. "We do not give them power or a voice by turning them into martyrs. We shall try them and put them in jail just like any other common criminal."

"Glad somebody learned that lesson."

"If you will excuse me, I have much work to do."

"If you need us, get in touch."

"I shall, *Kulhuka*.

"*Kulhuka*."

Allison ends the transmission.

"Well that certainly changes things," Dave says folding his arms across his chest.

"Rillius and the Empire were dangerous alone, but now that he is bringing back the Order of Draconius, he's taken this shit to a whole new level," Robert replies.

"Robert, our conventional Special Forces will not be sufficient," Rillius states as he returns to where they are standing.

"I know, *binzah*, plus dividing our forces will only weaken us. We will need to keep the Special Forces intact and continue with the original mission of infiltrating and liberating the occupied territory along with a team dedicated to fighting the order."

"Yes, other than Zerellus, I am hesitant to use other Bwentani."

"They'd be the easiest to train and become *Bahal'Zai*."

"And the easiest to be tempted to align themselves with my namesake. The power offered by the Order is a difficult temptation for a Bwentani," Rillius points out to them.

"Would Zerellus be tempted?"

"No, he has strong ties with Anamiok and his children."

"And you?"

"I have my friends to keep me grounded."

"Besides ourselves, who else do we git?" Ray asks.

"The original group that had their DNA affected, Paul, Mike, Ana, Ky'Holl—"

"Don't fergit me, Bob."

"Ryan are you up for this training?"

"Son, ya keep fergittin' that I'm only ten years older than ya, an' I can still open a can o' whup ass on ya, even with yer fancy trainin'."

Robert laughs, "True, and you're only a few years older than Dave. If his old ass can do it, I guess you can, too."

Dave puts his middle finger up, "Fuck you."

"Well we can't totally dismantle our senior command structure. Rico is a good tactician and we can use him. I would suggest that Keith take command and Jackie's the XO, Darrel Henderson is in charge of Special Forces and Samantha take charge of the pilots."

"Harry should maintain his post as liaison," says Ryan. "And leave Allison runnin' communications, but who do we put as Chief of Intelligence?"

"Miguel and Paul are too valuable in the field. I think Alex would make a good Intelligence Chief, besides, I think Liaok would kick our asses if we sent him undercover again."

"Bat'ai should stay where he is in R&D; but his workload is gonna double, if not triple."

"He's the ultimate workaholic and never sleeps, he'll love this shit," Dave replies.

"True. Let's check to see when Ky and Alex can return to duty. Allison, the command center's yours; let us know if anything else come up.

"Yes, sir."

The senior command leaves to check on the status of their two injured operatives and plan on implementing the changes to the Covert Ops Force and the newly designated *Bahal'Zai*.

CHAPTER 47

Imperial Base – Venpari Prime

The former Bwentani Imperium Commanders that have pledged their loyalty to 'Rillius' and the Order of Draconius are reciting an ancient Bwentani chant and circling Jen'Pway, who is tied to a table, with his arms and legs spread and he is blind folded, babbling incoherently in Kallaxian.

'Watson', 'Pasqualle', and 'Sanchez' observe everything from the balcony of the amphitheater used for fighting. They remain in the shadows so they can't be seen or heard.

"Ya mean Tucker let ya take 'im an' go?" 'Watson asks.

"Yeah, Jen'Pway was going to double cross Rillius and leave us to die," 'Sanchez' replies.

"Tucker returned my son unharmed and could have easily wiped us out by letting us die on that station."

"Tucker is a soldier, he wants to fight us on the battlefield, not kill us in cold blood," 'Sanchez' states.

"Well son, he's gonna have his hands full with Rillius an' his new friends."

"So will we," 'Sanchez' replies.

"So, what do we do?"

"Get the hell out of here while we can. Spread the word, we are leaving for our base in the Kolromi system."

"I'm all fer that," 'Watson' replies.

They slip quietly out of the amphitheater and using handheld communications devices, order an evacuation of the Venpari garrison, and make their way to the hangar where their Reapers are waiting.

Within minutes the entire Imperial garrison is cleared of their forces, with the exception of the Order.

The Order stops their chanting.

'Rillius' states, "The Terrans have left. They did not possess the will to embrace the ways of the Order."

"They will be our first target," Pomar Clavius states.

"They are not a concern. It is Commander Tucker and his *Bahal'Zai* team that is the main obstacle to our return to power," 'Rillius' replies. "They will oppose our claim to Bwentani Prime as our birthright."

"Once we complete the ritual and release the spirit of Draconius, all who oppose us will perish," 'Rillius' states, at the same time taking a knife, plunging it into 'Jen'Pway, slicing out his heart and then holding it above his head and allowing the blood to drip onto him.

A blue light engulfs 'Rillius' and the members of the order begin chanting his name.

'Rillius' slowly opens his eyes which are glowing blue and in that sounds completely different from his own says, "I am Draconius."

Other Books by Gary A Wilson

American Defense Force: The Triangle
Covert Defense Force: Sake of Time
Time Defense Force: 2025
Special Ops Force: Quantum Armageddon
Marshal Keller and the Black heart Gang
Covert Ops Force: Empire
Covert Ops Force: War Criminal

Coming soon

Covert Ops Force: Omega Defense
Marshal Keller: Adventures in Old Mexico

Other titles from Nightstalker Press

Navajo Repo by Jonathan Miller
Twilight in the Twelfth by Jonathan Miller
Rem: A Journey Within Dreams by LuAnna Garcia

Nightstalker Press
Albuquerque, New Mexico, USA

About the Author

Gary A. Wilson grew up in the town of Ogdensburg, New Jersey. He graduated from Sussex Vo-Tech in 1981, majoring in Commercial Art and photography.

He enlisted in the Army in 1990 as a 19K (M1 –AI Armor crewmen), serving for three years before leaving the service on a medical discharge for service connected injuries.

Wilson used his military experience to glimpse into the future of the military in the "Defense Force" series.

He has expanded into the steampunk genre with his first release, Marshal Keller and the Blackheart Gang – a Southwest novel that he describes as "Wild, Wild West meets Briscoe County Jr."

He currently lives in Albuquerque with his wife, Maria, stepson, Andres and two dogs.

They share in three businesses: Nightstalker Press, Wilson editing and Maria's Bracelets & More under the umbrella of W/A Enterprises.

Preview of Covert Ops Force: Omega Defense

Minarian Prime 04.01.2222 – 0800 Covert Ops time index

The Magistrate has convened the arraignment of Imperial Commander 'Robert Tucker' on the crimes against the Alliance and Bwentani Imperium: complicity in the genocide of fifty different species, dating back to the Empire's appearance in this reality in the year 2025, the annihilation of six planets, including Earth, atrocities committed during the time of war and wanton acts of destruction too numerous to cite.

'Tucker' is led towards the Magistrate's chambers, where Kaslo and the Council of Judges await his appearance to read the charges and to assign a defense council on his behalf.

They pass the detention block control center. 'Tucker' presses a button concealed in his pocket and a mini grenade is teleported, ending up on the panel for the cells and discipline collars worn by the inmates awaiting trial. The grenade explodes, killing the Minarians monitoring the controls.

'Tucker and the Magistrate guards are knocked unconscious.

The cell block force fields are disabled, along with the discipline collars worn by the Black Ops team, who remove the collars, collect the weapons they have stashed and make their way out of the cellblock, shooting any Minarian they meet and to aid 'Tucker' who was knocked to the ground.

Black Ops Commander 'Dave Walsh' and First Trooper Vince 'Colretti' pick him up and try to release him from the hand and leg restraints.

"No time for that, let's get the hell outta here," 'Tucker' commands.

The Black Ops team surrounds 'Tucker' and they move in staggered formation towards the hangar where the Minarian transport vessels are located.

They board the vessel and release 'Tucker' from the restraints. He gets into the pilot's seat, studies the panel, and finds the shield control panel. "Colretti, I need the access code."

'Colretti' immediately hacks into the Minarian database, "Code is two-seven-nine-six-four-one."

'Tucker' enters the code and then flies the transport towards the access port for the planetary shield.

They leave Minarian Prime and then proceed at maximum speed away towards the Moravin Nebula, a few light years away.

Covert Ops Command Center – Taqua Four

Communications Chief Allison Foster is doing her daily maintenance check of the system, when a Priority One alert comes in from Minarian Prime.

"This is Chief Magistrate Kaslo. I must speak to Commander Tucker immediately."

"Yes. Sir." She accesses the encrypted Covert Ops channel. "Command to Ops One."

"Ops One, go ahead, Allison," Commander Robert Tucker replies.

"Sir, I have a Priority One message from Chief Magistrate Kaslo."

Utilizing the base teleporter, Robert materializes and then goes to the communications monitor.

"Chief Kaslo, you wouldn't have contacted me unless Tucker and his men escaped."

"That is correct, Commander. He was able to escape while being brought before us for arraignment."

"The discipline collar failed?"

"Commander, you know Minarian law prohibits the use of the collar until the accused has been properly arraigned."

"I understand, but Chief. Tucker and his men are trained operatives that can escape from virtually any prison, just like myself and my people."

"He has been in our custody for several of your weeks and has made no attempt to escape before now."

"His men have been in custody for a few months, they probably planned for this when he was being led past the detention center and somehow triggered an explosive device to disable your security."

"That is precisely how they escaped."

"Well that's how I would have done it."

"And you must think of us as fools for allowing dangerous prisoners to go unchecked before they are arraigned."

"Chief Kaslo, you have maintained galactic justice for untold generations, but unfortunately you have never had to deal with a prisoner like 'Tucker' and his Black Ops team."

"There is one other, The Order of Draconius. We have heard rumors that the Order has once again attained power."

Robert replies, "Unfortunately yes; they have seized control of Bwentani Prime, expelled anyone not of their origins and sent them to Imperial detention camps."

"It is as you Terrans say, 'you have your hands full.'"

Robert chuckles, "That we do, Chief. I will have our best teams go after 'Tucker' and the other escaped prisoners. Were you able to track where he went?"

"Our transport vessel was seen heading towards the Moravin Nebula."

"He picked the perfect place to hide, spatial distortions and polaron radiation makes it impossible to scan and it's ten light years across with numerous planetoids to hide on, they could stay hidden for years."

"If anyone can bring Tucker to justice, it is you Commander," Kaslo states.

"We'll get on it right away."

"I shall await your progress report."

Allison closes the channel.

"Shit! How many fucking times have we told them to update their procedures, and they don't listen?"

"Preaching to the choir, sir," Allison replies.

"I know, Allison. Get a hold of the senior staff; we have another mess to clean up."

Covert Ops briefing room

Robert briefs the senior staff on the recent escape by his doppelganger and the Black Ops team.

"Dadgummit, Bob, how many damn times have we told them sum'bitches ta do a full search on people brought into them?" Ryan Dickinson laments.

Robert replies, "Too many, Ryan, but I guess it's difficult to change twenty-five thousand years of Minarian judicial procedures."

"As if we don't have enough shit with the Order blitzing Bwentani Prime and putting our people in Imperial detention centers," Commander Dave Walsh adds.

"Actually our people are safer there than on Bwentani Prime," Robert points out.

Commander Ray Watson asks, "What makes ya say that, Bob?"

"Commanders Sanchez and Pasqualle figured they owed us one since we returned Pasqualle's son to them, and they're willing to negotiate some kind of truce, seeing that the Order is a threat to the Empire as well as us."

"You think they'll actually return territory to us?"

"They won't return systems that will give them a tactical advantage, mainly the ones that put a buffer in between the Empire and the Order."

Commander Keith Sykes shakes his head, "I thought I'd never hear myself say this but maybe we should consider an alliance with the Empire."

"That's what we're working on. We're going to notify them that Tucker escaped, because we know they're just as motivated to catch the bastard as we are."

Ray nods, then adds, "I'd trust 'em as far as I can throw 'em, but if we can work some kinda deal, be a helluva a lot better ta only have two threats than three."

"Exactly. Darrel, you're gonna lead the Special Forces to start looking in the Moravin Nebula."

"We're on it," Special Forces Commander Darrel Henderson replies before leaving the briefing room.

"We need fresh Intel from Bwentani Prime. When was the last time Ky checked in?"

"Her last encrypted message was twelve hours ago."

Robert exhales sharply. "It's too risky to contact her. Z and Rillius are too recognizable. We need to get a small team in there to get a sit-rep and possible extract."

"You and me fit the bill, Bob," Dave says.

"Let's have Liz set our cover and then we're Oscar Mike (On the Move)."

Robert and Dave leave to have Doctor Elizabeth Burke alter their appearance using the Kallaxian metamorph device.

"Assuming those two yahoos don't git their sorry asses shot up, what's our next move?" Ray asks.

"Keep trainin' til the Order makes their move," Ryan replies. He pauses to consider the situation then speaks. "Return ta yer duties an go ta Alpha One Alert."

They senior staff reply in unison, "Yes, sir and then leave the meeting room.

To be continued …

www.ingramcontent.com/pod-product-compliance
Lightning Source LLC
Chambersburg PA
CBHW061318170626
46817CB00001B/220